A BIT OF CANDY IN HARD TIMES

A NOVEL

BLAINE BEVERIDGE

A BIT OF CANDY IN HARD TIMES

Promontory Press
www.promontorypress.com

ISBN: 978-1-987857-86-3

Cover Design and Typeset by Edge of Water Designs, edgeofwater.com

Printed in Canada
987654321

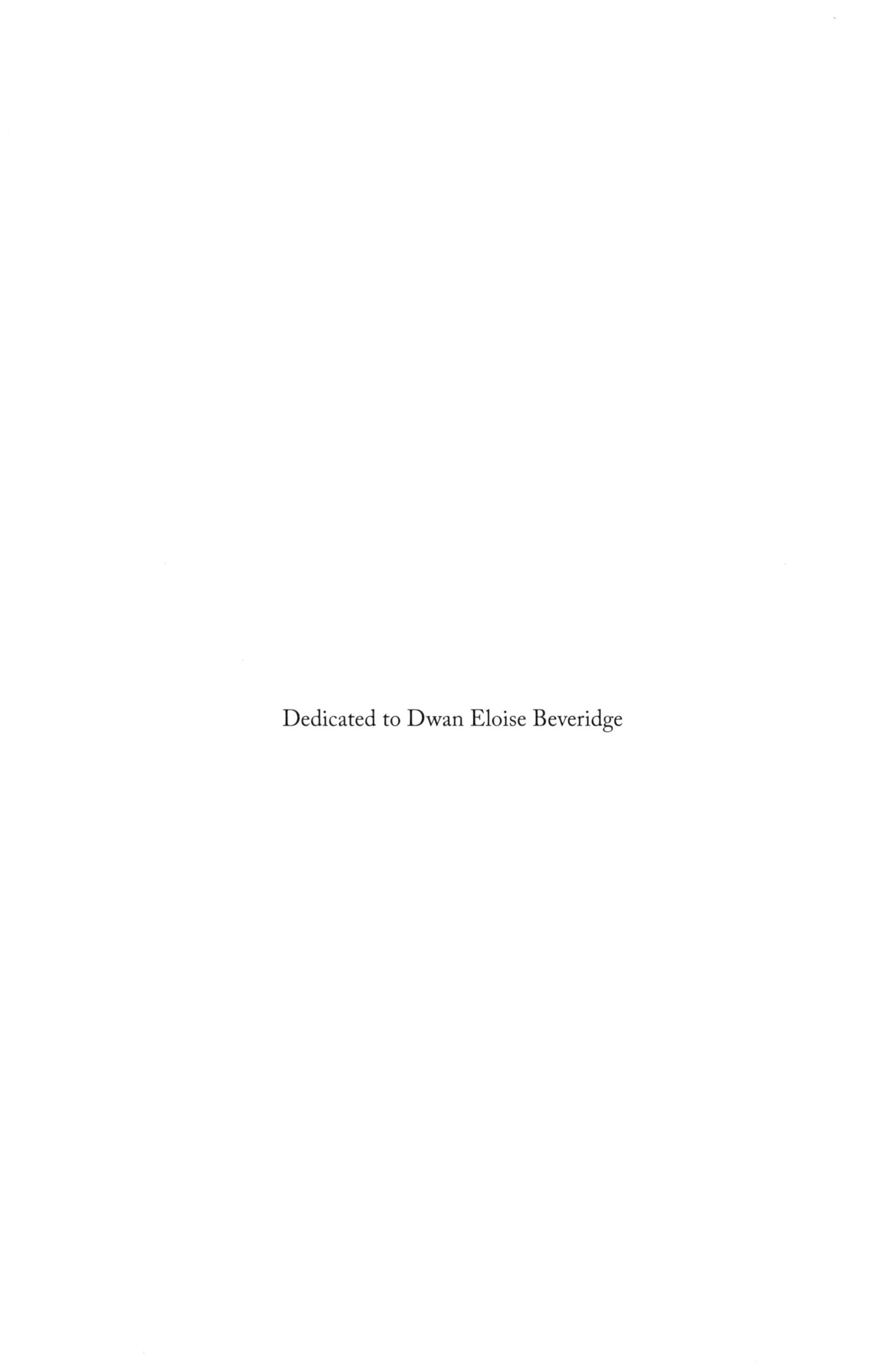

Dedicated to Dwan Eloise Beveridge

CONTENTS

ACKNOWLEDGEMENTS

This book has been a labor of love, but it would not have been possible without the great help and support from the following people:

My good friends at Promontory Press: Bennett and Richard Coles, and editor Michelle Balfour. Friends who have encouraged my writing over the years, including Felix and Karen George, Katy Keeslar, David Lema, Shannon Pinc, the wry Canuckian humorist Gordon Kirkland, Peter and Carol Bizlewicz, Robert Illes, Rena Youngblood, Teresa and Chelsea Elliott. The late Professor Edward Staniford, who taught me that history was a continuum and not restricted to the traditional linear narrative. The late Jiri Weiss, my mentor and filmmaker *extraordinaire*. Jennifer McCord. Theresa 'Soni' Guzman-Stokes. Writing instructors Lew Hunter, Jack Rowe, Dan Toft, Peter Zukowski, Dick Perkins and Frank McAdams. My erstwhile colleagues at UCLA Extension, especially Ronnie Rubin, Shannon Battle and John Bragin, and my fellow writers at Pacific Northwest Writers Association. And my family: my sisters Leigh Blake and Heidi Glosser; my kids, Benjamin and Melissa, my niece Kris Heckert and, particularly, my wife, partner and inspiration, Bretta. Daily attitude adjustments continue to be provided by my constant companions, Captains Nemo and Queeg, Circe the

Siren Queen, Captain Bligh, the finest retriever in the world, and the wonderfully enigmatic, and vocal, Calliope.

Finally, while this book is dedicated to an outstanding fine artist and loving mother, Dwan Beveridge, I must acknowledge the guidance, world view and love that my father, Benjamin Harrison Beveridge, Jr., provided me every day until his passing in 1995. No child could receive better life instruction than I did from these wonderful, caring human beings.

Blaine Beveridge
From somewhere offshore…
2017

OIL AND WATER

The night sky was dimly illuminated by a low, quarter moon as the *Blue Jacket* pushed her way south along the Nova Scotia coastline toward an expected rendezvous in Casco Bay where she would offload ninety-three cases of scotch, gin and Canadian whisky.

It was a good night for the run. There was just enough light to help navigation, and to detect any Coast Guard cutters on patrol. They had lain up in Clam Bay, just north of Halifax, after picking up the booze at St. Pierre et Miquelon, waiting for nightfall.

Bruge had pulled the engine cover and fiddled with the Liberty engines while his deckhands got some necessary sleep. The easiest part of the run was always between St. Pierre and Nova Scotia, unless it was bad weather; the second half of the trip was always the most stressful. But Bruge had made the run dozens of times over the past couple of years, and felt he knew the ways of the Coast Guard as well as anyone could.

Back out on the open ocean that afternoon, everyone was alert but in good spirits. Bruge kept the *Blue Jacket* well out in international waters, and he carried certificates of transfer — should they be stopped — indicating the booze would be delivered to an importer in Nassau in the Bahamas.

As dusk settled over the ocean Bruge steered his vessel toward the thin coastline of Maine, secure in his belief that the *Blue Jacket*, whose hull was painted a dull gray color, would be hard to pick up by any coast watchers in the employ of the Prohibition Unit; all too often, civilians were happy to take money from the government, which they themselves could reinvest in, among other things, illegal alcohol.

The illegal import of alcohol from Canada, whether down the coasts or across the Great Lakes, had made millionaires of a variety of businessmen and politicians, despite the occasional bust or hijack. Bruge thought of himself as a good citizen, and a good businessman, delivering a product that was widely desired and championed, despite the best efforts of the Women's Christian Temperance Union and its allies. The Volstead Act meant nothing to him; it was just an instrument intended to increase the difficulty of delivery, and thus the price of the commodity.

He was a church-going man, a good Catholic who attended mass weekly and shared his confession, as well as good scotch, with his parish priest. It was all good business: a business that had allowed him to forego the vagaries of seasonal fishing for a year-round business that promised no end to profit. And all he had to do was pick up the product, move it without detection, and deliver the goods. For that he got paid in hard currency, part of which went into an envelope that was handed to an unidentified agent in Bangor, who in turn passed it to the big boss man Laningham in Long Island.

It was nearly midnight when they approached Bailey Island and spotted the cutter coming out of Merriconeag Sound. At first Bruge was certain they hadn't been spotted, but then the 75-footer turned in their general direction. The *Blue Jacket* was running without lights and was closer to shore, making it difficult for the cutter's deck watch to spot them. But the cutter kept on coming, closing the gap.

It fired its warning shot when it was still a thousand yards off, the shell sailing over the *Blue Jacket's* wheelhouse by twenty-five feet. The cutter was rapidly closing the distance, and Bruge reacted by turning his bow toward the rocky coastline.

The second shell splashed fifty feet in front of them, but Bruge maintained his course, full throttle. Smoke began to escape from under the engine cover.

The larger of the two deckhands pulled the cover off, hoping that the smoke might cover their escape. Before the hatch was clear, the third shell took out the bow, and the entire boat disintegrated in a second.

The water was cold, its immediate surface covered by wreckage, marine fuel and oil. Fires burned on floating patches of decking, illuminating the complete destruction of the *Blue Jacket*.

A lone survivor struggled to catch his breath, pumping his legs to keep his head above water. He was glad for the oil; it covered him and kept him marginally warm. He turned in the water, looking for his companions, but there were no other signs of life.

The survivor wanted to call out, but the cutter had closed the distance and was now directing its searchlight into the midst of the debris. Its light swept slowly across the water, almost exposing him as he clung to a large piece of wood, which he quickly realized was the stern. The commander of the cutter would want to identify the craft, and its disposition, in the cutter's log, so staying with the stern was certain to land him in custody.

The survivor ducked into the cold water, under the remains of the stern, and swam undetected to another small raft of shattered decking. From this small refuge he could watch the cutter's deckhands use their gaffes to dislodge debris in their search for bodies and contraband. Their conversation was difficult to make out over the noise of the idling diesel engines, but he could hear brief outbursts of laughter as they hauled a couple of the wrapped burlap sacks of booze onboard. There would be a party as soon as they were off duty, the survivor surmised.

After identifying the boat but recovering no bodies, the cutter moved away from the remains of the *Blue Jacket*, easing off into the night, looking for more prey.

The survivor was left to himself, alone in the vast, dark, ocean; clinging to a small piece of wood that would not keep him afloat, or warm, long enough to be discovered by a friendlier vessel. And what was the likelihood that any boat would be in the general area anytime soon? The cold was seeping into his body, and he was glad that it was May, not December.

The last of the small fires burned themselves out, and his eyes began to adjust to the dimness. The survivor called out and felt a compulsion to search for his captain or shipmate, but the cold water was sapping his body heat and strength. He could already feel the muscles in his legs threatening to cramp. He scanned the horizon and could see the Maine coastline. It might have been a few hundred yards, or it could have been five miles: he couldn't tell.

He could hear a bell softly clanging in rhythm to the undulating swell. There was a buoy nearby. He was a strong swimmer, and he set course through the debris field toward the sound. After several strokes he could make out the dim, flashing light atop the buoy, and within a couple of minutes he was able to pull himself onto its floating base. His arms vibrated from the exertion and the stench of the oil finally overtook him, making him vomit.

He regained his composure and his breath, and looked around. The remains of the boat were lost in the dark, but small pieces had gathered around the buoy, held captive by the local current. A crate of bonded whisky drifted close to the buoy and he reached out to lift it onto the platform. He pried the top off with his hands, and tossed half the bottles into the water. He could use the crate as a float while he kicked to shore; a distance that he roughly gauged was a couple of hundred yards. The length of two football fields: could he make it? He'd pop a bottle open once he got to shore, just to warm up.

The sound of the bell refocused his attention to the buoy. He looked up and was startled by what he saw. A figure, Christ-like, was suspended, splayed out, on the upper structure of the buoy, dimly and briefly illuminated by the battery-driven light at its peak. The body, having been deposited there by the force of the exploding artillery shell, was held in place by its outstretched arms, which were caught in the buoy's superstructure. It reminded him of his Sunday school lessons and how the Romans had jabbed spears at the crucified figure of Jesus. Fortunately, this figure's torment had ended.

It was Bruge. In those brief moments of illumination he could see the look of frozen surprise on his captain's face.

The survivor's shoulders drooped and he felt a sudden sense of loss. He had only known Bruge for a few months, and had made no more than a dozen runs with him down the northeast coast after having been recommended to him by the boys out of Nassau. He had grown close to the captain and his family of six: he had been a frequent guest at their dinner table, and a playmate to Bruge's children. While it was generally wise to keep coworkers at an arm's length, Bruge had clearly taken to the tall deckhand. Now, in one fell swoop, the survivor's benefactor and friend was gone, hanging lifeless, a crucificial caricature, on a buoy too far out to be seen from the shoreline. Literally hung out like a rag doll on a laundry line.

He climbed the superstructure, struggling to free Bruge's arms. Suddenly, with the man's weight upon him, both of them fell back down onto the buoy and into the water.

He hoisted Bruge's body onto the platform and then struggled back aboard. He was desperately cold, and so he removed Bruge's mackinaw and worked his way into the jacket. It was tight, perhaps too tight to allow him to swim, but he kept it on, hoping to regain warmth.

The survivor propped Bruge into a sitting position against the superstructure and used the corpse's belt to hold him in place. Bruge's head slumped against his chest, suggesting someone too tired to stay awake. Then the survivor reached into the mackinaw and pulled out an oilskin packet that contained Bruge's merchantman's license and identification. There was no picture on the identification: only the certification, vessel name, and port of origin.

Once the license was secure, for anyone inquiring he was now Walter Bruge. He fished out Bruge's wallet and noted the number of bills. Thirty-six dollars. He left the driver's license and replaced the wallet in Bruge's hip pocket. Bruge's family deserved to know how this had all played out. Knowing was less painful than not.

"You won't be needing the money where you're going, Walter," he said, using the man's Christian name for the first time. He leaned down and grasped the muscular shoulder of the dead man, hoping that Walter, wherever he had gone, would note the affectionate gesture.

Providentially, the stern section of the *Blue Jacket* drifted within fifteen feet of the buoy. There would be no better time. Dawn was still hours away, and he could be ashore before first light.

He eased into the water, noting the weight of the waterlogged mackinaw, pulled the crate of remaining whiskey into the water after him and kicked to the *Blue Jacket's* stern. The small raft bore his weight, and that of the whisky, above the light swell that was on the crest of the ingoing tide.

He kicked until he was no longer conscious of kicking, while the current carried him northward, almost parallel to shore. His mind turned back to Bruge and his fellow deckhand, Gavin, whose last name he never knew. Gavin was a Canadian who had been working the St. Pierre et Miquelon routes for two or three years with whatever rumrunner had booze to run. He was a grizzled, middle-aged man who wore patched pants and spoke sparingly, sharing nothing about his family, if he had one. When the *Blue Jacket* returned from its runs, Gavin would take his cash and disappear until the next assigned sail.

Now he was fish food, and whomever he had waiting for him back in Nova Scotia would never know how his life had suddenly been cut short. The image of Walter Bruge, however, would always be etched in the survivor's memory. Now the counterfeit Walter Bruge floated atop a broken section of vessel, kicking away from the prevailing northern current, trying to catch the ingoing tide to safety.

A light fog settled over the sea near the coastline, and he was wary of getting too close to offshore banks of rock that might knock him off his float. The sound of breaking waves could not yet be heard over the churning swells that impeded his effort, or the gulls and other seabirds already busy at their breakfast.

In the predawn light, barely enough to see a hundred feet ahead, the Maine coastline was barely visible. He kicked harder, suffering cramps in his cold legs, willing himself to continue working against, and across, the current.

After another hour, while resting in place, he could hear the surf breaking against the rocks and knew that he was drawing closer to shore. As the light increased, it was now apparent that the entire coastline, now a mere twenty-five to thirty yards away, was made up of inhospitably high rocks that jutted out to sea, making any exit there near impossible.

The survivor was exhausted, cramping, and thirsty. For a moment, whispers of despair suggested that he just give up and submit to the dark, silent depths. But then his resolve returned, and he kicked harder, as though punishing the ocean for cruelly having spared him.

For an interminable time he continued to search for a safe break in the rocks without success. It was enough to make a man give up; but then, he became aware of an indistinct but bright colored image on the shore. It was some kind of animal, pacing the survivor's slow passage along the shoreline. After a few moments, he was able to see it was a dog. A big dog of some indeterminate breed, yellow in color: an animated warning sign seemingly meant to draw attention.

And then, there it was: a safe passage through the surf line. The survivor kicked hard toward shore. As he closed on the shoreline, he frequently looked up to keep the dog in sight. It was farther up the beach, alternately digging in the sand and then looking back toward him. It was as if the dog were waiting for him.

He kept at it, and soon he was in shallow water that covered small, round, unthreatening rocks. He stepped off the stern section and, legs exhausted, collapsed into the water. He held onto his float while regaining his strength, then hoisted himself onto his feet, grabbing the half-empty crate of whisky and hauling it onto the sand.

He lay back, wracked by sobbing gasps, and allowed himself to rest, only raising himself onto his elbows to examine the remnant of the *Blue Jacket*. The boat, or at least a portion of it, had managed to deliver him back to shore, and he silently blessed it and its captain. He turned to look back up the shoreline, but the dog was gone.

He managed to crawl up the beach, dragging the crate behind him, and into the scrub forest that bordered the beach. He found a dry spot affording safety and rest before he would decide his next move. He was done in the northeast. He had worn out his welcome. Perhaps it was time to start over. Perhaps enough time had elapsed allowing him to go home. That decision would have to wait until he had some sleep and his body had a chance to recover. He opened a bottle of whisky and took a short pull. The warmth spread through his stomach and he soon drifted off, thinking about Bruge, the big yellow dog, and home.

THE CHIEF END OF MAN

The new dress shirt itched mercilessly. Arlyn Dunne wasn't used to wearing a suit, unless it was for a wedding, a baptism, or a funeral. His daily attire for nine years had been a police uniform, a uniform that he had been trying to replace with the aforementioned suit for the past three years. After an inordinate amount of ass-kissing, shit details, and completion of all the requisite tests, the Seattle Police Department had seen fit — finally — to promote him to sergeant and to place him in Detective Lieutenant Virgil Glaupher's squad.

Virgil was a rarity on the force, born in Seattle, and of the mind that anyone who outranked him was to be silently loathed while those subordinate were to be overtly abused. He didn't like Dunne. He didn't like the fact that Dunne, a newly minted sergeant, was foisted on him in lieu of any number of other cops who Virgil knew were ... flexible. Dunne was an unknown quantity and Virgil meant to determine how far and how hard he could push the man.

Dunne's first assignment as sergeant was to work the security detail at Longacres racetrack. Upon receiving the assignment he thought it was a perk, a repayment for all the long, cold hours he had walked his beat. It was not. Instead of being posted in the grandstand or paddock he worked the gate detail, where there was no shade, no access to bathroom facilities, and where he was required to be the last man on duty until the racetrack closed each day during the season. Those nights he rarely got home until well after his supper had grown stale in the oven.

But, with a $12 per week pay raise his wife, Mary Elizabeth, did not complain. There were new curtains on the windows of their flat and a new settee being purchased on credit. The promotion afforded his family the opportunity to live a bit more comfortably, though he continued to suffer Mary Elizabeth's ongoing demands for more space so the three boys wouldn't be crammed into their one bedroom.

He didn't complain, of course. He bucked up, met his duty, and went out of his way to please his watch commander. Then he was assigned to Virgil, whose squad generally involved the special handling of very important politicians and businessmen. Members of the city's elite society often had need for police security at their place of business, or when members of the city council and chamber of commerce got together for poker.

Dunne was promoted from watching the gate at the racetrack to watching the front doors of Seattle high rollers. And he was no longer just a beat cop. He wore a new suit from Sears, with brown wingtips instead of the black brogue shoes he had resoled several times over the years.

Dunne pulled up the collar on his overcoat and scanned the street for the hundredth time. Five cars were parked on the block. One of them was their police cruiser, and he could see the occasional glow of a cigarette being drawn on. The driver was lucky to be inside the car with the windows, no doubt, rolled up. A strong, unrelenting breeze blew across Magnolia and up from Elliot Bay, seeming to focus on Dunne.

He checked his watch. Eleven forty-two. He wondered how long the game might go and whether he could inveigle his way inside even for a few moments. If he had to piss, he had been instructed by Virgil to use the bushes at the side of the house. Some things never changed except, perhaps, the scenery, and he remembered the dirty alleys and piers where he had been forced to squat during his rookie days on the beat along the waterfront. As a young cop he had envied the veterans on the force, who had long since developed relationships with saloon owners that not only allowed the cops to use their facilities, but provided them with hot coffee or whiskey on cold nights.

By twelve thirty he was pacing up and down the walkway, attempting to keep blood flowing to his feet. This was no longer just an assignment: it was now torture. He was surprised, therefore, when the front door opened and a man he didn't recognize handed him a mug of hot coffee: so hot that it burned his tongue when he tried to take a sip. He pulled off one of his gloves and wrapped his hand around the hot mug, allowing the warmth to do the job that his mouth couldn't. He finished the coffee but continued to hold the empty mug long after it had cooled. It was more a psychological effect by this time.

At one o'clock Virgil came out and motioned to the cruiser. Its engine started and it slowly pulled up to the curb.

"Everything go all right?" Dunne asked.

Virgil glared at him. "Why wouldn't it go all right?"

Another man appeared on the porch, and a car down the street immediately started its engine and pulled up behind the squad car. The man, well dressed and heavily smelling of whisky and Bay Rum, pressed something into Virgil's hand and made his way to the car, climbing inside as three more equally-attired men queued up for their rides. Each of them passed something to Virgil, who pocketed the exchange without allowing Arlyn to see what it was.

Arlyn knew what it was: no cop worked the street for fifteen minutes without coming to the conclusion that cooperation was best arrived at through the sharing of wealth. Virgil Glaupher had been with the SPD for two decades, and the gossip surrounding him more than suggested that Olmstead had put a great deal of money into the Lieutenant's pockets during the former cop's successful run as rumrunner extraordinaire.

Virgil lived well beyond the means of any police lieutenant in

Seattle—or New York, for that matter. Not that Arlyn knew any of the particulars. But Virgil's expensive suits, hats, and shoes, all of which mimicked the wardrobe of these influential men, provided enough evidence that the lieutenant picked up additional funding beyond his pay envelope. These gents of leisure, these captains of industry, out for an evening of enjoyment free of concern were all too happy to press a few bills into Virgil's hand in exchange for security.

When the last of them slipped a bill into Arlyn's hand, Virgil scowled. Once the gent was in his car the lieutenant held out his hand, and Arlyn handed the bill, unseen, to his boss. Glaupher glanced at the bill, wound it onto his pocket wad, pulled a fiver off, and handed it back to his subordinate.

Arlyn was surprised to receive the money and idly wondered how large the bill he originally received had been. Virgil further showed some latitude by dropping Arlyn off at his apartment rather than setting him loose at the station house. But then, Virgil didn't need to return to the station, because there would be no paperwork surrounding the evening's detail.

As he sat quietly in the back of the squad car, listening to the driver and Virgil make small talk, the matter of the five-dollar bill occupied Arlyn's mind. It wasn't an insignificant amount of cash: it could pay for extra groceries, or the electric bill. It could buy new shoes for their oldest boy, now four, who seemed to outgrow shoes as fast as they were laced and tied. But it could also go for something special, something that might earn some brownie points for him: a gift, a token, which might ease the ever-growing tension between him and Mary Elizabeth.

Virgil deposited him onto the sidewalk without so much as a 'good night', and Arlyn entered his apartment building on the north side of the Denny Grade. He could hear someone talking as he made his way upstairs; the sound of the man's voice was as clear as if he were standing on the landing. The voice said something about beating someone else within an inch of their life, presumably the man's wife or girlfriend—

Arlyn didn't know which, for he made a point not to mingle with the other tenants. He didn't intend to stay in this apartment any longer than necessary. Let Mary Elizabeth deal with the neighbors.

He ignored the muffled threat and attempted to quietly insert his key into the lock of his front door. The door opened without sound. He had long since oiled the hinges, since he generally arrived home after the boys had been put to bed.

He locked the door and took off his coat, unfastening his shoulder holster and putting his gun on the shelf in the coat closet. The kitchen was clean, dishes long since washed and put away; in fact, there was no hint of any recent activity. Mary Elizabeth was a stickler for cleanliness, something that he appreciated after spending a watch with a bunch of slobs. But even M.E. could go over the top. He drew himself a glass of water from the tap and drank it without stopping. Then, quietly, he went into the tiny bathroom and attempted a brief wash-up before going to bed.

After drying his hands he pulled the fiver from his pocket, climbed onto the toilet seat, pried a board loose above the water tank, and hid the bill inside. He still had no idea what he would spend the money on, but it just felt good to have the luxury of being able to do something for M.E. as a surprise. He climbed back down off the toilet seat and splashed some aftershave on his face and under his arms, hoping that the pervasive smell of cigarettes and cigars might be minimized.

M.E. was breathing steadily as he carefully climbed into bed. She was on her side, facing away from him, so he slowly snuggled closer to share her warmth. As Arlyn laid his head on his pillow he could smell her: the soap that she had used to wash her hair and her natural scent. His love for her drove him to succeed, as much as he might be able. She deserved a better life than she had. The only time, in recent weeks, that she had bestowed affection on him without solicitation was when he received his sergeant's stripes. The marginal increase in income might have warmed her feelings, but it was the implied promise of further promotions that compelled her to reach out to him.

Lately, however, she had once again withdrawn into her cocoon of measured apathy. She spent most of her attention on the boys, serving as primary parent while Arlyn took as many shifts as he could to better position himself for more authority and, hopefully, increased income.

Now her smell aroused him. He could feel the tightness in his pajama bottoms and he eased forward, pressing into the small of her back while his lips found her neck. Her response was to recoil without words, pulling a bit away from him without giving up the warm spot on her side of the marital bed. He wasn't surprised. She had, no doubt, had a hard day dealing with the boys, and his late entry probably woke her despite his efforts otherwise. Being awakened with an unspoken request for sex was probably the last thing she needed.

Arlyn rolled over onto his other side and closed his eyes. Things would be better in the morning. He didn't have to show up at the station house until noon, so he could spend the morning with M.E. and the boys. Those thoughts carried him to slumber.

In the dark, M.E. lay quietly, listening to Arlyn's breathing become shallow as he fell asleep. She didn't resent his attempted embrace, but she wasn't in the mood to meet his, or her, needs. As it was, it was the wrong time of the month, and the last thing they needed was another mouth to feed.

She could hear voices coming from the apartment next door. The Dentons were still up, talking in low voices about something. M.E. could hear Mrs. Denton's voice, insistent and shrill. Was that her future after the boys had gone? Would it be a mostly loveless home life, dependent on the pension of a man that she no longer wished to be with? She loved Arlyn, but had never been *in love* with Arlyn. He had provided an escape from her family of nine in Albany—she was one of two girls among six boys—whose mother had been forced to raise them all herself after her husband had been killed in a streetcar accident. Even that marriage had been unhappy, and her mother had noted on a couple of occasions that while she missed her dead husband's paycheck, she didn't miss him at all.

When Arlyn was introduced to her during the holidays, while he was in Albany from New York City to visit his mother's family, she was most taken by his cleanliness and manners. He immediately fell for Mary Elizabeth, and she recognized that his attentions might provide her escape from a troubled household. She used her understated beauty and nascent charm to woo the young man, encouraged by her mother's practical observation: "He's about as different from your old man as he can be. He don't look like the hitting kind. Any man who don't hit his wife and who don't drink up the rent can't be all bad."

That was seven years ago, and they still lived in the same tiny apartment. Arlyn didn't drink the rent, and he had never hit her, but she felt listless in his presence, persuaded by the fact that life had only offered incremental change during the course of their marriage. The boys had become her life, and she was amazed at how they sopped up her love and encouragement; a distinct change from the way she had been raised. And Arlyn loved her even more for her attention to the boys. A one-sided love affair was much better than a loveless marriage, and she appreciated his affection even if she felt no compulsion to return it to him.

She closed her eyes and willed herself to sleep. After a few minutes there was the combined breathing of two people dreaming of unrelated happiness.

In the morning there was no 'good morning' for Arlyn.

"When will we have enough money to get our own home?" M.E. asked. "There are bungalows on Queen Anne we could look at."

No offer of coffee or breakfast, just an imprecise demand that he work harder so that she could own her own kitchen, her own bathroom, her own home. That was it. It was that demand that he took with him to work later that morning, and when he stood before Virgil in the latter's office Arlyn immediately asked for additional details like the one the night before.

"Already spent the proceeds, eh, Dunne?" Virgil asked, carefully setting his mug of coffee on his desk, away from a stack of papers he had been scanning.

"The wife is talking about getting a home. My pay won't cover a down payment. I could use extra work."

"Maybe police work isn't for you anymore?"

Arlyn balked. He liked being a cop. He liked those few and far between moments when he felt like he provided value to his community. Truth be known, the job was all he felt he could do. "I'm a cop, Lieutenant, but I need more than my salary if I'm going to get her that house."

Virgil picked the mug back up and sipped at the coffee, looking over the rim at his subordinate. "Wives and police work have never been a harmonious pair," he noted, then put the mug back down. "I can swing you some more side work, but maybe you should consider looking for a more profitable occupation. Perhaps I can put you in touch with someone who could use a man like you. You interested?"

"I don't want to quit the force," Arlyn exclaimed.

"Maybe we can set you up with a special detail. There are people in this community that the city fathers always like to look out for. Give me a couple of days."

Virgil's grin—more a leer—was disturbing, but Arlyn felt gratified that he had been heard and not simply dismissed.

SWEET STRAINS AND CATECHISM

It was quiet in Reynard's office, and he was glad to have escaped the houseguests that were in his dining room. His office was not overly large, but it had been constructed so that he could manage his working needs in one space. The office contained his reference books, his collection of prints, maps, his Victrola Borgia and records, a comfortable lounge, and a fully stocked bar. But what comfortably dominated the room was a massive teak desk, with six side drawers and a japanned desktop on which one could set a small dinghy.

Reynard Delacroix sat at his desk and marveled at the set of plans in front of him. A site elevation detailed a large building on a busy city street. The plans were for a small hotel with restaurant on the ground floor. Included in the architectural schematic was a floor plan depicting a casino in the basement.

The drawings could only begin to suggest how Reynard imagined the finished structure. It would be showy but elegant; accessible yet engaging. No whorehouse red flock or dark wood paneling, but also no Mary Jane white wainscoting. People would *want* to come there to meet, to dine, to dance, and to gamble. The top floor of the building would house eight glamorous rooms, each with its own bathroom en suite, with plumbing to rival the best hostelry in New Orleans, New York, or Monte Carlo, for that matter. Reynard had grand ideas that he was now beginning to believe he could afford.

He rolled the plans up and secured them as Virgil Glaupher escorted a man into the office. The stranger was a bit over average height, and whose physicality his bad suit could not disguise. The way he carried himself indicated someone who was as capable as Glaupher, something like a man-sized Pinscher. The newcomer looked Reynard in the eye and the latter interpreted the look as one of curiosity rather than challenge.

Glaupher stepped forward, almost like a referee in a prizefight. "Monsieur Delacroix—"

"*Excellenté, Virgil!*"

"Monsieur Delacroix, this is the man I spoke to you about, Arlyn Dunne."

Arlyn stepped forward and stuck out his hand. "Pleased to meet you, Mr. Delacraw."

Reynard welcomed the grip with a broad smile. "Please sit down."

"I have places to be, Monsieur." Glaupher started to put on his hat and then stopped. "Unless you need me here?"

Reynard stood and amiably waved Glaupher off. He waited for the door to his office to shut and marveled, again, at the quiet. "Do you hear that, young man?" Reynard was, perhaps, four or five years older than Arlyn.

The latter turned his head from side to side.

"No? Marvelous, isn't it?" Reynard asked, smiling toward the half-shuttered and closed windows. It was gray, and probably raining outside.

Reynard saw that Arlyn didn't understand. "It's *quiet* in here. Outside there is traffic, people walking and talking. You can barely hear the drizzle against the glass. But, within these walls it's *quiet*."

"Yes sir, it is quiet."

Reynard smiled. "Never mind. So, your lieutenant says you are a good man who wants to get ahead. Is that true?"

"Yes sir. But if it's all the same to you, I would rather stay on the force. I earn half my pension in just a few more years."

"I understand. Entirely. And if I may be so rude, may I ask how much a police sergeant earns these days? Two hundred? Three hundred dollars per month?"

"Oh, no sir. Nowhere close to that. It's much less."

"So, in a few more years you will have earned a pension of less than a hundred dollars a month, perhaps two hundred … ?"

"Sure, perhaps."

"But you are an honorable man, a dedicated member of the police, a family man; someone who has to look out for many, many people with the hope of being able to scrape by when you can no longer get out to work … that is all very noble, Mr. Dunne." Reynard got up and walked to the office door, opening it and speaking out into the hallway. "Coffee, please."

"You'll stay for lunch," he announced, and Arlyn admitted that he had no other plans.

After the remains of lunch were removed from the office, Reynard retrieved a bottle of scotch from his bar and poured a dram for each of them.

"Thanks for the lunch, and the libation, Mr. Delacraw. You do know that it's illegal to possess this stuff?" Arlyn asked with a smile, before raising the glass and offering a silent toast.

"Old stock, Sergeant, old stock, I assure you." Reynard took the first sip.

Arlyn tossed his back.

"Arlyn—may I call you Arlyn? We might drink water, and we might gulp corn liquor, but we *sip* scotch."

Arlyn didn't savor the scotch any more than corn or rye whiskey. But he just nodded his head.

Reynard poured Arlyn another dram. "Have you given any thought to what we were discussing prior to lunch?"

"In what way, Mr. Delacraw?"

"About alternative employment, of course. Let me provide you with three alternatives, and you decide which of those appeals most to you. First, I contract with the city of Seattle to detail you as a security man for me, the details of which I will share with you if you find the first or second alternative most appealing. Upon which point you shall continue as a paid police sergeant with your current wages, working toward that pension. Second, that you instead leave the department to come work for me, full time, exclusively, and for which I will remit to you one hundred and fifty dollars each Friday evening, close of business; or, three, you return to your duties with the Seattle Police Department, thus precluding any formal relationship to Reynard Delacroix and Associates, with no hard feelings."

"One fifty?"

"You're right, too low; make it one-seventy-five. Did I mention that was per week?"

"That's—that's—"

"Multiples of what you earn now? Yes. And for that I demand loyalty. It is as if I welcome you into my family, do you understand?"

"One seventy-five?"

"With occasional bonuses as opportunity might allow. Lieutenant Glaupher suggested that you needed additional income …"

"But I never thought about that much money!"

"Of course not, but I think, perhaps, that it is not the amount that takes you off guard, it's what you might be expected to *do* for that money. Am I correct?"

"Well, one seventy-five, Mr. Delacraw, I doubt the *Chief* makes that kind of money."

"I can assure you he does much better than that, my friend." Reynard took a leisurely sip of his scotch and sat the glass back down in order to use his hands to talk. He could feel a familiar tightening at the base of his skull, so he tried to speed things up.

"In India they have this little snake, a small thing, so long—" he spread his hands outward about eighteen inches—" but they are very poisonous, these reptiles, and very prodigious breeders, meaning that as fast as one dies three more are born to replace it. They are everywhere, these *kraits*, and like to do their business late at night. When it is warm, and it generally is in India, one can easily deal with these snakes. It is as if the warmth quiets them down. But when it gets dark and cool these snakes will hunt anything that they can get into their mouths. Do you follow? My world is filled with these *kraits*, but we have different names for them. Grifters. Con artists. Flim-flam men. Strong arms. Hustlers. Assassins. *Les Truandes*. On occasion, even policemen.

"In India, these small snakes kill thousands of people each year, not to mention dogs, water fowl, fish, and virtually any amphibian upon which they might happen. But, when a water buffalo or elephant wanders into a *krait's* backyard, the reptile withdraws to its den and waits for the rumbling to go away. Now whether the serpent knows that the elephant is impervious to their bite, I can't say, but you can be certain they know that whatever makes the ground shake can squash them flat as a crêpe.

"Now, you can think of yourself as an elephant, or a water buffalo, if you prefer. You will accompany me into the fields of *kraits* and they will retreat to their dens, fearing for their safety while allowing me to conduct my commerce. Do you agree?"

Arlyn sat quietly, still chewing on the analogy, before looking Reynard in the eye. "Let's get this straight. One seventy-five each and every week, and I don't kill anyone."

"Let's hope not!" Reynard agreed with a broad grin.

Arlyn stood and offered his hand.

It had been weeks, maybe months, since Arlyn had happily climbed the stairs to his apartment, anticipating the warmth of his family and home. But this evening, lubricated by good scotch and the promise of a secure, well-paying job, he had to hold his sides to keep from laughing out loud.

M.E. was wiping up the baby's vomit on the kitchen floor when the front door quietly closed behind her. The footsteps, no matter how careful, gave away the intruder's presence. She leapt to her feet, stepping in front of the baby. "Arlyn, you beast!" she yelled, angry but relieved.

"You have to remember to lock the front door, Mary Elizabeth," he began in earnest before his face gave way to a broad smile. "I quit the force!" he yelled, still smiling, his arms outspread as though he were giving a testimonial.

"What? You quit? Now what are we going to do?" She gathered up the baby as if ready to flee. But even the tenor of her question couldn't dampen Arlyn's mood.

"What are we going to do? We're going to move!"

Reynard sat at his desk, plotting. Business was good. Income was steadily growing, and he foresaw a Seattle the size of San Francisco. Soon, he might have enough grit to move his businesses into Tacoma and, perhaps, Portland. That would mean more feet on the ground, more names on the payroll, and certainly, more palms to grease.

But in the time he had been in Seattle he had learned as much from his shortfalls as he had from his successes. He had been burned by crooked pols, cops, and business associates. Few of these crooks surprised him any longer, and the latest addition to his operation, the erstwhile cop, Arlyn Dunne, would only further strengthen his ability to make the most out of obscure opportunity.

He recognized the fiber of Dunne's loyalty in direct contrast to Glaupher's cynical and desultory obedience. One wanted to belong; the other wanted to be boss. Virgil Glaupher had run with the bootlegger Roy Olmstead too long, and sooner or later—probably sooner—he would end up like his former boss, incarcerated at McNeil Island or someplace like it. Dunne could be counted upon. Glaupher would just be counting …

He didn't hear the office door open, and didn't hear her at all until she was leaning over him, the scent of her *Lilas de Ressorts* perfume smothering the smoky smell that filled the room.

"Noémi, I've asked you to knock."

She playfully tousled his hair and laughed. "That's no fun."

He stood and admired his little sister. She was turning out much better, becoming more of a woman than he had ever expected. The good nuns at the private Catholic girls' college in Maryland had been successful at preparing her for life as a rich man's wife. She was schooled in the classics, knowledgeable of world affairs, and now carried herself as a fully-grown woman, even though—in his presence alone—she still often behaved as though she were twelve.

There was no hint that she, like Reynard, was once an impoverished orphan from southern Louisiana. She wasn't tall, but her frame suggested height. She had become a beautiful woman with a pleasantly round face, pouting lips, and a full figure that needed no fashion embellishment. She had green eyes, which almost seemed iridescent when she focused her attention on someone. Her dress was conservative but elegant, suggesting wealth without affectation.

Reynard, and Cozette, the erstwhile madam of a brothel in Thibodaux Parish, had raised Noémi. Reynard and Noémi's birth mother was an alcoholic who had done the laundry for two brothels on the tony side of New Orleans when she wasn't basking in the warmth of rotgut whiskey and laudanum. Their fathers were unknown, even to their mother. Reynard rarely attended the parish school but possessed a variety of books that had accumulated in and around the brothels, which Reynard had 'collected' while they were left unattended. He persuaded the whores to read to him and do their best to give him his ABCs. By the time he was nine he could read and write as well as any of the whores and quite a few of the johns.

When he was twelve, and on the verge of puberty, Noémi appeared, sired by yet another unascertained suitor, and Reynard immediately fell in love with the tiny infant. Which was well and good, for their mutual birth mother disappeared before Noémi turned three.

Reynard earned their keep by washing dishes, keeping the sitting porch clean, and running errands for everyone in the neighborhood. Along the way he picked up a variety of useful talents such as shoplifting, pick pocketing, and running numbers for Big Rudy Nagine, the parish boss who had solid connections in New Orleans.

When Reynard was old enough, Big Rudy introduced the young man to others who would help educate Reynard in the ways of a criminal life. He quickly matured and, as is the nature of life, violently displaced Big Rudy, venturing deeper into the world of Big Crime: protection rackets, usury, graft, and the miscellaneous thuggery that he hoped to one day forget.

Through all of his ventures, Noémi was kept at a safe distance. Cozette had her most educated girl serve as *au pair* when Reynard was away, though he kept his absences as short as possible. When she grew old enough to ask questions, his younger sister was led to believe he was a businessman, in a profession that she neither understood nor had any desire to understand.

When she was of age to attend the local Catholic school he was almost always home on the weekends, and he chaperoned her to the school fairs and events, as though he were her father. Over the years he began to recognize that she would need to leave Louisiana to get a better education. It was pure providence that when she was old enough to matriculate to St. Catherine's, just outside Baltimore, he had cause to leave Thibodaux Parish.

Or, rather, he had *need* to leave the parish.

On New Year's Eve, 1921, Reynard made a mistake. After having displaced Big Rudy, Reynard had become an associate of the Provenzano gang. The Provenzano family had run the docks and the fruit markets of New Orleans for three decades and, as business needs dictated—due to their losing control of the waterfront to the rival Matranga Family—they had included in their operations the running of the paddocks at many of the smaller racetracks in the South. This provided them with invaluable information regarding the health and status of resident or visiting thoroughbreds and jockeys. They handsomely profited from that inside information, and from activities attendant to those relationships. Reynard, like everyone in the Louisiana crime community, knew about these relationships and was generally content to accept the crumbs of information that the family might share in order to occasionally score some heavy bets.

Reynard was ambitious, but he was not driven by greed. His plans were long term, and he was capable of seeing the larger picture. He knew that as long as he provided his tribute to the Provenzanos they would continue to toss those crumbs his way.

Noémi had chosen to stay with a school friend's family in Philadelphia over the holidays, leaving Reynard on his own. He was invited to a New Year's Eve party in New Orleans at the Hotel Monteleone, hosted by the Provenzanos. It was a large, formal, gaudy affair with more than two hundred guests attending, many of whom would split their New Year's with a party hosted by the Matrangas, or someone else of influence at other nearby residences.

One of the Matranga lieutenants, Henry Beguille, had been a friend and accomplice of Reynard's since they were teenagers. Henry had a weakness for women of all shapes and age, and he had secretly taken up with one of the nieces, Gianna, of Angelo di Monasteri, a Provenzano captain. The *capo* had no idea that his niece was involved in this relationship, or he would have immediately stopped it—one way or the other.

Henry could not spend the evening with Gianna at either the Matranga gathering—where she was *proibito*—or at the Monteleone, where he would certainly be met with violence. So, he turned to his friend Reynard for help. Reynard was a romantic at heart, and he recognized the ardent request as genuine. Together, they laid out a plan, wherein Gianna's early presence at her family's gathering would be noted so that Reynard could spirit her out a side door, without detection, and into the arms of her beau.

The problem arose with the taxi driver that Reynard hired, who, unbeknownst to him, also worked for the Matranga Family. After he deposited the two lovers at a small, out-of-the-way hotel the driver made a phone call. Within a half hour, the two of them stood in front of Charles Matranga's chief lieutenant, who made a discreet phone call to the Provenzanos demanding a large sum of cash in order to guarantee the safe return of Gianna.

Of course, Reynard was rounded up, given a severe beating by the Provenzanos, and proclaimed *persona non grata.* His livelihood was taken away, and while he wasn't killed, he was ordered out of New Orleans.

Because of the Matrangas' close ties to New York, Chicago, Detroit, and even St. Louis, Reynard was compelled to seek opportunities elsewhere. The west coast, and particularly Seattle, was still a largely untapped source of easy money, but he never considered it until Cozette pointed out that one of her 'girls' had built a very profitable business with relationships tied to a variety of civic leaders in Seattle and Portland.

There was no time to investigate the region, so Reynard had to take Cozette's word that there would be ... *opportunities* ... for him in the Emerald City. The war between the Provenzanos and the Matranga family would continue to escalate, but Reynard was two thousand miles away, fighting his own battles.

It took two years for him to fully define his business in the region, taking partners when necessary, but generally absorbing the risks and rewards himself. Once Roy Olmstead's rum running operation was shut down, and the great man incarcerated, opportunities opened for Reynard that he had no idea even existed.

Noémi welcomed the move as another great adventure. She had balked when Reynard asked her if she wanted to attend college in Maryland, but once she was enrolled and gathered a new circle of friends that introduced her to Washington, DC, and, especially, New York, she took on the mantle of happy traveler.

Four years in Baltimore allowed her to blossom in ways that would never have been borne out had she stayed in New Orleans and attended Our Lady of Holy Cross. The relocation to Seattle would allow her to add a new roster of friends with whom she could share her cronies in the east and Louisiana.

She insisted on being included in the selection of a new house, and to be kept apprised of the businesses that Reynard would develop. It was her hope that she could keep Reynard on the straight and narrow path, which was surprising given how little she actually knew of his dealings in New Orleans. He had always gone to great lengths to ensure that Noémi was insulated from his businesses, and while Cozette had some inkling of his dealings even she rarely knew the particulars.

Noémi had grown into a young woman while in Baltimore, and as she became more aware of the world around her she began to recognize that her brother somehow managed to house, feed, and clothe her very well despite the lack of an established job. Moving to Seattle, she thought, would allow him to find something that was above reproach: a job or position that would be welcomed in the community. She felt that what he needed, besides a woman, was prestige.

Prestige he had earned or, better, notoriety. Reynard helped pick up the slack not long after Olmstead was thrown to the wolves, meeting with Canadian suppliers at Point Roberts to cement a new distribution network. The demand for hooch remained as great as ever, and he was able to devote his efforts to reestablishing the supply lines between Vancouver and Seattle.

Virgil Glaupher kept the heat off him for a healthy allowance and Reynard was soon taking more than his share of the market with little notice from the WCTU, Prohibition Office agents, Mayor Bertha Landes or her successor, Frank Edwards. He had become part of the landscape over a short period of time, and his well-placed philanthropy had garnered enough communal support to overshadow any concerns regarding his dealings.

Noémi leaned over his shoulder and examined the plans, as if she were able to divine what the plans were for. The key in the lower corner indicated a site elevation for a four-story hotel, that much she could understand.

"A hotelier? We are opening a hotel?"

"We have talked about it."

"Yes, but I had no idea that it would actually come to pass."

"I have never been an idle talker, little sister."

She turned the sheet and looked at a detail sheet for the lobby. At one end of the depicted room was a double doorway labeled 'restaurant.'

"And a restaurant—"

"Not just 'a restaurant.' A four-star restaurant. A destination for weary travelers in need of *haute cuisine*, something no other hotel in Seattle can offer."

"Like Delmonico's?" Noémi had been introduced to that eatery by the wealthy parents of one of her schoolmates at college. "Real French cuisine?"

"The best. Perhaps we can persuade Monsieur Duchamps to relocate to Seattle. Can you imagine what he would do with the fresh seafood that is so easy to come by here? Ah! Do you remember the pastries?"

"Who could forget, Reynard? You used those treats to get me to behave. Oh, what would I do if those pastries were here in this very hotel? I would gain ten pounds within the first week."

"I'll just have to declare the restaurant off limits to you then, *mademoiselle.* I shall have to lock you into our new house on First Hill, and keep you like Rapunzel."

The mention of the new house was a sore subject. The interior, except for marble tile being imported from Italy for the foyer, was done. Telegrams arrived almost daily, offering lame excuses for the ongoing delay in delivery. Reynard frowned at his own mention of the house.

Noémi pulled on his ear and stepped back. "You are having too much fun, Reynard. It is like you are building your own little city here." She returned to the plans and turned page after page until he attempted to stop her. "Why? You have something you don't want me to see?"

"You don't *need* to see everything. There can be surprises, you know."

What she didn't know, and what he intended to keep her from knowing, was one page detailing the construction of a very private series of subterranean rooms which would house a speakeasy and gambling parlor: the haven for very special guests of Reynard's hotel. These would be guests who would never hobnob with Noémi, if he had anything to say about it. But they would be guests who would provide additional wealth to both of them. He rolled the plans up and retied them, ending her interest.

"What will you name it?" she asked.

He turned back, thought for a moment, and smiled. "I was thinking *La Belle Grande.*"

She smiled and pinched his arm, her mark of approval.

After she left him alone he went to his Victrola, pulled a lacquered disc from its paper jacket and listened to the warmth of Piaf's voice. He sat in his chair and allowed the music to soothe him, taking him to his special place, a place where ideas flowed like water, where questions were intercepted by answers, a place where Reynard could pretend that everything would always be all right. Soon, after closing his eyes, the familiar jagged lights that presaged the pain began to appear at the corners of his vision.

A PASSAGE OF SORTS

It was the sun that woke "Bruge." Not the heat, but the light in his eyes. He had huddled beneath an empty boxcar, wrapped in a blanket beside his rucksack, fighting the cold, incessant wind and watching for yard bulls. In the all too brief moments between dawn and early morning, he had slept soundly, only to have the morning sunlight dispel whatever slumber he had achieved.

He had worked his way north and into Canada once he made the Maine shore. He wasn't sure whether or not the law was looking for him, but the homeward transit from east to west would be easier above the border. Hopping freights took him to Edmonton, where he nearly got caught napping in a boxcar in the Walker Yard by a railroad cop.

He took a job at a wheat farm west of town and bucked hay for three days, earning some large meals, a dry bed, and a few bucks, before thumbing rides out to Hinton, a small rail town near the eastern slope of the Continental Divide. He needed to restock his portable larder, and made his way into the company town that abutted the small yard.

With his dwindling funds he bought a pound of coffee, a small sack of jerked beef, a loaf of crusted bread, and some apples, all of which he stuffed into his rucksack.

The store manager watched him with suspicion, even to the extent of ignoring two young boys pilfering penny candy from jars at the far end of the shop counter in order to keep track of the stranger. The moment that he left the store, the manager phoned the Mounties and a Model A closed on him as he walked out of the small whistle stop. Once the Mountie noted the direction the stranger was heading, obviously on the march elsewhere, he abandoned his pursuit and drove back to the one small café in town.

Noting that the cop had turned back 'Bruge' altered his course and headed for the most likely spot to hop the next westbound freight. In this case, the best spots would be a mile up the line, where the train would be struggling to pick up speed and yet far enough from the yard that few bulls or railroad cops would be lingering.

He made his way through an adolescent spruce forest, across a steep knoll, and found himself on a bluff a hundred feet above the tracks. The tracks were on a raised rail bed here, paralleling the Athabasca River. Not a good spot for attempting to board. The rider would have to sprint—totally exposed—up a rocky slope to get to the slowly accelerating train.

And yet, from his vantage, he could see a half dozen people hiding in the scant brush paralleling the tracks. It was as many people as he had ever seen queued to catch a moving train. He smiled, for he knew the conductor and his bulls would be focusing on these easy pickings, leaving an opening for him farther up the incline.

He followed the tracks a few hundred yards farther to the west, finally angling down the rocky slope and into a small meadow surrounded by spruce and aspen. He was surprised to find another five people waiting in the shade of the trees. One was an elderly hobo who looked as if he had spent his entire life riding the rails. Another was a man with a young boy, probably a father and son who had been forced onto the road. The other two were burly but well worn: the kind of men who manage to make a go of it when there is no go to be made.

He casually inspected them, gauging for weapons and ability. No one acknowledged his arrival save for a couple of stolen glances, so he knelt down, removed the linen sack of jerky and gnawed at a piece, scanning the distant rail bed. Between their resting place and the tracks was a hundred yards of open grassland. There was no hidden approach to the tracks from that position.

After swallowing his last bit of dried beef, he casually stood up and strode off through the trees to find a better spot. The two burly men watched him, looked at the others, and then followed him at a safe distance. He was aware of their presence but felt no threat. He recognized that they, too, were simply looking for a safer, and easier, place to board the train without detection.

Another hundred yards west, and he found a wooded bank that overlooked the tracks. He wedged himself into a tight copse of aspen and watched for the other two men. They apparently found a spot of their own, for they were nowhere to be seen.

He picked at his teeth, liberating the last stubborn bits of meat with the fingernail of his index finger. In the distance he could hear the train's whistle as it departed the yard in Hinton and began its slow excursion onto the backside of the Rockies. After another few minutes he could hear the sound of a shotgun — sometimes the bulls loaded rock salt to fire at those who tried to sneak onto their trains. Another shotgun blast indicated that those in the meadow below had made their attempt to board, and had either made it or were now suffering from the salt pellets that had been fired at them.

The train continued to come, taking the moderate grade at a slowly accelerating pace. He saw the two men emerge from brush fifty yards down track and attempt to swing onto an open boxcar, where they were met by a bull that clubbed at them until they fell away from the train.

He took this opportunity, with the bull's attention focused on the two men, to slide down the embankment below the aspens and dart under a passing freight car. He climbed onto a suspension bar, shoving his rucksack into a dead space below the floor of the car.

The train continued to pick up speed, and there were no more disturbances. The bulls were probably sitting on top of the freight cars now, trading pulls from a bottle and enjoying the cool breeze flowing over the top of the train. They had probably concluded that they had repelled all those who sought free travel on their train, and that the ride would be relaxing until they slowed in Jasper where another group of freeloaders would attempt to board.

'Bruge's' back was killing him by the time the train slowed down while passing through Jasper, the last stop before crossing the Continental Divide. As the steady drone of the boxcar wheels across expansion joints slowed, he altered his position to stretch out his long body and nearly lost his balance. He wasn't built for this kind of life.

The train entered the Jasper rail yard and passed a small outbuilding. He grabbed his rucksack and dropped onto the sloping rail bed where he waited until the train slowed further before darting between the wheels and onto the far side of the train, watching for bulls on the ground or the top of the cars.

He was safe, and he found a group of stacked redwood ties to hide behind. The train was watered, and more coal was loaded into the tender. There wouldn't be any more water or coal available until the train passed onto the western slopes. He didn't notice any other illegal riders; they would be waiting farther up the line, away from the yard, so he knew the bulls wouldn't be watching that closely until the train continued its journey.

He carefully made his way along the line of boxcars, searching for one with an unlocked door, which would mean it either held little in the way of valuable cargo, or was empty. The railroad didn't like moving empty cars so he was pleased when he found a car that contained pallets of millet and wheat. He hid behind a stack of the sacks, creating a comfortable bed on top of the grain.

After fifteen minutes the train began to move, lurching forward due to the incredible weight the engine had to pull. No one came to check the car, there were no shotgun blasts, and everything seemed quiet until a group of five, one at a time, leapt into the open car. One was a hobo whose age was uncertain, covered in road dust, clothes crusty from constant use; the others were four men, two of whom were obviously traveling together.

Those two stood at the door, watching the shadow of the train on the ground for evidence that bulls were inspecting the cars from the top. They appeared particularly more nervous than their fellow riders, none of whom were aware of his presence.

The five settled down, and from his hiding place he heard them pull down grain sacks to create comfortable seating. The two nervous men stayed by the open door; ready to escape should a bull happen upon them.

Ten minutes out of Jasper and their demeanor changed. Making the assumption they were safe, they turned their focus on the other riders. Through a narrow space between the sacks that fronted his resting place, 'Bruge' watched the larger of the two men pull a knife from his belt and advance toward one of the other riders. The knife was brandished and the victim pulled a well-worn billfold from inside his shirt. He took out a dollar and handed it to his assailant. The scoundrel seemed pleased and went on to his next prey. Coins were placed in his hand. The third victim, the hobo, only had some apples, which were taken. The thief and his traveling partner stood in the doorway, munching happily on the apples, firing the remnants at passing bridge abutments.

'Bruge' had to piss. Badly. His first inclination was to urinate on the floor at his feet, but that urge was overtaken by anger at feeling captive to a couple of thugs. He stood up and they immediately noticed him. The knife reappeared. "Pony up. You want to ride, you got to pay."

'Bruge' quickly advanced toward the men and the knife wielder stepped forward, but before he could utter another threat he was seized and thrown from the boxcar. His companion looked at 'Bruge', shocked to have seen his larger friend so badly treated.

"Jump."

"I ain't gonna jump. It'll kill me."

"You got a choice. Either you jump, or I throw you off. Don't care which way this goes."

The man looked at him and knew he meant what he said. "Just give me a second. At least let me find a soft spot."

"There aren't any soft spots—" 'Bruge' pushed the other out of the boxcar, sending him bouncing, uncontrollably, down a rocky embankment and into a slough.

Standing in the door, he relieved himself. The other riders made it clear that they wanted no trouble. But even as they recognized him as a legitimate threat, they concluded that he had no interest in them. They left him alone until that evening when, as the freight passed over the Divide, one of them woke him and offered him a slice of crusty bread with a tin full of something passing as soup which they had heated over a small fire they built in the lee of the open door.

He had no interest in the food, but took it as a good faith offering for the protection he had provided, though both of the robbery victims would have liked to receive their money back. With a bit of food in their stomachs, and the reassuring rocking of the freight car, all of them fell back into troubled slumbers, never forgetting that they were one mistake away from apprehension by the bulls.

The next morning, after stops in Blue River and Barriere, the train highballed into Kamloops, where two of the strangers departed without a word. There were other connections, and decisions, to be made.

'Bruge' and the soup man stayed with the train, knowing that it would be more difficult to remain out of sight of the bulls as the train moved down the Fraser Valley and into Vancouver. Given the heightened security, he took to the undercarriage again, suffering the pain in order to avoid detection.

When they rolled into Vancouver ten hours later, his back ached so much that he was forced to sleep sitting up on a park bench, dodging the city cops when they passed close by on their rounds.

The next day he was in Seattle, but it was not the Seattle he remembered. The skyline was changing. What had long been the promise of a city had become that city, or rather, a city faintly resembling the visions shared by founding fathers Henry Yesler, Doc Maynard, and Arthur Denny. Before he had been forced to flee the Puget Sound region, many of those more important changes had been realized: new neighborhoods in Washington Park and Mount Baker had matured, and new businesses spurred by the Great War had expanded, providing more employment and a means to buy into those preferred neighborhoods.

The downtown seemed even busier: more pedestrians, more cars, more trucks clogged the thoroughfares in places that he remembered as still being vaguely pastoral. The manufacturing sector had overtaken the south end of town, and the mud flats along the Duwamish River already housed a small collection of outcasts: the first indicators of what was going to be a hard economic downturn.

The Northwest was the last region of the continental US to mature. The Puget Sound embodied the ultimate shoreline over which Manifest Destiny finally swept. He had grown up outside of Seattle, on an island in the Sound, but had been close enough, and visited often enough, to witness the city's evolution from township to metropolis.

Some real changes, the changes that helped to define the city, had occurred during his expatriation to Canada and the Northeast. There were many landmarks that he recognized, and an equal number that were new to him as he climbed off the bus that deposited him downtown. He walked down to Pioneer Square just to get his bearings, parted with two bits to get a sandwich and coffee at a small diner, and then headed for one place that he knew well: the Sailors' Union Hall down along the waterfront.

He was amused by his predicament. He had spent the past three weeks as Walter Bruge, making his way across the continent and now, having arrived, he was aware he had no real plan of action. But fishing was his career, his profession—his *chosen* profession, having made that decision to spite his father's wishes—despite the fact that he had only fished a few times since leaving Seattle.

He had been born into a settler's family on Vashon Island, the second son of a farmer and lay minister whose plans for his sons were embedded in civic duty. But he had no interest in either farming, policing, or mercantile: the choices he, as youngest son, was offered. Going to sea and escaping the tyrannical tantrums and sermons of his father was much more appealing.

So by the time he was fourteen he was working a seine boat out of Dockton, learning the life of a deckhand, living in a storage shed, and feeling a sense of pride that his Calvinist father seemingly wanted to destroy. Fishing in the Straits, or in the blue waters of the North Pacific was hard, dangerous work, but it gave him a sense of independence that he would never have experienced had he stayed within reach of his old man.

Not surprisingly, this upset his father a great deal, and after Steven—his older brother and proverbial acorn—became a deputized county sheriff, the latter made his life even more miserable. Steven found excuses to show up in Dockton, the small fishing town on Quartermaster Harbor, to harass him. Cain showed as much affection to Abel as Steven showed him. Despite his family's interference, he fished for seven years before the real trouble started.

Fishermen, particularly those that fished the deep, dangerous waters of the North Pacific and Bering Sea, had formed a union just as he had started his career as a deckhand on a short draft seine boat. Though he felt he was treated fairly by his boat owner—as well as a deckhand could expect to be treated at that time—he joined the union out of solidarity to his fellow fishermen. The group in Dockton was small, but they spent time together during bad weather, or when the fleet happened to be harbored at the same time.

He listened to the older fishermen, some whom carried lifetime reminders of mistakes they, or their skipper, had made. Scars, limps, missing fingers: these were all the hallmarks of a working deckhand in the early part of the century. The union intended to make working conditions easier and, more important, safer for their members, and it didn't take long for him to become a stalwart member, albeit still a hard working fisherman.

His brother often shadowed these meetings, hoping for the opportunity to 'speak' privately with an unsuspecting union representative, or to find a good reason to break up the meeting before it could even get started. It wasn't long before the young fisherman tired of his brother's heavy-handed behavior and came to blows with his sibling.

That landed him a night in the island lockup at town center before being transported to King County jail to await arraignment for the charge of disturbing the peace and assaulting a deputy sheriff. In the lockup he met up with an acolyte of Eugene Debs, and the militant inside him was born. What was once a dedicated fisherman, with no axe to grind, had become a radical who happened to be a fisherman.

When he met his first Wobblie at an Industrial Workers of the World meeting in Tacoma, the die was cast. One year later, at the Everett Massacre, he became a wanted man and a fugitive.

Now, he was hoping to find work, once again, as a fisherman. He was willing to take any job that was offered; he knew that his work ethic would keep him employed, and his knowledge of fishing would get him promoted.

The trouble, he realized when he entered the hall, was that there were literally hundreds of men looking to hook up with a boat. Another issue was that the papers he carried belonged to the real Bruge, and what fishing boat captain, and owner, would be looking for work as a deck hand on the opposite coast? He found the right line and waited patiently for his turn with one of the union representatives. When he presented his papers the rep looked him up and down.

"You sure look familiar. You're out of Maine?"

"Yeah. Buck's Harbor."

"Lobsterman, huh?"

"I did some lobstering, yes. Also worked a dragger down the coast."

The rep looked at the papers, as though they might offer some additional bit of information about the man sitting in front of him.

"And now you're willing to scrub decks?"

"If that's all I can get. I need to get back to sea."

"What happened to your boat? The *Blue Jacket*?"

"Lost her off the Massachusetts coast last year."

"But you left Maine to come to Seattle?"

"Yeah. Change of scenery. Bad memories, losing my boat and all ..."

"Okay. Well, I can put you on the list. No one has a vacancy right now, and you need to bring your dues up to date, Captain."

"How much?"

"We'll have to check with the main office in San Francisco. If you need casual work, we can probably line something up at one of the canneries on the north end of Elliot Bay. Not much in the way of pay, but plenty to eat, and they have bunks. That suit you?"

'Bruge' nodded.

"Check back with me in three days. We'll get something for you, Captain."

Work in the cannery was brutal. Outside, it was in the low sixties. Inside, with the canning machinery running, and with a large mob of women working the cleaning and packing tables, the atmosphere was hot and humid. The smell was overpowering: a smell that he had always enjoyed, until he was reduced to cleaning scrap bins and removing the inedible debris to collection bins for fertilizer and farm food.

The work was endless. He got one half-hour to eat his lunch, and two fifteen-minute breaks during each ten-hour day. And the pay was minimal: 35 cents per hour. But as long as he did his work, no one bothered him, and when anyone took a quick smoke break he would join them, eschewing the tobacco for a quick pull at someone's flask or pint bottle. In the evening those that were bunking at the cannery grilled tuna fillets and augmented that with stewed greens purchased for a few cents from a local grocer.

After three days he reappeared at the hall. He saw a policeman standing along the wall behind the seated union representatives. He had never seen a policeman inside a union hall, and wondered at this one's presence. Were they aware that he was not the real Bruge? If so, would they suspect foul play? Had the Coast Guard found the broken stern of the *Blue Jacket*, tied that wreckage to Bruge's body on the buoy, had the corpse identified by Bruge's wife, and passed that information along to the union and the Seattle Police? Had someone identified him for who he really was, and to his involvement with the IWW and the *Verona* on that bloody Sunday ten years earlier?

He wasn't going to risk his freedom finding out. He carefully backed his way out of the hall, and back onto the street, where he noticed a beat cop casually walking toward him. He froze, watching the cop, and the latter smiled at him as he passed, swinging his baton in rhythm to his walk.

He turned and walked in the other direction, toward downtown. He couldn't risk going back to the cannery, even though his rucksack was secure in one of the lockers there.

He made his way back to Pioneer Square, and found a seat at the counter of the diner where he had eaten upon his arrival in Seattle. There he assessed his belongings: the clothes on his back, a jackknife, and his wallet, with Bruge's papers and six dollars and eleven cents. Whether the cops were onto him, or not, he couldn't be sure, but if he returned for his belongings at the cannery they might be there, ready to take him into custody. He wondered about the statute of limitations—hell, he didn't even know if he was a killer, it had all happened so quickly.

The Wobblies were largely reviled by society, as was the labor movement in general. The big boys in business, who owned the papers and pulp rags upon which most folks drew their news and information, had poisoned the image of union members. While Eugene Debs had many supporters who were mainstream members of society, he also had a roster of enemies ranging from railroad to mine owners, to hard-core conservative news columnists, and even the US government. From the moment Debs formed the IWW in 1905, his enemies conspired to destroy the union, its membership, and, especially, its leaders.

But the organization's membership grew despite the efforts of big business, and held meetings across the country to expand that enrollment. Trades people from all stripes, including fishermen like him, attended those meetings, even while belonging to other unions. The organization coalesced primarily in the Northwest, and managed to disrupt a variety of enterprises through their actions; overall improving working conditions for migrant workers, and fostering the establishment of unions for loggers and other laborers.

But the government vilified the IWW, and his father and brother, once they learned of his involvement with the IWW, made unimaginable threats, not the least of which would be to ostracize him from his mother and sisters.

When the authorities in Everett, with a level of violence that no one could have predicted, attacked the steamer *Verona* the ensuing confusion muddled both the responsibility for the attack and the identities of those who were actually involved. He knew that he had shot someone—an *ad hoc* member of the county sheriff's deputation.

Once the dust had settled he stealthily returned to Dockton, secured his small collection of belongings, and then made the mistake of returning to his family's home on Vashon Island to say good-bye to his mother. Surveying the home before announcing himself, he noted the presence of his brother and another, obviously armed, deputy. They sat on the front porch. His brother balanced a lever action carbine across his knees, waiting for something: waiting for *him*. He hadn't seen or contacted his mother again for a decade, leaving for points east where he might start over, leaving her to wonder whether her son was even still alive.

And now he was back home. Well, not home, but close enough.

He finished an egg sandwich and walked down to the Mosquito Fleet dock to catch a ferry for the island.

If he accomplished nothing else during this return, it would be to say hello to his sisters and mother. Ferry passage was a dime, and now he was counting them. There were a variety of places he could stay on the island for free, without detection. He doubted that the authorities knew who he really was, so the notion that they might have alerted his brother seemed improbable.

Once the ferry left its landing he immediately felt better, being on the water and away from anyone looking for him in Seattle.

BARTERED SOULS

If Arlyn believed that the purchase of a new home would salve the state of his marriage, he was mistaken. There seemed even less opportunity for them to share intimacy. M.E. had made finding the new home her holy mission, securing the help of a broker to first locate a few choice selections, then to focus on the actual purchased property.

Following the purchase, Arlyn knew that she would devote her time and resources to outfitting the house, a three-bedroom bungalow on the south slope of Queen Anne. And she did, generally to the exclusion of any attention directed toward him. Enjoying his larger paychecks, she often spent the money before it was earned, surprising Arlyn, for he had expected that the increased income would be more than enough to sate her growing appetite for finery.

But as M.E. continued to finesse her surroundings, her interest in Arlyn seemed to diminish. There had been a time when he would appear, presenting a simple bouquet of flowers bought at the corner grocer, and she would be ecstatic. Now, any simple expression of affection was swept aside as she focused on something more immediately important to her.

Her saving grace was her undying concern for the welfare of their boys. He noted, with great satisfaction, how carefully she dressed them, and had the eldest boy, named Charles after his grandfather, enrolled in a decent school not five blocks from their new home. He felt a sense of pride, then, in the decision he had made to leave the force.

His relationship with Delacroix was solid, and his sense of loyalty could not be shaken. The latter had all but adopted him, inviting him to his new house on Capitol Hill to share dinner, and was sharing substantial amounts of the business operation with his new chief of security. Delacroix ensured that Arlyn felt important, already deferring to him on matters that he, personally, did not feel the need to oversee.

Delacroix was a shrewd man, who clearly knew the value of loyalty, and was able to identify the needs of those around him. Arlyn was blooming: his appearance was more polished, and his demeanor much more confident.

It wasn't that Mary Elizabeth wasn't proud of Arlyn, in light of their recent rise up the social ladder. She just wasn't sure that Arlyn's career change was entirely good. She knew little about Mr. Delacroix, but she held automatic distrust for anyone whose intentions she couldn't divine. *Why* had Delacroix hired her husband away from the police? *What* was there about Arlyn that made him attractive to a man like Delacroix? These things puzzled her, and while his appearance had become more polished, in her eyes Arlyn's new suits seemed to be a lame attempt to make him something he wasn't.

There was something else. Arlyn rarely brought a gun home when he was on the police force. Generally, he locked the gun up at the station, and it only made its way across their threshold on those late nights when he came directly home from a shift taken in another part of the city. Now he always had a gun. He even carried it when the five of them went out for dinner, or even to church. And it was a larger gun than the .32 he had carried with the police. If she had had the chance to look at the gun more closely, she would have been mortified to see an engraved message along the barrel: *"Bienvenue à la famille!"*

When he attempted to be intimate she gave in, more frequently now.

First, it was because he represented something new, though the routine remained predictable. Lately, it was because she was a bit fearful that if she refused him he would go elsewhere. No amount of resentment, or fear, was going to take her husband from her.

Over time their marriage, their life together, had become a mixture of missed opportunities and unspoken promises. But the need for money had been answered: there was no dripping faucet in the middle of the night (and the kitchen was no longer adjacent to their bedroom); there were no cardboard inserts in the hand-me-down shoes that the boys wore; her closet contained more dresses than she had owned during the course of her lifetime; and there was the promise of more, much more, if Arlyn kept his employer happy.

But there was something missing from their life together that had once made up the fabric of their relationship. She no longer implicitly trusted Arlyn, and he could tell. No matter what gift he brought her, no matter what assurances he offered of his love and devotion, a line had been crossed when he left the force. And, try as she might, even her newfound focus on a better life for herself and her boys did not measure up to the disappointment she felt toward her husband.

His marriage damaged, and with no idea how to repair it—short of the gifts and groceries—Arlyn focused his attention on his new job. At first, he looked past Reynard's questionable business practices. He refused to be involved in what he recognized as outright illegal activity—the loan sharking, the numbers games, the illegal off-track betting—and told Reynard that he would not be a bill collector.

"That presents no problem, Arlyn," replied Reynard with a broad smile. "We have others to do that kind of work. I want you to focus on the political aspects of business, and find out what you can about those who would work against our legitimate interests. You can do that. You've done it for the force. You have friends and contacts that can help us stay one step ahead of the competition. Think of this job as your finishing school."

Reynard gave Arlyn a new edition of *The Prince* in which he inscribed: "*Power is only a tool. It can be used for good or bad, but knowing people and how they think is the real power.*"

Arlyn tried to read the book. He kept it with him in his coat pocket, and when there were breaks in his day he would crack it open to his bookmark and read sections over, and over again, attempting to find and digest the kernels of wisdom that generally remained hidden on the page.

One day in the car, when they were on their way down to Tacoma to look at a potential warehouse site along Commencement Bay, he brought it up.

"Stay with it," replied Reynard. "Take notes. After a while you will begin to understand the greater message."

"Which is?"

"You must read the book. But I will tell you this, Arlyn: the world isn't as easy to define as the government, or the Vatican, will tell you. Nothing is, as people like to say, black or white."

"I know that, I don't need to read a book to know that."

Reynard smiled. "Consider reading, and coming to understand what has been written, part of your job."

And it was. Arlyn finished the book, having written notes in the margin, some of which he would share with his employer. Then he read it again, in the evenings when Mary Elizabeth was asleep, or when she was at church, her latest refuge from her husband. He came to understand the flexibility of morals, and the contradictory application of codified laws that had been handed down for generations. He began to question the very mores that had compelled him to become a policeman.

The relationship between Arlyn and Reynard fully matured one afternoon when they were leaving Chauncey Wright's restaurant on Third Avenue with one Frank Ander. Ander was one of Reynard's business allies, visiting from San Francisco.

Little did any of them know, an enforcer named Jacarusso, working for one of Ander's North Beach competitors, had followed Ander to

Seattle. Quite coincidentally, Jacarusso's employer was connected to the Matranga family in New Orleans. Jacarusso had been given the order to take out Ander once the latter was off his home turf, and the visit to Seattle presented such an opportunity.

Jacarusso watched where Reynard Delacroix's driver parked, and situated himself at a newsstand between there and the restaurant. Leaning against a brick wall while pretending to read a copy of the *Post-Intelligencer*, he kept his other hand on a revolver in his pocket.

Jacarusso was a patient man, but the moment his quarry appeared on the sidewalk outside the restaurant he advanced, pulling his gun.

Arlyn, who walked ahead of Reynard and his guest, noted the movement and reacted immediately. He knocked the gun to the sidewalk and threw the would-be assassin to the ground.

Before Jacarusso could react Arlyn rolled him onto his stomach, placed his knee in the middle of the man's back, and pulled hard at the man's shoulders, threatening to dislocate both sockets.

Screaming, Jacarusso went limp, and he remained that way until the Seattle Police arrived, led, not surprisingly, by Virgil Glaupher.

"We'll take care of him, Monsieur Delacroix."

And everyone, especially Jacarusso, knew what that meant.

Ander was impressed, but not nearly as much as Reynard, who now held Arlyn in greater esteem. Arlyn's reflexes were quick, and his uncanny eye had picked out the danger before anyone else was aware of it. As he climbed into his sedan, Reynard smiled at Arlyn, a genuine smile that reflected his satisfaction in his selection of a bodyguard.

"We could use a man like you in 'Frisco," said Ander.

"He has a home here. Are you happy here, Arlyn?"

"Yessir, Mr. Delacraw."

While it was not a friendship, it was a close association that both men, for different reasons, wanted to limit to a professional relationship. For Reynard, trust could only be meted in careful increments. For Arlyn, Reynard was out of his league: alien to his culture, to his experience.

What little he knew about Reynard's past persuaded him to think that too close a relationship might become troublesome, if not burdensome. On those occasions when he was in the Delacroix household, he had noticed Cozette's careful deference to her employer. She had been with the Delacroix's for years, while he was only in his first month, still on probation.

However, sitting on the front seat of the sedan, feeling the admiring gazes from both Ander and his boss, Arlyn allowed himself to bask in a sense of security that had largely been absent from his life.

In a moment of celebratory exuberance, Reynard straightened in the back seat and announced, "This heroism calls for celebration. We dine in tonight, at my house, to mark the actions and goodwill of our associate, Mr. Dunne. Arlyn, I will not take any excuses. You bring your wife, by whatever means necessary. It shall be delightful."

Arlyn was uncomfortably aware that his employer had previously noted Mary Elizabeth's dedicated absences on two occasions when reading her nearly illegible notes aloud in Arlyn's presence. "She uses the term 'familial obligation' quite often, doesn't she?" he had asked. "Aren't there any babysitters up there on Queen Anne?" Reynard would joke, but Arlyn could only shrug.

Mary Elizabeth, of course, struggled to find an acceptable reason not to go, but there were none. There were several teenage girls living in the neighborhood around them, and Arlyn rounded up one fifteen-year-old who was thrilled to have the opportunity to make some money.

Then there was the matter of what to wear: Mary Elizabeth had expanded her wardrobe, but she complained that she had nothing suitable for the occasion. So, Arlyn dispatched her, via taxi, with $30 to spend on a dress at *The Bon Marché* at Second and Pike.

She returned, rather quickly he felt, with a red party dress that he concluded was not appropriate, so he rounded up the boys, left them with the sitter, and drove Mary Elizabeth back downtown where they shopped, and found, a more suitable—more conservative—dress for

Reynard's dinner party.

The meal was extravagant. Following aperitifs, Arlyn and Mary Elizabeth joined the gentlemen, Noémi, and Cozette in Reynard's grand dining room for a catered meal of oysters, crab soufflé, roasted capons, and a variety of steamed root vegetables, all followed by fresh fruit and brandy.

Mary Elizabeth was at once entranced and overwhelmed by the demonstration of wealth that Reynard's home presented. She marveled at the paneling and imported carpets, and giggled when Noémi complained about the still-absent marble for the entryway. The bond M.E. seemed to be making with Noémi encouraged Arlyn, yet he couldn't help but note that with every sweep of her eyes around the room she was counting dollars. She needed to realize that even with their new affluence, this lifestyle would never be hers.

"You certainly have a beautiful home, Mr. Delacraw," she observed, sipping at her brandy.

"De-lah-qua. Thank you, Mrs. Dunne. It makes coming home so much more pleasant, and Noémi deserves to have a comfortable home, as do you. And how is your new home, to your liking?"

"Very much so. We'll invite you up for dinner once we've finished our decorating." The mention of new decorations caused Arlyn to flinch. Their very serviceable, and affordable, dining room set could only seat six, which limited the number of guests, and M.E. had already made it clear that she wanted a larger, solid oak table which would cost a small fortune. He knew that she was going to leverage this visit into another series of purchases.

"You put on a nice spread," noted Ander, "equal to anything I've enjoyed in Pacific Heights. I hope to return the hospitality when you visit San Francisco."

The evening remained devoid of business, with Reynard and Ander inquiring into the quality of schools on Queen Anne, the best places to shop for furniture—with Reynard offering to put the Dunnes in contact with his suppliers in New York—and upcoming cultural events that they might together attend. It was, for most of them, a pleasurable evening.

As the night wore on, Mary Elizabeth became a bit more uncomfortable in the presence of the younger, more attractive, worldlier, Noémi. M.E. found that she had little to share with Noémi other than the tribulations of motherhood. Noémi had been college-educated while she, M.E., had not even finished high school. The former could speak two languages fluently, while Mary Elizabeth had trouble following the conversations of her husband and his employer. Mary Elizabeth realized that she was resentful, and growing more so, of Noémi the longer she was in the presence of the younger woman.

Every question seemed a challenge, no matter how innocent the subject or the tenor in which it was asked. Every seeming physical affectation, from Noémi's perfume to the style in which she kept her hair, provided some level of discomfort.

And so, she was happy to announce, at nine-fifteen, that it was time for the Dunnes to make their way back up to the safe refuge of Queen Anne.

"Did you enjoy yourself?" Arlyn asked during the drive home.

"How did he get so much money? What is it exactly that he does, or that you do for him?"

Arlyn was taken aback. He recognized that this was an attack on him more than on Delacroix. "He's a businessman. He buys, he sells. He has investments in the housing projects up in Shoreline, and owns a piece of the logging business east of Tacoma. He owns a car dealership—that's where this car came from. What is it, exactly, that you're disturbed by, M.E.?"

"Did you see her clothes?'

"Yes, very nice. You should go shopping with her."

"She shops in New York! When would I go shopping with her? And you didn't answer my question!"

"Which question was that, honey?"

"What is it you *do* for him that he would pay you all that money?"

"I'm his security. It's that simple. I watch out for him; I do background checks ..."

"And for that he pays you more in one week than most people make in month?"

"I'm not going to question our good fortune, Mary Elizabeth. And you would be wise to accept and embrace this opportunity. Why have you become such a crab? You used to complain all the time about the apartment, how we had no piped in hot water, how the boys all had to share one room, and one bed. Now, for some bit of good luck, we have our own home, we have hot water, we have our *own* bathroom, and you want to second-guess the reasons for that? Get a hold of yourself, woman."

The silence that followed carried on for two days.

At the end of that second day Arlyn drove Ander to Union Station. Ander invited him in to have a drink before the train departed, and the two of them found a quiet corner in the bar to have a beer.

"Reynard likes you," Ander began, "and that incident outside the restaurant put you in good sway."

"I'm glad he's happy with me."

"It's good for him to have an ex-cop working for him. Provides him with a different perspective that helps him to avoid the usual pitfalls in business."

"If you say so."

"I do. Listen, a man like you is valuable. You'd be valuable in my organization. If you ever decide to relocate to the Bay Area, we would gladly take you on."

"Well, I like it here in Seattle. Mr. Delacroix takes good care of me."

"I'm sure he does. But nothing lasts forever, kid. And the money you're making, while it's gotta be head and shoulders better than what you made as a cop, isn't that much. You can do better. We would do better by you."

"I appreciate what you're saying, Mr. Ander. And I'm glad I've made a good impression, but until something changes, my loyalty is to Mr. Delacroix."

"No problemo, kid, just a word to the wise. Say, what do you think the chances are I find a professional working girl on this train?"

"What did you think of him?" Reynard asked after Ander's departure.

"He seems to be pretty smart. He must be, for you to be doing business with him."

"Well, sometimes we have to do business with people that we wouldn't normally be associated. Ander is no fool, and he's done all right for himself in San Francisco. He's tight with the unions, the pols, and a couple of big business types. He's a very clever man, but a dangerous man. He will likely do all right for us, but only if we keep him on a short leash."

"What, exactly, is he doing for 'us'?"

Reynard laughed. "Good man. You recognize the pecking order. Did he offer you a job? Better make sure he pays up front!" He laughed again. "Take it easy, Arlyn, I'm just joking. I *know* where your heart is. I believe we're coming to know each other better each day. But there are things that you don't yet need to know—not because I don't trust you, but because too much information can make decisions more difficult. I just need you to focus on my security for now … though I believe I might have you spend some time with Noémi on our next trip east. Have you been to New York? No? Then it's high time you became acquainted with that den of delights."

HOMECOMING

Bells ringing. He slowly escaped a dream—which he immediately forgot—and became aware that it was the phone ringing. He lay in bed, hoping the ringing would stop so he could grab a few more winks. But then his wife Elise came in and gently shook him free from his slumber.

"What?" he demanded.

"Steven, it's Annie Post, says that Warren has taken to beating her again. She's managed to get him locked in their smokehouse."

Deputy Sheriff Steven Dougal sighed and swung his feet to the floor. He massaged his eyes with the heels of his palms and forced himself to shake off the cobwebs. "Coffee."

"It's there on the nightstand. Annie says it's really bad this time."

He struggled to his feet. "It's always bad, goddamn it. I should lock both of them up with a baseball bat and let out whoever survives."

Elise went to the bathroom and returned with some aspirin. Dougal was already on his feet and in his pants. He buttoned up a clean shirt and pinned his badge to the left side pocket before taking the two aspirin and washing them down with the coffee.

"Make me an egg sandwich to eat on the way," he said on his way to the toilet.

While Elise worked quickly to get him his breakfast, he checked his revolver and strapped on the holster. Another day in paradise, he thought.

The Model T, a few years past its prime, sat in its tiny garage, daring him to make it start. He had been petitioning the county for a new car for five years, but the sheriff's office in Seattle figured it still had one or two good years left in it.

He retarded the magneto, adjusted the throttle, and palmed the crank, giving it a hard, swift turn. Nothing.

He played with the choke and tried the crank again. The T refused to respond.

"Fucking piece of shit," he announced, slamming his fist on one of the fenders.

He was rubbing at his hand when Elise came out and handed him his sandwich wrapped in brown paper. "Won't start?" she asked. His glare told her what was patently obvious.

"It won't with you standing there gawking!"

Elise knew better than to hang around when her husband was in one of his blacker moods. It was Saturday morning, a day when he could generally stay in bed until eight-thirty or nine, but today he was going to have to go deal with one of his least favorite constituents.

Steven waited for her to return to the house and gave the fender another shot, then pulled the choke open and reset the throttle, checking to ensure that the magneto was, in fact, retarded before giving the crank another pull, this time accompanied by an angry grunt.

The T finally caught, struggled, and then caught again as Dougal closed the choke and played with the throttle, revving the engine to life. Convinced the damn thing wouldn't quit on him, he quickly climbed into the cab and engaged first gear, urging the car to move before it had a chance to argue with him.

The sun was still below the trees, and the road was cold. He hadn't brought his jacket, but this time of year he shouldn't have to bring a jacket, he thought.

From the Dougal house at island center the road ran east to Dilworth, passing planted fields. The warmth of the early morning sun considerably helped his mood enough so that he was aimlessly whistling by the time he reached the Posts' property, which sat on a bench overlooking the Eastern Passage. Annie Post was sitting in a chair in front of her house, well distanced from the building in which Warren smoked his salmon catches.

"Good morning, Annie," Dougal called from his car. "Are you okay?"

She stood and pulled up the sleeve of her housedress, revealing a black and blue welt on her shoulder. He turned off the engine and climbed down to examine the injury.

"Nothing broken?"

"No, Steven, nothing broken, as if that's any consolation."

"It's something. He still in the smokehouse?"

"He can stay in there till Heaven finds its way to the island for all I care."

"Let me talk to him."

He walked around the house and across the yard to the outbuilding that jailed Warren Post. "You okay in there, Warren?" he called.

"Get me the hell out of here, Sheriff!"

"Well, we got to talk about things first, Warren. Why'n you go and hit Annie for?"

Silence.

"Warren, no one's letting you outta there till we get some things settled? How's the smell, it getting to you yet?"

"Damn woman poured out my whisky!"

"She must've had a good reason. You do tend to get over-excited when you drink, and you do know it's illegal to possess whisky anyway, don't you?"

"Like you don't partake. I seen you bolt down a glass or two."

"Look, I'm gonna let you out, but if you do anything to make me nervous I'm gonna lay you out. You understand?"

"Let me out."

"Okay, then."

Dougal lifted the hasp and pulled the door open. Shielding his eyes from the bright morning sun, Post emerged, holding a nearly empty bottle of Everclear.

"Was that thing full when she put you in there?"

"She knocked me cold, sheriff! Hit me when I wasn't looking. I wouldn't of had nothing to drink if I didn't have a bottle stashed in there for when I'm hanging the fish. Woulda died from thirst for all she cares."

Annie appeared at a safe distance to witness the exchange.

"You go on and get out of here!" Warren shouted. "Hit me when I wasn't looking, not sporting like at all!"

"From what I understand, you started it."

"Didn't start nothin'—!"

"Here's the thing, Warren. I could lock you up right now, I should lock you up right now, I've got evidence—" Dougal snatched the bottle from Warren "—and I'll bet if I looked hard enough I could probably find your still. But—" Dougal threw the bottle against a short wall of granite, and was satisfied when it smashed, spilling the last of its contents, "—I'm going to give you one last chance to turn things around with your woman. She's put up with enough—*I've* put up with enough from you. If I have to come back, I'll be bringing shackles, and I'll make sure you have more lumps than you've given her. Understand?"

"She's evil!"

"Yeah, and I'm Santy Claus. Sober up, Warren. Find the Lord. Find something besides the booze. Or I'll make you pay."

Dougal was preparing to crank the T when Annie hurried out of her house carrying two bottles of the Everclear. "I found these where he hid them. You better take them, but I know he's got more."

Dougal noted Warren watching from the rear corner of the house, frowning. The deputy made a great show of bundling the bottles in the backseat of the Ford. "You've got my number, Annie, you've used it once already today. See if you two can't get along for the remainder of the weekend. Warren," he shouted, "don't make me come back out here anytime soon."

Post watched silently as the T was cranked back to life. Dougal drove back out the quiet road toward the main highway. He stopped at the intersection, abandoned except for a lone freight truck that slowly passed him.

Once the truck was fifty yards past, Dougal pulled one of the bottles from the backseat and uncorked it. First he tested the liquor with his nose, then he took a dainty sip: just enough to wet his lips. The stuff wasn't horrible; it was drinkable, but it wasn't quality. Still, he took a short pull and then another, feeling the liquid burn its way to his stomach.

"That'll kill the worms," he said to no one, and then took another long pull before replacing the cork. He wouldn't report the seizure of the booze, any more than he would write up the Posts for a marital squabble. There was no blood and no broken bones, so, officially, nothing had happened, except that his Saturday morning was ruined. The booze, however, might prove to help out Saturday night.

He unwrapped his sandwich, which was now cold but still delicious, and worked at it, taking small bites so that the runny yolk couldn't escape.

In the distance, coming from the direction of Vashon Heights and the ferry landing, he could see a figure walking toward him. He wiped some yolk from his stubbly chin and waited. The person might need a ride to town center. He finished his sandwich and took another quick pull to wash down the last bite before securing the bottles in the back so that a passenger wouldn't know they were there. Tired of waiting, he got out, cranked the T back to life, and pulled out, heading for the stranger.

"Son of a bitch!" Dougal leapt from the T, causing it to lurch to a stop. "No, no, no! Turn around, asshole, you're not welcome here!"

The figure stopped to assess the threat, preparing to defend himself. "Hello, Steve."

"No hellos here, asshole, only good-byes. You're good at good-byes, Emmett, now get off my island!"

Steven closed on the newcomer. His hand traveled to his gun and Emmett attempted to calm him down. "I'm just here to see Ma and the girls. I'm not staying."

"You're fucking-A right you're not staying, not one more minute past the next departing ferry—"

"It's been a long time, Steve. Let me at least say hello to Ma."

"She thinks you're dead, Emmett, and that's the way it's going to stay. You leave now or I'll arrest you."

"For what, for something that happened almost a decade ago? Where's the brotherly love? Let me say hello to the family, have a sit-down meal, and then I'll happily be on my way. I don't mean any trouble."

"You've always been trouble, Emmett. You broke the old man's heart. You broke Ma's heart when you disappeared. Not a word, not a fucking word ever came to her from you. Who you running from now? I'll bet I put out a description for you to Seattle, something bad comes back, you gonna tell me different?"

"Just a visit and a meal, Steve. What's that gonna cost you? Who's gonna know whether I've been here or not? Let me see my mother one more time before she's gone. I deserve that. *She* deserves that."

Steven weighed his options. He hated Emmett. He had hated Emmett since he was eleven and watched his parents dote on a spoiled, six-year old kid. But he loved his mother, and it *would* please her to no end to see her youngest son one more time. Still, a happy reunion didn't sit well with him.

"You armed?"

Emmett shook his head and lifted his jacket to show his brother.

"Okay, you have one day—you leave on the first ferry in the morning, you got that? And don't say anything to upset her. You tell her you've got a life elsewhere—far away—and a job that won't let you come back here for a long time. But I don't want you *ever* coming back. Do we have a deal, or do I tote you back to the ferry landing?"

"Sounds okay to me. Am I walking, or are you giving me a ride?"

"You walk. It'll give you time to think up a good story."

The sheriff cranked his car back to life and backed it out of the ditch where it had come to rest. He didn't even offer a glance at his brother as he drove away. A mile down the road, along a deserted stretch of the highway, he retrieved the bottle and took three long, hard pulls from it, hoping that the liquor might salve the anger that threatened to consume him.

"What a fucking way to start the day," he muttered.

Emmett arrived at the Dougal homestead just before noon. It was a four-mile walk from the point where Steve had encountered him, and he was hot and thirsty.

"Can a stranger get a drink of water?" he called out to the house from the gate.

His sister, Amelia, with a baby in her arms, appeared in the doorway where she peered at him for a few moments before the realization hit home. "Emmett! Ma, it's Emmett!" Still holding the baby she rushed to the gate, nearly crushing the infant in her embrace of her big brother. "Oh, sweet Jesus, where have you been, Emmett? We all thought you were dead. Come on inside. Ma, Emmett's come home!"

An elderly woman, stooped by her years, appeared in the doorway, her face masked in disbelief. "Emmett?" She nearly fainted when she recognized him, and only the doorjamb held her up. "Oh, Lord, my boy's come home."

The simple meal was welcome. They plied him with warm, fresh baked bread, butter, blackberry jam, and hot coffee. "We'll kill a couple of chickens to roast for this evening—maybe Steven can join us," announced his mother.

"Heck, Ma, this is wonderful!" he said between mouthfuls. "It's like a holiday for me!"

"It *is* like a holiday—my birthday and Christmas all rolled into one.

It's so good for this old body to see you. You finish what you have, and Amelia will get you more. When you're done eating, you're going to catch me up on what you've been doing—and why haven't you written? I taught you better than that. A note, something, would've gone a long way."

Emmett shoved the last of the bread and jam into his mouth and washed it down with coffee, cheerfully waving off his sister's offer for more. "It was confusing, Ma. Bad things happened that I didn't plan on, and there were a lot of good reasons not to bring the trouble to you and Pa."

"But a postcard—"

"I'm sorry, Ma. I'll be better from now on."

"You just come home. What would keep you away? Do you have a wife? Kids? What have you been doing?"

"Mostly fishing, some other odd jobs, very odd jobs. Doing what I can to survive. No family. Couldn't afford a family if I wanted one."

"You come back home, someone will get you a spot on one of the Dockton boats."

"Already went to the union in Seattle. They have me on a waiting list. But don't get your hopes up, Ma. This island isn't big enough for Steve and me."

"Steven! Does he know you're home yet? Lorraine is living up in Everett now, with her husband—did I tell you she got married? But then, you didn't know Amelia was married with two kids until an hour ago! Amelia, call Elise, tell them we're having Sunday dinner a day early. Elise will be thrilled to see you, and Steven has grown up a lot over the past few years. He's a good law man, people respect him—he'll be glad to see you."

"I wouldn't bet on that. But it would be nice to see Elise and her kids."

Dinner was a huge success, mainly because Elise and her children arrived without Steven, who had 'urgent' business in Tahlequah, but promised to stop in on the way back. Emmett knew that wasn't going to happen. His older brother had been clear about his feelings—as he always had when it came to Emmett.

He, Emmett, would enjoy this reunion dinner, get caught up on all the family doings, play with the kids, sleep on the divan, and then be gone before anyone else was awake in the morning. He wasn't sure if this would be his last visit home or if, somehow, Steve could come to see that he wasn't just another criminal on a wanted poster.

Still, if the Seattle police were looking for him, the union was not a good place to revisit anytime soon. Perhaps after things cooled down a bit, he could go back as Emmett Dougal and try to pick up where he had left off nearly a decade earlier.

In the meantime, he intended to absorb as much familial love and affection as he could. It *had* been a long time, and he relished the punishment that Elise's boys inflicted upon him throughout the afternoon. He hadn't realized how badly he missed the aspects of daily family life, including childish arguments coming from the kitchen, or the wide-eyed questions the young kids asked him about fishing on the big blue ocean.

After dinner was finished, and the kids finally in bed after an hour's worth of amusement with their Uncle Emmett, Amelia brought out some homemade loganberry wine. The four adults sat on the front porch in the dim light of dusk.

"What happened up there, Emmett?" Amelia asked quietly. He chewed on the question for a few moments, trying to fix an image. But it was too long past.

"A lot of angry men—and some women—decided to tempt fate. You know, on the way up, on the *Verona*, it was almost a party atmosphere. We actually thought we were going to get our way with the law and be able to speak our piece. Of course, some of us were drinking—I had a few drinks myself—and almost all of us were armed. The first shot was a surprise, but, really, what followed was hardly surprising. It was confusing. A lot of shooting, shouting, and running around. I ... may have shot someone. To this day I don't know for sure."

Emmett drained off the last of his wine and shook his head. "But the moment the shooting stopped it was obvious that the local sheriff had us outnumbered, and they were loaded for bear. They put a lot of holes in that boat and I skipped out before the rest of the reinforcements showed up. They were in a hanging mood, and I wasn't going to be at the mercy of some lynch mob. Communists, they called us. I never even met a commie, how could I be a communist? Hell, I don't even really know what a commie is, other than the Russian kind, and we didn't have any Russians on that boat. The *Verona*. I wonder what happened to her?"

"And for that you felt the need to disappear?" Emmett's mother shook her head and frowned. "You don't know what would have happened if you answered to the law."

"I was young, and didn't know much about anything, Ma. Maybe I still don't. But I knew my brother wouldn't take up for me. He would have enjoyed seeing me get locked up."

"Emmett!"

"It's true, Ma. There's no love lost between us—with all due respect, Elise—there hasn't been a kind word between us in more than ten years. He doesn't want me here. You know that. Steve wanted to run me off this island, and he got his wish."

Elise shook her head. "I think you're wrong, Emmett. He's hardheaded with a mean temper, but he's fair. People wouldn't keep him on as deputy sheriff if they didn't like the job he was doing."

"Most people aren't related to him," Emmett said, chuckling.

"So, what now, son?"

"I'll get settled somewhere in the area. Steve can't keep me off the Sound. I fished for nearly a decade here. Someone will hire me on. Wherever I hook up I'll find a place to live, you'll know where I am. I'll visit when it's not a bother. I won't be disappearing again anytime soon. I do have to say, though, it's good to be back on the island."

In the morning, before the first hint of daylight, Emmett left his blanket neatly folded on the divan, stole into the kitchen, and grabbed a couple of cold biscuits from the previous night's dinner. He turned around slowly in the kitchen, cataloguing past memories, both good and bad, of events that had been centered in that room. There was a perennial smell of fried bacon, even though everything had been washed and put away during the previous evening before the kids were asleep. The room had once been the central part of his family life, yet now it felt alien. He had been away so long.

Emmett closed the front door quietly and made his way around the house: a familiar track that he had traveled daily for many years. He hopped the picket fence at the side of the property and headed down the dirt road that would ultimately lead to the south landing at Tahlequah.

He was taken by surprise when Steven suddenly appeared, sitting on the running board of his T. He had, obviously, been waiting for him.

"Figured you might come this way. There's no ferry service the west side of the island, Emmett. Hop in, I'll take you to Vashon Heights."

"You already been to church?" Steven ignored the humor. So Emmett walked a bit closer. "I'm not going to Seattle."

"Oh, then where you headed?" Steven stood; his intent was to be menacing.

"Thought maybe I'd walk down to Tahlequah, grab the ferry to Ruston, and check for work with the fleet in Commencement."

"You thought wrong."

"You're offering to drive me to Tahlequah? Great!"

"You're going the other way, back to Seattle."

"Drive me down there, I'll buy you lunch."

"You bastard, this isn't a joke. Get in the fucking car!"

"What is it with you, Steve? Don't you ever get tired of leaning on people?"

"I'll never get tired of leaning on you. Once you're on that boat, I'll be through with you."

"Go away. I'm not bothering anyone—certainly not you or yours. I had my visit, now I'm on my way—"

"You're going back to Seattle!" Steven wound up and aimed a short right cross at his brother's face.

What he had not bargained for, however, was a grown-up Emmett, a man who had long since learned to defend himself. Emmett had the pleasure of watching the elegant French heavyweight and war hero, Georges Carpentier, dismantle Battling Levinsky in Jersey City almost a decade earlier. Carpentier had style more than power, and Emmett had been taken by the Frenchman's ability to step inside his opponent's attack and quickly land straight rights and jabs. In the brief lulls aboard fishing boats or the *Blue Jacket*, Emmett would often shadow box, attempting to emulate the fistic combinations of his hero.

Emmett stepped inside Steven's punch and landed one quick pop on his brother's chin. Steven went down like a sack of potatoes: out cold.

"Jesus!"

Emmett looked down at the still shape of his brother and then bent over to ensure he was still breathing. He looked like a man lost in deep sleep.

"Boy, will he be surprised when he wakes up," Emmett thought, smiling. He hoisted the limp figure onto his shoulder and carried it to the T, where he propped his unconscious brother behind the steering wheel. He picked up Steven's worn-out fedora and placed it backwards on the sheriff's head. Then, fingering some lubricant from one of the wheels, he smeared a wide, black moustache across his brother's face.

Emmett picked up his jacket, checked his pocket for his wallet, patted his brother on the shoulder, and began to walk toward the south end. A bank of heavy gray clouds moved overhead, and within a few minutes heavy rain was coming down. Emmett smiled at the heavens, and began to whistle. It *was* good to be back home.

He rode *The City of Tacoma* ferry to Point Defiance, and worked the waterfront on the north side of Commencement Bay, angling for any kind of deck job with a seine boat. He knew seiners, and had worked for a dragger on the east coast for two years before the man's drinking had cost him his boat and Emmett's job. Finding a similar job had proved difficult, prompting him to take work with another rumrunner that led to his introduction to Bruge and—for that time being—left fishing in his wake.

But in Tacoma there were no job offers, and only a couple of lame suggestions that he check back at a later time. '*Later time*,' he thought, *what does that mean*? He left his name and his mother's phone number for contact information, hoping that someone might turn up sick or injured; that's what the world was coming to, having to rely on someone else's misfortune in order to get ahead.

He thumbed a ride back to Point Defiance, where he was faced with a decision. Should he return to Seattle, to Vashon, or to where? There were boats running out of Bremerton, Port Townsend, and even up out of Everett. But would the prospects be any better there? To return to Seattle would be hazardous—who knew if they were looking for him—and would either require him to ferry back to Vashon, hitch rides to the north end of the island, and then take the ferry back to the city; or, head back through Tacoma and hitch rides up the highway to Seattle.

He chose instead to take a four-car ferry west, which would land him above Gig Harbor. Perhaps one of the few fishing operations on the Kitsap Peninsula might have an opening. Few job applicants—those who weren't desperate—would make their way to the peninsula seeking a deck job.

Once on the peninsula, he found that the few boats out of Gig Harbor were already manned. He was hungry and disappointed. He found a general store, bought some apples, and counted his cash while he munched at the fruit. He was running out of resources and the first pangs of desperation began to set in.

He was in no mood to wait for another ferry back to Point Defiance, and the road that led north to Port Orchard, Bremerton, and Port Townsend was traveled, primarily, by logging trucks that rarely—if ever—stopped for hitchhikers.

Emmett walked along the waterfront and noticed an untended dory. He was in the mood for some hard work so, after watching to ensure that no one was paying any attention to him, he untied the rope securing the dory to the dock. He climbed in, placed the oars in their locks, and began to row away, waiting for the yells of an angry boat owner. But no yells came. No one noticed, and he hugged the shoreline until the docks were out of sight. If there were no better prospects up the Sound, he'd return the boat and wait the ferry back to Point Defiance.

The Colvos Passage was calm, and as the afternoon grew late, the clouds cleared. A magnificent sheath of light swept over the water, reflecting up at his face, so that he had to squint to see where he was heading.

After a half hour he stopped rowing, finally tired, and ate his last apple. He was committed now. Vashon sat to his portside, a mile away, and there were no houses, no settlements in sight along this stretch of the Kitsap Peninsula.

He tossed the core into the water and watched the current pull it into his wake as he began to row again, taking his time, hugging the shore, and enjoying the last traces of warmth from the sun before it dropped behind the Olympics to the west.

He pulled around a small point covered with madronas and came upon a collection of buildings perched on a steep shoreline. In front of one of the buildings was an Indian, perhaps a Puyallup or maybe Skokomish, who was cleaning a mess of fish on an elevated table.

The Indian barely looked up to acknowledge Emmett as the latter beached the dory. Emmett noticed a short hull seine boat moored to a rickety dock that extended a few yards out into the Passage. Emmett felt the day giving way to the chill of dusk as he walked up the gravel beach toward the Indian. "Looking for work," he started to say.

"No work."

The gutting continued, and that was the total acknowledgement of his arrival.

"Is there someone I can talk to?"

"You not talking to me, white boy?"

Emmett felt his anger rise like gorge in his throat, but he held it in check.

"I mean, the *owner* of the boat. Are you the owner?"

The gutting stopped and the Indian looked at him, his wide, yellow eyes suggesting jaundice, and the set of his mouth suggesting potential violence.

"I said, no work."

The Indian was not physically impressive, but the way he held his knife suggested that he knew how to use it for more than just gutting fish. Emmett felt compelled to establish some sort of pecking order.

"And you're *not* the owner of that fishing boat. Where is its master? Where is *your* boss?"

"*I'd* be that boss," said a voice from behind.

Emmett turned and faced a burly man who could have been in his seventies. The man was picking flecks of rice from his overalls, but in one swift movement offered his hand in welcome.

"Urquhart's the name. Kenneth Urquhart. Who might you be?"

Emmett responded with a firm grip. "Emmett Dougal, Mr. Urquhart."

"What can we do for you, Mr. Dougal? Looking for work?"

"That I am. Deck hand. Dock man. I've worked as a fisherman here on the Sound and in the northeast. Mostly seine boats but also sword boats."

"Well, Dougal, we're dead in the water here. This here's Angel, he's the last of my crew. Had to lay everyone else off when I couldn't come up with the money to have my boat's engine repaired. You a mechanic, too?"

"I've spent my share of time in the bilges."

The older man lightly grasped Emmett by his elbow and steered him up the beach toward the dock.

"You get that beast running and we'll go fishing. Can't offer much of a wage, but I've an unoccupied cabin you can use and all the fish you can eat. Sound good?"

"You know nothing about me ..."

"You said you were looking for work, I have work, take it or leave it."

The Aberdeen was her name, and she had been kicked around a lot during her life of service. The decks were worn and in need of paint, and her hold covers were chipped and split. Urquhart, with Emmett's help, struggled to dislodge the engine cover. Somehow it had warped, suggesting that not enough time had been spent below decks to complete maintenance.

"Hell, Saint Peter himself must have used this engine on the sea of Galilee."

Urquhart chuckled. "It's been used and abused some. She should be in dry dock, but I just can't afford to have the work done. The market's down. Has been since the end of the last war, but it's pretty bad now. I checked the gaskets and seals when we docked her two months ago. I had enough grist to pay the boys to keep her scrubbed, but that was just throwing good money after bad. So, here she rots in the water. You have a go at her. In the meantime, I can feed you and give you a roof. Other than that, you're on your own until we catch us some fish. Okay?"

Emmett looked at the filthy engine and the shallow pool of water that covered the bilge. This, ordinarily, would not be a job he would want or take. But, for some reason he couldn't immediately determine, he liked this gruff old man.

"Sounds okay. Tools?"

"Gotta shit load of tools in the tool shed. You'll have to move all the nets that we got stored in there, but you should have everything you need, excepting parts. I can barter with a fellow down in Gig Harbor. By the by, that appears to be Samuelson's dory you rowed up in."

"Don't know the man, but I'll be glad to return it."

"We'll tow it down after you get this pleasure yacht running again. But first, let's have Angel grill us some dinner. Then we can get you situated in the 'guest house.'"

The fish was good, accompanied by corn that had been canned the previous summer. They ate, without conversation, in the cramped dining room of Urquhart's small, wood-frame house. Hinged windows that opened out surrounded the room, allowing the cool sea air to filter through the house. Despite Urquhart's rough exterior, there were many feminine touches that decorated his home, evidence that a woman had once shared the house.

With only the light from the fireplace and a hanging lantern, Emmett couldn't readily make out the people in the framed pictures that lined the walls. But there were a lot of pictures, and a lot of people in those pictures, most of whom had their arms around a large man, obviously Urquhart. All of them were smiling. Why would Urquhart, whose popularity was apparent as evidenced by the number of photos depicting such a variety of undefined relationships, remove himself so far from society?

After dinner, Urquhart had Angel lead Emmett to his new home: a dilapidated cabin full of cast-off furniture and debris. Once Angel left him, Emmett removed a couple of heavy boxes from a cot and sat down in the dark, hoping that the bedding wasn't infested with fleas, or worse.

In the morning light he could see how badly run-down his cabin really was. On his way to the main house, where he hoped there would be hot coffee waiting, he picked up an armload of rags and debris and set them outside. From his vantage point, on the steps of his new home, he had a panoramic view of the Passage and the western shore of Vashon Island. He had never spent any time on this side of the water, and it seemed alien to see the sun rising over the tops of the firs on the far shore. But it was beautiful, and placid. The only sounds were birds, the breeze through the surrounding trees, and Urquhart yelling something at Angel down below.

"You got that boat running yet?" Urquhart asked with a smile when he found Emmett pouring himself a cup of coffee.

"Almost, give me another five minutes," Emmett responded.

After a small breakfast of tinned biscuits and coffee, he lowered himself into the bilge, emerging only to retrieve specific tools, or to write out a list of parts that would need to be replaced. He stripped the engine of its head, examined the gaskets, noting replacements, and determined that he would need to hoist the block free to remove and examine the under-workings. He also had to ensure that no water had entered the cylinders.

He found some timbers used for shoring and, with Angel's help, he was able to affix a chain and a come-along to lift the engine, very slowly, free from the hold. A small fountain of brown water trailed the engine from the boat to a skid on the dock.

Angel seemed to have accepted Emmett. He didn't say much, but was more than ready to lend a helping hand whenever Emmett asked. Emmett had proved that he was handy with a wrench and was more than willing to get dirty—traits that seemed just as scarce in bad times as they were in good.

The Indian was wiry, hardworking, and always able to find some chore to take care of. Emmett wondered if the old man was still able to make Angel's wages or if the Indian, like he, had nowhere else to go and worked simply for room and board.

With the engine on the dock, and a new problem facing him with the need to get the engine onto sawhorses for the strip-down, Emmett signaled for a break. The two men slumped against the side of the storage locker at the foot of the dock.

"Angel ... your mother named you that?"

"Never knew any mother. Or father. Raised in a Catholic orphanage. Nuns called me Angel. Like I was their little angel."

"Which you weren't."

"Not hardly. I liked to ... *collect* things, you know? They had us locked in like animals at a zoo, but I got good at getting into places that were locked. Found plenty things that little angels shouldn't find. They used belts on my legs, but that didn't take, so they worked their way up to bigger, *meaner* things. Still wear those stripes across my ass and back. Got big, and they stopped calling me Angel. My name became 'Hey You!' Then, they stopped calling me anything, and just put me out. The old man, I just happened upon, the old man took me in and gave me this job. I was thirteen. Angel is what I'm called, that's all."

"He seems like a good old guy."

Angel nodded, talked out.

They slid the engine along the dock on wood rollers, using a timber and a large iron persuader to lever the block onto hard ground. The next morning, they used the same A-frame of timbers with the come-along to hoist the engine onto their makeshift stand, and began to remove the oil pan. The work was arduous and time consuming.

Neither man noticed that the day had largely elapsed, broken up only by the occasional piss break or a plate of sandwiches brought out by Urquhart, who smiled when he noted the amount of progress that had been made.

"What's the verdict, Dougal?"

Emmett welcomed the sandwich that the old man offered him, taking half of it in one bite.

"No damage to the cylinder walls. The pistons are pitted, but serviceable. What it needs more than anything is a complete cleaning and overhaul. The carburetors need to be rebuilt but they won't need to be replaced, so that's good news." Emmett shrugged his shoulders to ease the ache in his lower back. "There's a good possibility we have this back in the boat in two days and the boat on the water in three."

"Looks to me like you're gonna get to go fishing, Dougal."

"Suits me. When can I get these parts?" He handed a scribbled list on a piece of cardboard to Urquhart, who examined the items noted.

"I believe we can cannibalize these parts ourselves."

"Cannibalize? From what?"

Once again, Urquhart took Emmett by the elbow and led him back behind the dock, along a set of wooden tracks nearly obscured by pervasive blackberry cane. The tracks led to a wood-framed and canvas-walled building not easily seen due to the banks of berry vines and overgrown salal that surrounded it.

Urquhart pulled open the double doors to reveal the hull of an unfinished, deep V-hull boat, nearly forty feet in length. The top deck was not finished, so they clambered up a ladder to stand on the vessel's sub-flooring. Urquhart pulled a couple of tarpaulins free, and Emmett saw two seemingly new Liberty engines.

"What the hell is she doing in here? She should be on the water."

"This hull will never sit on water. I'll be damned if it does. But the parts are there for the taking. Use what you need." Dismissing any further questions, Urquhart quickly climbed down the ladder and made his way back to his house.

Emmett watched the old man for a moment and then yelled down to Angel to bring wrenches, pliers, and drivers. He climbed down into the engine hold and examined the engines. They seemed intact; no damage was evident and, from what he could see, they'd had little or no previous use. The gaskets were all tight, with no sign of leakage, and the carburetors showed no evidence of corrosion, grit, or oil.

Angel appeared at the hold opening with the tools.

"Climb down, friend. We've got some work to do."

The next day, the *Aberdeen's* engine was again in one piece, and the three men labored to get it back into its hold without further damage. The smell of oil, gasoline, and sweat commingled in the tight space, but it seemed like home to Emmett. The old man mostly stood clear, kibitzing, or running for food and water and by evening, the work had been completed.

"Five full days of work done in three. Great job, boys. This calls for a libation. But before you come into the house, I suggest the two of you wash off three days of stink."

They stood in the yard, stripped to their shorts, hosing each other off and using powdered soap to work the grease from their hands, arms, necks, and faces. It felt good to be clean but Emmett would have preferred a hot bath.

Afterward, they sat on the *Aberdeen* and ate more tinned biscuits and hard cheese, washed down with hot coffee. Emmett sat, amused, watching Urquhart reacquaint himself with his pilothouse: moving things around, marking his territory. *Captains and their boats*, he thought. Ultimately, which was more important: the house on shore, or the home on the water? For Emmett, the answer wasn't clear. But the old man came out on deck with a wide grin on his face.

"Boys, we may be back in business. Time for a celebration."

They packed up the remainder of their dinner, such as it was, and followed the old man back to his living room.

There he produced a bottle of bonded scotch and three glasses. "Guess it's illegal to give whisky to an Indian, but then, these days, it's illegal to give whisky to anyone," he said, pouring three fingers of the amber liquid into a glass and handing it to Angel.

The stuff was good, Emmett noted, as good as anything that Bruge had run out to Bill McCoy on Rum Row. He sipped at the liquor and looked at Urquhart.

"There are perks to fishing in the Passage off Vancouver," Urquhart noted.

NOEMI AND REYNARD TAKE MANHATTAN

It had been an interminable three days confined to her compartment and the dining and observation cars. The trip had, at first, proved engaging as the train made its way through the Cascades and then through the Rockies. However, once it entered the northern Great Plains, the trip was as dull as a plate of cold pasta without sauce. Gone were the sheer faces and golden landscapes that Bierstadt had successfully captured in his paintings, and Noémi was left with a seemingly endless flat landscape that rushed by her compartment window.

Noémi had exhausted her initial supply of magazines, as well as the additional stock provided by the solicitous Dunne, and had abandoned a Booth Tarkington novel that she had purchased exclusively for the trip. Cozette recognized the restlessness and gave her ward her space, remaining in the coach car as much as possible.

The four of them, Reynard, Noémi, Cozette, and Arlyn, met for meals where they would exchange casual commentary about the countryside, or observations of other passengers. If Noémi had been ten years old, the trip would have been fun, but much as a ten-year-old waits for Christmas morning, she longed for arrival at Grand Central.

Reynard had unspecified business in New York, and the trip provided his sister an opportunity to have a reunion with some of her college friends from the Baltimore area. They, too, would train up from Maryland and share the same hotel in Manhattan, compliments of Reynard.

But, after a train change in Chicago, Noémi had grown weary of the endless rattling of wheels crossing expansion joints, of overly-solicitous porters, of whistles or rail crossing bells rousing her just as she dropped off to sleep. Outside of meals, Reynard was keeping to his compartment, leaving her to the company of Cozette and Arlyn.

The latter didn't talk much, and refrained from any of the card games that Noémi and Cozette played in the club car. While she didn't resent Arlyn's presence—he had protected her brother once already—the dedicated distance he maintained did not allow her to know him any better than she knew the back cover of a magazine.

He wasn't an extraordinary sort; he was of average height and average size, with a pleasant, if reserved, demeanor. He was always polite, and showed as much deference to her as he did to her brother. He was, as yet, a blank page to her.

Arlyn, for his part, was still unused to living among such overt wealth. His compartment was large enough for four, yet it was his alone. The porters visited frequently, leaving fresh fruit, cigars, and newspapers.

Arlyn was somewhat disturbed that Reynard was not spending time with any of them. He kept to his compartment, appearing only to share dinners with them during the transit. For a week or so, Reynard had spent a lot of time alone and, at midday on the previous Wednesday, Arlyn had been sent home early. There was no explanation. At the time, Arlyn concluded that it was his good fortune, and he intended to spend it with Mary Elizabeth and the kids.

He arranged for a sitter for the baby, and took M.E. and his older two boys out for a chicken dinner at Yesler's Chop House: a favorite of the kids. After the boys rampaged through a plate of chicken legs and mashed potatoes, Arlyn ordered pie for the table. It seemed like this was the best time to alert M.E. to his trip to New York in the next week.

"Why do you have to go?" she demanded.

"It's my job, M.E. If Mr. Delacroix goes somewhere, I'm to go with him. This is not a vacation, it's work. I'll also be escorting his sister and her attendant. I'd much rather be here than back in that city."

The meal was ruined, though the boys slumbered peacefully in the backseat of the car on the way back up to Queen Anne. M.E. undressed the boys and put them to bed, refusing Arlyn's assistance; then she, too, retired without another word.

Mary Elizabeth was less easily appeased since their arrival onto the upper-middle-class rungs, and his parting from her had proved difficult. She cried, strategically, and refused to kiss him good-bye, choosing, instead, to pout in the bathroom while he packed his valise.

Reynard's driver arrived to take him to Union Station, and the bathroom door remained locked. He telegrammed from a stop in Omaha, reminding her that everything he did was for her and their boys. Another telegram from Chicago offered hints as to what surprises he might return with from New York. Not having her in front of him, so that he could wrap his arms around her and reassure her, was discomforting, and he wondered how she would punish him for the perceived abandonment.

He sat in his compartment, with the action of his .45 automatic stripped down to pieces on the small side table. He carefully cleaned and oiled each piece, testing the spring with his fingers, and reassembled the weapon again; it was the third time he had done so since they left Seattle.

He was even happier than Noémi when their train finally pulled into Grand Central Station, though his return to the city of his birth and youth did not come without misgivings. He had been back, infrequently, since he first departed for the West Coast a decade earlier.

As a teen Arlyn had watched his father descend into alcoholism. The old man turned to violence and, after beating Arlyn's mother and killing Arlyn's younger brother, ended up spending the rest of his life in Ossining. His mother's subsequent instability landed her in New York state's Women's Lunatic Asylum. Arlyn couldn't bear to face her there, and she died without ever exchanging another word with her eldest son. His sister had turned her back on Arlyn after her mother, her lone advocate, withered away.

There were people in the city that he should see, but probably wouldn't, using his employment as the handiest excuse not to revisit his troubled past.

They lodged at the Waldorf-Astoria, close to Grand Central and the theater district, so that Noémi and Cozette could take in a performance of *No, No, Nanette* and still have easy access to the shops and boutiques of Manhattan.

Again, Arlyn was given his own room—not a suite, but a room much larger than his living room at home. His immediate reaction was one of unease; it was just too large a space for one person. He still had not come to full terms with his ascension to affluence. But he was smart enough to know he was merely a retainer, and that the grandeur of his surroundings had everything to do with his employer and nothing to do with him.

Noémi was in her element. Reynard had seen to it, since she was a little girl, that she would have almost anything she wanted. And the first thing she wanted, now that she was in New York, was to gather her friends in her room to strategize their assault on the eating, entertainment, and retail establishments of Manhattan.

Cozette arranged for a fine meal that was enjoyed on the large terrace that abutted the grand suite shared by Reynard and Noémi. Squeals and champagne were the order of the afternoon. When Reynard and Arlyn entered, one of the girls screamed, "Man on the floor!" The table erupted with laughter and giggling.

"Ladies, welcome," Reynard said, with a slightly affected bow. "While you are out and about, Mr. Dunne here will escort you."

This was news to Arlyn. He expected to spend some time with Reynard, certainly with hopes of learning the real reason they had traveled three thousand miles. Now, he was being shuttled off to chaperone a group of giddy young women.

"The shops and then dinner at Pierre's?" demanded Noémi.

"It has been arranged. Seven o'clock, a private room, before the masses arrive."

"Thank you, big brother!" She hugged him and he noticeably winced. "Are you all right?"

"I'm fine. Three days confined on a train and I'm sore. You ladies go out and lay siege to the town. I'll join you this evening."

Arlyn and his flock found a limousine waiting for them on Park Avenue. It was a tight fit in the back of the vehicle, which had to accommodate the five young women, Cozette, and himself.

They traveled from store to store, window shopping, and spending what seemed like hours to Arlyn trying on all kinds of clothing and shoes. He struggled to remain attentive to their safety, without ever wondering just who might represent a threat. Men often approached the periphery of this chattering gathering, drawn by the collective beauty of these refined young women like moths to a flame. At which point, Arlyn would present himself in a manner that informed the would-be interloper that no further advance would be allowed. He quite enjoyed the looks on the faces of these young men once they realized that the cluster of women was attended by security.

After exhausting the possibilities at each store, Arlyn would herd them back outside to the waiting limousine, wrangle packages into the car's trunk, and direct the driver to the next destination.

Noémi obviously enjoyed the reunion, especially her position within that reunion. She opened her purse on more than one occasion that day in order to purchase some delightful trinket for one of her friends. That they allowed her to do so demonstrated the fondness that they held for her and each other. It was like a gaggle of sisters, happily fighting for mirror space in a small bathroom, and the happiness was infectious. Cozette and Arlyn caught each other smiling often during the course of the day.

At six-thirty, after having spent an hour inside Tiffany's, where store security was watching *him*, Arlyn escorted the women back to the car and on to Pierre's. The restaurant, the New York watering hole *du jour*, was only lightly populated when they entered, but the maître d' was expecting them, and immediately ushered the group into a private dining room.

The table was round, so that everyone could easily see everyone else; its centerpiece was a floral explosion of lilies and pink roses. Several ice buckets, each with a bottle of imported champagne, were set at intervals around the table, and wait staff ensured that everyone had a full glass of the bubbly; except for Arlyn, who politely waved away the offer of a glass. He sat in a very comfortable chair off to the side and near the dining room entry. A waiter placed a pot of hot coffee on the side table nearest his chair and poured him a cup.

He watched the young women, still energized from the afternoon he had spent with them. They were all from upper-crust families, who had sent their young ladies off to a good Catholic women's college to prepare them for lives as wives and partners to the scions of American industry.

Cozette sat with them, centering the table, a constant reminder that, while Noémi was a free spirit, she remained under a watchful eye at all times. Arlyn smiled at this observation. Cozette was the conscience and he was the muscle. They both had their work cut out for them.

Just after the salad course had been brought to the table Reynard appeared. He swept into the room and stopped at the side of each young woman to gently lift her hand in greeting. His smile was broad and he playfully picked at pieces of the salads in front of the ladies, commenting on the dressing or a bit of walnut. He didn't even acknowledge Arlyn until he had made the entire circuit of the table and taken his seat.

"Mr. Dunne! You look so lonely. Please come join us."

"I'm fine right here, Mr. Delacroix. Pretend I don't even exist."

"Ah, but you do. Waiter, bring another chair and place setting.

Girls, scoot around a bit, let's find Mr. Dunne a spot, perhaps next to you, Beverly?"

"I can find room for Arlyn—Mr. Dunne," offered Noémi.

But before she could move her seat, Beverly stood and quickly shoved her chair to provide the necessary room. Arlyn was compelled to join them and, after wedging himself in between two of the lively young ladies, had to admit that Beverly was an attractive young woman. Despite her seeming impulsiveness, she had impeccable manners. He noticed the slight frown on Noemi's face, and recognized it as similar to the stiff-lipped pout of his oldest boy when the lad didn't get what he wanted.

Noémi watched Arlyn settle in between her friends, Beverly and Viola, surprised at her own jealousy. He was obviously uncomfortable, and she enjoyed that discomfort, smiling as he awkwardly accepted a plate of food as it was set in front of him.

She noticed that her brother was watching her, obviously aware of her interest—innocent though it may be—in his bodyguard. She smiled at Reynard, who returned the smile though his eyes were suggesting something other than amusement.

"Arlyn, why don't you share with the ladies who you were before entering the Delacroix family?"

Arlyn had just begun to lift some steamed vegetables to his mouth when Reynard spoke, but he instantly returned his fork to his plate. "Not much of interest there for young ladies, Mr. Delacroix."

"Of course there is. These young women have lived privileged, sheltered lives. I'm sure they'd love to learn what it's like on the streets of Seattle. Why don't you share your *genèse*, your beginnings, with our assembly?"

"All right." Arlyn looked around the table, taking in all their engaging faces before his eyes met those belonging to Noémi.

"My father was a steam fitter for the city, who felt the need to nightly support a local saloon in our Brooklyn neighborhood. My mother was a laundress, which she took in, and also worked as a seamstress, happily doing alterations for a haberdasher because that meant she could get out of the house as often as possible. My father got drunk one day in 1911, beat my mother senseless, and then started in on me and my little brother with a broom handle. I was faster than my brother and escaped. He wasn't so lucky. His name was Timothy. He was six. My mother went to a hospital, and my father went to Ossining. I never saw either of them again. My father died from drinking Sterno, which had been smuggled into the prison. My mother was institutionalized, and I got word later on that she died there. My sister has only communicated with me once since then, informing me of our mother's death."

Arlyn scanned the table to see what effect his story was having, and was most surprised to note Reynard's wide-eyed response. "I went to the streets, robbed groceries, rolled drunks, and lived in the subway near the Lexington station until I was nabbed by the police. I was in a juvenile offenders' home upstate when I got the letter from my sister, but she never mentioned my little brother. It wasn't for a few years until I found out about Timmy. One night … I don't know what brought me to it, but I decided to become a cop—maybe to help people who can't help themselves, but probably more because that way I could avoid being victimized by others—"

"Or maybe so you could victimize those 'others'?" joked Reynard, but his eyes were still showing the effects of his surprise. He had assumed that because Arlyn had been a cop, he had enjoyed a secure, middle-class upbringing.

"No sir." Arlyn was quietly angry at the suggestion. He glanced around the table, embarrassed. The young women sat, frozen in place, surprised at the suddenness and severity of Arlyn's personal tale. "I apologize. I didn't mean to upset anyone."

"I am the one who should apologize, Mr. Dunne. That was rude of me to ask such a personal question, and I applaud the trust you've shared with us. For that, I will attempt to reward you in an appropriate fashion."

Reynard signaled the waiters to bring in the main course, which was a choice of the restaurant's signature beefsteak, accompanied by a mélange of seafood, with side dishes of aspic and creamed corn. But the young ladies were rattled, and paid very little attention to their plates. Reynard had more champagne poured, decidedly angry at himself for not having learned more about Arlyn since his hire.

After they finished dinner, the company returned to the main section of the restaurant and camped at another large table in order to enjoy the live music provided by a string quartet. While the ladies sipped at some after-dinner port and carried on with their reunion, Reynard signaled for Arlyn to join him in the lounge. He nodded to the barman, who obviously knew him, and the latter provided them with teacups liberally filled with scotch.

"To your health, and future happiness, Arlyn," Reynard toasted.

Arlyn returned the salute and sipped at his scotch, surprised to hear Reynard use his first name.

"You and I are more alike than I had any idea."

"We're very different men, Mr. Delacroix. You're a man of ideas. I'm just your muscle."

"Nobody can survive without muscle. I am happy that you are here to look out for us." He sipped at his liquor, running his tongue along the rim of the cup. "I have to meet with someone in the morning, so I would appreciate it very much if you would look out for the ladies until I can join you. But"—he reached into his vest coat to pull free a thick, rolled wad of bills, pulling off several—"you should enjoy yourself. I suggest you take the women to Coney Island. That should serve as adequate distraction."

"Can I ask who you're meeting with?"

"There's no need for you to know. It's … something very personal. Keep Noémi and her friends amused and I'll see to our entertainment this evening. Do you like music?"

"I guess so. Shouldn't we get back to the ladies?"

"That's another reason why I hired you, to keep me focused. Drink up!"

Reynard sat on the edge of the examining table, still in his slacks, but bare-chested. The doctor listened to Reynard's chest with his stethoscope, thumped on his back, and then pulled the scope away and sighed.

"The lungs sound good. That's a plus. But the blood work isn't telling us enough. Despite the x-rays, a complete diagnosis is still difficult, and I really recommend you seek a second opinion. I can get you an appointment at the Mayo Clinic."

"Can I get the other opinion while I'm already here?"

"Mr. Delacroix, the Mayo is in Minnesota. They have a fine staff, on the leading edge of oncology—"

"I can't go to Minnesota. I've never been to Minnesota, Doctor. Can you not refer me to anyone here or, perhaps, Seattle or San Francisco?"

"Yes, I have colleagues here and in San Francisco, but I truly recommend going to Minnesota. This is going to require an operation—a delicate operation—perhaps even a series of them if we're going to effectively treat this."

"I can't afford to leave my business unattended, doctor. What's the fastest way to handle this?"

"This is not an engine tune up, Mr. Delacroix. This is life threatening. The growth must be dealt with as quickly as possible. If left unattended, the tumor might grow quickly enough to render you unable to continue to do business anytime in the near, or distant, future. Am I making myself clear? This is not to be trifled with, and you came a great distance to receive this advice, which we provided in quick fashion. I would hope you heed it.

"In any event, I will be glad to forward the x-rays and diagnosis to any physician you would like. Would you like a recommendation for a San Francisco oncologist?"

"Get me an appointment. In the meantime, what can you give me for the headaches?"

After the doctor left the examination room Reynard pulled on his shirt, carefully buttoning it: calm as though he were home in his own closet.

The doctor reappeared and gave him a small, unlabeled box. "These are not candy, Mr. Delacroix. Do not take more than four pills each day. They are a highly addictive opiate, which will affect both your mood and your ability to successfully interact with your family or business associates. I'll provide a prescription for a refill.

"You wanted to keep these appointments confidential, which leads me to believe you've not shared your condition with anyone else. It would be wise to confide in someone you can trust if you're truly concerned about your ability to conduct business."

"Thank you, Doctor. I'll give that some thought. You've been candid with me, and I appreciate it."

"It's what we do. Do yourself a favor, Mr. Delacroix, don't put off the surgery."

Reynard nodded. The gravity of his health weighed heavily on his shoulders. "I always wanted eighty years. Now, I'd settle for fifty."

"Do the surgery. There's nothing written that you can't make it to eighty."

Arlyn unbuttoned his shirt and loosened his tie. It was warm on the boardwalk. The girls—who had left Cozette behind to take in the city on their own—were enjoying another turn on the Wonder Wheel. He remained stationed on a bench across from the ride. The sun beat down on his shoulders, at first relaxing, and then irritating, him.

The young ladies seemed impervious to the heat. In their light, fashionable dresses they moved with no seeming concern for the temperature or humidity, while his wool suit seemed suffocating. He was distinctly aware of his full bladder and needed to find a restroom, but he didn't want to leave the ladies alone for even a moment, although there seemed to be no need for immediate concern.

They sat in one of the inner rail cars, screaming as the car slid forward coming over the top. He could see one of the girls leaning slightly out of the car's windows and, at first, he couldn't make out who it was. He shielded his eyes from the sunlight and squinted as the car completed another circuit. It was Beverly, the most outgoing of the group. She was looking down at him and waving frantically.

His initial response was to ignore her, but he offered a small, half-hearted wave that, somehow, she could see from the car. She began to yell something, but the sound was lost among the amusement zone cacophony.

But then Arlyn saw the accident about to occur: Beverly's long, gauzy scarf had come loose and was now hanging out the window. As the car once again started its descent along the inner rail, the scarf became caught in the sliders.

Without hesitation, he sprang to his feet and launched himself across the boardwalk, through the waiting queue, and onto the loading platform. The ride operator had just become aware of the danger, but hadn't yet responded.

Arlyn pushed the man aside and yanked hard at the clutch and brake handles, stopping the wheel with a lurch that caused yelps and screams from above.

"The scarf, man." Arlyn pointed.

"I'll bring it down—"

"You do, you'll kill someone. Leave those handles alone." He climbed onto the nearest spoke, finding the footholds that the maintenance men used. He was halfway to the car when he realized how high he was. He stopped for a split second to catch his breath and felt the wheel begin to move.

"Stop it, you son of a bitch!" he yelled down.

He climbed out onto a perpendicular spoke and reached the car. Beverly's scarf was caught and was forcibly being pulled from within the car. By the look on her face, it appeared she was in serious distress.

Arlyn pulled out his jackknife and sliced through the fabric. Beverly was freed. She fell back against her cushion and began to cry.

Arlyn squeezed through the window, and then motioned back down to the operator. "Now!" You son of a bitch, he added under his breath.

The car descended to the platform, the operator passing the other cars in order to let the ladies off first. No one spoke. The girls felt embarrassed, and Arlyn was still breathing hard.

The moment the car stopped on the platform the door was opened, and the girls rushed away from the ride and onto the Boardwalk.

"I warned 'em to keep inside the car," the operator noted.

"I'll bet you did. You were lucky—we were lucky today, chum."

Half an hour later, as they waited for their car to pick them up, Beverly began to laugh. She pulled at the damaged scarf as though it were a noose. Everyone laughed, even Arlyn. Beverly made a series of comments about chivalry, and contrasted Arlyn's behavior with that of a variety of young men that the group had come to know at their nearby men's Catholic college. With the increasing volume of laughter, Arlyn became more light-hearted, and was able to join in the conversation, serving as bits of punctuation to their happy arguments.

They met for dinner in the hotel, and Reynard took the opportunity to celebrate Arlyn's latest heroic effort. "Frankly, I have no idea how I or my sister have survived all these years without the gallant Mr. Dunne."

For her part, Noémi had ambivalent feelings about Arlyn's performance that day. While the event was unfolding, she'd had no inkling of how dangerous, and how imminent, the situation had become. Witnessing Arlyn's climb was both exhilarating and frightening.

And, certainly, Beverly's repeated gestures of affection for him infuriated her. Her territorial imperative had been awakened, but she recognized that any exclamation on her part would be bad form. So, she dutifully sipped at her champagne and watched Beverly all but drool on Arlyn's shoulder.

At the conclusion of dinner, Reynard again took Arlyn aside and presented him with a gold Patek Philipe pocket watch.

"This is too much," protested Arlyn.

"It's merely a token, Arlyn." Once again Reynard's use of his first name caught him by surprise. "I had no idea how much you would bring to the job. First, the assault in Seattle, and now, today. I must say, I don't pay you enough."

"I just do my job, Mr. Delacroix. As for today, I would have done the same thing if it had happened to anyone. That's my training. But I do appreciate your kind words, and this extravagant gesture. With all due respect, I'm curious to know what my employer has been up to during this visit."

"In due time. We shall return home in two days. In the meantime, all of the drama has tired me out. I'm going to my room. Please make my apologies to the ladies for me and, again, thank you so much, Arlyn."

Arlyn returned to the group to find the additional presence of two men, dressed like what he would describe as 'dandies.' They wore the latest three-piece suits, with silk shirts and ties. Their hair was held in permanent position by an accumulation of scented pomade, which they had combed again after leaving their matching fedoras with the hatcheck girl.

One stood and offered his hand, aware that this was the hero of the hour. "Louis Ferrini," he said, "theatrical producer."

Arlyn shook the proffered hand, but said nothing. Noémi noticed the subtle snub and rose to take Ferrini by the arm and lead him back to the table. "Tell me about your play," she insisted.

"Well, we haven't finished the financing stage yet, but we have a completed script and a well-known director—"

"We may be able to get George Abbott!" exclaimed his partner.

"—might be interested. If the financing comes, so will the director. Abbott would," he allowed, "be a good choice. He's had some success."

"Some success?" Beverly was amused. She was the most knowledgeable Broadway devotee of the group. "He directed *Chicago* last year!"

"He would be a big catch, that's for sure," said Ferrini. "So, Mr. Dunne, do you follow Broadway?"

Arlyn shook his head. "How do you spell your name, Louis, with one 'r', or two?"

Ferrini blanched, and Noémi came to his defense.

"Don't badger an artist, Arlyn. It's a business with which you're unfamiliar. Ignore him, Louis, he lives in a different world." But she glanced back to see what effect, if any, her words had on Arlyn. The latter simply shrugged, got up and flagged down a waiter to retrieve a scotch. When he returned, glass in hand, Noémi and Louis had wedged themselves into the corner of an adjacent booth.

"It's getting late, ladies," he announced.

Ferrini stood. "We would like to make a formal presentation to Monsieur Delacroix, Mr. Dunne."

"I don't make his appointments, Ferrini. But I suggest you look elsewhere for financing. Mr. Delacroix has his interests elsewhere."

"Arlyn!" Noémi was furious. "How would you know whether Reynard was interested or not?"

"With all due respect, Miss Delacroix, perhaps *you* should put the two of them together." He turned to the rest of the party. "Ladies, say good night to the gentlemen, it's time to retire."

He caught Noémi's eye, and she recognized the futility of arguing. She rose in resignation, and offered her hand in farewell to the struggling Broadway producer.

Two days later, at seven in the morning, they boarded a train bound for Chicago, where they transferred to another train that would deposit them at Union Station in Seattle. During the return trip, Reynard never joined them for meals, and wouldn't even allow Noémi into his compartment.

Mary Elizabeth was attempting to size up the young housekeeper applicant sitting in her living room when she heard the knock at her front door for the second time. She excused herself and, swearing under her breath, strode down the bare hallway to the ornate front door. When she opened it she was faced with the tall, imposing figure of Lieutenant Virgil Glaupher.

Virgil was holding a bouquet of flowers and had his hat in hand. "Is this a bad time?" he asked.

A WANTED MAN

Emmett leaned against the bulkhead and listened to the engine. Hearing was difficult because Angel had steered the *Aberdeen* into the part of the passage where the current was strongest. The hull pounded into the small swell, and the thudding almost overwhelmed the sounds of the engine.

He stuck his head out of the hold and yelled toward the pilothouse. "Full throttle!"

Angel looked back toward him and nodded, opening the throttle all the way. The engine sped up, and Emmett touched the business end of a screwdriver against the valve cover. The steady vibrations indicated all was well inside. He smiled. They were one step closer to fishing.

When they returned to Urquhart's dock, Emmett was ready to go pick up ice and fuel.

"Not yet, boys. That seine reel needs to be reconditioned, and the winch should probably be taken down as well. And who's checked the nets?"

"The nets okay," said Angel.

"We can't be dragging with damaged nets," responded the old man. "Pull them out and check for frays and tears. We're not going out half-assed."

"Is it just me or is the old man getting all fired up now that he's got a boat under him?"

Angel laughed. "But he's smart man. Can't be draggin' with holes." The way he said it made it sound as if he said 'whores.' Emmett laughed back at him.

"Well, let's pull the goddamn nets. I'm ready to fish." They pulled all of the nets from the storage shed and laid them out along the gravel beach. Emmett took large rocks and set them where the tears were largest. They took to mending the entire length, replacing missing or damaged floats, kibitzing while they worked. Women. Boats. The land. Boats. Women. They got to know each other through a short hand of language and common experience. By now, they both knew the other was genuine, and it made working not just easier, but more enjoyable.

A day of mending only led to a second for Angel. Meanwhile, Emmett tore down the gurdy—the seine reel—and checked and replaced a burned bearing before lubricating everything. The winch was in fine shape, though he played with the carburetor. After reassembling everything he ran the winch engine hard, revving until the old man came out of his house, frowning and gesturing. But each time he attempted to yell at Emmett, the latter just revved the winch engine and laughed. Finally, Urquhart couldn't stop himself from laughing, and waved before returning inside his house.

That evening, after supper, Angel sat with Emmett on the steps of the latter's cabin. The night sky was clear, and stars carpeted the expanse. The Sound was quiet, save for the plaintive cry of one loon in the distance.

"Why's the old man letting that hull rot?" wondered Emmett.

"He say he going to burn it, but he don't. I think maybe it's like a tombstone for his son. Could be."

"His son? He has—had—a son?"

Angel nodded and pulled out his makings to roll a cigarette. "The old man loses his wife, then two years later the kid. Hard on Urquhart."

He pronounced it 'Oarquit.' "But it was the way the kid went. Bullet to the brain. Left a mess that the old man had to clean up. He ain't been the same since."

"What's that got to do with the kid?"

"Long story short. Kid ran a still farther up the peninsula, for a couple a years before getting busted. Went to court, and the kid promised to go clean. The court gives him probation, and holds the old man responsible for the kid. For a couple a years—I wasn't keeping track—the kid seem okay. Fishing was good, and the kid took his shares and talked the old man out of money to build a second boat. It was gonna be the kid's boat, only the kid is building something other 'n a dragger. He's building a rumrunner, and the engines cost more 'n the kid could keep in his pocket.

"Turns out he's working with some crook out of Everett who's smuggling booze. Someone ratted him out, and the old man threw him out on his ear. Old man found him in the woods back there, brains splattered on the tree he was sittin' against. Door on the boat shed got locked, and it weren't open again till you came along. Still think he'd like to burn the damn thing."

"Wouldn't take much to make it a good fishing rig. Deep hull means open ocean. Larger deck space. We're talking some big money, Angel."

"The old man, he ain't gonna go for it. And don't push on him, Emmett. Things're just gettin' settled again."

Professional curiosity got the better of Emmett. "Tell me about the kid's still? Do you know where he had it?"

Angel looked at him and a smile slowly spread across his face. "You thinkin' running booze? You think the big men in Seattle let you do that? Here's one thing maybe I tell you I shouldn't. The kid? He weren't no sideways case. No way he put a gun in his mouth. No way. His backbone weren't that stiff. I think someone had business with the kid. Think his name was Randall, or maybe it was Russell. Never talked to him much, or him, me and the old man. He call his own son 'kid.' I think pretty sure the old man's son, he crossed *someone*—but don't bring that up with the old man. Let it go. The boat, she rots in the shed, I'm sure."

Two days later, the *Aberdeen* made her way out of the Colvos Passage and headed north toward the Juan de Fuca Strait for a shake down at sea. Their intent wasn't to fish so much as to ensure that the boat was truly ready for hard work in big seas.

Still, the old man knew where to drop his nets, and they began a sweep along the Dallas Bank, hauling up a medley of cod, flounder, and a few smallish halibut. Emmett manned the winch, and Angel rowed the skiff in a wide arc to envelope the school of fish. As the heavy net came back on board, Urquhart and Emmett sorted the catch, keeping the halibut for supper.

They made their way back down the Sound, stopping in Elliott Bay to sell their small catch and refuel before cruising back to the safety of their fish camp. Urquhart pressed $20 into the palms of his two-man crew. It was the first real wages Emmett had received since Walter Burge paid him. At dinner, Urquhart produced an unopened, bonded bottle of Black & White scotch to wash down the halibut.

Fishing was even better when they traveled back out onto the Strait two days later. The old man's ability to gauge water temperature, current, and fish migration was uncanny. They filled their hold with cod and a small crab-pot that had been caught in the drag. They kept the pot, filled with a small raft of Dungeness crabs. When they again returned to Urquhart's they were able to throw a crab cook, inviting a few of the old man's neighbors. One of these was a Kitsap County deputy sheriff, named Ralph Gerritson. His wife, Betty, and Urquhart's closest neighbor, Janie Ferrady, also joined them. The entire party sat on planed log benches, drinking cold beer and getting stained by buttered corn and cracked crab. Betty had brought plenty of apple cobbler, and it was while Emmett was wolfing down his portion that the sheriff focused on him.

"Dougal? Sheriff on Vashon is named Dougal. Know him?"

Emmett smiled. “He’s my brother.”

Gerritson smiled broadly, took another small bite and washed it down with a pull from a cold bottle of Bevo near beer. “Thought so. You know, you’re wanted.” It was more a statement than a question. Gerritson was a patient man, a *measured* man, emotionally grounded and perfectly suited to his profession.

“Wanted? For what?”

“According to the circular, assault on a peace officer. Family fight?”

Emmett nodded. “Never thought he’d go that far. How much?”

“Oh, no reward listed, just a general bulletin. If there *was* a reward, I might get interested.” He laughed, and Emmett recognized Gerritson meant no threat. “I’d recommend—if you was open to recommendations—that you go and square this with him. I know him well enough to know he won’t let go of this.”

“Then you know him as well as I do. I don’t think he’ll let this go in any event. Still, I owe my Ma a visit … maybe he and I can finally settle things.”

“That’s your business. Say, does the old man have any decent liquor? I’m parched and the good woman’s attention is elsewhere.”

The next morning, Urquhart took the boat to Gig Harbor for supplies and to give Emmett a chance to call his family. There was no answer, and someone else was using the party line.

Disappointed, he joined Urquhart in the chandlery, where the old man was clearing his account and picking up some needed hardware. “Everything okay?”

“No answer, boss. Think maybe I need to take a visit, and see if I can clear things up with Steven.”

“I’d go easy, Emmett. If Gerritson lays no claim on you, you’re safe on this side of the water. I’d say let sleeping dogs lie.”

“Well, I need to let my ma know where I am and that I’m safe. I haven’t talked with her in almost two weeks.”

Urquhart smiled, walked to the sales counter, and picked up a postcard from a rack by the register. A blurred image of Mount Rainier adorned the front side. "Don't get too specific. Just tell her you're working for an old man somewhere on the Kitsap and that you'll visit soon. If your brother sees the card, it won't tell him enough to bring him calling."

Emmett put a nickel on the counter and took the card.

Prior to mailing it at the Gig Harbor post office, he wrote in pencil:

"Ma, got work in Kitsap. Fishing. No troubles here. Will see you soon. Love, Emmett."

They were fishing nearly every day of the week, staying out for two or three nights at a time, chasing cod, herring, and hake along the Strait. They had yet to venture out into the Pacific. Urquhart seemed antsy and unsettled, but he knew where to lay his nets, and Angel was a marvel in the skiff, acting in unspoken unison with his captain. Emmett watched his fellow fishermen, getting a sense of their timing, and the three of them continued to haul in profitable catches.

They set their nets out early in the morning, as soon as there was enough light to see. Angel pulled the net in a wide circle, rowing against the lumpy swell, and Urquhart angled the *Aberdeen's* course in the opposite direction, encircling a swarming ball of herring.

Emmett manned the gurdy, waiting for the signal from Urquhart once the boat had nearly closed the distance to Angel's skiff. Then his work began. The old man joined him on deck to loosen the net from the gurdy, and to help guide the full net onto the boat, where they quickly sorted out flatfish from herring and cod. The fish were shoveled into the hold where the men laid ice on the catch.

After two days out, they unloaded their catch at the processor in Elliott Bay, took on another load of ice, and then headed back to Kitsap. The three of them sat down to a late dinner after hosing down the boat and pulling the nets for mending. The summer solstice was growing close and dusk lingered later each evening. They built a fire on the beach as the dwindling light gave way to a low ceiling of dark gray. A light drizzle began to fall as they ate from plates full of fish and potatoes, oblivious to the moisture.

Something moving beyond his cabin caught Emmett's eye, and he squinted in an attempt to see what it was. But it had receded back into the dense forest of firs.

"Bears over here?"

Urquhart looked up, amused. "None that I know of. You goin' skeezy on me?"

Emmett shrugged. "Something up by my cabin."

"Then I'd check under the bed before I lay down." The old man laughed. He got up and struggled through the beach rock and gravel to his house and returned with a bottle and glasses. "This should help you sleep through," he said, and poured a liberal amount into each glass and handed one to Emmett. Angel got up, took his whisky and departed for his cabin.

"Goodnight to you, too, Señor!" called out Urquhart.

Angel waved without turning, exhausted and intent on his warm, dry bed after two nights in a cramped bunk on the *Aberdeen*.

"So, when do we head to sea?" asked Emmett.

"What do you call where we've spent the better part of the last two weeks?"

"I mean the deep blue, old man. The albacore will be running down off Humboldt. Big money. We'll never get very far ahead netting baitfish and cod. We need to rig for tuna and salmon."

"You got big plans, boy. We're doing just fine. We got to take enough to pay for that rigging. You priced hardware lately? I'm not pulling out my last jar of pennies just so you can stick some albacore. We fish the Strait for a while longer. Plus, I been watching you work the deck. You're so slow, we're lucky to haul any fish at all." He laughed and drained his glass.

"You are one mean old man, Urquhart," replied Emmett. "Bed for me. Don't go getting caught in the tide. Don't want to have to haul your iron-keel carcass to the morgue." He tugged the bottle of Black & White from the old man's hand and poured another dram into his glass before heading up the hill toward his cabin. In the doorway, he stopped and looked back down at the old man, straddling a log and quietly singing a refrain:

"What do you do with a drunken sailor, shave his belly with a rusty razor, what do you do with a drunken sailor, throw him in the bed with the Captain's daughter ..."

Emmett smiled, saluted with his glass, and closed his door. Before he crawled into bed he peeled off his salt-encrusted oilskin pants and opened the cabin's one window, allowing the cool breeze off the Sound to cleanse his body and his head.

In the morning, sunlight streamed through the window, forcing Emmett out of bed. He struggled into a pair of canvas dungarees and a light wool shirt before opening his door to the world. Down on the beach, Urquhart and Angel were preparing breakfast over an open fire, rather than using the indoor stove. The smell of bacon—where had they come up with bacon?—along with a fresh pot of hot coffee, permeated the atmosphere, drawing him like a moth to a flame.

"Bacon?"

Urquhart stood up, stretching his back. "Neighbor wife come by while you were still in dreamland, traded a slab for the use of my churn. Make yourself useful and crack them eggs."

Angel was working *masa* flour into a flatbread, which he laid out onto the griddle suspended over the fire. He smiled at Emmett—the bacon was a real treat, and all three of them worked quickly to create a breakfast big enough for the most hardy logger or farmhand. As they gorged themselves on their eggs and bacon, Emmett's eye was again drawn toward his cabin, where a huge, shaggy animal—apparently a dog of undetermined breed—was sniffing around, drawn by the smell of the bacon and fried eggs.

"Holy cow." He stood, and this drew the other men's attention.

Angel laughed and went back to work wrapping his eggs and some bacon in some flatbread. "Scavenger. Make sure we clean all this up. Ignore him, Emmett, he just come around for the fish guts."

"He looks big enough to make one of us a meal."

"Mebbe. I seen blood on him, could be man blood. More likely raccoon or possum. He big enough to kill and eat just about anything short of moose."

"But he doesn't belong to someone around here?"

Urquhart sniffed and took a mouthful of coffee. "He comes and goes, has nothing to do with us. He's after what he can get into his mouth. Wouldn't be surprised to learn that he's killed more'n a few of Ferrady's chickens. I'll have to ask the next time I see her."

Emmett began to mop his egg yolk with the flatbread and stopped. He stood, and walked up the incline toward his cabin, where the dog had taken position, reclining in a nearby salal bush.

"Leave him alone, Emmett. Those are big teeth," called out Urquhart. The old man was amused by Emmett's interest in the dog.

The animal watched Emmett approach, tensing in anticipation of an assault, his large brown eyes focused on the man as he drew near. About fifteen feet from the dog, the animal appeared huge. He had to stretch the better part of six feet from nose to tail, and Emmett guessed the dog was easily 150 pounds.

Man and beast stared each other down for a few seconds before Emmett set his plate, with the remains of the fried eggs and bacon, on the ground before retreating farther back down toward the beach.

The dog lifted his muzzle and took in loud drafts, smelling the food. He slowly lifted himself into a sitting position and seemed to consider the hazards and rewards surrounding the short trip to the plate. His big brown eyes took in Emmett, the men on the beach, and the surrounding yard. Slowly, he gained his feet, and took a couple of tentative steps toward the food.

When no trouble seemed to meet his approach, his confidence grew, and he carefully walked to the plate, sniffed at it, looked at Emmett again, and then nosed into the yolk and licked at the bacon before beginning to eat in earnest. In a matter of seconds, the plate was licked clean. The dog looked at Emmett, attempting to assess this adversary. He wagged his tail twice, and casually wandered back into the woods.

Emmett grinned and picked up the cleaned plate. When he looked again, the dog was nowhere to be seen; a phantom of the breakfast, he thought.

"Waste of good food," was all that Angel said.

Urquhart took them on a grand tour of the Inland Passage over the next week, ducking in and out of the San Juans and Orcas. They followed schools of herring and cod, dragged for flatfish, and ran troll lines for salmon. They sold their catches at processing plants in Nanaimo and Vancouver. After the final run off the Strait, they made their way into Elliott Bay and sold that catch before berthing near the foot of Broad Street. They were only a couple of blocks from the cannery where Emmett had briefly worked a month earlier, but he resisted the urge to reclaim the meager belongings he'd left behind. He also decided not to join the old man and Angel when they headed toward a local fisherman's saloon along the waterfront.

He needed new oilskins and, with a pocket full of money, he headed toward downtown to shop at a well-known outdoors supplier, with the promise to join them for dinner at a cafeteria on Second Avenue.

He took his time shopping, but quickly picked out a new set of oilskins, noting how much stiffer they were than the tired old gear he had been borrowing from Urquhart. Then, feeling extravagant, he bought new undergarments and socks. He could feel the darning on top of darning that held the soles of his old socks together, even in heavy weather rain boots.

On his way out of the store he noticed an ice cream parlor across the avenue, and decided to treat himself to a soda.

Inside, the parlor was all pink and white, and the gent behind the counter sported a pink-striped apron. Emmett felt like a kid again. He ordered his ice cream soda and took it to a small table at the back of the parlor, sipping slowly to savor the cold, sweet flavor.

From his table he could see the boulevard through a large pane of glass, and was taken by the sudden appearance of a beautiful young lady, escorted by an older woman.

They entered the parlor and strolled to the counter. Emmett couldn't take his eyes off the young woman; the older of the two, scanning the interior, caught his glance. Her eyes narrowed, silently warning him to maintain his distance. She guided her young charge to another table at the other side of the room, and purposefully took a seat that required the young lady to sit with her back to Emmett.

The older woman, dressed in funeral black, was a distinct contrast to her ward, who sported the latest finery. Emmett's glance was met by a cold stare from the woman, and he saw in her eyes the impossibility of an introduction.

Then the young woman noticed her companion's fixed glare, and turned to see the source of her displeasure. In that instant Emmett forgot all about his soda. This young woman's countenance held no mystery for him: she was a living delight, a promise of pleasure, warmth, and intimacy, unlike any that he had known.

From her chair, awkwardly perched, Noémi caught her first glimpse of a strange, intense young man, spoon poised above his soda, eyes locked inextricably on her. He was unkempt, forward, verging on rude, but absolutely attractive.

"Noémi!" Cozette pulled at Noémi's cuff to regain the young woman's attention. "Don't stare. Don't encourage him. He's nobody to you."

But she could see that he was. His gaze wasn't unnerving; it was reassuring, as if she knew this man she had never met. When he stood, she heard Cozette rise in unison with the clear intent to cut off his advance.

But Noémi was not to be restrained.

Defiantly, she stood, impeding Cozette's interference. "Sir? Would you like to join us, sir?"

Emmett nearly knocked over his soda, grabbing the glass. "I beg your pardon, miss?"

"Would you care to join us at our table?"

"I'm sorry, we haven't been introduced …"

"The man is correct, he is a stranger, Noémi—"

Noémi's sudden and unmistakable glare stopped Cozette mid-sentence. "Are you diseased? Do you smell funny?" she asked Emmett.

Emmett sniffed, considered, and laughed. "Well, I'm a fisherman. I suppose I smell like a fisherman. Don't know about any diseases. Your—sister?—is right, I'm a stranger, but I do appreciate the invite."

"I'd love to hear about … fishing. For just a few minutes?"

Emmett looked to Cozette, whose face was that of one who's lost an argument. He awkwardly picked up his packages, and his soda, and moved to their table. He carefully set his glass down before holding Noémi's chair as she sat back down. He remained standing, wondering if it was polite to offer his hand, kiss hers, or just what protocol demanded.

"My name is Emmett Dougal, miss … ?"

"Noémi Delacroix, Mister Dougal. And this is my … *aunt* Cozette."

"Ma'am. Pleased to meet you both."

"Sit down, Mr. Dougal."

He pulled the offered chair to a point central to both women, maintaining a careful distance, and checked to see if the soda jerk or the other customers were paying attention. They weren't.

"What kind of fishing do you do? I've always wondered how the fish arrives at my plate." She was looking at his hands while she asked, and he immediately withdrew them below the table. They were not attractive hands; they were the hands of a workingman, with dirt under the remaining nails that hadn't been torn or damaged, and with calluses that threatened to engulf his palms.

"I work on a seiner, a net boat that we call a dragger. We drop large nets, hopefully, around schools of fish, mostly cod, herring, or mackerel, then close those nets and haul them onto the boat."

"I'm sure it's more difficult that it sounds."

"Not really. Just a lot of hard work. But it all depends on where the captain tells us to drop the nets." His hands had worked their way back to the tabletop, where they caressed the evaporation clinging to his glass.

"And how does one know where to drop the nets?" Her eyes were locked onto his.

"Takes a long time to learn how to think like a fish." He laughed, hoping for a mere smile from Cozette, but got nothing more than her hardened scowl. "Currents bring warm water up, like rivers in the ocean. Little fish are attracted to the warmth and food, luring even bigger fish that hunt the smaller. Fish in a place long enough, and you get to know when those currents are strongest … but you aren't really interested in any of this, are you?"

Noémi's eyes flashed. "I asked. I'm interested. My life is generally free of concerns surrounding the supply of my food or clothing. Tell me more."

Emmett continued, talking about seasonal migrations, storm fronts, and the laws that had been established to protect from overfishing. "Since the end of the war, the government has started putting in rules that govern size and limits of catch, meaning more work for the deckhands. We throw a lot back now that used to go home with us. And prices have been down for a while. It's not an easy life, but for a lot of us, it's all we know."

"How long have you been fishing? Was your father a fisherman?"

Emmett laughed. "I went to sea to escape my father. Put him or my brother on a boat deck and sooner or later you'll need a bucket and a mop, pardon my French."

Cozette caught a laugh before it could escape her mouth.

"And on shore you come to ice cream parlors rather than men's clubs?" Noémi's smile showed a set of lovely, straight, white teeth that sent a shiver up Emmett's back.

"A special occasion, Miss Delacroix." He reached down and pulled up the bag of new garments. "New clothes. Normally, I'd be passed out in some corner of a saloon in Pioneer Square."

At this Cozette couldn't help herself. Her laugh burst free, and both Emmett and Noémi were startled. "Excuse me," she said, attempting to regain a measure of stern watchfulness.

Emmett grinned. He was welcome at the table. "And you ladies?"

"We, too, are shopping today, but not in order to avoid debauchery."

"I beg your pardon?"

"We limit our imbibing to the parlor, Mr. Dougal. My brother would find it unseemly for us to take alcohol in public."

"Meaning you don't spend much time in bars."

Both women smiled. He was no longer the crude reprobate in the corner, but a gentleman—a *soiled* gentleman—capable of repartee. The conversation drifted to the general topics of the day, as viewed by ladies or by those whose prime focus was putting food on the table. Emmett forgot all about his soda. The ice cream melted, and the soda water warmed to room temperature, but he never ventured another sip while in the presence of his newfound friends.

When they were ready to leave, Cozette found that she wasn't surprised or disapproving of the fact that Noémi provided Emmett with their address on First Hill; trusting that a down-to-earth man like Emmett would realize he was of lesser status and would not have the gall to actually call upon the address.

They said good-bye on the sidewalk, with Emmett gently grasping both of their hands; both women immediately missed him as he strode north toward his supper with Urquhart and Angel.

"What's with the smile?" Urquhart asked when Emmett found them in the cafeteria. Emmett ignored the question, went to the serving line, and assembled a large, hearty meal of potatoes, stew, creamed corn, and pie.

When he returned to the table, it was Angel's turn. "So, new clothes, new man, *happy* man?"

"Fresh, clean underwear will do that to you," was all he said.

They took their time eating, joking around, speculating about the next trip out, and what they had to do to prepare for that trip. He didn't mention Noémi or the slip of paper with her address on it, which he had secreted in his wallet. He didn't let on, during the joking and noisy eating, that he was already debating the possibility of visiting that address, or what he might be looking for there. Mostly, he didn't want to jinx any possibility that he might, at some future time, be in the presence of that beautiful young woman again.

After they finished eating, Angel returned to the *Aberdeen*, taking Emmett's parcel with him. Urquhart and Emmett found their way to a speakeasy located behind a laundry on Western.

Frowning at the quality of the gin, Urquhart noted that Congressman Volstead was likely responsible for more people going blind or getting rot gut than any other reason. But that observation did little to keep him from quickly tossing down a couple of shots.

"Rather drink good bonded whisky on the boat, but these days the Coast Guard will sink you if they see an empty bottle."

Emmett winced. He thought of Walter Bruge, his good friend and employer, strung up on the buoy, left to the elements and the gulls. "I could make better stuff than this," he said.

"Maybe. But you're a fisherman, Emmett. We both know you're even better at that."

Emmett winced again, this time due to the unvarnished compliment.

"Some people are meant to be accountants, some firemen or politicians, but you're happiest when you've got a rolling deck under your feet. I seen you out there, Emmett, you belong on the ocean. Hell, you'll die out there, just like me."

"Hardly. You'll die in your bed, all warm and cozy."

"Maybe. I hope not." Urquhart signaled for a refill, and a waiter came to take their teacups to the counter. "The fact is, I was ready to throw in the towel until you showed up. Me and Angel, now we got a reason to crawl out from our bunks each morning, and we thank you for that, despite all the trouble you cause."

Emmett smiled. That was as good as it was going to get, coming from Urquhart.

The waiter returned with two fresh cups full of gin. Urquhart sipped at his, almost daintily. "Used to take Russell to that cafeteria we ate at when we would come to town to shop for his school clothes. He was a good kid ..."

Emmett bit his tongue, waiting for the old man to continue.

"What's so frustrating is how temporary things are. One second, you got life by the balls, and the next it's cutting your legs from underneath you." He drained his cup and signaled again. "They can hurt you, you know, children? You don't have any, so you've been spared. But they get to know your weaknesses while overlooking theirs. That boy played me like he was cheating at solitaire."

"What happened?"

"Oh, I suspect Angel's already told you the particulars. What happened? The boy got a hard-on for money is what happened. Took to lying, even to me. Lived a life full of lies that all caught up to him. Eventually, someone took the bother of blowing out his brains ..."

Emmett stiffened. The old man *knew*. "They say you get all the rope you need to hang yourself, and Russell had two or three coils waiting. I love that boy. I always will. He cheated himself a helluva lot more than me or anyone else."

Emmett sat, thankful for a brief pause in the conversation. Urquhart seemed to be considering what he should say next, or whether to say anything at all.

"Look, the thing is—and I don't mean to embarrass you—but you're the closest thing I've got to a son now. Don't go fucking it up."

A BIT OF CANDY IN HARD TIMES

Unlike other wards in the prestigious hospital, this one was quiet. One patient occupied the white room, just off the nurse's station–only one of four rooms in the wing, and none of the others were occupied. The room was filled with flowers, but the pervasive smell of disinfectant obscured any aroma those blossoms might have afforded. On the bed stand was a short stack of books, newspapers, and magazines, as well as a pad of paper and pencil. They were accompanied by a pitcher of fresh drinking water and a glass. Other than that, there was total anonymity, and only a name card on the outside of the room's doorway identified the patient.

Reynard lay quietly, awake but with eyes closed, attempting to ignore the appearance of his nurse. He called her 'Miss Uppity,' because she would brook no nonsense from him.

"This is *my* ward," she had announced when he was delivered into her hands following the surgery. "My ward, and my rules. And they're simple. Don't fight me. Take your medications without complaint. And no visitors after seven PM. Got it?"

Of course, Reynard had no memory of that fiat, having just returned from a compulsory visit with Morpheus at the time. His head was wrapped in gauze, and a perpetual headache fogged both his vision and his thinking. Whatever Miss Uppity had said, it never gained any conscious traction.

But he couldn't forget her: either she or her counterpart on the night shift checked his vitals every hour on the hour, waking him to dispense medication or encourage him to use the bedpan. He had little control over his bladder and the discomfort vaguely reminded him of his early youth.

He wasn't certain how long he had been in recovery, but the three issues of the *Chronicle* stacked on the side table was an indication.

He kept his eyes closed, waiting to hear Uppity's leather soles scrape their way out of his room, having left his breakfast tray next to his bed. When he was sure he was alone, he carefully edged his way onto his elbows in order to survey his situation. His head throbbed painfully when he lifted it from the pillow, and he hesitated, allowing the blood pressure to stabilize.

He was in a corner room on the southwest wing of the hospital, and out his window he could see the dim tree line of Golden Gate Park. Noémi and Cozette had departed in the late afternoon, chased by Miss Uppity well before curfew because she had happened to catch him closing his eyes during the visit. By the look on Noémi's face, it was obvious that things were still very serious, and he had begun to worry about her future if things didn't work out for him.

Once again, he took stock of his situation. The businesses were doing fine. While the national economy was touch and go these days, their corner of the world continued to function without so much as a hiccup. He was glad he hadn't invested in agriculture; that market was in deep trouble, having slumped as the Great War receded from recent memory. Coolidge had corrected some of Harding's postwar excesses, but the President's decision to turn over stewardship of the national economy to Hoover had reawakened Reynard's misgivings about the doings in DC. The boys in office were funneling money in virtually every direction, doing what they thought would motivate the economy without overlooking the inescapable fact that there was a ton of money to be had.

Reynard knew he *had* to get better, to get over this bump in the road, to ensure that their holdings were safe and grab his share of the largesse. He had no one else on whom he could rely, not even the imperturbable Dunne.

Arlyn had been magnificent once Reynard shared his condition with his lieutenant, arranging their transit to the Bay Area, ensuring that Reynard got the best private room, and seeing to it that SFPD had men in the halls and at the doors for security. But Arlyn was no businessman.

Reynard picked up the top copy of the *Chronicle* and noted the date. Ander was due to visit him that afternoon, dependent upon his condition. He turned toward a small mirror on the open door to his bathroom, angled his head, and forced a smile. The smiling face, looking back at him, was alarming: almost garish.

He would have to do better. He grabbed the pad of paper and pencil from the side table and lay back, nearly exhausted from the minimal effort. He began to take notes regarding Ander's potential for success: mostly in the gathering of outside support for Reynard's proposed hotel. From there he analyzed who those potential suitors might be, and what their support would cost him.

While scribbling his thoughts, the headache took on greater proportion, and he was forced to drop the pencil and close his eyes, attempting to will away the ache that was gathering behind his eyes. He was tempted to push his call button, but knew that Miss Uppity would simply bring morphine, and he needed his mind to be clear. He was beginning to accept that the pain would never, entirely, go away, and that he would simply have to deal with it, no matter what difficulties he might face.

Finishing his outline, and examining it, made him feel a lot better. He called out to the hallway, and Arlyn, ever vigilant, appeared in the doorway. Arlyn had taken his turns on watch, despite Reynard's insistence that he return to the Fairmont for rest and refreshment. Instead, Arlyn had slept in chairs and completed his toilet in the restroom of the doctors' lounge, changing his shirt every other day and relying on Cozette to have them laundered. It was obvious, from his rumpled appearance, that he had just been asleep, but he came to Reynard's bedside with a look that expressed great concern.

"Get me a barber."

"A barber?"

"Yes, a barber. I need a shave before Ander arrives. And grab a doctor or nurse. I want them to redress this bandage. Afterward, get back to the hotel, take a bath, and put on a fresh set of clothes. Four days in one suit is too much. You might try *leaning* on that razor as well. You're starting to go bohemian on me."

A barber was ushered in and performed his function, carefully shaving Reynard with as little contact as possible. Then a doctor rewrapped his head bandage, affecting an almost jaunty turban. Reynard examined himself in the mirror on the door and was satisfied.

"Do I look … less *tragic*?" he asked Arlyn.

"If he weren't dead, people would think you're Valentino."

Reynard laughed, satisfied.

Noémi was thrilled and deceived, believing that her big brother was making a rapid recovery. She made a fuss about his silk pajamas, not aware of the pain he had suffered shrugging off the stale hospital bedclothes and donning the lightweight PJs.

"Okay, ladies, we've got a business appointment in fifteen minutes," announced Reynard. "Go have lunch in the cafeteria, or go see a movie …"

Arlyn returned from the Fairmont, looking much fresher. Before Ander's arrival, Reynard sat him down to discuss the deal.

"Ander knows a certain, unnamed politician in Seattle who has *aspirations* which—not for lack of trying—he has been unable to meet. Ander suggests that someone who could provide this pol with financial resources would be in a position to recoup that investment, in a variety of ways."

"Who's the politician?"

"Ander isn't saying. I have my suspicions about two or three gents, but it doesn't matter. I only need one more vote to get the zoning variance we need to move on the hotel. Ander is going to deliver that vote, but he wants something in return, beyond the skim he'll be taking."

"What does he want?"

"Nothing from us. But, again, it doesn't matter. He won't get whatever it is. I've done business with Ander long enough to know that he'd leverage his mother's life in exchange for the political influence he doesn't know how to use. What I want you to do is watch him. In a way he doesn't notice. See how he reacts to what I say. Blinking. Shrugging. Shifting his weight or impulsively interrupting. Make mental notes. You're a cop, think like a cop."

Arlyn understood before Reynard finished speaking. Ander wasn't all that he pretended to be, or pretended *not* to be. Arlyn also understood the importance that Reynard gave to his appearance, his mien.

Ander arrived on time. He believed that punctuality was the hallmark of integrity, though integrity was a flexible position, which he could set aside when necessary.

"You're looking well," he exclaimed on his entry. He made great show of shaking Arlyn's, then Reynard's hands. He examined the silk pajamas and the fashionable head wrapping and waved his hand. "You needed to come to San Francisco for a massage?" He laughed. But he had already slipped a five spot to the nurse on station in order to get the real prognosis.

"A minor readjustment," Reynard joked back. "Mr. Dunne?"

Arlyn produced a bottle of scotch and poured a dram into two glasses. Ander took his whisky with delight, saluting both men before tossing it back. Arlyn took and refilled the glass.

"So, news?" Reynard sipped at his glass, making a show of enjoying the liquor. He would have much rather had a glass of milk.

"The news is good. I've spoken with the politician in question, and he assures me that your needs would be met. He requires the help that you can provide, of course."

"Of course. And has the amount of that help been determined?"

"Ten grand, in cash."

The moment Ander quoted the amount Arlyn knew the man was lying.

"I assume as soon as possible?"

Ander nodded. "He has campaign costs already. Your donation would put him over the top. It would allow him to grease the tracks, so to speak."

Reynard nodded. He opened the bed stand drawer and drew out his checkbook.

"A draft will do. I'll make it out to you, and you can convert it to cash in Seattle. You don't want to be carrying around a lot of green these days, do you—not after our little adventure in Seattle last month?"

Ander would have preferred cash, but he reached to accept the check. Reynard held it just out of reach. "Who is it?"

"I can't tell you that right now."

"Meaning you don't trust me, Ander? After all the business we've done? You think I'd forego our relationship just to strike a dime on the dollar business deal? This is a lot of money I am trusting you with. I should think you'd trust me at least as much."

"I'll tell him you want to meet with him, but I know he wants to maintain a distance from you."

"Why?"

"I can't speak for him."

"Well, you tell him that the money comes with a face-to-face meeting. Do you understand? From what you've told me, he doesn't have a lot of patrons stepping up with checkbooks. No meeting, no money. I want to make sure I get what I'm paying for."

Arlyn watched Ander with interest. The man knew something that he didn't want to share. He wondered what that was. More than likely, the would-be politician wanted to maintain a squeaky-clean public persona, while striking deals with those who could bankroll his political career.

Arlyn had mixed feelings about Reynard's dealing with Ander and the anonymous pol, but he wasn't naïve. It was how politics worked. Better someone like Reynard pulling the strings than some clown whose only intent was profit. No, he knew Reynard had a vision and a desire to improve the community; that Reynard was willing to oil some palms to do so didn't bother him at all. Perhaps it was a newfound sense of loyalty: this man had invested in him, had made it possible for his family to own a home and, recently, a new Chevrolet.

Ander delivered the message. When Reynard arrived at Union Station three days later a chastened, if outwardly affable, man met him and conveyed his thanks. Reynard recognized the man as a Seattle furniture manufacturer who had been working hard to increase his stature within the Chamber of Commerce and other fraternal organizations. His name was Harry Gosford, scion of one of the merchant families that had earned vast wealth by outfitting men on their way to the Yukon goldfields.

"May I join you at your office?" he asked, and Delacroix enjoyed the gravitas his pocketbook provided during introductions. For a man concerned with his public image, Gosford was taking a chance meeting with Delacroix in such a public place, and Reynard appreciated the gesture.

"Of course. Do you have a ride, or would you care to join me in my car?"

Reynard had removed his head dressing even before leaving the hospital in San Francisco, insisting on a smaller bandage that he could hide beneath his homburg. Once they were inside his office, he removed his hat and Gosford felt compelled to comment.

"I trust you're on the road to recovery," he offered, waiting to be invited to sit.

Reynard motioned to a chair, and signaled to Cozette to have coffee brought in. "On the road, yes; to recovery … hopefully."

"The prognosis is good?"

"The doctors are satisfied. Their bills have been paid, so they are in good spirits. I, on the other hand, still harbor a headache the size of Elliott Bay. So, Mr. Gosford, I have invested in your run for office. Shall we discuss that?"

"Thank you for your generosity, Monsieur Delacroix." Reynard was pleasantly surprised by Gosford's obvious, and obsequious, use of the honorific. "Mr. Ander suggested that there might be more forthcoming? I had no idea how expensive political campaigning—even at this level—could be."

"You run a good business, Harry. Politics is like any business, there are start up costs."

"Yes, indeed. I believe we're going to see eye to eye."

Reynard waited for the coffee to be brought in, carried by Arlyn, who retreated to a chair at the back of the room after pouring coffee for the two gentlemen.

Gosford seemed uncomfortable, squirming slightly to gain a view of Arlyn, and Reynard noted the glance. "Harry Gosford, Arlyn Dunne. Mr. Dunne is my lieutenant, late of the Seattle Police Department."

Gosford quickly smiled, concluding that Arlyn meant no threat. "Pleased to meet you, Mr. Dunne. You look a bit too young to have retired."

"*I* retired him, Harry. He's doing much better by me than he did by the city fathers."

"And the PR value is undeniable, yes?"

Arlyn nodded, offering a weak smile as well. He was taking in Gosford's expensive, tailored suit. He certainly looked the part of upper-crust Seattle.

"Mr. Dunne has been an indispensable part of my family for several months. He helps to protect the good work that we do. That might well extend to you, Harry."

Gosford appraised the remark and smiled. "But he's just one man. Is that enough to protect all of our 'good works'?"

Reynard ignored the question and pulled some paperwork from a folder. Included were some sketches and draft elevations of his hotel, a break down of costs, and a list of the inspection schedule, most of which was moot if the council did not grant a variance, and much less applicable if Reynard did not have any support on that council.

"Take a look at this, Harry," he said, shoving the page with the frontal elevation of the hotel toward Gosford. Gosford examined the hotel, and then the other sheets. "Very impressive, Monsieur, and I see nothing that would catch any snags in the building department."

"I need a variance to go that high, for one thing. Another issue exists in that I intend to excavate below elevation, and this depiction doesn't illustrate that fact."

"Why on earth would you need to dig down below foundation level, Monsieur Delacroix?"

"Call me Reynard. To be frank, I want to house a large wine cellar there. I intend to provide my customers with the finest continental cuisine available on the west coast, and a large selection of Bordeaux, Burgundy, and Estate appellations would complete the menu."

"Again. I don't see why there would be any problem."

"It will require an additional variance, and I don't have many friends in the building department or review panel. The fact is, I am not all that well connected. That is, of course, the reason for our meeting today, is it not?"

Gosford sat back and sipped at his coffee, now cool. He regarded the paperwork, and its author, with a measure of calm that he hoped would disquiet his potential ally. "If I am elected then, surely, you will have one more favorable voice in city hall."

"I'm afraid I will require more than that, Harry. This will be a substantial investment, and I do not wish to have anything, or anyone, tripping me up once it is underway. I will need to have some assurance from you that this project will move forward, unimpeded, if I am to provide further financial assistance to your campaign."

Gosford smiled. He listened to Reynard's mellifluous voice, weighing the level of education the man must have achieved in order to arrive at such a ready vocabulary.

"You are from New Orleans, Reynard?" The latter nodded, wondering where this might lead. "I have several associates from that fair city, but none of them have your mastery of the language. Were you born well?"

"You're surprised that I don't lean on *yat*? The Creole *patois*? To be honest, I *was* well born … into a well-known and well-patronized house of ill repute. One of the house's regulars was a professor at Tulane, and he took some comfort in introducing me to literature and political theory—I would suppose to offset whatever guilt he felt from cheating on his wife with the various ladies of our house. I probably know your associates, but I have little or no dealing with those in New Orleans. There are enough of those that you know, personally, here in Seattle that will gladly thwart my plans for this hotel. Competition for the dollar is just as keen in Seattle as it is in New Orleans or New York."

"Why, Monsieur Delacroix!"

"Mr. Gosford, I am happy to help underwrite your political campaign, but don't for a moment conclude that I am an easy mark. This is a transaction. May I ask how much money Mr. Ander delivered to you?"

"This is most irregular—"

"Well, this is also my first foray into politics, Mr. Gosford. I simply need to understand what the prevailing tolls might be."

"Mr. Haller delivered five thousand dollars to my campaign manager."

"Who is Mr. Haller?"

"He is an associate of Mr. Ander."

"All right. So half of my investment is getting to you through Ander. Perhaps we should deal with each other on a more direct basis. Do you agree?"

"Half? You were donating ten grand?"

"I *did* donate ten grand. It's up to you to get the other five from Ander. Or I will. Believe me, you want to take care of this yourself. Mr. Dunne is a man of limited patience."

Sweat was beading on his brow, and Virgil Glaupher realized he was overheating. He stopped to unfasten his Sam Browne belt and unbuttoned his police officer's tunic. He took his handkerchief and carefully wiped the peak of his brow before tucking the linen into his back pocket. Harry Haller, an unimpressive young man crammed into a cheap wool suit from Monkey Ward, was seated on a hardback chair. He wasn't tied to the seat. His feet could shuffle, and his arms flinched at his sides. He knew there was no escape. He could only hope that Glaupher wouldn't beat the shit out of him.

"C'mon Lieutenant, you know as much about this as I do. I don't know nothing more. Come on, Lieutenant." He leaned forward slowly to the edge of his chair. "You know I don't want to get fucked up. I'd tell you if there was anything else going on. I don't want no broken teeth—"

Virgil stepped forward, and the kid slumped to the back of the chair, half pulling up his arms in a meek effort to defend himself.

"Haller, it don't matter if you tell me or not. I know. There's no punkass on the street that can think of something I myself haven't thought of. You think you're smarter than me? You may be smart enough to scam assholes on the street, but you're not smarter than me. I know. You got nothing to bargain with. But I ain't gonna break your teeth."

Virgil's fist arced forward and smashed into Haller's ribcage, knocking the wind out of him. Haller fell onto the floor and gasped for air, struggling to pull himself into a sitting position by the chair.

Virgil leaned down. "See? I know."

ATLAS, AT LAST

It was a brilliant morning when the *Aberdeen* forged her way across the Strait and merged with the traffic heading back into Elliott Bay. The sun shone so brightly off the glassy water that Urquhart had to shield his eyes while making his way to the docks to sell his catch.

It had been an eventful three days. The holding tank was full and they had, somehow, managed to net a good-sized swordfish, an unexpected bonus that would cover the costs of the trip's fuel. Urquhart was in an excellent mood, and didn't even bother to dicker with the fish broker at the dock.

After selling the catch, and filling the fuel tanks, the *Aberdeen* stood nearly $700 in profit. After they docked at Urquhart's, and after they had scrubbed the decks and rinsed the fish hold, Emmett and Angel hauled the nets onto the dock reels for repair. Then Urquhart gave them a couple of days off. He pressed ten dollars into Angel and Emmett's palms.

"It's a bonus. Buy a book. Get drunk. Relax for a couple of days. It's gonna get gray again soon, so enjoy the sun." Inside his house they heard him put a record on his phonograph and Signore Caruso's voice lifted above the yard. Soon the old man was doing his best to obscure the Maestro's voice.

Emmett didn't know what to do. He pocketed the tenner and headed up to his cabin. The sun shone brightly through the doorway and the small east-facing window. He sat down on his bed, smoothing the coverlet. What he really wanted to do was once again find the beautiful Noémi. He had no idea, of course, where to begin. He pondered the problem. How could he inquire? And even if he did have her address, would he be welcome—a fisherman, calling on a lady?

"Bullshit," he exclaimed, "of course I'm *good enough* for her. I'm a man of means," he laughed bitterly, surveying his one-room world. That life should take so long to introduce him to a woman he could love, while making that love unattainable, he found unacceptable.

He stood and walked down the slope to Urquhart's weathered, wood-frame house. He knocked at the door, though the clashing voices raised in song seemed to drown out his knock.

Urquhart did hear the knock, and stopped singing long enough to open the door and invite Emmett in while resuming his duet. The old man sang his way across the room to the cabinet where he kept his liquor and pulled out a bottle of scotch, underscoring the sweeping move with a hopelessly limited attempt to reach a note that only Caruso could manage.

He laughed while pouring out a dram into a glass and handing it to Emmett. "Too early? Nah, it's a day off. Sit down, drink some whisky, sing along. You know *Tosca*?"

Emmett sipped at the whisky and shook his head. He knew nothing about opera.

"It's about the French invasion of Italy by Napoleon. There's more to be sure, but that's enough of an explanation. The man singing is no longer with us. Listen to that voice! His name is Caruso. The Italians would have Caruso sainted if they could get the Pope to forego the religious crap they use to identify such folks."

He poured himself a drink, turned the volume down on the phonograph and sat next to Emmett. "My wife, she loved to listen to opera on the phonograph. She always wanted me to take her to New York so she could see the greats—Caruso, Patti, Ponselle, Gigli—she wanted to hear them in person, and when I balked at such a trip, she insisted I purchase this phonograph and these records. She would sit in the chair you occupy each evening after doing the dishes, playing these records. At the time, I hated them. But they've become part of her, and when I hear Caruso sing, I see her face, smiling there, and my losing her doesn't seem to be so unbearable."

Emmett nodded and drained his glass. He was beginning to learn about love, finally. To live without having shared such a thing was a frightening prospect.

Urquhart noted the darkened mood on Emmett's face. "What's troubling you on a day such as this?"

"You talk about love, you've *had* love in your life. For you, love has been something you've shared."

"Twenty-seven years. Some people would think that was a long time, but it was the blink of an eye!"

"I've never known a minute of that kind of love."

"Ah. You have regrets no young man should have. Go to Seattle, or Tacoma, and get yourself a woman for a night. That should ease the need."

"I don't mean that kind of love. I've had my share of women, paid or otherwise. I'm talking about someone to share your life with."

Urquhart poured more whisky into Emmett's glass. "You have someone in mind? Some farm girl here on the peninsula, some shop worker or waitress in Gig Harbor?"

"Seattle. But I don't know her, I don't even remember her last name. Something foreign sounding."

"And how did you run into this young woman?"

Emmett recounted the chance meeting in the ice cream parlor.

"I've always said a sweet tooth leads to nothing but cavities."

Emmett did not laugh, much less smile, and the old man realized how serious his young friend was.

"And now you want to find this young child of privilege?" It was more a statement than a question.

"I can't think of anything but her when there's no work to occupy me."

Urquhart sat back and sipped at his scotch. "You realize that more than good can come from this? Is she married?"

"I would never approach a woman wearing a wedding ring."

"Some don't. Some wives troll, do you understand what I'm saying?"

"She isn't anything like that. She had a chaperone, a woman twice her age."

"And this woman allowed you to talk to her ward?"

"She had no choice. Noémi—the young woman—insisted I join them. All we did was talk."

"And apparently fall in love."

"I can't speak for her, and I'm not certain I know what that means. She seemed to like me, but how could I know?"

"So all you have is a young, seemingly wealthy young woman named . . . ?"

"Noémi." Emmett pulled out the piece of paper with the address.

"Unusual name, and from a wealthy family, given the address. Her last name sounded foreign you said? I can make some inquiries. Over the years I've come to know folks whose contacts in the city are fairly broad. Won't promise anything, and you shouldn't expect anything. Think too hard on her, and you might miss something else even better. Now drink up, and let me get back to Caruso."

Emmett straightened his room, did a hand wash of his fishing gear, and hung the coveralls, shirts, and underwear outside in the sun. Then, as the image of the fair Noémi reinvaded his mind, he took a walk away from the cabin and into the interior of the woods that surrounded their fish camp.

The day had grown long, and the sun that made its way through the firs, spruce, and maples was golden. Bees, damsel flies, and midges flitted through the shafts of light, and Emmett thought of a similar afternoon in Nova Scotia when he and Bruge spent the day salmon fishing on the Chezzetcook River. But this light was more brilliant than any day he remembered from Nova Scotia, Newfoundland, or Maine. Perhaps it was his mood.

The track led to a lightly used road, and as he walked along on the grassy ridge between wheel ruts he was surprised by a sound from behind. It was the yellow dog, shuffling through leaves and debris at the side of the road. It trailed him by ten yards, a safe enough distance.

When Emmett stopped to face the dog, it stopped also and sat down. Sitting, the canine was more than two feet high at the shoulder. He was an impressive animal. His large mouth hung open, and his long tongue hung to the side; an almost maniacal smile formed by the tensed lips and raised muzzle.

Emmett smiled and returned to his easy walk and he heard the dog begin to shuffle through the leaves again, maintaining that same ten-yard distance.

Finally Emmett found a stump adjacent to a wide meadow, filled with grass and brush. The grass was no longer green, the result of a dry summer, and animal trails crisscrossed the expanse, perpetuated, perhaps, by the dog.

Emmett sat, carefully, on the stump. The tree had not been cut down, it had fallen, but the trunk was no longer there; probably harvested for firewood or building material by one of the peninsula's citizens.

The dog approached and lay down in the grass, about fifteen feet from Emmett.

"Look at you, you're huge. What do you eat, besides fish guts, to get that big and stay so healthy?" The dog didn't answer, he simply continued to pant and leisurely wag his tail at the sound of Emmett's voice.

There were large mats of hair formed on the dog's chest and along his flanks. Emmett was tempted to work on the mats but he wasn't certain what the dog would do if he approached. The dog's disrepair was so evident that Emmett felt compelled to go back and retrieve a filleting knife to cut the mats and balls free.

When he stood, the dog stood as well, and when Emmett started back toward the camp the dog followed, but this time at a nearer distance; it was as though he were loosely attached to this human, who had never thrown anything at him, or cursed at him, or chased him.

Emmett found a knife while the dog kept a respectful distance, obviously mindful of Angel, who sat on his stone stoop, nursing a bottle of beer and absorbing the warmth of the late afternoon sun.

Angel was at once both amused and disturbed by the big dog's presence, and the animal's focus on Emmett. "Emmett, don't encourage that dog. He never go away."

As Emmett carefully approached the dog, speaking in a soft voice that Angel couldn't quite hear, Angel was fearful that the dog might attack his friend. When there was no barking or biting, and when it was obvious that the big animal was welcoming Emmett's effort to groom him, Angel laughed in relief. "That dog, he gonna get the idea he's welcome 'round here. You gonna have to pick up his shit, Emmett, I ain't doing it."

Emmett managed to cut out a large mass of matted fur and chuckled. "By the size of this guy I'll bet those piles will require a snow shovel."

The big dog, unfazed by the tugging and cutting of his fur, lay down on his side and sighed, accepting Emmett's care. He panted in a relaxed cadence; his large brown eyes gazed upward and focused on his new friend.

After a few minutes, though, he'd had enough, and pushed himself into a sitting position. He faced Emmett with what appeared to be a broad smile splitting his muzzle. Then, without warning, he leaned forward and licked Emmett from chin to forehead, an act that at first startled, but then delighted, Emmett.

Emmett stood and walked to Urquhart's cabin, went inside, and then returned with a handful of salmon jerky. He offered a piece to the dog, and the animal gingerly accepted it, dropping back to the ground to enjoy the treat. Piece by piece, the bond was set. Emmett had himself a dog.

"What's a good name for an animal like you? You're almost as big as a bear. Certainly larger than any pup I've ever seen. Goliath? Nah, he was a villain. But you're no villain. You're just a big old puppy in need of a bath. But you're almost big enough to carry me around on your back ... that's it! Atlas. I'll call you Atlas." Emmett stood and made a sweeping introductory motion. "Angel, meet Atlas."

Angel took another swig of beer. "Don't care what you call him. I ain't cleaning up his shit, and damn dog not welcome in my cabin ... ever. You live with his fleas. I take a pass."

Angel finished his beer and threw the bottle into the Sound, admiring the splash it made. "By the way, what you gonna feed him? The old man ain't gonna be happy you take all the jerky to feed that mutt."

Emmett thought about it. What would he feed the brute? Maybe it was wrong to think he could domesticate the dog. By its looks it had been on its own a long time: perhaps from the moment it had been kicked from its mother's teats. Somehow, during that time, Atlas had managed to feed himself and find places to sleep, hide, or wait out the weather. Despite his tangled coat, still festooned with burrs, leaves, and bits of pitch, the big boy appeared all too healthy. How could he, Emmett, do any better for Atlas than Atlas had done for himself, and why did he feel the need to do so?

His family had had dogs while he was growing up, but they were essentially farm dogs: never allowed into the house, and used primarily as alarms around the chicken enclosure. His siblings were never encouraged to show any affection for those dogs, and he couldn't recall his father, or his mother, calling them anything but 'dog.'

Still, he felt a distinct kinship with Atlas. And, apparently, Atlas felt the same way toward him; or perhaps the canine just enjoyed the fact that there was at least one human who didn't feel the need to chase him off.

But, besides the mats that Atlas hadn't allowed him to cull, under the forelegs and on the withers, the animal was filthy. Emmett felt compelled to clean him up, so he built a fire on the beach and set a cast-iron Dutch oven filled with water above the flames. Then he dumped the hot water into the holding tank over the outdoor shower that Angel and Emmett used after coming in from days at sea.

All the while, Atlas watched in seeming amusement, unaware of what was in store for him. But when Emmett dispensed water from the tank into a bucket and began to pour it over him, Atlas balked, jumping to his feet and retreating a safe distance. Emmett spoke in a low voice, cajoling the animal, attempting to keep Atlas from disappearing into the woods.

It took several minutes, about the time it took Angel to finish another beer, before Atlas allowed Emmett to soak him with the warm water and suds him up with a bar of soap. By the time Emmett was finished Atlas was a different color—now a brilliant golden yellow—and Emmett was as wet as the dog. The sun reflected off Atlas' coat, and Emmett was pleased.

As Emmett doused the fire in the pit, Atlas swaggered down to the water's edge and lay down in the shallows. He wasn't used to life without a fine patina of dirt enmeshed in his coat. But at least for a few days he would be a different colored pup.

When Emmett offered the ten dollars he'd received as a bonus for the salmon jerky, the old man waved him off.

"We'll just have to smoke more fish. Or is the brute only partial to salmon?"

Emmett laughed. "That dog will probably eat anything that it can get into its mouth. Wasn't that Ferrady woman saying she would shoot the dog if it came around her hen house again?"

Urquhart grunted. "She's threatened to shoot *me* on a number of occasions. For that reason alone the dog is welcome—so long as you take care of him and keep him out of my house. Consider the dried fish an ongoing bonus. But you're gonna have to come up with something more, he can't live on the jerky alone. Go see the vet in Port Orchard, he'll fix you up. Should maybe check the animal for other things, too. Get the Ford running, you can take him in that."

Emmett coaxed Atlas into the old car with more smoked fish and made the half-hour trip into Port Orchard. The sign on the office door said "Walter Christenson, DVM," and Emmett concluded that it was the place.

The vet didn't seem fazed when Emmett led Atlas into the office, but smiled broadly when Emmett told the dog to sit and was ignored.

"Had him long?" he laughed.

He ran his hands around the dog, which made Atlas nervous at first. But then he realized the human meant him no harm and relaxed, collapsing into a heap on the floor. Both men had to hoist Atlas back to his feet, and the big dog seemed amused by their efforts.

The conclusion was that Atlas was in fine health, and had been getting plenty of exercise. The vet gave Atlas a vaccination against distemper, explaining to Emmett that the treatment was relatively new, but that it was important to take the precautionary steps to protecting Atlas' health. In the end, after the purchase of a large bag of Spratt's Dog Cakes, the bill was eleven dollars. Emmett pulled out the tenner.

"This is all I got, Doc. Can I owe you for the rest?"

"Sure, get it to me when you can. But you're going to need another bag of food in a couple of weeks. Is that going to be a problem for you, money wise?"

"Nah. I fish. I can handle the food, and I'll be sure to bring along the extra buck."

The ride back was even less eventful than the drive in. Atlas had grown used to the automobile and reclined, quite content, in the backseat, his head resting on the sill of the open window.

A casual bond had been struck, and when they returned to Urquhart's, Atlas bounded out of the backseat like an over-sized puppy, happy to have returned to familiar ground. He attempted to approach Angel—something he would never have done in recent times—but the Indian made it clear he wanted nothing to do with the dog. Atlas didn't seem to mind, sticking to Emmett, though he brushed up against Urquhart, much to the old man's amusement, whenever he came outdoors.

Atlas became—much to Angel's disgust—a member of the shore crew. He learned to stay out of the way when they hauled and repaired the nets, and showed less interest in the fish guts that Angel tossed to the crows and gulls that waited patiently along the waterline. His menu had been improved.

The big dog slept in the doorway of Emmett's cabin, allowing himself to be closed in, but choosing to sleep away from his human, stretched out across the threshold. The first night Atlas slept indoors, Emmett tripped over him on his way out to the outhouse in the dark. Sprawled on the ground in front of the cabin, Emmett watched the dark silhouette of Atlas' large head lean over him and then lick him, as if apologizing.

Atlas would also nuzzle Emmett in the mornings before the sun was up. Emmett would crawl out of his warm bed and open the door so Atlas could wander over to a nearby bush to relieve himself before returning to the cabin.

The loosely bundled bale of golden yellow fur followed everyone around the property, splitting off from one man to another if the big dog thought that person was doing anything involving food.

But, when he was invited onto the *Aberdeen*, Atlas balked. There was no way he was going to board the boat; instead, he sat resolutely on the dockside, as if to announce that he would be there waiting for their return. When they were going out for more than a day, Emmett left his cabin door open with a wash basin full of dog cakes and another with fresh water, though there was plenty of standing water nearby for Atlas. When the *Aberdeen* cleared Blake Island on the way back into the Passage, Emmett could swear he could see Atlas waiting patiently on the distant dock.

The big canine made Emmett's desire to see the mysterious Noémi easier to bear. But he found that he missed Atlas when he was fishing, no matter how busy he might be.

And, though he would hesitate to agree, Urquhart did as well. When they were on shore, he felt a sense of security when Atlas was around; not because the canine might protect them, but because Atlas filled the place out. He made it whole; not as whole as a woman might, but whole as an ersatz family. Perhaps that was it: he was part of a larger family, now. Angel, Emmett, and the dog provided him with a proscenium of life, something that had been missing since the murder of his son.

While he came to feel affection for the oversized mutt, it really pleased him to see the attachment grow between Atlas and Emmett. Emmett never ate before making sure that Atlas had eaten; for one, if Atlas had a full stomach, he was less likely to bother everyone else while they ate. It had grown cooler, and meals were taken indoors now, but Urquhart left the front door open so Atlas could keep an eye on them from the postage stamp sized porch.

One evening, the drizzle turned to a hard rain, and Urquhart brought the dog inside himself. Angel, who was camped in an overstuffed easy chair near the fire, began to complain, but the look on his employer's face told him there would be no argument.

From that night forward, rain or no rain, Atlas came inside and was allowed to stretch out on the gray shale hearth that fronted the fire. Angel, recognizing the *fait accompli*, took to pulling off his boots and resting his feet on the warm, shaggy flank of his erstwhile antagonist.

They were tucked into books and magazines one evening, a light rain pattering on the roof providing counterpoint to Brahms, when Atlas went ballistic, letting loose an awful combination of bark, whine, and growl. Emmett was on his feet in an instant, ready to discipline his charge, but then they heard a loud knock at the cabin door. He opened it to find a sodden figure: it was Helfing, one of their neighbors from down the Passage, dripping onto the old man's threshold.

"Evening, fellas," he said, pulling off his sopping wet hat. "Wanted to let you know, I was down to Gig Harbor to get a telegram, and they told me at the office they was one for you, too, but they wouldn't let me take it. Something about privacy and saying that if you had a phone you wouldn't have to count on someone like me alerting you to the fact that you got a telegram. Hope it ain't bad news."

Urquhart motioned him inside and Helfing gladly entered, dripping onto Urquhart's linoleum floor.

"Thanks, Helfing. Get you a warm up?"

"Well, sure, no pro cops around I'm guessing."

"Do *they* look like cops to you?"

Emmett had returned to his chair and was holding Atlas by the scruff of his neck to keep him from jumping on the stranger. He wasn't sure what Atlas' intentions were. Atlas wasn't growling, but his tail twitched. Angel, eye deep in the latest issue of *Life*, ignored the intruder.

"You didn't get a look-see who it was from?"

"No, they didn't even show it to me. They ask 'You know an Urquhart up there?' and I says sure, and they tell me to tell you about the telegram." He took the proffered glass of whisky and thoughtfully sipped at it. "Mebbe you *should* get a telephone. But, then I'da had no excuse to come sample your liquor. Mmm, good stuff, not homemade. You got any more of this a fella could buy?"

"Limited supply, Helfing. But take the last of the bottle to keep you warm on the way home. Thanks for the heads-up and stay out of ditches."

Helfing shuffled off through the rain to his car, cradling the bottle more carefully than he had cradled any of his five children.

"I guess one of us is going to have to go down to Gig Harbor."

Neither Emmett nor Angel looked at him. Bad news was infectious. If the old man got bad news, who's to say one of them wouldn't be the next recipient? Both men knew it was only superstition, but telegrams rarely brought *good* news.

"Why not we all go?" asked Angel. "We ain't going back out for a few more days. You say so yourself. We hang around here all the time. Maybe we get a restaurant meal instead of fish cakes. Maybe see a movie."

"We don't need three people, much less two, to go pick up a telegram. There *is* work to get done, Angel. But hell's bells, why not? Okay, we go in, pick up the telegram, grab a sandwich, and maybe a movie. Maybe they got a good western there at the *Empress*. Could use me a little Tom Mix."

Angel grunted, waiting for a dig about his Indian background, but none was offered.

In the morning, they decided to take the *Aberdeen*, concluding that the ride would be more pleasant than being jostled in a car for nearly an hour. Despite the higher prices, they could fuel the boat at the Shell Marine depot at Gig Harbor.

Atlas, seeing his humans getting ready to board the boat, waddled off to carefully nose at a feral cat that sat at the edge of the woods, an approach that the cat accepted as if they were old friends. Emmett noted the combination, smiling at the absurdity of the relationship.

He would have made comment, but Urquhart was obviously feeling some anxiety about the telegram and what bad news it might contain. The old man fussed about the boat, entered and then reentered his cabin several times, before finally climbing onboard and firing up the *Aberdeen's* engine.

The passage was calm, glassy as any lake on a summer day, and they eased out onto the southbound current. Gray skies had broken up, and there were patches of intense light spotting the water. A cold breeze flowed over the boat. They cruised toward Gig Harbor and, as they passed out of Colvos and across Dalco Passage, a southeasterly headwind took them from the port side, giving them a taste of the winter to come. The water fairly danced as the wind pushed against the prevailing current.

Angel stood precariously at the side deck while Urquhart steered through the chop, heading for the Narrows. The Indian grinned, happy to be on the water; he was even happier thinking about meatloaf and mashed potatoes waiting for him at the Lily diner.

They pulled into the Shell depot at ten, and Urquhart hopped onto the pier to pay for the fuel in advance. Then, leaving Emmett and Angel to fuel and find a temporary berth, he strode off toward the telegraph office on Front Street.

After the tank was full, Emmett maneuvered the *Aberdeen* into a berth, and they secured her well, before trotting off to find the old man and hear his news. However, they found he wasn't at the office and learned that after he had picked up the telegram, he had left immediately. They looked up and down the street, looking for a despondent, perhaps grief-stricken elderly man, but the only people on the street were a scrap metal collector and two men loading a truck in front of the feed and supply store.

Emmett began to get worried. They split up: Angel headed toward the north end of town and Donkey Creek, while Emmett went back to the waterfront. There he located the old man sitting comfortably, sipping applejack, in Vottenberg's marine repair shop. A happy, at-ease Urquhart was not who Emmett had expected. "What the hell's the news? You win some contest?"

Urquhart offered the glass of jack to Emmett, who waved it away. Enjoying Emmett's impatience, the old man pulled the telegram from his shirt pocket and held it out to him. "It's for *you*, sent care of me. And I read it. No bad news today, Mr. Dougal."

Emmett read the telegram:

"Son, didn't know how else to reach you, but had name of your boss. Stop. Come for turkey. Stop. 'Steven says OK.' Stop. Call or write. Stop. Love, Ma."

"You ought to be better about keeping you mother informed of your health and whereabouts, Emmett."

Emmett nodded, relieved and yet somewhat angry.

"You going?"

Emmett stopped and wondered about it, taking a glass of cider from Vottenberg and nodding in thanks. "Steven says OK." All of a sudden, Steve was fine with him? Was this some brief break from the fighting, or perhaps a trap? "I don't know."

"Well, you got to let her know one way or another, and to let her know you got her telegram. I have to ask, why a telegram? Why not a letter sent to general delivery?"

"Who knows? How'd she know I was at your place?"

"Gerritson must have passed the information. But, why not a letter?"

"Never known her to write a letter. Don't remember her ever getting a letter. But it got us down here for a moving picture and a hot meal. We might as well go find Angel, he's probably all the way up to Port Orchard looking for you."

The three men reunited at the boat and made for the small diner on the main drag. The place was well lit, even though there was still plenty of light outside. While tight quarters—it sat no more than twenty—it was comfortable, and the food was reliably good.

They sat at the counter and placed their orders, drinking coffee to offset the hard cider. While they kibitzed about family Thanksgivings or, in Angel's case, institutional Thanksgivings, a lanky man wearing a well-worn canvas jacket over coveralls sat down next to Urquhart. He made his helloes and started to introduce himself to the old man.

"I know who you are, Bud."

"Well, that's good. Then you know what I'm going to ask."

"No point. I been fishing the Sound, the Strait, and the Inside Passage for nearly three decades, longer than your cooperative has been around. What are you going to do for me? Fix my nets? Overhaul my engines? Show me the best places to drop net?"

"Well, we don't offer most of those services, but we *can* ensure that no one else damages your nets, your boat, your house, your cat ..."

"Get the fuck outta here," Urquhart muttered. The man obliged, saying a good evening to the newest group of loggers entering the diner.

When Angel and Emmett looked at him, Urquhart filled in the blank. "Been after me to pool with them for three years. I guess they're running out of patience. Best we be watchful for a while."

The Lily was nearly empty when they arrived, but by the time they had finished, dawdling while waiting for a start time at the theater up the street, it had filled with workingmen. The loud talk and heavy smoke that followed soon compelled their exit.

Angel decided to wait for them on the boat, probably because the billing was a Hoot Gibson film, *Burning the Wind*, running with a Laurel and Hardy short. He was sound asleep in the pilothouse when they arrived back at the boat early that evening. They made their way back up the Colvos Passage. Urquhart nudged Emmett, and they left the pilothouse to stand at the fantail. "Your ma's telegram wasn't the only news you might be interested in," he said.

"What now?"

"This girl of yours, Naomi—"

"Noémi."

"Yeah. Vottenberg does work with suppliers out of Seattle and spends time in speakeasies when he's in town. Thinks she's related to a certain Delacroix. Bigshot of some kind."

"So, she's rich. Her clothes told me that much."

"It's *how* he got rich. It's how he *stays* rich."

"Don't string me along, old man, get to the point."

"He's a hood, apparently a well-connected hood. You don't want to be messing around with that kind of character."

The wind at their back seemed to grow colder, and Emmett shivered, as much by the information as the temperature. "What was the name?"

"Delacroix. Reynard Delacroix."

Emmett nodded. "Doesn't make her any less attractive."

Urquhart nodded; his face was almost imperceptible in the near darkness. "Figured as much."

When they eased up to the dock at Urquhart's fish camp, Atlas was waiting, his heavy tail thumping on the weathered dock planks.

MIXED BLESSINGS

Thanksgiving morning crawled out from under a thick gray blanket, promising a day of happy family gatherings. But the Dunne holiday was starting as something less than happy. Mary Elizabeth was in one of her moods. Arlyn wouldn't point this out, however, for he knew from her mien that any attempt to cheer her up would simply make things worse.

She muttered under her breath as she fed the boys, and angrily shut the bathroom door when he volunteered to bathe them. He knew why she was angry, though why she would object to going elsewhere for a feast—a feast that she wouldn't have to prepare or clean up after—was beyond him.

"When am I going to get to show off my kitchen? We never have company. Whenever we do go out, it's with that Reynard. Frankly, I'm tired of it. We could have invited others here for dinner."

"Who? *Who*, M.E.? We don't have family within hailing distance. I could invite someone from the force, I suppose, but why would I when my employer has graciously invited me to share his table? It's one day, M.E. One day. You'd think we were moving in with them for all the fuss you're making."

"Well, we're coming home early, and that's all there is to it."

"We'll come home when it's time, and not a minute before. Mr. Delacroix has a game room that the boys love, you know that. They'll have good food and lots of treats."

"And I won't be able to get them to go to sleep." Her voice was rising in volume, and Arlyn noted some concern on Teddy's face. Teddy, being the middle boy, was the most sensitive to her outbursts.

"You quiet down now, M.E. *Now*. I won't have this. They'll be able to catch a nap after dinner. You go get ready, and I'll finish up with the boys."

He could feel her cold stare as he pulled clean shirts out for his two oldest. "We're leaving in fifteen minutes, M.E., better get a move on."

The drive across Queen Anne was quiet except for the boys playing in the backseat. He hoped she would become a bit more responsive after a glass or two of wine, but lately she had been sullen and withdrawn whenever he came home. They had already hired a housekeeper so she wouldn't have to cook or clean up after the boys, but that hadn't seemed to help one bit.

He had opened an account for her at a women's store in Seattle, and she had made liberal use of the opportunity. She relied on Annie, the new housekeeper, to watch the boys while she was out. Her closet and wardrobe were filling out, but often she came home with nothing, having spent the day just window-shopping. Even those liberated afternoons seemed to set her on edge. He had no clue what to do, or say, that would mend their situation and, lately, she had been refusing his advances in bed.

During the prolonged silence he wondered if she even loved him anymore. Was it a case of too much too soon? She had grown up in lesser conditions—hell, they had spent the first decade of their life together in lesser conditions and now she was lady of the manor, a position that she had never anticipated, even if it was something about which she fantasized.

He looked across at her, staring out her window as if to pretend that he didn't even exist, sitting pretty in a forty-dollar dress decorated in expensive, but tasteful, costume jewelry.

He told her she looked lovely as he opened the passenger door for her, and she offered him a wan smile. He marshaled the boys onto the porch, holding them aside so their mother could precede them to the beautiful oak front door. The porch was bigger than their kitchen and dining room combined, and this wasn't lost on Mary Elizabeth. But when the door opened she forgot all about it.

Holding the door open, sporting a grin that he never wore to work, was Lieutenant Virgil Glaupher. "Come on in, folks. The party's just getting started."

He stood to the side and motioned them in. He patted Arlyn on the back, a typically un-Glaupher action.

They moved into the foyer, where Reynard and Noémi greeted them with small favors for the boys, small die-cast soldiers painted in garish colors.

"Samuel is too young for those," Mary Elizabeth noted, taking the toys away from him. "He'll just try to eat it."

"We'll find something to keep him occupied," said Reynard, who picked up the toddler and strode off to find him a distraction. Normally, Mary Elizabeth would have objected to Reynard's hijack of Samuel, but she was still regaining her equilibrium. Virgil's unexpected presence was unnerving.

Arlyn followed Noémi down the hall to hang his, and M.E.'s, coats in a closet, and when they were beyond the foyer Virgil's large hand grasped M.E.'s buttocks in a very familiar fashion.

"Stop it!" she whispered, brushing his hand away, but she noticed that Charles had seen the movement. "Run along with Mr. Delacraw, Charles. Go see what goodies he has in his play room!" Charles' eyes widened, thinking of the possibilities, and dragged Teddy with him to catch up with Reynard and Samuel.

Virgil roughly turned M.E. toward him and planted his mouth upon hers. He pressed his body against her, and she found herself allowing him to explore her body, perhaps excited at the prospect of being caught; Arlyn was probably no more than two rooms distant.

"Not now," she whispered gruffly, forcing him away.

She checked her makeup in the hallway mirror and waited for him to enter the living room a few moments before she joined the party. Arlyn was already drinking, she noticed, holding a short crystal goblet filled with some amber liqueur. He stood next to a seated Noémi, who was sharing a photograph with him.

"Lookee here, M.E., here's a picture of me, Noémi, and some of her friends at Coney Island." He stood away so she could seat herself next to Noémi. Mary Elizabeth had no desire to sit next to the young woman, but realized that her reluctance to do so would not be viewed favorably by the company. She carefully sat down and took the photograph. The picture showed a group of five young, well-dressed women, all smiling like idiots, while her husband stood to the side like some gabardine-clad eunuch. She wondered at the timing of the photograph, perhaps taken at the same moment that she and Virgil had been locked in amorous combat at the Rainier Hotel. She handed the photograph back without comment.

"Would you like a tour of the house?" Noémi asked. Mary Elizabeth realized she was trapped; it was going to be a long day. She nodded, and the two women deployed to the kitchen to inspect its latest gadgetry, leaving Virgil and Arlyn to themselves.

"Got quite a family there, Dunne." Virgil's attempt to engage Arlyn was clumsy and hardly heartfelt.

"Thanks, Lieutenant."

"You can call me Virgil. You don't work for me anymore."

"Virgil it is. I thought you were married."

"Technically. We're separated, but she'll fight a divorce. She gets a hefty share of the salary, and she ain't gonna give that up for a lesser amount of alimony. But she's also stuck with the kids. I'd say good riddance, but I really miss my little girl. I cover the mortgage, the food, and her clothes, but the bitch makes me pay to see the kids."

"She makes you pay to see your kids?"

"Well, not exactly. But when I want to take the kids for a weekend, she finds things that she needs and has me get them for her: a new icebox, new wool rugs ... hell, I even got her a used Buick in July—course, I got that out of the impound lot. I'd have her knocked off, but babysitters would cost just as much in the long run." Noting the look on Arlyn's face, he added: "I'm kidding, Dunne, that's a joke!"

"But you don't share the holiday with them?"

"Nah, she took the brood to her family in Portland for the week ... on my dime, of course. Say, you want to change out that prune juice for some good stuff?"

Virgil went to a side table, pulled a couple of glasses and a decanter of whisky from the cupboard, and poured liberal amounts into each glass.

"Cheers," he said, handing a glass to Arlyn.

Reynard reentered and, noting that the men had poured themselves a drink, followed suit.

"Those boys are awfully quiet," Arlyn said.

"They're fine. They're playing miniature ten pins."

"And Samuel?"

"*Mère* came and retrieved him. I think she thought he'd eat one of the pins. I don't think she's happy here, Arlyn."

"She's been pretty antsy lately. Don't know why. Give her another glass of sherry and she'll settle down."

Virgil stifled a smile. *He* knew what would settle her down.

Mary Elizabeth returned to the living room with Noémi, holding Samuel and using him as a shield from the younger woman.

Cozette entered to announce dinner, and the party went inside. On the long dining room table was a large roasted goose set on a platter, surrounded by a variety of roasted root vegetables. There were bowls of mashed yams, sweet corn, and French green beans, along with a platter of fruit and cheese. The settings were formal, and Mary Elizabeth, who had seen some of the preparations in her brief visit to the kitchen, was still nearly overwhelmed by the variety and quality of the food.

Cozette produced a highchair for Samuel, which she set next to M.E.'s seat. It was new, and obviously had been purchased specifically for this occasion. Despite her predisposition, M.E. found herself thanking Cozette, and then Noémi, and meaning it. She wasn't used to being around people who were so thoughtful.

Reynard waited until everyone was settled and then said grace. It was short but profound, and Arlyn sensed his employer's sincerity within the well-worn words.

The meal was enjoyed by all, though the boys fought over the drumsticks and engaged in potato warfare, catapulting the starch back and forth until Reynard almost laughed himself sick. Even Mary Elizabeth had to restrain her own laughter as she lightly slapped Charles' wrist to get him to behave.

While passing bowls of the potatoes and carrots to Virgil, M.E. allowed her hand to briefly rest on the lieutenant's arm, an act not lost on Noémi. The two women's eyes met, and M.E. blushed. Noémi quickly directed her attention to Teddy who was sitting beside her.

"Don't you like the stuffing, *chéri*?" she asked, and Teddy made a face, eliciting another round of laughter.

After dinner, they were all seated in the living room again, sated. Cozette had produced decanters of port and sherry, and everyone had tippled. The boys were asleep on the floor of the game room. Conversation was slight, but everyone was comfortable.

The phone rang in the distant hallway, but was quickly answered. A few moments later, Cozette entered and told Virgil that someone wanted to speak with him. He took the call, and returned only to thank Reynard and Noémi, and to say good night to the Dunnes.

"Trouble, Lieutenant?" Reynard asked.

"Not for me. For somebody else," was Virgil's grim reply. Noémi and Mary Elizabeth found themselves looking at each other, and in that instant Noémi recognized the bond that existed between the latter and Glaupher. She tried to smile but Mary Elizabeth could see the disappointment on Noémi's face.

"We ought to be going home, too, Mr. Delacraw."

"Understandable," he said, standing. "Allow me the privilege of rousing the troops." He hurried down the hallway while Arlyn went with Cozette to retrieve coats and mufflers.

"You have a lovely family, Miss Mary." Noémi offered her hand.

"Yes, I do, thank you." Mary Elizabeth did not offer hers.

"You must do all you can to protect it."

M.E. looked at her, divining what Noémi had seen. "Yes, I must. Thank you for a most pleasant afternoon and evening, Miss Delacraw."

As soon as Atlas realized that his human meant to take the dinghy out on the water he lost interest, and retreated to the stone steps in front of their cabin. Emmett struggled to start the outboard engine, waved back at him, and departed toward the distant shore. Atlas didn't share the human's attraction to the water, though he identified it as the place from which many of his meals had come. He sniffed at the air, tasting the acrid discharge from the engine.

Urquhart came out of his cabin, having been alerted by the sound of the engine. Looking at the dinghy now fifty yards offshore, he smiled. Emmett needed family, just as he needed his. He looked out toward Atlas. The big boy was poised, sphinx-like, at the door to Emmett's cabin, and was looking back at him. He whistled, and Atlas struggled to his feet and wandered down toward him. Unlike Angel, the old man was usually good for a scratch and a treat.

Urquhart met him halfway and playfully pummeled the big dog on his shoulders, stopping to scratch behind the ears and beneath the new leather collar that Emmett had purchased for Atlas. He had burned in the name "Atlas" along with "Urquhart" on the leather, hoping to further tie the dog to his new home.

Urquhart strode across the wide yard and pounded on Angel's door. There was a murmur of sound inside and then a loud "All right!" when Urquhart repeated his pounding.

"We got us a bird to pluck!" Urquhart yelled. "Play with yourself later!"

Atlas sat, content. Things were normal.

The two men cornered the tom they had purchased and quickly dispatched it, immediately hanging it out of reach from Atlas, who was convinced the best time to consume the bird was then and there. Then they set to plucking and eviscerating the bird, setting aside the giblets for gravy.

The general fare at Urquhart's fish camp was just that: fish. Whenever they went to Gig Harbor, Tacoma, or Seattle they generally found a place for red meat. Poultry was an extravagance: holiday fare. They both took to their tasks with happy anticipation of the afternoon's meal.

Once the bird was plucked and cleaned, Urquhart produced a large roasting pan, filled it with potatoes and onions, and placed the bird on the nest of vegetables. He primed his wood-burning oven with dried apple wood and set the pan inside while Angel was skinning a large bowl of yams. The air inside the cabin soon became redolent of roast turkey and memories. Urquhart could fairly see his beautiful Lillian bustling about the kitchen, shooing him from the proceedings.

It wasn't yet midday, but he produced a bottle of Black&White and poured a dram into Angel's coffee. The Indian slurped at the mixture and smiled.

"Sweet enough for ya?" Urquhart asked. He nearly tripped over Atlas, who had encamped himself directly in the middle of the kitchen floor so as not to miss one dropped morsel of food. Urquhart placed his foot on the animal's flank and gently pressed, bringing a grunt of affection from Atlas.

Emmett guided the dinghy along the shoreline of the island. He knew a spot, where he had often played as a kid, just below Lisabeula where he could hide the boat: a direct, one-mile shot to the Dougal homestead. He brought with him a rucksack filled with jars of jam and honey, penny candies for his nieces and nephews, and a bottle of scotch from Urquhart's pantry. His mother had taught her children to arrive with gifts, and Emmett wasn't going to let her down.

When he was within fifty yards of the property, he found a place where he could scan the site for potential danger. There were two cars parked on the roadside in front of the house, and he recognized one as Steven's. Perhaps he had a couple of men with him, intent on taking Emmett into custody; perhaps the invitation had actually been sent by Steven to lure him out into the open.

He worked his way closer to the house and he could hear the happy arguments coming from inside: the sounds a family makes when it gathers to celebrate itself. The front door burst open, and two boys bolted outside, ki-yi'ing and chasing each other around the yard. It appeared to be safe. Still, he was wary as he approached the front door, and looked down the back yard before climbing onto the porch.

When he knocked at the doorjamb there was an immediate, loud explosion of affection from the women within. The door was opened.

"Emmett! Ma, Emmett's here!" They surrounded him like hungry puppies rooting for a vacant teat.

Steven appeared and offered his hand; his badge was in his pocket. Emmett took the hand and warily looked his brother in the eye, hoping to detect the actual intent.

But Steven just smiled and asked, "Truce?" He offered his brother the easy chair he had been occupying.

Emmett soon had the entire family, less those working on Thanksgiving dinner, surrounding him in the large living room. He handed out the penny candies to the kids, telling them to wait until after dinner, but smiling at the empty wrappers left on side tables or the floor. Even his mother and sisters forgave him this indulgence.

Steven watched from a corner of the room, amused by his younger brother's attempt to engage his kids. He thought *the idiot doesn't realize that they don't really like him, only the things that he gives them.* He appraised his younger brother: work clothes, not dress clothes, but laundered; boots well-worn but recently soled, lightly caked from his cross-country walk; hair cut white-wall style and combed from the left side; hands clean and nails trimmed. If he didn't know better, he might have thought his brother to be on the square, just a hard-working man.

They were all called together into the dining room, which wasn't really large enough to accommodate the entire group. But somehow they managed to squeeze in a couple of small side tables around the dining table and there was enough room to lay in the turkey platter with all the traditional side dishes.

Emmett's mother beamed, not from the success of her menu, but because it was the first time in many years that that many Dougals had been in the same room. She insisted that Emmett say grace, and he searched for and found the litany that had been repeated thousands of times during his youth. When he was finished he looked up to see Steven looking at him, his furrowed forehead leaning forward; the look of a man trying to figure something out.

"Steven, you dish up the bird now," their mother said, and Steven regained his smile. He picked up the carving knife and fork and carved the turkey just as his father had, slicing down the breastbone and then carefully cutting through the white meat. A plume of steam escaped the bird, accompanied by a collective oohing. The bird smelled even better than it looked.

The room was loud with conversation and playful argument. They plowed their way through turkey, cornbread stuffing, potatoes, canned green beans and carrots, and two types of pie: pumpkin and spiced apple.

When the belts had been loosened and chairs pushed slightly away from the table, Emmett started taking plates from the table and heading for the kitchen.

"Emmett, you leave that alone. Go relax in the parlor with your brother, and let us clean this up."

He smiled and gave her a hug. "You know best, Ma, you always know best."

She laughed and hit him on the arm. He surveyed the table and the damage they had done. It had been a remarkable feast.

He breathed in the smell of home, attempting to memorize it. Then he shuffled toward the largest stuffed chair in the room and slumped into it. Steven sat on a divan opposite to the chair.

"Pretty good eats." Emmett nodded. "You relaxed?" Steven asked.

Emmett smiled. "Thanks for agreeing to my visit."

Steven smiled back. "Didn't have much choice. Ma said either I don't make a stink, or I'm not invited. Haven't missed a Thanksgiving in this house, and wasn't gonna start now." The smile disappeared. "So, what're you doing now, Emmett? Still scraping by?"

"I work a boat on the Kitsap. Been with that boat for the past few months."

"Where?"

"Like I said, on the Kitsap."

"Yes, but where? Who's the boat owner?"

"I'm guessing this visit is about over." Emmett stood up, and Steven motioned for him to sit back down.

"I'm just curious is all, Emmett, it's not official. But if something were to happen to Ma—"

"I'll be in regular touch with Ma."

The old Dutch wall clock chimed twice, and Steven thoughtfully looked at it. "Okay, okay. We gotta finish this business between us, Emmett. This can't go on, it's not good for the family. We hafta *resolve* the issue."

"Are you saying let bygones be bygones? Is this square one? I can agree to that."

Steven stood up. "No, I mean I'm glad you enjoyed the visit, but now it's time for us to go." He went to the front door, and opened it to expose three well-armed men on the porch. "There's two more out back, Emmett."

"You bastard!"

"Hush, there're kids about. Come quietly. There's no good in getting everybody all riled up. Sorry, but I gotta put these cuffs on you."

He stepped forward. Emmett quickly shoved him into the men standing behind the door. Then he launched himself up the stairs, past his old bedroom, and scrambled up a drop ladder into the attic.

Steven struggled to his feet, and the commotion brought his mother from the kitchen. She saw the men, with guns drawn, standing behind her eldest. "Steven, what's going on?"

"Sorry, Ma. He's gotta come with us."

"You *promised*!"

"I said he could come to Thanksgiving. He came, he ate, and now he goes."

"You cannot take him from this house, Steven!"

"Sorry, Ma … " he pushed past her toward the stairs. "Come on down, Emmett. There's no way out." He started up the stairs, followed by the largest of his fellow deputies.

His mother reappeared with a shotgun pointed at him. "So help me, Steven, I will shoot you. You may have not said the words, but you meant to make me think you did. Emmett is welcome here, and you are not. Now, git!"

Steven decided not to test her goodwill. "Won't mean a thing, Ma. He can't escape this time, and he's going into my jail until I can transport him to Seattle. With a little luck, you'll be able to see him on McNeil."

"Well, if that's the case, it'll be more often than I see *you*. Now git out of my house."

Steven good-naturedly put his hands in the air and said, "Don't shoot." He backed out of the hallway and made his way to the front door. "We'll just be waiting outside."

They went out to their cars and smoked, maintaining close surveillance of the house.

His mother joined Emmett in the attic, but she wasn't prepared for what she found. Holding out a lantern, she could see him in the attic's far corner. He had carefully pried loose the wallboards that surrounded a wall vent.

"What are you doing there, Emmett?"

"Don't worry, Ma," he said with a smile. "I'll come back and fix it like new." He worked at the boards, prying carefully. Using his pocketknife, he levered the nails, and a large piece came free. He placed his boots against the outer boards and pushed slowly, forcing away the exterior planking and creating a large enough hole for a man to squeeze through. "Don't bring that lantern any closer, I don't want them to see this new window."

She smiled and withdrew. "Don't let your brother make you a stranger."

"Never again," he replied, throwing a kiss.

Emmett waited for the last of the twilight to die before wedging himself through the opening. After he hit the ground one of the deputies picked up on his escape. "Over here, the son of a bitch's heading for the woods!"

"Stop, Emmett!" Steven yelled, grabbing his shotgun and running toward the dim figure about to disappear into the line of fir trees. "Goddammit, Emmett!" He stopped and pointed the shotgun in the general direction of his brother and pulled the trigger.

The shotgun blast prompted a scream from the house, and Steven stopped in his tracks. His deputies continued to race into the trees in a hopeless effort to capture Emmett.

Steven returned to the porch where his wife and one sister were bent over the collapsed figure of his mother.

"Heart attack? Is she dead?" he asked.

"Not yet, you liar," she replied. "Get off my porch!"

Emmett ran south through the forest, a forest he had been running through since he was four years old. He knew the dips in the trail, where the roots emerged in unforgiving tangles, and where the low branches hadn't been cleared. Behind him he could hear swearing, and it wasn't long before he knew he was entirely beyond their range.

He stopped and listened. He could barely hear their voices, probably fifty yards behind him in the gloom. Then he headed back north through the woods, flanking his pursuers and emerging along the edge of Kellum's pasture. He followed the fence line until he came to a road that would lead him back down toward Lisabeula, just north of where he had hidden the dinghy.

Emmett put the dinghy out and started the outboard. He was hot, dirty, and sweaty, but a mighty belch forced its way up and he tasted, again, the wonderful dinner to which he'd been treated. He grinned. All in all, not a bad adventure, he thought.

But Steven was out of hand. Emmett had no idea what had transpired between his mother and her oldest son, but he knew that the family was supportive of him. He would just have to be a lot more careful whenever he came to visit them. Steven wasn't going away anytime soon.

When he was within a hundred yards of the camp, he cut the engine and rowed the rest of the way in. If the old man or Angel had already gone to bed, he didn't need to disturb them.

As he got closer to the beach he could see that someone had built a small bonfire on the beach and was standing just beyond it. It might have been the old man, or Angel; he couldn't tell.

The fire was bright enough to illuminate the figure, but not enough to identify him. As Emmett pulled the dinghy onto the rocky shoreline, the figure noted his arrival and quickly ran up the slope. Emmett made his way into the camp, and he heard a car start up and drive down their road into the gloom.

It was then that he saw Angel lying at the base of the fire, apparently unconscious.

"Angel, get away from the fire!" he yelled. He ran up the beach and pulled the inert Indian from the fire's edge. Angel's hair was singed, and the smell was obnoxious. He shook Angel until the Indian came around. He immediately began to struggle before he recognized Emmett.

"What the hell happened, Angel? Who was that?"

Angel sat up, still unresponsive. Then Emmett thought about the old man, and ran toward Urquhart's cabin.

There, on the floor of his kitchen lay Urquhart. There was blood on his gray shock of hair, but he responded with a loud grunt when Emmett tried to lift him into a sitting position.

"Take it easy, boss," Emmett said. He took a pillow from Urquhart's easy chair and slotted it under the old man's head.

"Whisky," Urquhart requested.

He sipped at the glass of liquor that Emmett held for him and slowly hoisted himself onto his elbows. "How'd it go?" he asked.

It took Emmett a few seconds to realize the old man was asking about his holiday. "Not bad," he replied, grinning.

TO HEAR MERMAIDS SINGING

Once Angel had regained his equilibrium, he joined Emmett in helping the old man onto his well-worn sofa. Angel blanched at the sight of the blood on Urquhart's scalp, and was compelled to sit down.

"What happened here?" Emmett asked Angel.

The Indian shrugged. "I mebbe drank too much, went down and built me a fire. Next thing I know, you're standing over me."

Emmett used a wet towel to clean Urquhart's head wound. There was a large lump, but only a small cut had been opened, and Emmett stanched the slight bleeding with a styptic pencil, causing the old man to wince.

"What happened to you, boss?"

Urquhart looked up, then took another long pull from his glass. "I assume it was a visit from the 'Association.' Before he clocked me, he put something on the kitchen table."

Emmett retrieved an envelope and opened it to find a note that simply said:

"$50 every two weeks."

"What does this mean?"

"What does it mean? What does it *mean*? It means I'm being strong-armed by a bunch of thugs." Urquhart swung his legs up onto the sofa and stretched out, cradling his glass as carefully as he would an infant.

Suddenly, Emmett remembered Atlas.

"Where's Atlas? Did they hurt Atlas?" He rushed out into the darkness and called out. The animal did not respond. "Where was Atlas when this asshole showed up?"

"Assholes," Urquhart corrected. "After dinner he took off. I suspect to find himself a comfortable spot to take a nap. Why? You think they hurt him?"

"I hope not. If they have, I'll kill them." Emmett rushed out into the darkness.

Angel looked at the old man; he'd never seen Emmett like this.

Emmett ran into the woods, checking where the big dog liked to wander, calling his name every few seconds. He dreaded what he might find or, worse, that he wouldn't find Atlas at all.

There was no response, and after fifteen minutes of scrambling about in the undergrowth, he gave up and returned to the camp.

As he drew near the lights coming from Urquhart's cabin, he made out a dark shape in the middle of the yard. As he drew near it approached him. It was Atlas, apparently unharmed. Emmett knelt on the moist gravel and hugged his dog.

When he returned to the cabin, Angel was standing over the old man. "He just went to sleep kind o' sudden. He's breathing, but he twitches every so often."

Emmett checked the old man's pulse and it was strong. "Probably took something out of him, getting clobbered like that. All he needs is a good night's sleep." Emmett retrieved an afghan from Urquhart's bed and spread it out over the unconscious figure. Atlas loudly thumped to the floor in front of the sofa and laid his head down. He wasn't going anywhere.

Angel and Emmett left them alone and walked back down to the beach. A fine mist was falling, but it had little effect on the fire.

"Why a fire?"

"Seemed like a good idea. Felt maybe the liquor was gonna force out the food. Man, we ate good. You?"

"Ma puts out a good spread. You never saw or heard nothing?"

Angel sat down on a large piece of driftwood. He pulled up his collar as the mist turned to an intermittent drizzle. He poked at the fire with a stick, making the flames dance. "Nothin'. Wish I had. My head hurts, but the old man looks bad. What'ya make of it? Think he should go to the doctor?"

"In the morning. Let's let him get some rest. The real question is, what are we going to do about these gangsters? The boss forks over fifty bucks, and that kills a good bit of our pay. That fifty will become one hundred if Urquhart gives in, and I'd bet they're willing to do worse if the old man doesn't come across. What do we do? What does he do?"

Angel leaned over and quietly retched into the gravel, spit a couple of times, and then shook his head while wiping his mouth.

"Assholes left us alone when we're scrimpin'. Then you come along, get things up to speed. Now they wanna bleed us. Pretty much the way things always been, so's I don't know what we should do. Could be they okay with killing. Are you?"

Emmett thought of the massacre in Everett, and of Bruge, hung on the buoy, killed by the impersonal blast of a naval gun. Violence had followed him around a good portion of his life. Then he thought of the old man, attacked by a thug in his own kitchen. Sure, he thought, he was okay with *some* killing. He had it in him. Would the world miss thugs who extorted money from old men?

"I like it here, Angel. We may not have a lot, but what we got is good. And even if it wasn't, I'm not inclined to let some thug in a wool suit strong-arm someone who's been good to me. But we aren't gonna get it figured out here in the rain. You best get into your bed, and sleep off that headache."

Angel stood up slowly, swaying, and Emmett placed his hand on the Indian's shoulder to brace him. Angel smiled in the firelight. "Hope I don't puke in my bed."

He struggled off toward his cabin, and Emmett watched him go. Things had changed in Urquhart's fish camp. Things had changed in his life. He kicked at the edge of the fire and thought about Noémi before dismissing her image as nothing more than fantasy.

Contrary to popular thought, things did not look better in the morning. The lump on Urquhart's head had swollen, and he had trouble focusing. Even Atlas' enthusiastic licks barely evoked a smile on the old man's face.

They bundled him up, packed him into the backseat of the car, with Atlas, who lay across Urquhart's legs, and drove him into Port Orchard. The GP there took one look at the swelling and glazed eyes and said one word: "Concussion."

"Okay," replied Emmett, who thought he knew what that meant, "is he going to be okay?"

The doctor took his time, keeping a coughing patient waiting, and performed some basic tests on the old man before taking a blood sample and dressing his head wound.

"How'd he do this? A fall?"

Emmett hedged his reply and nodded his head.

"Well, these things tend to be temporary. He might be a bit disoriented for a few days, suffer from an ongoing headache, and might even be nauseated. But give him some time to mend, and he'll be all right. Can you keep him off his feet?"

"That'll be difficult."

"Do your best. He needs time to mend, and by that I don't just mean the concussion. At his age these things can become more … complicated. If you can't tie him down, at least limit his activities. And you can give him"—he handed a small bottle to Emmett—"two of these every six hours, preferably after he eats something. It'll keep him quiet."

On the way back, under the heavy warmth of Atlas, Urquhart fell asleep, despite the jostling of the car. His arms spread around the big dog's shoulders, and Atlas seemed to smile at the embrace.

Angel looked at the two of them and thought how different the big dog had become: once a homeless scavenger, now a trusted and seemingly devoted member of their pack. He felt a little envious of the big dog, but had to admit—if only to himself—that he had grown to like Atlas. What a cobbled pack they were.

Urquhart wanted nothing more than scotch. Solid food didn't interest him, and broth was left to chill in untouched bowls. Emmett scoured the cabin for any hidden bottles, but only found three. Later in the day, Emmett found yet another half-empty bottle stashed behind the sofa.

"Can't I leave you alone long enough to take a piss?" he asked angrily when he found the whisky.

"I guess not, Junior."

"Well, at least eat something solid. You need fuel, old man, and whisky is not gonna help."

"It helps just fine. But make me a cheese sandwich and I'll eat that."

Emmett did as directed, and the old man wolfed down the food. When he was done, Urquhart asked Emmett to fetch Angel and the three of them sat together at the kitchen table. Urquhart was wrapped in his afghan, stroking Atlas and trying to ignore the cup of hot tea that Emmett had placed in front of him.

"We need to get fishing boys," the old man said. "The larder's getting thin, and we need to make some scratch. Not to mention, this galoot is eatin' us out of house and home." He playfully pulled at Atlas' ears.

"*We* meaning Angel and I—*you're* not going anywhere, says the doc. We can drag the Strait for a couple of days, but you're going to have to draw some charts. Neither of us know the grounds like you do."

"The doc can say whatever he wants. The *Aberdeen* is my boat, and when she goes out, I go out on her. I ain't gonna argue about this, Emmett. You can tie me to the wheel in the pilothouse and I can piss my pants the whole trip, but I go where she goes."

"The doc says you just have to stay quiet for a while, not forever. You don't trust us to go out *one* time without you? You think we'd sink her?"

"Takes two on deck to work those winches and haul nets, Emmett, you know that. You need someone at the wheel."

"We need you to get better. Seems to me either the two of us go alone, or none of us go at all. And then how do the bills get paid, much less the extortion money? You're not going out on this trip. Plus which, you got a dog to take care of now. Who'd feed him if all three of us were gone? Probably get into that old lady's chicken coop and get shot."

Urquhart laughed and looked down at Atlas, who was looking back up at the three of them, happy to be part of the discussion. "All right, Emmett," Urquhart said quietly, "you win. One trip. But I guess if my fishing days aren't over, we better get this galoot used to life in a pilothouse."

That evening he complained again of the unrelenting headache that had plagued him from the night before. Emmett gave him more of the tablets and made sure he washed them down with water and not whisky. The medication slowly took its effect, and Urquhart dropped off to sleep.

Emmett, worried about the old man, spent the night in the adjoining easy chair, regularly stirring to check on Urquhart's condition. The steady breathing evolved into a sonorous drone that helped to keep Emmett awake.

In the morning, the old man seemed refreshed, and his headache had largely dissipated. He got up while Emmett was finally sleeping and quietly made a pot of coffee. Atlas followed him outside, where he assayed the weather. The sky was a uniform medium-gray, promising some good fishing if the conditions held.

When Emmett appeared, coffee in hand, Atlas meandered to him and allowed his head to be scratched.

"Think it'll hold?" Emmett stretched his shoulders and back. The chair had taken its toll.

"Not much of a breeze, and what there is ain't out of the southeast. Yeah, I think it'll hold for the day. But who knows what's going on up on the Straits. I think I can go out with you."

"No way. The doc said to take it easy."

"I will take it easy. Doesn't take much effort to read a chart, plot a course, or steer a boat."

"One trip, that's what you said last night. Give yourself a break, boss. Trust us this one time, we'll bring *The Aberdeen* home in one piece, with enough fish to pay the rent. *Trust* me."

Urquhart scanned the Passage, the far shoreline, and the sky again, looking for an argument to counter Emmett's. There was nothing there, so he nodded. "I'm the same man I was three days ago, Emmett, hell, the same man I was ten years ago. I ain't ready for the dry dock. But I can sit here a few days if that'll make you happy."

"It'll make me happy."

They took the rest of the day to outfit the boat, repair nets, and check all the running gear. Emmett wouldn't even allow Urquhart to police the pilothouse, insisting that he remain in a straight chair on the dock to supervise.

After a light dinner everyone went to bed. The next morning, at three-thirty, *The Aberdeen* cast off and headed north up the Colvos Passage. They stopped in Seattle only to fuel and pick up ice, along with some provisions for the galley. Then they were out into the traffic, heading for the Straits.

Urquhart had made some notations on the charts, information based on many years of fishing those grounds, but he warned them.

"There's no guarantee that fish will be running at any of those points noted. Be prepared to pull up nets and move on. This is no Sunday drive, boys."

His two hands just looked at him with empty smiles. They knew what they had to do. One less hand, particularly the one main hand, would increase their workload and demand their full attention.

Once in the Strait, they dropped their nets three miles northwest of Dungeness Spit. The dragging was fitful, and they pulled very little worth throwing into the hold. They moved farther into the Strait and closer to Vancouver Island, mindful of freighter traffic.

At five in the morning on the second day, they hauled in three hundred pounds of pollock, flounder, and a few halibut: a less-than-promising start. They decided to drop a few crab pots in an area where they had previous luck, and headed northeast toward Hein Bank.

The seas were choppy, but *The Aberdeen's* deep hull carried her well into the swell, and Angel worked the deck as though he was on a sidewalk in Seattle. When they got to the Hein Bank, they were met with the sight of a dozen fishing boats, draggers, and seine netters spread out across the Bank.

"Who's directing traffic?" Emmett asked Angel. "No way we wander into that mess. Let's head over to Salmon Bank."

"The boss don't like to go up there. Too busy."

"The boss ain't here. Let's try something different."

They sidled up the Strait, toward San Juan Island, and a southeasterly swell made for a rough ride. Angel was quiet, obviously unhappy.

"I suppose you'd rather have got in line and waited to drag whatever those pikers might leave behind at Hein Bank, eh?"

Angel held onto the doorway of the pilothouse and frowned. "I hope we get us some fish. A couple hundred pounds of bottom feeders and baitfish won't cover fuel. You better be right 'bout Salmon Bank."

They arrived at the grounds as dark fell, so they dropped anchor and fried up a flounder with hard biscuits and jam for dinner. Angel produced some whisky for their coffee, and they turned off all but their running lights. It hadn't rained since they turned out to the Straits and now, overhead, the clouds parted, exposing a thick ceiling of stars.

"The old man must be miserable," Angel said, sipping at the hot coffee.

"He's got good company, probably better company than what we give him."

"No, he live for this. You seen him. He prob'ly happiest when he works that wheel in hard weather."

Emmett nodded. He could almost see the old man propped on the wheel, feet set wide, swearing at the sea. "So we best make the most of this trip. I'll take the first watch. I want to be setting nets no later than five, so don't let me oversleep."

Angel went forward to the small, angled bunk under the foredeck, leaving Emmett to watch for marine traffic. They weren't far off the shipping lanes, and there had been more than one close call in this stretch of the Sound. The running lights on *The Aberdeen* could be seen from more than a half-mile in calm weather, but freighters ran close to twenty knots, and could run up on a smaller boat if the deck watch wasn't paying attention.

But there were no freighters and only one other fishing vessel arrived just after midnight and anchored about a mile to the south. Emmett hoped that few other boat captains had the same idea of running up to Salmon Bank. Being there first never meant getting the best run, but Emmett had hoped to make a couple of sweeps to find the most profitable drag.

Angel shook him hard. "Wake up, lover boy. She be waitin' for you again tonight!"

He handed Emmett a cup of hot coffee, and Emmett balanced the cup in one hand while peeing over the bulwark. He finished his coffee and opened the engine hatch. He lowered himself down to check the oil level, and then the bilge to ensure that the pump was working. Once he was satisfied, he fired up the engine, and they began a slow cruise across the bank, dropping their nets and holding a straight course for more than a mile.

At the end of the run Emmett began a slow turn of the boat while Angel engaged the winch and began pulling up the net. The boat slowed in the water, and Angel realized that the net was heavy and full.

He hoped it wasn't a pile of junk fish. He yelled with glee when he saw that they had netted cod, sablefish, and even some mackerel. He winched the net aboard and opened the catch to release the fish onto the deck.

Emmett put the boat in neutral, letting the engine idle, while he went to help Angel sort the fish. He pulled a couple of small flounder from the pile and tossed them into the pilothouse. Lunch.

They made two more runs during the morning and nearly filled the hold. Angel noted that they were running out of ice, so that cancelled out any argument for staying longer. Outside of the other boat, the *Ginnie Mac* out of Bellingham, they had the banks to themselves, and they regretted having to head for home. But when they got to Seattle late in the afternoon the payout was good, and they looked forward to showing the old man the transfer receipt.

They picked up some fresh vegetables at a nearby market, along with some baked goods for a treat, and headed around Alki and toward Colvos Passage. It grew dark quickly, and they had to navigate through small rafts of driftwood that had been liberated by recent storms.

Once they were in the Passage Angel produced the bottle of scotch that had spiked their coffee and they each took turns nipping at the liquor.

When they drew nearer the fish camp, they noticed that no lights were on and both men were instantly alarmed. Had the thugs returned? Was the old man all right?

Emmett increased the throttle and reversed the engine when they were drawing close to the dock. *The Aberdeen* nearly slammed into the dock, and the jolt could be felt through the entire length of the boat.

Angel jumped off, leaving Emmett to secure both bow and stern to the dock. As Angel came into the yard, Atlas stood, loudly growling and holding Angel at bay. When Emmett arrived, the growling continued until Emmett was able to put the big animal at ease. The tail wagged, but it wasn't a happy wag.

"Where's your buddy?" Emmett asked, attempting to walk around Atlas, but the big dog kept cutting off his advance. Emmett recognized that Atlas was attempting to protect Urquhart.

"Boss! Where are you boss?" Emmett called out. No answer.

He was finally able to get by Atlas and the big dog immediately joined him in going into the dark house. He found a lantern and got it lit, and found Urquhart on the floor. There was no indication of a struggle, only the inert figure.

"Boss," he said quietly, hoping for the best as he knelt down. Urquhart was breathing, but in very shallow drafts. Angel came in, after Atlas checked him, and helped Emmett drag Urquhart onto the sofa. Emmett had Angel hold the lantern and he pried open the old man's eyelids. He was unresponsive.

"Goddamnit, this doesn't look good. He needs a doctor."

"Take him in the car to Port Orchard?"

"No, you need to go fetch the doctor. I'm not taking any chances by moving him. Go, now!"

Angel trotted into the darkness, and a few moments later the Model T was coaxed to life. Emmett propped the old man up and attempted to rouse him. "C'mon, old man. Time to put up or shut up."

One bleary eye opened, stared at him for a brief moment, and then closed.

"C'mon, help me out, Urquhart!"

But the eye did not reopen.

Angel returned in an hour with the doctor. A frazzled, unkempt man, the doctor opened his bag and pulled out his tools, checking Urquhart's pulse, his eyes, and reflexes.

"Looks like a stroke, but we need to get him into the hospital at Bremerton. They've got what we need to make a legitimate diagnosis. Help me get him to the car."

Angel drove with the doc in front while Emmett cradled the old man in the back seat. Atlas was determined to go along, but they forcibly left him behind to watch them disappear into the dark.

The hospital was at the naval base, and Emmett was somewhat

concerned when they asked for identification and he had none to offer. As far as he knew, there may have been a warrant put out by Steven. But they were passed without a hitch once the doctor vouched for Emmett and Angel.

The waiting room was lined with four ranks of hard, straight-backed, wooden chairs, unsuitable for sitting for any longer than fifteen minutes. Emmett found himself pacing up and down the short stretch of hallway that was accessible to them.

Every time someone with a white uniform came through the swinging doors, Emmett turned to confront them, but no one made any attempt to communicate with him. The lingering odor of Izal disinfectant was so pronounced that he and Angel were finally compelled to wait at the outer entry of the emergency ward.

"Wish we had a drink," said Angel. "Don't suppose there's anywhere we can get a beer?"

Emmett shook his head. "Even if there was, we can't leave. We got to be here when the old man comes around."

Angel shook his head. The whole thing was more than he could wrap his head around. The old man was invincible, or had been for longer than Angel could remember. Urquhart had become the rock of his life: the one thing on which he could depend. Now, seeing the old man reduced to an inert mass of flesh had left Angel rudderless. He needed that drink. The cold night air felt constricting to him, and he longed for whatever clarity dawn might bring.

He looked at Emmett, who sat on the stone steps of the entrance with his hands clasped tight. Emmett's arms rested on his denims and his head hung down. Was he the rock now? It seemed that the old man had borne all of their past sins, and provided whatever redemption was necessary for them to continue in life. He had become mother-father-priest for them, even for his son, though that had not been enough for the kid.

Like stray cats, he and Emmett, and the old man had taken them in. Angel couldn't bear the thought that the old man might not be there for him to depend on any longer.

There they remained, moving little and not noticing when an ambulance arrived, bearing the half-burned body of a sailor who had been involved in an accident aboard one of the ships berthed nearby. Nor did they respond when the doctor from Port Orchard came out, patted them on the shoulders, and climbed into a taxi.

When it was light, a nurse found them outside and brought them cups of hot coffee, but she could offer them no update on Urquhart.

Finally, midmorning, a doctor found them perched on the hard chairs in the waiting room. "He's stable now. We don't know the extent of the damage yet—we'll keep him here for a couple of days for observation—but it's obvious that he's going to need help, or be institutionalized."

"What's that mean?" Angel demanded.

"He's not a young man. Do either of you know his age? And there's evidence of blunt force trauma, as though he was attacked. Do you know about that?"

"Yeah, some thug thumped him some nights back," said Emmett. "He's been complaining about a headache—"

"Probably the source of the stroke. Look, I'm not going to sugarcoat this. He'll never be the same. He's not a vegetable, though we're still unable to gauge how bad the stroke was, but he's going to have physical limitations. You, or his family, need to start making plans."

"What kind of plans?" Emmett was suddenly frightened.

"He'll need care, constant care, and even that might not slow down his deterioration. Now, go home. He won't be having visitors today, not that he would be aware of your presence, anyway. The two of you look like shit. Go home and get some rest."

The ride back was quiet until they reached the turnoff for the camp.

"What are we gonna do, Emmett?"

"Whatever we can, Angel." Tears welled at the corners of Emmett's eyes, making the drive difficult. "The old man has been there for us. We can be there for him."

When they pulled into the yard Atlas sat, erect, at the door to Urquhart's cabin, waiting. The big dog examined the interior of the car after Emmett and Angel got out, obviously looking for Urquhart.

"He'll be home soon," Emmett said, scratching Atlas' head. "C'mon, let's get you some breakfast." Angel left them alone, heading down to the boat to find busy work.

Emmett led Atlas into Urquhart's cabin and began to scrounge through the kitchen. He found a bottle of Black&White and set it on the kitchen table, but didn't open it. The temptation was there but, for some reason, he felt it necessary to remain sober, even though a drunken stupor seemed particularly attractive. They had no phone, so he knew he would have to ask their neighbor, Janie Ferrady, the chicken lady, to call the hospital for updates during the day.

Emmett pulled his oilskin jacket back on and headed out the door with Atlas at his heels. He looked down at the boat, noted the open deck hatch, and knew that Angel was going to get himself immersed in whatever work might distract him.

Emmett crossed the yard and began to plow through the bracken and undergrowth that would ultimately lead him to Ferrady's property.

He was so deep in thought that he crossed the half-mile in what seemed like the blink of an eye. His knocking brought her to the door, and she could see the trouble on his face. "What is it? Everything okay over there?"

Emmett began to explain, but had trouble with the words, and she grabbed him by the arm and pulled him inside. She sat him at her table and shooed Atlas back outside. She poured a cup of tea for him, giving him time to regain his composure.

"The old man is in the hospital for a stroke."

"Kenneth! Will he be all right?"

"The doctor said he's stable, whatever that means. Said we should be making plans."

"But he's going to live, isn't he? Poor thing. Who's with him now?"

"No one. They sent us packing. I guess we can go back tomorrow, but the thing is, they have no way to contact us, and I was wondering … "

"Of course." She stood and went to her phone. "Where, Bremerton?"

Emmett nodded and Ferrady turned the crank and spoke to the operator. She was connected to the naval hospital and had a quick conversation before hanging up.

"They'll call here if anything comes up. The nurse said we could visit him tomorrow morning."

"We?"

"I've known Kenneth for almost thirty years. We may not always get along, but we are neighbors, and neighbors stand by each other. When you drive in, I'm going with you. But you keep that mutt in the backseat."

She looked out the kitchen door at Atlas, who was lounging on her porch to avoid the drizzle. "You have cleaned him up, though, and he hasn't been after my chickens for a while."

"He's a good boy, a good watchdog, and he and the old man have grown close. Maybe they'll let us bring him in so the old man can see him."

"I doubt it. Look," she got up and pulled some cold, fried chicken from her icebox, "you boys are probably hungry. Take this chicken, and go get some rest. He'll be okay. They know what they're doing. Your worrying won't get anything done, so go on. Vamoose!" She shoved the covered plate of chicken into his arms.

Emmett and Atlas were soaked by the time they traversed the woodlot separating Urquhart's fish camp and Ferrady's farm. Atlas was drawn by the smell of the food, and he hounded Emmett's attempts to dodge from tree to tree to avoid the drizzle.

Man and beast shook off as much moisture as they could before entering Urquhart's cabin, where they found Angel sitting at the kitchen table. "Where the hell you go? I couldn't find you. Thought maybe something else bad happened."

"Yeah, I should have come down to the boat. I went over to see Mrs. Ferrady and have her take phone messages from the hospital. We need to know when we can go see the old man."

Angel nodded. "Good thinking." He rocked in his chair and drummed his fingers on the table. "What do we do now?"

"Well, I'm gonna feed this guy, so we might as well eat, too. Brought some of her chicken."

He found the bag of Spratt's kibble in Urquhart's pantry, and Emmett saw that the old man had stashed an additional bag without his knowledge. He smiled, remembering when Atlas was an unwelcome guest on the property, and how much his fortune had changed. The big animal was sprawled in front of the dead wood stove but his nose was bent toward the plate on the table.

"Get a fire going, Angel."

The latter hauled himself up and set about making a fire in the fireplace. Once a blaze was well established he knelt in front of it, almost as if he was praying. There was an intense look about his face. "What if he doesn't come out of it?" Angel asked.

"Don't start that—"

"But what if he doesn't? You saw him. He's half-past dead."

Emmett hadn't given that possibility any thought. He had managed to miss his father's long, drawn-out battle with cancer, about which he had often felt guilt. He had rationalized this 'failing' through a variety of half-assed self-explanations, but the fact remained, outside of Bruge, he had not found himself within an arm's length of death.

"He'll be fine, you'll see," he said, almost believing it himself. The bottle of Black&White beckoned. Would a good drunk alleviate the fear and anguish both men felt? Or would it make it worse? He felt compelled to find out and opened the bottle, taking a long pull before handing it across to the willing Angel.

The liquor burned the Indian's throat, and he welcomed the slight pain; it suggested that he was still capable of feeling something other than dread.

They exhausted the bottle with no conversation. They were after the numb, the state of comfortable indifference.

Angel thought about his tethered youth in the orphanage and the compelling need to find some sense of family; not family in the communal sense, but family as something mystical and unobtainable. The old man was as much family as he had, and represented the part of his life that was more than merely tolerable.

He scratched at his scalp and knew he needed a bath, but that would wait. Everything would wait until the old man did whatever he was going to do. His glass was empty again, but he could do something about that.

Emmett reflected on the dysfunctional state of his family, of his life. For the better part of a decade he was a free agent more by necessity than by choice. The path of his existence had no more meaning than the paths traveled by steel balls when batted about inside pinball machines. For a time, in his teens, he really believed that an open eye and the strength of his efforts would be the sole genesis of his success.

It never goes as expected: that point had been driven home. Emmett had clung to that free agency; it served as his security blanket as he ran from the law, dodging from job to job, committing petty larceny in a variety of ways: working the decks of Great Lake freighters, running rum from Kingsville, Ontario to Toledo, Ohio, fishing in the North Atlantic, running rum again, this time out of St. Pierre et Miquelon, off Newfoundland to Maine and points south, all the way to Long Island.

Bruge had been an employer first, a friend second; but it was the opposite with the old man. Emmett didn't know how to intellectually address all that had gone on in such a short time. Life had become more flavorful, more rewarding. Yet it fomented something that he long feared might happen: he had become happy. And now he was going to have to pay the price.

In the still darkness of the cabin he could barely make out the sounds of an ethereal chorus. The voices were barely discernible. He tried to make out the lyrics to the song they sang, but couldn't decipher the sounds. The music was, however, intoxicating.

Emmett stood and went to the door, quietly pulling it open. He stepped out into the yard, but the sound faded away. He felt an unusual sense of calm, but he reckoned that was the whisky. The drizzle had been reduced to a mist and he stood, allowing the moisture to collect in his hair until it ran down his neck and drove him back inside.

Ferrady showed up at their doorstep early the next morning, rousting them from their sleep. When she entered the kitchen, she noted the plate of chicken bones and an empty whisky bottle on the table.

"Help much?"

Emmett carefully observed that, indeed, it had.

"They called me a little after six–*I* was already up, had even fed the chickens and collected the eggs." She held out a basket with six eggs in it. "They told me we could see him at eleven. So, let's scramble these and make you presentable for a visit."

She rummaged through the kitchen, produced a cast-iron frying pan, and scrambled the eggs, mixing in some of the mushrooms they had purchased in Seattle. Then she made a pot of strong coffee that finally brought Angel around. After eating, the men took sponge baths and put on fresh shirts.

By ten they were ready to drive to Bremerton. Their concerns were each kept to themselves, and Ferrady focused on changes to the road, or kibitzed about other neighbors whose properties they passed.

"She finally put an arbor on the side porch. That wisteria was threatening to take over her back door ... Betty started paving her driveway, until she realized the road in front of her house wasn't likely to get paved any time soon ..."

Emmett focused on the weight of fur collapsed across his legs. Atlas hadn't needed an invitation to go along: he'd waited at the car door until it was opened, and then leapt onto the backseat as if it were his bed.

Emmett forced his way in, and the big dog made himself comfortable on Emmett's lap. Ferrady looked back at the two of them and was compelled to smile. Emmett was burdened, but he didn't appear the least bit uncomfortable.

It was then that Emmett first noticed the state of Angel's scalp. The hair, where it had caught fire, had burned down to tiny, shriveled, black stubs. Angel's head resembled a small topographic map and, in close quarters, Emmett could smell the burnt hair.

"What the hell, Angel!"

Ferrady turned sharply, startled.

"What?" Angel asked.

"Your head!"

"It's okay, Emmett. I dip my head into Sound to put out fire. Worked good. Saltwater good for burns."

"Yeah? Well, it looks horrible. You got to get your hair cut. After we see the old man, let's go get a haircut and a shave."

Urquhart was semi-reclined and somewhat responsive, though he wasn't given to speaking. He grabbed Janie's hand and offered a broad grimace passing for a smile. He patted each of the men's hands when they were offered.

"You look so much better, Kenneth. We're looking forward to getting you home."

"Haythass?"

"Of course not, Kenneth. This is no bother. And we're so glad to hear you talking again."

Urquhart looked toward Emmett. "Haythass?"

"What's that, boss? I don't understand."

"HAYTHASS!"

Emmett shook his head.

"HAAAYTHASSS!" Frustration overtook him. Still, the old man managed, "Woof!"

"ATLAS!" replied Emmett and Angel in unison.

Urquhart offered another grimace and nodded.

"He's okay. He's in the car. Probably destroying what's left of the leather on those old seats. He sends his best regards."

Urquhart smiled and nodded. "Nuhs?"

"News? Mrs. Ferrady here is going to help us get you through this."

Urquhart shook his head. "Uh…uh. Embaba."

"Not a baby, no, but some of your parts need fixing, and that's gonna take time, old man. Me and Angel, we got to fish, so we worked out a deal with Mrs. Ferrady to make sure you're all right while we're away. You got to do your part too, boss. You're gonna have to help all of us. You understand me?" Emmett leaned closer, looking into the old gray eyes.

Suddenly, Urquhart leaned forward with hands extended as claws and roared.

Emmett laughed so hard, and so loud, that two nurses came quickly to put an end to the fun. Urquhart was leaning back against his pillow, pleased with himself, having glimpsed a bit of his former self.

The nurses brought in some orange juice and glasses, and three of them bantered while Urquhart simply enjoyed the company. When they were asked to leave the timing was perfect: Urquhart could no longer hold his eyes open, though he smiled whenever he reopened them.

"The boss looks okay?" Angel asked.

"He'll be okay," Emmett responded from the back seat.

As they drove back through Port Orchard, Emmett spoke up. "Park over there. There's the barber shop at the corner."

They left Atlas with Ferrady while they went for a quick haircut. She waved them off and leaned her head against the window to take a nap.

The sun peeked through the clouds as they entered the shop. There was one barber and one chair, with two chairs lining the wall next to the sink. Emmett had visited twice, and the barber remembered his face, and smell.

"White walls and a close shave, right?"

Emmett nodded and smiled. When the barber noticed Angel he

frowned, but recognized that the two men were together.

As Emmett peeled off his weathered Filson and wool shirt, Angel sat down and leafed through a couple copies of *Life* and *Colliers*, until a year-old copy of *Field and Stream* advertising a fishing contest caught his eye. He found the article and scanned through it, laughing.

"What's so funny?" the barber asked, irritated by the nasal tone of Angel's snort.

"These guys. They get all fancied up, go out on lake somewheres, catch a fish, and get a bunch a money," said Angel, smiling.

"What's funny about that?"

"Well, it says some guy gets two hundred dollars for fish I can hold in my goddamn lap. *That's* funny."

"I don't see anything funny about it, at all. Keep your snorting and swearing to yourself, please."

Emmett sat down on the barber chair. "Well, what he finds funny, maybe ironic is a better word for it, is that we go out on the ocean, get tossed all over hell's half acre laying and pulling nets, only to get a couple hundred dollars for a roomful of fish. And we don't get to wear no fancy clothes to do it, as you can see. You gotta admit, Harry, it's a bit goddamn funny."

"Yeah, maybe. So, the works?"

Angel was bored by the magazine, and seeing that the barber was going to take his time with the white man, decided to get some air. The sun was out, glaring down with an intensity that made Angel further squint his eyes. What to do, what to do? Emmett's visit might take an hour, by the look of things. And that fat-assed barber would probably butcher what was left of his scalp. What to do?

He took his time and walked up Bay Street. There was the hardware store, a couple of rooming houses, the Central Hotel, a drugstore, an American and Chinese restaurant, and a movie theater. The *Dragonfly* wasn't open yet, and the movie poster in the street display advertised a romantic comedy. At least he thought it was a comedy, the stars' grim smiles didn't offer enough of a clue.

Anyway, it didn't matter; he didn't have time for a movie. He was hungry, but he thought he should wait for Emmett. He stopped and stepped off the boardwalk, deciding that there was really only one thing to do. The *High Spirits* bar offered lunch with a beer, a pretty good deal: cheese sandwich, pickled egg, and a draft. He headed in.

The interior was dark; there was only one small window that opened onto Bay Street, and the walls were paneled in fir that been stained a color somewhere between brown and black. The bar was short, but ornate. There was a weathered pine plank counter, and brass rails for elbows and feet.

Half a dozen men sat at the nearby tables: workers from the naval yard or fishermen. The bartender was a tall, thin man wearing a stained white shirt and black apron.

"What'll it be, chief?"

"Beer." Angel was inured to the slight. He put a dime on the bar and then downed the beer in about fifteen seconds.

He put another dime on the counter. "One more." The beer was delivered, and Angel reached for the egg jar, opened it, and removed an egg.

"Hey, nigger," a voice called from the dim recess of the bar.

"I'm no nigger," replied Angel, biting into the egg while peering toward the voice.

"Same difference. Doesn't matter. Did you wash your fucking hands before dipping into our eggs?"

Angel smiled; he could already see where this was headed. He quickly finished his second beer so it wouldn't go to waste.

Emmett had been busy catching the barber up on Urquhart, and didn't notice Angel leave. As Harry dusted his neck with talc and spanked his cheeks with Bay Rum, Emmett wondered where his partner had disappeared. The damn Indian needed to have his head cleaned up, or the ride back would be just as smelly.

He was putting on his shirt when Sheriff Deputy Gerritson entered the shop. "Morning, Harry. Morning, Dougal."

"Morning, sheriff. Don't tell me you're here to serve my brother's warrant."

Gerritson didn't laugh. "No, but I am here on official business. I'm holding your Indian at the jail."

Emmett quickly paid Harry, and he and the deputy walked down the street to the sheriff's office.

"What's the charge?" Emmett was walking quickly, making conversation difficult.

Gerritson was struggling to keep up. "Drunk and disorderly."

"Drunk? Angel didn't have enough time to get drunk."

"That's not the story I got."

They entered the building, and Gerritson unlocked the holding cell so Emmett could go in. Angel sat, propped against the cell wall, holding a red rag to his head.

"You hit him?" Emmett asked Gerritson. The deputy shook his head.

"No," interjected Angel, "the fuckin' bartender coldcocked me. I was takin' it to the sons of bitches, Emmett, and then the bastard hit me with somethin' heavy."

"Sap," said Gerritson. "Could have shot you, Angel, he was within his rights."

"For a bar fight? Son of a bitch could shoot me for a bar fight?"

Gerritson shrugged. "Well, at least he didn't."

"How'd all of this get started? You couldn't sit tight in the barbershop? You thought maybe tying one on was a good idea, this time of day?"

Angel removed the sodden rag from his head and examined it. "Went for a beer, that's all. Son of a bitch called me a nigger and it went further, that"—he looked pointedly at Gerritson—"all there is to it. Four against one, and I was holdin' my own till the fuckin' barkeep coldcocks me."

"He needs to be cleaned up," Emmett said to Gerritson.

The deputy agreed. "Go see the doc, get some stitches and then get him to the barber. He looks a mess."

Emmett nodded and reached down to grab Angel. The Indian, startled, shoved Emmett against the far wall. Emmett was amazed at his friend's strength. He had never given much thought to the way Angel worked the winches and maneuvered full nets of fish about the deck. His power was deceptive. "Take it easy, Angel. Let's go get you cleaned up."

"That barber don't like me, Emmett. Don't let him open my neck with no straight razor."

"I'll watch him. C'mon now."

They found Janie Ferrady in the front of Gerritson's office. She was surprised to see them. "I thought the two of you had left me high and dry. What's happened?"

"Nothing to get upset about, Mrs. Ferrady. Angel here just had an accident, and the good sheriff brought him here until he could find me. Let's get him over to the doctors, and then home. How's Atlas?"

"I think he needs to relieve himself."

"Well then, we better make this fast."

After having the doctor clean the wound and give Angel a couple of stitches, the three of them marched back toward the barbershop. Emmett could see that Atlas was scratching at the car door as he approached.

"You two go on in—Angel, Mrs. Ferrady will make sure Harry doesn't cut your throat—while I see to Atlas."

The big dog was thankful to get out and immediately went to the nearest wall to relieve himself. It was obvious that he had been holding it a long time.

"You're a good boy, Atlas."

The big dog managed a couple of tail wags as he finished his business.

"Okay, now you have to get back in." Atlas wasn't having any part of it. "C'mon, big fella, get back in."

But Atlas sat down and looked at Emmett, resolute.

Finally, Emmett had to grab him by the collar and tug until the dog was forced to his feet and pulled into the backseat of the Model T. Emmett climbed back out on the street side of the car.

"We'll get you something to eat soon, I promise." Atlas looked forlornly at him, taking the man at his word.

Harry shampooed Angel's scalp, carefully working around the stitched wound. Then he clipped the singed area on the back of Angel's head until it was essentially symmetrical, though shorter than in front.

"That'll have to do. I don't think Gilbert or Valentino will feel threatened."

The Indian grinned. "Movies not in my future, Harry?"

Harry's face reddened at the familiar use of his name by the Indian.

Angel chuckled, feeling that, at least in this small way, he'd won. He left the shop feeling slightly better than when he'd come in.

Two days later, they were allowed to take Urquhart home. The hospital couldn't send an ambulance on the bad roads that led to the Colvos shoreline. So they bundled up the old man in the backseat. Atlas, who straddled both Urquhart and Emmett, held him in place. Ferrady rode up front with Angel, whose hair no longer smelled, though its appearance was still disturbing.

When they turned off the main road onto the track that led to his house Urquhart managed one clear word: "Home."

Ferrady and Emmett smiled, hoping that some clarity had returned to Urquhart's cloudy brain.

Emmett left Urquhart in the car with Atlas, who seemed a willing car blanket. Inside the cabin, they removed the table and chairs so that they could move the bed from its dingy room over to the short bank of windows near the kitchen that looked out over the yard. They situated his bed so that he could just catch a glimpse of the Sound.

The old man was luxuriating in the warmth from Atlas, as well as the dank marine odor that filled the atmosphere. His body was inert, but his eyes wandered over the landscape, rememorizing those parts that he had long taken for granted. When it came time to pick him up, he good-naturedly shoved Atlas from his lap.

"Guh woof," he said and Atlas grunted a bit in reply. Emmett wondered if the old man and dog had already worked out their means of communication. He hoisted Urquhart carefully in his arms and the old man managed an air kiss, followed by "Honey."

"Don't get too familiar, old man, and don't get too comfortable. Mrs. Ferrady's got a regimen from the hospital that you're gonna follow, like it or not." He turned Urquhart's body to avoid bumping the old man's head as they passed over the threshold. Urquhart smooched the air one more time.

The next few days required a great deal of patience for all of them. Mrs. Ferrady managed to keep his bed neat, and to feed him, but she needed help with the bedpans and changing his bedclothes.

Angel wondered how long this might go on. Emmett did as well. With Urquhart bedridden, and perhaps out of commission indefinitely, he had found himself going through Urquhart's desks, sorting out bills and unpaid invoices. He found that one fish wholesaler was in arrears for nearly $500 to them, a debt that had accrued over several months, and he wondered why.

When he attempted to have a conversation with Urquhart, the latter squinched up his face in an attempt to formulate an answer, but nothing he said could be deciphered. Even the old man recognized that changes were going to have to be made.

One morning, the third week he was home, Emmett mentioned that he and Angel should get back to the fishing grounds. Urquhart refused the food Mrs. Ferrady was trying to feed him and motioned for Emmett to come closer. "L-l-l-yawn."

"Again?"

"L-l-l-lyawer."

"Lawyer? Why do you need a lawyer?"

"Ab-ur-bur-deen."

Emmett knew the old man had to get someone to sort things out with the business. "Okay. You care which one? You got one you prefer?"

Urquhart shook his head violently, and Ferrady and Emmett laughed.

"Okay, I'll get a lawyer to come out. There's a couple of them in Port Orchard and Gig Harbor. I'll find someone."

Three days later a Samuel Berman, Attorney at Law, arrived in a shiny new Chrysler sedan. His cologne preceded him to the front door, and when he was admitted Urquhart made a great show, waving his hand in front of his nose.

The lawyer, who was a careful observer, took in the entire setting and knew what his task was. "Mr. Urquhart, Samuel Berman," he said, offering his hand.

Urquhart shook it without much enthusiasm, and Mrs. Ferrady playfully pinched him in rebuke.

"Ouch!"

Emmett pulled up a chair next to the bed, and the lawyer sat himself down and opened his briefcase. "Do you have a will?"

"He's had a stroke, he's not dying!" exclaimed Mrs. Ferrady.

"Still, it's good to have these things prepared in advance, Missus, so the state cannot claim the remains of the estate. It's a simple matter, and we have enough witnesses. I truly recommend preparing a will—that's what you called me out here for, isn't it?"

"I think he's more concerned about the business end, aren't you boss?"

Urquhart nodded at Emmett. "Ab-bur-deen."

"I beg your pardon? Aberdeen?"

"The name of his boat. I think he wants to make sure it's okay for us to be working the boat even while he can't captain. Is that right, boss?"

"O-kay, no!"

"You don't want us to be able to fish?"

Urquhart nodded again. "Own."

It took a few moments before Emmett realized what the old man was talking about. "You want to give us the boat?"

"Angel."

"You want to give Angel the boat?"

Urquhart shook his head and then pointed at Emmett. "Two. Two."

"He wants to give the boat to you and someone named Angel."

Urquhart shook his head again. He tried to form a word but was frustrated, so he waved his hands around, pointedly looking at the cabin interior and then out toward the yard.

"Everything? You want to give us everything? Why? You're not going anywhere soon. This is all yours! You've shared it with us. That's more than enough!"

The lawyer pulled his legal pad and began making notes. "I believe he feels that if the property, its contents, and the tools of the trade are in your hands, you'll continue to care for him. Is that correct, Mr. Urquhart?"

The old man nodded and a small smile formed on his face. "Two. And Haythass."

"The dog," Emmett interpreted, laughing.

"One more question, Mr. Urquhart, how do I know if you're mentally competent enough to make these changes?"

Urquhart's face gave him the answer.

'TIS THE SEASON FOR FOLLY

Kenneth Alexander Urquhart. Kenneth Alexander Urquhart. He heard the words over and over in his head. The woman had read them to him, shown him the embossed letters on the cover of his Bible. Kenneth Alexander Urquhart. Well, he knew who he was; he just couldn't *say* who he was.

He tensed his mouth and constricted his chest, trying to form some familiar sound. However, except for the odd moment of clarity the filters allowed, only grunts and jibberish escaped his lips. No one was around now to hear his attempts, which made him oddly comfortable. They rarely left him alone anymore, manipulating the bedpan in and out of the bed, not even giving him the privacy to evacuate his bowels. He wondered where they might have gone.

A lone robin, stalwart annual winter visitor, landed on the fender of the Model T, directly in the old man's line of sight. He watched the bird surveying the yard for possible sources of food. Outside of crows and ravens, the robins seemed to be the most adaptable. This one had come in from southeastern Alaska, and would head back north in April. For a moment their eyes locked, and then the bird flew away.

"Bird," he said, startling himself. He said it again. The word was clear. "Bird sing," he said, feeling the words form and disappear.

The old man smiled, proud of his accomplishment. He wished then that somebody had been there to share the moment. "Bird fly."

He laughed. Maybe he was going to be all right. He decided to take a piss without the bedpan that sat on the chair next to the bed. He carefully swung his legs over the side of the bed, remembering that it had been sometime—how long?—since he had been on his feet. The cold floor felt good underneath him, and he pushed himself slowly off the bed, feeling weak but enthusiastic.

He stood erect and waited. Nothing happened. He was still conscious, and no stars cluttered his vision. He turned and scuttled around the bed toward the bathroom, and was fine as long as he had something to hold onto. The moment he let go of a chair and made for the doorway, he lost his balance and fell ass over teakettle.

He immediately sat up. He was embarrassed, but there was no one there. He felt his hips and then his legs, and everything seemed to be in place. So, he pulled himself back to his feet and carefully shuffled the last few feet to the toilet.

After finishing he washed his hands, and they felt clean for the first time since he had been home. He negotiated his way back to his bed and climbed back in.

'A' for effort, he thought. "A for enborth," he said, and was immediately dispirited.

He was feeling hungry, and hoped that someone would come with something to eat pretty soon. He remembered his father pulling out his well worn, folded packet of Sen-Sen and giving him two or three to stave off his twelve-year-old's hunger. The childhood brand of hunger tended to be more ravenous than that which plagued him now. He wished he had some Sen-Sen. What would his dad say if he saw him now, lying up in bed with no broken bones, no fever, just an addled brain, complaining about a little hunger?

He would tell him to get on his feet. "Better to die on your feet than laid out in bed," he used to say. Ironically, his old man died in his sleep on a Saturday morning. He had been retired from the manufacturing plant he had managed in Lowell for less than three years.

His father had gotten up early that morning, put on tea, read a day-old Boston Herald, awakened his wife to make breakfast, and then lay down to die. Really, what more point was there to life for him? He had no hobbies. He had no real friends. His only son was three thousand miles away on some fishing boat, and they hadn't spoken in half a decade. There wasn't any compelling reason *not* to go, so go he did. His son Kenneth wouldn't learn about his passing for the better part of a year, when his mother would calmly note the death in a Christmas card.

"Your father died this past April. It was mercifully quick. He just went to sleep. The funeral was just me and the undertaker. You didn't miss anything. Thanks for the money, I'll use it wisely. Merry Christmas, Ma."

He felt himself sliding into melancholia, starting to reassess his life: looking back through the kaleidoscope of embellished and half-forgotten memories, weighing blame, responsibility, failure, and success. He still thought of himself as a thirty-year-old, an indestructible force of nature. Now, every time he looked into the mirror he saw a stranger. No color to the beard, not much on his head. There were hairs springing out of his ears, and wrinkles on top of wrinkles. Inside, he knew the thirty-year-old still existed, but the machine was beginning to break down.

He lay there in bed, feeling sorry for himself, only to sit up erect and swear. "Get over it, goddamn it!"

"Get over what?" Ferrady asked as she came through the door. "Kenneth, was that you? Where's Angel, I told him to watch out for you!"

"Nope," was all he said, shrugging.

Then Angel appeared, wet from the drizzle. "Sorry, I was doing work on the boat. He okay?"

"He *swore*. Kenneth, you're going to have to watch your language around me. You might think you have some leeway due to your condition, but I won't have it, you hear me?"

"God...damn...it." It felt good to say it, and it amused him immensely to see her reaction.

"Hey, the old man is talking!" Angel pounded him on the arm.

"Goddamnit."

Angel pounded him again.

The room was nice enough, and in one of the better hotels in Seattle. Virgil had given her the key to the room, and she inferred that he *always* had the key to this room, though there was nothing within that room that would identify it as belonging to the man. She took her third tour of the room, impatient for his arrival.

She had used the excuse of Christmas shopping to get away from the house, leaving the boys to be tended by Annie, the maid. But, if Virgil took too much longer, she would have to leave without seeing him in order to actually do some of that shopping.

She had stopped at a jewelry store next to Frederick's and picked up a diamond studded tie-pin for Virgil's Christmas present; she intended to give it to him today after their lovemaking. If she had to leave early it would disappoint both of them: she wouldn't get to give him his gift, and he wouldn't get to have her.

When he arrived he was sweaty: strange given how cold it had been lately. And three of the knuckles on his right hand were bloody.

"I slipped and scraped my hand on a wall," was how he explained it. He was in no mood for any preliminaries, so they got to the sex immediately. When he was finished, he sat up in bed and lit a cigarette.

She took it from his mouth and took a deep drag, enjoying the sinful feeling it gave her. What would Arlyn think if he saw her lying naked atop a bed, smoking a cigarette with another man? She reached over Virgil and pulled down the sheet to expose him and then boldly grasped his penis. Virgil smiled at her and stubbed out the cigarette.

He was no kid, but she was getting a second rise out of him. He took his time and worked her around the bed, dallying in places that he knew would, ultimately, send her over the top. He could tell as she tensed her lower belly that he had been successful and finished the work.

Whether it was the heat from the radiators or his abilities, M.E. was soaked. Perspiration lingered on her forehead and the back of her neck, and she continued to lightly tremble in the afterglow of her orgasm.

She knew that Virgil had ruined her for Arlyn. The latter was steadfast, but predictable. Virgil played her like an instrument. She basked in his attention as Virgil roughly pulled her into position in order to mount her. She looked back at him and smiled, but he only grunted and entered her, speeding to his own finish.

While he was cleaning himself up in the bathroom, M.E. set his wrapped gift on the side table next to the small wrapped present he had brought for her. Christmas was still three weeks away, but they had decided to exchange early in case family plans precluded another tryst before the holiday.

Virgil came out of the bathroom, naked, and she moved toward him to caress his body. His penis began to stiffen and he pulled away from her.

"Haven't got time for another go-round, M.E," he said, pulling on his under shorts and then his suit pants.

She helped him button his shirt. "I just like touching you. I like being with you. I wish I could be with you more."

"Me too. Okay, let's hurry this up, I've got to see to some things before I go off duty. What's that you have there?" he asked as she picked up his gift and handed it to him. He calmly, without expression, ripped the wrapping paper from the box and opened it.

"Whoa," he intoned as he examined the tiepin and held it up to the light to better see the gem. "The old lady is gonna wonder where this came from."

"Tell her a secret admirer."

"Yeah, let's keep this secret. Well, you got taste, that's for sure. Here," he said, handing the other package to her. By contrast, she took her time, carefully opening the paper so that it could be used again and set it aside. Then she pried open the small box to find a pretty, rhinestone-studded silver brooch.

There was a small gift card inside, and Virgil blanched, realizing that he had brought the wrong gift. He attempted to seize the card but she held it out of his reach and opened it to read:

"For Betty, a good kid and a great fuck. Merry Christmas, V."

M.E. dropped the card and sat down hard on the edge of the bed. "Who's Betty?" she managed. "I thought your wife's name is Miriam."

Virgil recognized his predicament and decided to take it head on. "It is. Betty is just a … *former* … friend."

"A 'former' friend, as in a fuck friend? You asshole!"

"It's been over for some time—"

"Apparently not that long, otherwise, a Christmas gift?"

"It's nothing. Forget it. *Your* present is much nicer."

"But with similar sentiments?" She began to gather her clothes to dress.

"Look, Miriam and I don't get along all that well. Over the years I've had girlfriends, and she's known about them. We don't share the same bed. It's no big deal. It's just sex."

"Does she know about me?"

"She knows there's someone … "

"Does she know my name? Does she know that you work with my husband?"

"We don't work together. He's no longer on the force."

"So that makes it all right?"

"Look, sister, you're the one who grabbed my dick in the first place!"

"And I was *wrong*! What was I thinking? And you're no better than a whore, sleeping around. How many have there been? How many are there *now*?"

Virgil and M.E. finished dressing without another word, and as they prepared to leave the room he said, "You'll get over this."

"I hope not," she said, departing toward the elevator. She didn't look back, and he watched her swaying backside, beginning to wish he had taken her up on thirds.

Half an hour later, Virgil had forgotten about the blow-up. He stood on the concrete floor of a warehouse along the waterfront. A cold wind blew underneath the walls, traces of an Arctic low front that had swept down from the Bering Sea. It pushed with it a wall of moisture that manifested itself in heavy rain on the steel corrugated roof above.

Sitting on a chair at an empty table was a young man, perhaps twenty-five or twenty-six, wearing a rack suit from some inexpensive Seattle haberdashery. His brown hair was still neatly combed, despite the smack he had taken to the side of the head when Virgil's men grabbed him at a bus stop on Capitol Hill. He sat erect with his hands calmly folded in front of him on the table, and he stared straight ahead, attempting to forge the image of an unconcerned and innocent man. But Virgil could see that the young man was chewing the inside of his mouth in steady cadence. He was lying.

"I happen to know that you met Ander on the eleventh in the lobby of the Sheridan Hotel. You deny that?"

"I told you, I don't know anybody named Ander."

Virgil strolled around the table and stood behind the young man. "Think hard, and while you do, think about missing Christmas with your family. I can't imagine celebrating the Lord's birthday in intensive care could be much fun. What do you think?"

"I think you can beat me to death, but I still won't know this person to whom you're referring."

"To *whom you're referring* ... gotta say, kid. You must've got something out of that college. But your boss thinks you've been giving secrets to the competition—"

"I just do his books, that's all! I was hired as an accountant and you, you make me out as some sort of spy!"

"That's glamorizing it a bit, kid. We both know what you are. And you're gonna tell me everything you've shared with Ander over the past six weeks, down to the last dot and period. Frankly, I hope you make the process more ... *enjoyable*. But, either way, I'm going to know everything that Ander knows. How's your head?"

"It h—" Virgil looped a closed right fist against the kid's head and both man and chair flew two feet through the air before crashing onto the cold concrete floor.

A burly sergeant picked the chair and man up and set them in front of Virgil.

"Hurts? I'll bet it does. Gonna hurt more. Tell me what your deal with Ander is."

"I don't have any deal—" This time a short left hook to the other side of the kid's head sent him flying off the chair onto the floor, where the kid lay whimpering.

"Now *that* had to hurt."

Virgil didn't wait for his sergeant this time. He reached down, grabbed the young man by his lapels, and slammed him back down onto the chair.

"You'll tell me everything, or you'll never leave this building. Spill it."

The kid looked up at him, tears rolling down his face. "He just wanted numbers, I gave him numbers, maybe not even the right numbers."

"Oh, so you were willing to fuck Ander over just like you fucked over Mr. Delacroix? How fucking *democratic* of you!" This time the assault came from the front, Virgil's bruised knuckles smashing into, and breaking, the kid's nose. Blood spurted from his nostrils and he instinctively attempted to protect himself, which triggered Virgil's temper. The big man set on the boy, pummeling him from all angles.

The kid fell, limp, onto the floor, and Virgil aimed the toe of his oxford at the young man's bloody pulp of a nose. There was a shriek and then quiet. The kid was breathing, but it was very shallow, and he didn't respond to the nudging from Glaupher's shoe.

"I think you killed him, Lieutenant," said the sergeant, a big Irishman named Bradley.

"Hardly, he's still breathing." Virgil stepped away to let the sergeant check out the inert body.

"He's not long for this landscape. If we don't get him to a hospital, he's dead in an hour, I'm sure."

"I'm sorry, Jack, I didn't realize you'd been through medical school. How the fuck do you arrive at that conclusion?"

The sergeant turned the head of the unconscious kid toward the overhead light. "It sure looks like you smashed his nose up into his brain. He's breathing, but he's shutting down. I've seen enough guys die to recognize the signs."

"Yeah, yeah. All right, take him down to the Duwamish and dump him." Virgil removed the kid's wallet from his jacket pocket and withdrew the cash, fifteen dollars in all. "Leave the wallet on the ground. It'll look like a robbery. Finish him, though. We don't want any deathbed convictions."

"You want him dead, you do it, Lieutenant. I go only so far ... "

Virgil looked at the sergeant, incredulous. Bradley had never questioned his orders, much less his actions, prior to this evening.

"I'm in a generous mood, Jack, it being the holiday season and all," he said. He stepped forward and kicked the unconscious body hard in the head twice. He squatted and checked for life. There was none. "Otherwise, you'd be joining him. Get him into the trunk of your squad car and make him disappear, you understand?"

Bradley bent down and checked. Yes, the breathing had stopped. "He's dead."

Virgil stood, pulled out a handkerchief, put his foot on the table and wiped the blood off his shoe. "You know, I forget just how much I enjoy that. My pants'll need cleaning, though."

Without standing, or looking at his boss, Bradley began to button the dead man's coat in order to lift him. "What are we going to tell the boss?"

"You mean what am *I* going to tell the boss. I'm going to tell him that this bag of meat stole from him and split the take with Ander. That should liven things up a bit, focus the boss on Ander, which should generate some extra juice. Is that all right with you, Jack?"

Bradley knew that the question didn't require an answer, that Virgil didn't *want* an answer. He had hoped to be home early enough to spend time with his kids. Now the drive down to the Duwamish would mean he wouldn't get home until an hour past their bedtime. Goddamn lunatic Glaupher.

Noémi looked at herself in the mirror and smiled. Her new dress for their Christmas party had arrived from New York, and it was gorgeous. She couldn't wait to wear it for real. She held it up and imagined her long, dark brown hair up, held in place by the understated diamond tiara that Reynard had given her the previous year. Her friends would be arriving in little more than a week, and she anticipated a grand gathering, a coming out, and had worked with Reynard to develop a guest list that would rival any parties taking place in the northwest over the holidays.

The dress accented her full but compact figure. The fashion industry's lust for anemia had finally died down, and women with curves were beginning to be noticed more by the press and, more importantly, Hollywood. She couldn't wait to wear it, fantasizing about the Christmas party, how gorgeous she would look, and the happy jealousy of her friends.

Yet there was something missing. She had plenty with which to accessorize: a diamond necklace, pearls in strings, earrings of all shapes, sizes, and construction. She had a closet dedicated entirely to her shoe collection, with built-in drawers for her purses and hosiery. Decking herself out would be easy. No, there was something else missing, something that she couldn't begin to identify.

She looked at herself. She was no longer the young lady-in-waiting. She had become a woman, not just in appearance but in demeanor. She was bored with the men that her brother brought around, though she knew that he would only introduce her to men he thought were worthy of the introduction. They came in all shapes and sizes, though there were no Italians or Irish among the bunch. Some had the pedigree, identified by college or family. But all those that she had met were self-absorbed, generally callow, and obsequious, waiting for their turns as custodians of the status quo. So, men had not yet been the answer to whatever it was that kept her on edge these days.

She needed to do something with her life. It wouldn't be enough to be someone's wife. It wouldn't be enough to bring children into the world, to marshal their upbringings, and prepare them to repeat the cycle. The face looking back at her in the mirror wasn't someone who would willingly settle for a subordinate role. Why would Reynard, on the one hand, prepare her with an education, and on the other, be anxious to marry her off?

And why wasn't he keeping company with women? She supposed that he dallied with professional women, but he had never shared any information about those relationships, and she couldn't bear the image of him with a woman. It just seemed unnatural. With no interest in a sustained personal relationship of his own, why was he so dedicated to finding her a man? Perhaps he envisaged some form of royal marriage or partnership with one of his colleagues?

She took the dress back into her closet and hung it on a hanger. As she did, she caught her reflection in a small mirror on the closet door and quickly turned away, tired of its accusing glare.

Arlyn was beat. He and Reynard had spent the day on the move. After Reynard's request for a code variance had been voted down, no one wanted to talk on the telephone, it seemed. The meetings would be face to face, in quiet places. And Reynard didn't trust anyone, not even Arlyn, to stand in for him anymore, although he insisted that the latter accompany him not just for security but for more objective observation.

They had met with a police informant—unknown even to Virgil Glaupher—on the flats southeast of Seattle. They had lunch with another member of the city council, and then met Ander in a hotel room on Third Avenue.

Ander didn't look as grand as he had in the hospital a couple months earlier. He had reached out to Reynard, and had made some interesting accusations involving Glaupher. He seemed relieved to see Reynard but he made it clear he didn't trust Arlyn. "How do I know he's not in league with that murderer?"

"How do we know you're telling the truth, Mr. Ander? Lieutenant Glaupher told me an entirely different story, and he says one of his men watched the missing victim board a train bound for San Francisco. Don't you do business in San Francisco? Is that a coincidence, or is the lieutenant lying to me?"

"Because he's skimming from you! He's been playing us both!"

"Both? What game have *you* been playing with Lieutenant Glaupher? Does it involve me?"

Arlyn went to the door and locked it, magnifying each gesture to make a point.

Reynard simply smiled. "I would have thought you knew who I am, certainly by now. I believe in rules, but rules that can accommodate unforeseen needs. That's just how a good businessman operates. I understand and accept a little bit of theft. That's human nature, to be sure. But you have exceeded what is an acceptable level of larceny. Moreover, you made promises on which you haven't delivered. I had hoped to make an official announcement regarding the hotel at a holiday event, and now I cannot."

Reynard leaned forward in his chair. "Make no mistake, I have an investment that I intend not only to protect but see come to full fruition. You are going to find a way to deliver those promises, and you will pay me back what you've stolen, with interest. Mr. Dunne will work out details with you. Mr. Dunne is an easy man to work with, aren't you, Arlyn?"

Arlyn motioned toward the suite door, and Ander quickly scurried toward the exit.

Arlyn grabbed him by the shoulder, bringing him up short. "There's no place you can hide from me, Ander. I'm tight with every law enforcement agency in the western states. I know where every one of your relatives lives, where their kids go to school—hell, where *your* kids go to school. I can be a relentless son of a bitch, or I can be a good friend. Your choice, but I'd recommend you go along with the program. You might even get to keep some of the money. But, don't fuck with me, Ander, for your own sake, okay?"

Ander had seen Arlyn in action. And he had looked him in the eyes. Those eyes promised a sudden reckoning. In them, Ander could sense a cold, reptilian certitude in that deviation from promises made to Reynard would bring about something worse than what Virgil Glaupher might do to him.

Arlyn leisurely followed Ander to the elevator in the hall. "I'll see you soon," he said as the doors closed.

When Arlyn reentered the corner suite, Reynard was already putting on his coat. "I hope you weren't too rude, Arlyn."

"We have an understanding. Dinner?"

"One more stop. Ever been to Virgil's house?"

Virgil's home was also on Queen Anne, overlooking Elliott Bay. His Buick was parked in the driveway of a large, yellow, wood frame house. The house had a large porch which was painted a contrasting dark brown. The yard was neatly maintained, with clipped border hedges and a row of junipers topping a low, whitewashed wall along the sidewalk. It looked more like the home of a police chief rather than a detective lieutenant. The residence represented the collection of two decades worth of mercenary moonlighting, but no one who knew Virgil would ever picture him in such a place.

Virgil was surprised to see them when he answered the front door. At first he hesitated, but then invited them inside. His shirt was unbuttoned, hanging out of his pants, and it was apparent that he had been drinking.

"The place is a mess, and the kids aren't in bed yet. Why don't I meet you at your office in, say, half an hour?"

"Why? We're here. No need to clean up. It doesn't shock me, and Arlyn knows what it's like to have a bunch of kids running around. Any coffee on the stove?"

Reynard brushed past Virgil, who was tucking in his shirt, and headed down the hall toward the kitchen. Virgil's wife, Miriam, was at the sink washing dishes. Their five kids were spread out from kitchen to living room, the eldest reading, and the youngest play fighting with his twin. Miriam didn't hear them enter, and was startled when Reynard lightly put his hand on her shoulder.

"I apologize, Miriam. Good to see you. Do you have any coffee on the stove?"

"I'm afraid not, Mr. Delacroix. I can make some, though."

"No thanks, it's not necessary. We would, however, appreciate it if you could take the children upstairs so we can talk a bit. Would that be okay?"

Miriam knew it wasn't a question, but she nodded just the same. She herded the kids up the stairs, and at first they made noisy arguments about going to their rooms, but soon it was silent. Reynard motioned to the table and chairs, and they all sat down.

"Something goin' on?" Virgil lit a cigarette. "You guys want a beer? I could use a beer."

He got up and went to the icebox, jerking it open and grabbing a bottle. Arlyn recognized the low level of fear and confusion. Virgil was a big man and a dangerous man, but he was no fool. He knew that short of killing Reynard, he would always be subordinate to him; much of his wealth was directly due to the Cajun, and he had no intention of killing the golden goose. Arlyn, on the other hand …

He popped the bottle top and sat back down.

"I thought you were getting divorced," noted Arlyn.

"No law against trying again, Dunne." Virgil said.

He looked at Reynard, waiting. Reynard remained silent until Virgil set the bottle down. "Had an interesting meeting earlier this evening."

"Oh?" Virgil picked the bottle back up and took a long pull on the beer.

"Ander is in town."

"He is? Where?"

"Well, to be honest with you, Virgil, he doesn't want you to know where. Why is that, Virgil? Why would Ander not want you knowing where to find him?"

"Because he knows I'm on to him. I told you what that kid told me. He and Ander were ripping you off. He didn't say how, and I don't know how, but the kid told me, with a bit of persuasion, that Ander was behind you not getting the vote you wanted. I already told you this."

Reynard nodded. "True, that's almost verbatim what you told me yesterday evening. I commend you for your memory."

Virgil nodded and finished off his beer, feeling much better.

"Ander says you killed the kid. You kill the kid, Virgil?"

Arlyn watched Virgil tense, then relax. The man was working to maintain control of himself. Virgil looked over at him and Arlyn smiled, hoping to disarm Virgil's hair-trigger temper.

"We put the kid on a southbound train at Union Station. Five-fifty. Track two. You can check it yourself."

"I'm sure you're right about the departure time and track. But the kid never arrived back in San Francisco, according to Ander. Fortunately for me, I keep my books locked up, and the kid doesn't have access to them unless he's in my office. I hate to think who all could get caught up in the firestorm if those books got leaked to the public, much less the police. Could end a lot of careers here in Seattle, and other places. But, as I said, that isn't the case. Still, Ander has made some damaging accusations about you, Virgil."

"Such as? Hey, give me his location and I'll make him talk. He'll spill everything he's been doing with the kid and the politician—"

"Ah. The second part. The politician, Gosford. I thought you were holding his hand?"

"I can't go into the chamber with him, Mr. Delacroix. What he did in there was without my knowledge. Hell, if I'da known what he was going to do, he and I would've been having a private head-to-head in some dark corner. Let me deal with him, Mr. Delacroix. I guarantee that he'll be with you from this point forward."

"I'm getting a lot of promises tonight, promises about other promises. I can't build on promises, Virgil. I can only build on results. Can I count on you getting me results?"

Virgil nodded his head and held out his hand to shake Reynard's. After they shook on it Reynard stood, joined by Arlyn.

"And from now on, Virgil, you work through Arlyn, here. Keep him apprised of your activities, and he'll pass on the important stuff to me. Now, enjoy the rest of your evening!"

Before heading home for the night they stopped for a quick meal at a diner on Mercer.

"Which is lying, which is telling the truth?" Reynard asked, over a spoon of split pea soup.

"Both of them are lying, and probably only telling enough truth to cover their asses," Arlyn replied.

Reynard smiled, liking Arlyn's talent for observation as much as his trenchant use of language. "I'm worried about Virgil. I get the feeling he's playing both sides against the middle."

Arlyn nodded.

"What's your take, Arlyn?"

"Don't know enough to say. You've known him better than me. He's a self-serving bastard, but as far as I know, he's been loyal to you. If I was guessing, I'd say he's been a shrewd player in this game, angling for a bigger piece of the pie. I'd bet he killed the kid, but who knows? Maybe the kid is drunk in some whorehouse on North Beach. I'll watch Virgil, but I don't think he likes the idea that I'm his contact."

"I have to say, Arlyn, that it was fun watching your lack of reaction to that tactic. Shall we get some pie?"

Arlyn pulled his car into the driveway behind M.E.'s and turned off the engine. The house looked quiet. The boys were all asleep, and the only light on, besides the porch light, was in their upstairs bedroom.

He got out and carefully closed the car door, mindful not to wake the boys. As Christmas drew near, his evening returns home had become loud riots, with demands from the boys to give hints about what they were getting for Christmas. Someone at school had disabused Charles of the belief that Santa was real, and he had been determined to share that information with his younger brothers. Arlyn had playfully restored the legend, but Samuel pointed out that their chimney could not accommodate any person closely fitting the description of jolly fat St. Nick.

He entered the house and then locked the door behind him. He went to the kitchen and checked the back door, drank a glass of water at the sink, and then went upstairs.

At the first door on the hall he opened it to look in on Charles. His oldest boy, his pride and joy, was sleeping on top of the covers. He carefully lifted the boy's legs, slid them under the sheet, and then pulled up the blanket. The boy was blissfully asleep. His shiny brown hair looped across his forehead, and Arlyn carefully swept it back into place.

He was about to leave, but something on Charles' bed stand caught his eye in the glow of the nightlight. It was a jackknife with a beautifully carved antler handle; the blade was open, revealing a sharp, four-inch clip blade.

Arlyn picked the knife up and closed the blade before putting the knife in his pocket. Normally, he would have said that Charles was still too young for such a knife, and finding the blade left open validated that opinion. But the question in Arlyn's mind was, where did Charles get the knife?

He went to the other bedroom and kissed his little boys on their foreheads, adjusting the covers that had been kicked off. He saw no knives.

He was beat and fell asleep immediately, and was not aware when M.E. rose in the morning. She noticed the knife sitting on the bureau next to his wallet and revolver and took it, leaving it on Charles' bed stand so that he'd find it when he awoke.

Arlyn was soon roused from his sleep by the sounds of small boys getting ready for school—the last day before Christmas vacation—and the smell of fresh-brewed coffee. He struggled into a robe and went downstairs to get a cup. As soon as he had filled his cup he noticed Charles using the knife to cut something on their new kitchen table while his younger brothers watched.

"HEY!" he yelled, and Charles dropped the knife onto the table and hid his hands between his backside and the chair.

Arlyn picked up the knife, closed the blade again, and held it up. "Charles, where did you get this knife?"

Charles froze. He hadn't seen this look on his father's face before. But before he could begin to stammer, M.E. came into the room to see what was going on. "Virgil gave him that knife." She reached for it, but Arlyn held it out of reach.

"Virgil? Virgil Glaupher? When did he give this to Charles, and why did you allow it?"

M.E. stopped and put one hand on her hip to indicate her displeasure at the tone of his voice. "He came by yesterday, I guess looking for you, and gave that to Charles. He said every young boy should have a pocketknife."

"Why would he be looking for me here? He knows that I spend my days with Reynard. I don't like that he dropped by, and I certainly do not want Charles to have a knife like that, not yet. What would you do, M.E., if Charles cut himself or one of his brothers?"

"I guess I would do what most mothers do. Wrap the bloody finger in a towel, and take him to the hospital for stitches. Jesus, Arlyn, you're becoming an old lady! Let the boy have his knife."

Arlyn felt his hackles get up. "I will decide when my son is old enough to have a pocketknife. You don't get to make those decisions without me, and certainly not with a bastard like Virgil Glaupher." He tossed his cup into the sink, breaking it, and went upstairs to bathe and dress for work.

M.E. recognized that a line had been crossed. She had pushed too far, and the last thing she needed to do was bring too much attention to Virgil. Sooner or later, that attention would also be drawn to her. She picked up the pieces of the broken cup and put them in the trash bin under the sink. Then she made some chocolate milk for the boys, all of whom seemed shell-shocked by the argument they had just witnessed.

Emmett realized that it was only a week until Christmas when he was turning over the calendar on Urquhart's kitchen wall. At first he didn't know whether it was December tenth or the seventeenth, and had to ask Janie Ferrady when she showed up to take her shift with the old man.

"It's the seventeenth. Monday. You want to write it down so you don't forget?" she asked, teasing.

"Christmas a week off." He looked around the cabin's dreary interior. "What this place needs is a Christmas tree."

Janie agreed and her encouragement set the boys into motion. In a flurry of activity, pausing only long enough to get the old man's opinion or approval on the removal of some dust gathering bric-a-brac, they cleared unused pieces of furniture and piles of books and magazines, ultimately leaving enough space to accommodate a good-sized fir. Atlas assessed the space and determined that it was an excellent location to nap.

Angel retrieved an axe, and they went out into the forest to search for a candidate. It was lightly drizzling, and the salal bordering the path was heavy with moisture. They plowed through the brush without complaint, excited about getting the tree. When they returned to Urquhart's with a lush seven-footer the old man smiled and mustered an "Okay!" Atlas relinquished the space with a fair amount of grumbling, relocating to his standby spot in front of the stove.

If the old man and his wife had ever owned Christmas tree ornaments he had no idea where they might be. He still had trouble verbalizing, and it took some time before he blurted out a loud "No!" So, they rummaged through drawers and cabinets, looking for smallish, shiny objects that they could attach to the tree. Angel started cutting shapes from the colored advertisements in some of his magazines.

The cabin did seem more festive and the Christmas tree—festooned as it was—recreated an ambiance with which all but Angel were familiar. The tree's smell permeated the entire cabin, mingling with the smell of stews, soups, and roasts that Janie cooked up for them.

Emmett and Angel made the *Aberdeen* ready for fishing, taking shifts to work and to watch the old man. One afternoon, Angel was washing out the fish hold to ready it for a load of ice, and Emmett was sitting in front of the fire, reading an article in *Reader's Digest* about fly-fishing in Idaho, when the old man decided to examine some old wounds.

"Went fishing to escape my dad. You know my dad? Hard man. Cold man. Only liked machines. Nothing living. Maybe not even my ma. No pets. Dirty. Eat too much. He smelled like oil, maybe something else. Couldn't tell 'cause I couldn't get close. Hard man. Bastard. Only place further than here from him would be China, and I don't speak the language. Kids. Shouldn't a had me. I shouldn't a had Russell." He raised his rheumy old eyes toward Emmett's. "There's fathers and there's fathers. We shouldn't be fathers."

Emmett was amazed by the soliloquy—as much by its meaning as the fact that the old man was speaking in whole sentences. "You're just tired," was all he could say.

Urquhart bent his head, lifting his good ear to hear better. "You hear that?" But Emmett could only hear the strong, regular breathing of Atlas, who was sleeping next to the old man's bed.

"No."

Urquhart wondered at that and laid his head back on the pillow. He knew with certainty that this would be his last Christmas.

Emmett and Angel went back out on a Thursday. The skies ran from light gray to gray-black, and the wind blew hard out of the southeast. The upside to the bad weather was that there were fewer boats navigating the Sound or the Straits. Sane sailors had enough sense to stay in the harbor. They went to their favorite hole on the Straits, a couple nautical miles north of the Dungeness Spit, and attempted to lay their nets.

Unfortunately, the currents were much too rough, and they were forced to pull the nets back in and run counter to the wind, making for the head of the Inland Passage where the winds might not be so strong. The slogging was rough; swells were running to eight feet, with tight troughs, and Angel had Emmett help him hold the wheel.

"If wind picks up more, we're going to have to run before it, meanin' Vancouver Island," said Angel, looking into the face of the storm.

"You're right, the rate we're going, the sea is going to beat the *Aberdeen* to a pulp. I think we should make for Victoria."

Angel nodded, watching the sea, timing the best moment to turn into the surge. The *Aberdeen's* large fantail offered itself up to the swells and the boat was propelled forward, picking up speed. Everything was battened down, so the pressing seas would just pour over the decking while the boat quickly made its way toward sanctuary in Victoria.

They were lucky to find an available berth in the harbor right off Montreal Street. They were exhausted, and both were in need of a bath. They found an affordable rooming house and each took a quick soak, changing into clean but wrinkled clothes. They had fifteen dollars, but all but three was budgeted for fuel and ice. So they went to a diner and had the fifty-cent special, and then returned to the waterfront to find a tavern.

From the safe haven of the tavern, they watched the wind continue to pick up. They could see the Red Ensign flying sideways atop the harbormaster's building. According to other sailors in the tavern, the Canadian navy had already pegged the winds at a steady 40 knots on the Straits with gusts running into the 70s.

"Good thing you found a place to park," one of them noted when they related their run to Victoria.

"There's a lot of places to park out there. All the smart fishermen are at home under the covers. We'll be in a rented bed," noted Emmett, sipping at his beer. "The question is, how long is it going to blow? It's a good thing I don't have a hold full of fish, but I'm losing ice while we sit. Sure would like to see gray skies and chop tomorrow. Gray skies and chop would be a holiday compared to this."

After a few beers, they knew they had to get some sleep on the off chance that they'd be able to get back out to the fishing grounds. But they had a restless night, listening to the wind whistle and howl, and a neighbor's unfastened shed door opened and slammed shut a dozen times, rousing them from shallow slumber.

Around five-thirty the next morning, the wind had died down enough that they hurriedly dressed and made their way through a stiff drizzle to the *Aberdeen*. They were lucky to find the owner of the marine fuel and supply store, taking the advantage of the storm to take inventory.

"Ten for the fuel and ice," he noted as Emmett pulled out his wallet. "You boys serious about heading back out?"

"Well, look at it this way, old timer, all the smart fishermen will sit on shore, leaving the grounds to lunatics like us."

The other man just shook his head. "Better make sure the navy knows where you're headed, so's they can find the wreckage later."

Emmett smiled sarcastically. "Thanks."

As they made their way out of Victoria, the wind seemed to abate a bit and they could see lighter skies to the east, in the direction of the sunrise.

"Red sky at morning," intoned Angel.

"Shut up," said Emmett.

The skies remained gray, but the chop leveled off and they were making twelve knots against the wind. After three hours Emmett took a reading and estimated their arrival at the grounds. Small flocks of herring gulls worked dark patches of water, indicating the presence of smelt or other small, bottom-of-the-food-chain fish.

"Let's drop," said Emmett. He took the wheel from Angel and steered a hundred eighty degrees away from the wind, so that the final arc of their circle would put the wind at their backs.

Angel braked the reel for a better spread, and Emmett began a slow turn to port, into the flank and then the teeth of the wind. It was halfway through the drop when the wind began to noticeably increase in strength.

They fought their way back to the initial drop and Angel hooked the lead buoy. Emmett put the boat in neutral and threw out a drag anchor so the boat wouldn't quickly drift while he worked with Angel to close the net and bring it on board. Being a man short made the task even more of a challenge.

The net was fairly full, mostly of cod and Pacific whiting. Angel grinned and clapped his hands. They sorted through the haul, one third at a time, filling the hold only with money fish.

When they were finished, the wind had strengthened to the point where they could no longer ignore it.

"We gotta run, Angel. If we go back to Victoria, we'll lose most of the catch. We head for either Everett or Seattle. What's your vote?"

"We get past Port Townsend, we be okay," Angel shouted through the wind. "We gotta deal with the net first. I do that, and you put more ice on fish."

Emmett nodded and lowered himself into the fish hold. The sight and smell of the full hold made him overlook the serious pitch of the boat. With an eight-pound mace he smashed a couple of ice blocks, and then shoveled the ice in between layers of fish. He did this twice before feeling the need to go topside.

He climbed out of the hold and looked around the deck, but there was no Angel. He ran to the rail, and as the *Aberdeen* lifted high on her portside, he could briefly see the Indian in the water, waving frantically.

Emmett hauled in the drag anchor and went into the pilothouse, pulling the boat hard into the opposite direction. The Sound was littered with small whitecaps, which made picking out Angel difficult. He headed in what he hoped was the right direction as growing swells picked up the stern and forced him forward. Emmett realized that he was only going to have seconds to grab his mate. The water temperature was probably already sapping whatever strength Angel needed to remain at the surface.

He scanned the horizon and the water in front of him, feeling that perhaps he had already passed Angel. But, suddenly, there he was, bobbing on the water, launching himself at the top of the white caps that swept past him.

Emmett cut back the throttle to a high idle, steered the boat right at Angel, and lashed the wheel. Then he went to the rail with a gaffe and waited.

For a few moments he thought the *Aberdeen* might roll right over the Indian, but the swell was pushing just a few feet to the left of his mate. The gaffe went out. Angel grabbed it and almost pulled Emmett into the water with him. Emmett set his feet on the deck. Angel pulled hand over hand up the shaft, grabbing the rail just as Emmett grabbed his collar to drag him aboard.

Both men sat on the deck for a moment, catching their breath and thanking their lucky stars. But the storm was increasing in severity, so both of them quickly returned to their work without a word.

This time, Angel worked in a jury-rigged lifeline lashed to the side rail of the pilothouse, and Emmett stuck his head out of the hold every couple of minutes until he was finished icing the catch. Then, the drag anchor was pulled up again, and they ran their engine to its limit, making for the Point Wilson lighthouse.

"You better change," suggested Emmett.

"All I got is dirty clothes. These *were* my Sunday go to meetin's."

"Well, then, you better make some coffee. This is going to be a long slog."

"Mebbe an hour to Wilson?" Angel asked hopefully as he pulled out the percolator and filled it with coffee grounds.

"Closer to two if everything goes accordingly."

"What does *accordingly* mean? No fuck ups?"

"Pretty much. We aren't done out here. We could still run into trouble. I'll need your eyes up here, so hurry it up."

The seas continued to pick up, and Emmett was glad his course allowed him to run directly into the teeth of the storm. When they arrived at the lighthouse, they knew they were into the inner Sound and, as they expected, the waves and wind lessened enough to make the passage nearly tolerable.

By the time they reached Elliott Bay, they were both exhausted, and the adrenaline rushes they had endured left them weak. When they got to the docks, the broker was taken aback by their appearance.

"You boys look like death warmed over," he said.

"Wish I was that warm," replied Angel.

They cleared nearly seven hundred dollars, but both were too tired to appreciate their good fortune. They refueled and headed back across Elliott Bay. A reverie had settled over them; the satisfaction of a successful trip combined with the exhaustion and relief derived from Angel's rescue.

As they passed Blake Island, both looking forward to a hot bath and a dry, stationary bed, they failed to see a raft of driftwood in their course and plowed into it. A long, thick, liberated length of Douglas fir managed to plunge into the hull of the *Aberdeen*, right above the draft line.

The impact was clearly felt in the pilothouse, and Emmett immediately put the boat into neutral. With the help of a flashlight they could see the hole: an opening four inches wide and three feet long. If the boat was idling in the water, as it was then, there was no problem. But if the boat was at running speed, anything above a couple of knots, water was going to pour into the bilge. They were going to have to patch the boat in order to get the final few miles home.

They had planking, screws, a hand drill, and some formaldehyde-based sealant that they brushed on between the planking and the inner hull. Emmett made sure all of their running lights were on while they remained within the edges of the shipping lanes, and they went to work.

They wedged the planking in place and screwed through the pilot holes into the hull. Finally, they brushed the sealant onto the new planking. It would hold long enough for them to safely cruise the remainder of the way home.

Once he restarted the engine and put his hands on the wheel, Emmett felt the pounding of his heart at the tips of his fingers. He had earned his keep for the day.

As they approached the landing, no lights were on at the dock. Of course, Janie wouldn't think to turn them on, so their approach was slow and careful. Angel fended off the dock with the gaffe as they drew near, then leapt onto the pier to secure the bowline. Emmett shut down the engine, climbed off the boat, and pulled the stern line taut to the bumpers of the dock.

Then, with the aid of the flashlight, he took a closer look at the rent in the hull. It was more serious than they had been able to see out on the water. What had appeared to be a somewhat small puncture was obviously more significant. The planking beyond the tear was cracking, and might need to be replaced as well. Repairs would be extensive, just to ensure the integrity of the boat's structure.

"Think we can fix it?" he asked Angel.

Angel got down on his hands and knees to better examine the damage. "I don't think so, Emmett. We don't got the tools here. Engine work one thing, but shipbuildin' and repairs—I can't do those. You don't think patch will stay?"

"I just plucked you out of an angry sea, what do you think? I don't want to head back out onto the Sound, much less the Straits or the big blue, without that hull fully repaired. Damn it. I'll bet this gets expensive."

Urquhart was asleep when they finally entered his cabin. Janie had been sleeping on the sofa, but had awoken when they docked and listened to their conversation from the front door of the cabin.

"Trouble?" she asked. Atlas had joined her at the door and went into the yard to meet Emmett.

"Some," replied Emmett, stopping to rub the dog's ears and pound him on the flank. "But we banked nearly $700 on a full hold of hake and cod, and we brought some home for a fish fry. How's the old man?"

"Sometimes better, sometimes worse. Just when I think he might never say one more intelligent word, he spews a whole paragraph. He was talking about his wife earlier this evening, and I could have sworn she was in the room with us. I think he's doddering and then he talks about cold fronts or fishing off California. It's like someone keeps lifting the needle off the phonograph record just as you get used to the music. I don't mind saying, it's disturbing to me. Can't tell if he's coming or going."

Angel made his way to the stove and pulled the top off a cast-iron Dutch oven.

"Beans with bacon and maple syrup if you boys are hungry."

Angel didn't wait for an invitation and spooned out a large bowl of the beans, sitting down on the arm of the sofa to wolf down the food.

"So what was the trouble?"

Emmett retrieved a bowl and was ladling out beans. "We managed to put a Titanic-sized rip in the hull of the *Aberdeen*. That won't please the old man. I'll bet we'll hear how he's managed to sail the boat from pole to pole without incident, and now the cubs come along and nearly sink her."

"Can you fix her?"

Emmett shrugged and shoveled a spoonful of beans into his mouth. Janie knew how to cook beans. "Don't think it's a matter of 'can.' It's more a matter of money. We need to get someone to come out and tell us how much."

“Maybe it’s time for Kenneth to sell the boat.”

“Well,” Emmett said, laughing through a mouthful of food, “according to a lawyer and a piece of paper, Angel and I own the *Aberdeen*.”

“He left you the boat?”

“No, he signed her over to us, so one of us has got to go to Seattle and register with the Coast Guard as master. Angel doesn’t want to do it. He thinks someone is looking for him. I don’t want to do it because I *know* someone is looking for me.”

“The law?”

“Well, my brother’s the law on Vashon, and he’s sworn a warrant for me, at least according to the sheriff over on this side of the water. Anyway, I don’t see how having Master’s Papers for the *Aberdeen* will help us fish any better, or fix that hole. But, we got to come up with something. The old man’s larder is getting skimpy, and even though we just picked up some dough, that money’s probably going to go back into the boat.”

Urquhart stirred, noted their presence, and struggled to sit up. “Fish?”

“Lots of them, old man,” said Angel, happy to see Urquhart awake. “Even kept a couple. How’d you like me to make some fish stew?”

Urquhart beamed at the idea. “Atlas?”

The dog came over to the bed, looked up at the old man and, without warning, leapt up onto the bed which creaked under the new weight. The old man laughed and pulled Atlas into a hug. The dog allowed the affection for a few moments and then pulled away to straddle the foot of the bed.

“He pretty much owns the place now, doesn’t he?” asked Janie.

Urquhart leaned forward and stroked Atlas’ fur. “Good boy. He owns all of us.”

In the gray morning light Angel and Emmett were better able to assess the damage, and it was sobering. Behind the tear in the hull there were fractures already separating the stern side planking, which would introduce moisture beyond the marine paint. Repairs were beyond their ability, and both men knew it.

Emmett went to Janie's house and made a call to a shipbuilder and repair specialist on Vashon that he had known since he was a kid hiring out to fishermen at Dockton on Quartermaster Harbor.

The next morning the specialist, a second generation Finn named Miles Maakinen, pulled up in his runabout. He made his sentiments to Urquhart, whom he had known for more than two decades, before heading to the dock. He took the dinghy and rowed around the boat so he could examine the breach up close.

"She needs to be taken out of the water, gents. Without even going into the bilge, I can tell you that the batten seams will have to be pulled and replaced, and additional bulkheads will have to be installed to shore up the new planking."

"You do that?" Angel asked.

"We build boats. We fix them, too."

"What would it take to get the repair made?" Emmett asked, knowing Maakinen's capabilities.

The Finn looked at the boat, did some internal calculations, and then looked back at the boat again. "Let me look inside." He rowed the dinghy back to shore, and then strode up to the dock and leapt onto the *Aberdeen*, disappearing beneath the deck. When he reappeared he was biting his lip while he added figures in his head.

"For Urquhart I can do it for fifteen hundred, and I'm throwing in material that I happen to have on hand. Take about three weeks, though I know I have three other boats scheduled to come in for major overhauls. Should we tow her over to Vashon now?"

"How about we give you five hundred to get things started, and then pay out the remainder as we fish?"

Maakinen shook his head. "I can't do that, not even for the old man. I've got people to pay. Tell you what. Give me seven-fifty up front, with final payment upon delivery. That work for you?"

Emmett shook his head. "Don't have that much money right now.

And we won't have more until we get back out to fish."

Maakinen shrugged and stood there. He wasn't going to adjust his offer. Emmett took a couple steps closer. "I can go six hundred, tops. That's all we have, no grocery money left. Six hundred, and we pay you the difference when you deliver her back."

Maakinen knew they were in deep shit and empathized with them. He had seen fishermen in all economic states over the years. This crew was in trouble, and with their boat out of commission they would have to take odd jobs or hire out to other boats in order to keep money coming in. It was a bad bet, taking on this job, but his feelings for them, and a sense of loyalty to Urquhart, compelled him to make an exception.

"Okay, Emmett. I'll take the *Aberdeen* and you give me five and a half. That'll leave you with grocery money. Though how you'll make up the difference remains unclear. What are you going to do to raise the balance?"

"Rob banks," Angel said, smiling.

The Finn's smile was short lived. "You may have to. I hear the economy's going tits up in the Midwest. Anyway, we only have so many berths over there, so you're going to have to come up with the money in short order. Do we have an understanding?"

Emmett took the proffered hand and shook it. "We'll come up with the money somehow."

Maakinen and his mate attached a towline from the bow of the *Aberdeen* to the stern of their boat and pulled her down the Passage until they could no longer see her. Emmett began to stew.

Where *would* they get the money?

"Maybe we can sell off tools and car?" suggested Angel.

"We need both. Too bad there's nothing else on the property that we could liquidate to cover some of that balance."

"There's the other boat," said Angel. And the mention of Russell's boat made Emmett's heart jump. Of course, somebody would want that hull and engine.

"Good thinking, Angel. But we have to find out who'd have interest in the thing. It's not rigged for anything but running liquor. We need to do some careful snooping, see who's in need of a fast rum running rig."

The most obvious candidates were in Seattle. Tacoma had its share of rum runners, but the great bulk of those involved in running illegal booze out of Canada were headquartered in Seattle, what with its close proximity to Everett, Shoreline, Burien, and Des Moines—the best spots to bring the booze ashore. The question was who could they approach, and where would they find those potential buyers.

It was determined that Emmett was the best party to make those inquiries, and he cleaned up and dressed for his long drive up north to Bremerton, where he could pick up the ferry for Seattle.

AN EARLY CHRISTMAS PRESENT

Christmas was still a week away, and things had been going downhill for Virgil since Delacroix and Dunne had shown up at his door. Dunne's wife had cut him off, and his other girlfriend, who had already opened up the gift intended for M.E.—a real diamond brooch attached to a black, silk chemise that Virgil took back—was also not speaking to him, and wasn't answering his calls.

But the really bad news was that the Coast Guard had blown the *Marionette* out of the water up at Deception Pass, where the forty-two-foot rum runner was attempting to stash its contraband liquor at an abandoned quarry. The *Marionette* had survived a three hour chase that began just inside US waters off Saturna Island and ran between the San Juan and Orcas Islands. The cutter was much slower than the *Marionette* and had simply lucked into finding the runner inside the pass.

When the order that came from the Coast Guard vessel, a new seventy-five-footer mounted with a deck gun and machine guns, to cease unloading was ignored, the machine guns fired a warning burst above the runner's stern. The *Marionette* made the fatal mistake of firing back, and was quickly shot to bits, along with its cargo.

The surviving three of the five-man crew were arrested, and remained in custody in the Seattle Police Department jail. Two of them knew Virgil by name and by profession. If they talked, he was screwed. He had no intention of going down like Olmstead, busted and caged inside McNeil Federal Prison. His concern was great enough that he considered ordering the three prisoners' murders inside.

And he had lost the *Marionette*. She was a custom-built boat, out of Vancouver, BC, running two Liberty aviation engines that enabled her to cruise in excess of twenty-five knots. She had a deep V-hull that made running in heavy seas much easier, yet still allowed for shallow landings in water no more than four feet deep.

His rum running operation, on a much smaller scale than what Olmstead had built, relied on a steady supply of booze—he even had a long-standing order from Reynard for several thousands of dollars worth of liquor for his nascent hotel-slash-restaurant-slash-speak-easy—and losing half of his "fleet" might destroy him as successfully as a few chosen words shared between his employees and the District Attorney.

The loss of the boat compelled him to negotiate with Reynard. Ultimately, he would probably lose whatever profits he might make on the next several shipments to cover the cost of a new boat. But, with the demand for product, it wouldn't be long before he was back in the long green.

But the new boat itself prompted key questions: what kind of boat? Should he seek an existing vessel, or have one be built? Would his needs be better met with simply a speed runner? The *Marionette* was the latter, and while she had enough speed to outrun the Coast Guard, particularly in the shallow straits between the Orcas and San Juan Islands, her configuration clearly identified her for what she was. He knew of fishing boats that had been outfitted for rum running, though they carried reels of net or trolling outriggers in hopes of dispelling the suspicions of the authorities.

He met with Reynard at his office, running into an openly angry Councilman Gosford as he was leaving. The two locked eyes, and Virgil screwed up his face to reflect what he thought was most menacing.

"Everything kosher over at city hall, *monsieur*?" he asked as Reynard motioned him to a chair. Arlyn was nowhere to be seen.

"We're not quite back on track yet, but I have good feelings, Virgil. Now, what was so urgent?"

Virgil outlined his loss and his plans to replace the *Marionette*.

"What does one of these boats cost?"

"I spent nearly ten grand on the *Marionette*. That's American. She was built in Vancouver. But she took six months to build, and I can't afford the wait time. I need to find something local, whether it's built for running or needs to be converted."

"Do you have any leads?"

"I've got my ear to the ground, and I've got my guys checking the builders and berths from here to Olympia. We'll find something."

"How much will you need? Will five thousand do the trick?"

Virgil shrugged. Inside he was jubilant that Reynard was ready to pull out his purse, but he didn't know if, in fact, five grand would be enough, so he shrugged again. "I'll know what's what in a day or two. You never know what my guys might come up with."

On the bulletin board on the wall next to the front counter of the chandlery at Elliott Bay was a crudely drawn sketch of the hull of Emmett and Angel's unfinished boat. Under the image of the hull was the notation:

2 liberty engines, twin screws/rudders, no bridge deck

Janie Ferrady's phone number was under the brief description.

The third day it was on the board the paper was ripped down, but no one noticed its absence. An hour later the paper was on Virgil's desk.

"Did you call the number?" he asked his man.

"No. Thought you'd want to do that."

The man was right, but it still angered Virgil that he had to rely on such poorly motivated subordinates.

Janie happened to be at home, baking bread and rolls to take back over to Urquhart's, when the phone rang.

"Interested in the boat," said the voice.

"Who is this?" she asked.

"Someone who is interested in the damn boat."

"There's no one here right now who can help you. Can I get a number and name? I'll have them call you as soon as I can get the message to them."

Again, a reasonable response, but this one angered Virgil even more. "Okay, tell them someone who wanted to buy their boat called." Then he gave her the number of his private line and hoped he would be there when the jokers finally got around to returning his call.

Goddamn life seemed to be getting more difficult every day.

Emmett listened to the phone ring. He let it ring ten times and was about to hang up when Virgil picked up the receiver. "Yeah?"

"You called about the boat?"

"I did." Virgil sat down, pulled open his desk drawer, and poured himself a snoot. "Tell me about this boat. I have a drawing which doesn't really tell me much."

"It's a forty-eight footer, V-hull with a six foot draft. It's fitted with two Libertys, about six hundred horsepower according to the spec sheet, with twin screws and twin rudders."

"This a fishing boat?"

Emmett laughed. "You could use it for some form of fishing, but it's definitely not a fishing boat. Think 'sport' boat, or pleasure craft."

"With six hundred horses?"

"Well, you aren't going to say it, are you? Okay, this hull was built to run liquor. It's never been on the water. The project got sidetracked two or three years ago. You a cop, or a Fed?"

Virgil laughed and nodded. The guy was being straight with him. No cutesy shit. He found that refreshing. " A ... businessman with *legal* connections. I'm very interested. When can I see the boat?"

"Well, she's on support blocks in a boat shed on our property. If you take the starboard side of Vashon you'll see our dock a mile or so below the head of the Colvos Passage. You'll know by the size of the dock that you're at the right place. When?"

"Tomorrow. Asking price?"

Emmett was stumped. He hadn't really thought this through. What was the hull and engines worth? "You come see the boat and make an offer. We'll be here."

After he hung up he sat down at Janie's kitchen table with paper and pencil and began to tally up the amount they needed to keep things running.

Urquhart was propped in a chair, enjoying the warmth of a brilliant sun break, when the smallish runabout pulled up and tied onto his dock. Four men, all dressed in suits, climbed onto the dock from their boat.

"No salesmen!" he heard himself shout and the men turned toward him. The largest, a man over six feet, wearing a dark brown suit and matching fedora, strode quickly toward him.

"You who I talked to?"

Urquhart was confused. He thought about the question. Who had he talked to? And when? There was Ferrady, of course, she always seemed to be around. He might have talked to her. Then there was Emmett, Angel, and Atlas. He was sure he had talked to them, but this man was a stranger. "Don't think so."

Before Virgil could ask about the boat, Emmett emerged from his cabin, buttoning his jacket and squinting up at the bright sun. "I'm your man." He closed to Virgil and held out his hand. "Emmett Dougal."

Virgil looked Emmett in the eye as their hands clasped and recognized a worthy adversary. "Glaupher. Where's the boat?"

"Hold on a minute." Emmett helped Urquhart to his feet, and helped him stumble back to his cabin and then onto his bed. "They might take those Libertys off our hands," he said to the old man, noting Urquhart's concern.

Janie watched and when Urquhart had reclined, she tugged on Emmett's jacket. "Are they dangerous?"

Emmett looked back out at Glaupher, who stood in the middle of the yard, surveying the entire property.

"Probably. He looks like a cop, don't he—a city cop."

"Haven't had a lot of experience with city cops, but he looks like he'd have no trouble putting a bullet in someone."

"I think you've spent too much time with the police gazette, Mrs. Ferrady."

She punched him on the arm. "Be careful. Don't turn your back on him, Emmett."

Angel unlocked the boat shed and the six men crowded inside, working their way around the support blocks to inspect the hull, screws, and rudders. Then Glaupher and Emmett climbed the ladder and lowered themselves into the hull next to the new Liberty engines.

"You can still see the packing lubricant on the blocks," Emmett pointed out. "And check out the shaft guides. This boat was built for speed in heavy seas. Is that something you're interested in?"

"I'm interested in a lot of things, mister. For one, how'd you come by this heap? You build it? You got papers?"

"You sure do sound like a cop. No, she's not registered, but there's nothing illegal here, just the *promise* of something illegal. Now, if you come up with enough cash, that promise goes away as far as I'm concerned."

Glaupher walked the interior of the hull, noting the tight construction. It needed the top deck and flying bridge built and installed, but Glaupher could see it was potentially a better boat than the *Marionette*. "How much?"

"You were going to make an offer."

"Three thousand."

Emmett was astounded. He wasn't ready to hear that large an amount.

He thought the dickering was done and not just beginning. Glaupher mistook Emmett's silent reaction and quickly said, "Five thousand, and that's my top offer. There's just too much to do yet, and this boat isn't ready for the open sea."

"Five thousand?"

"Okay, six thousand and you deliver her. I'd have to pay a crew to come get her otherwise."

Emmett held out his hand. We're *rich*, he thought.

Glaupher left them with two thousand in cash—neither Emmett nor Angel had ever seen that much money before—with the promise of the other four grand upon delivery to a well-guarded berth below Harbor Island on the Duwamish River.

On Christmas Eve, it took them more than six hours to line up the trucks and lift the hull off its blocks, and onto the trucks. Once they got the hull out of the shed they had to slowly work the craft across the uneven paving stones that had been emplaced several years earlier.

When they finally slid the hull into the Sound, they held their breaths and watched for any leakage. But the hull's integrity was above question; it was both well engineered and well built.

Then they had to borrow a twenty-five-foot cuddy boat from Maakinen to tow the hull across the Sound to the Duwamish; something Maakinen was happy to lend once the balance of the *Aberdeen's* repairs was tendered. He even told Emmett to hang onto the runabout until the *Aberdeen* was delivered. Money went along way toward Christmas spirit.

Their plan was to wait until dusk, which was around four o'clock in late December, and then tow the hull past the Vashon landing. They would hug the eastern shore of the Sound, and then make a mad dash past Alki Point and into the Duwamish before any Coast Guard boats might detect them. They ran without running lights, and were glad the runabout was small but powerful enough to make nearly fifteen knots, full throttle, with the hull in its wake.

When thcy closed on Alki, Emmett cut it close, pulling within thirty yards of the rocky shoreline. There was traffic on the Sound, but it was Christmas Eve, so whatever boats were on the water that afternoon were making for port; if one couldn't be with family on this night, they would spend it in a bar with other dispossessed souls.

The lights from the Seattle waterfront reflected off the water, taking on an eerie appearance. Soon, the mist evolved into a light rain. Still, the moisture couldn't dampen the enthusiasm on the boat, and Emmett and Angel looked forward to turning over the hull to the man with the money.

Angel produced a bottle of Dewar's scotch, and they each took nips. They weren't ready to tie one on; that would have to wait until they returned home. But they were enjoying themselves when a distant light flashed across their pilothouse. Emmett watched the beam of light sweep away, and hoped that whoever was manning that light thought that the runabout and hull were anchored rather than running without lights.

The light swept from view and for a moment Emmett breathed a sigh of relief; then the beam came around again, and this time it slowed and trained on them. The cutter was too distant for them to be clearly seen, even with binoculars, but their presence and apparent movement had already compelled the cutter to change course. It might have been wiser for them to run with lights, just on the off chance that a well-lit boat wouldn't require a rundown and boarding. But the die was cast; the light remained on them and the cutter blew its whistle twice, three times in succession, ordering them to halt.

Emmett gauged the distance to the mouth of the Duwamish before opening the cuddy boat's throttle to full speed. The cutter completed its turn and was coming on, gaining on them, but not quickly enough to overtake them before they were able to enter the Duwamish.

Emmett hadn't navigated this channel before, and he scanned the shorelines for depth indicators, sticking to the center of the channel. In the dark, without the use of the cuddy boat's floodlight, it was difficult to tell just how fast they were going. As the river curved below Harbor

Island, they escaped the light from the cutter, and switched on their own directional light to maintain their position in the channel.

Up ahead they could see some lights along the shoreline, and then they could see someone waving a lantern or flashlight, indicating they had arrived. Emmett backed off the throttle and sent Angel to the bow to watch for pilings or debris. The hull plowed into the back of the runabout, nearly throwing Angel into the river, but he held onto the bow railing. Emmett threw the engine in reverse in order to slow the hull.

"Drop the line!" he yelled at Angel, and the Indian ran to the stern where he began to unfasten the towline from the stern cleats.

"What now?" Angel yelled.

"Hold on!"

Emmett increased the throttle and pulled away from the drifting hull, turned the cuddy boat and maneuvered to the hull's stern and began to gently push it toward what appeared to be a group of men waiting by a large boat shed on the shore. Emmett turned his head and could see the sweep of the cutter's floodlight as the vessel neared the entrance to the Duwamish.

With the cutter coming into the river, he knew he had less than a couple of minutes to deal with the hull. He was forced to extinguish his floodlight in order to not give away his position. Emmett could feel a sense of panic, but was careful not to push the hull too hard—there was no practical way to steer it.

He let the hull drift again, then ran the cuddy along the starboard flank of the hull, pushing it away from the stubbed pier on the shore and toward the doors of the boat shed. He reversed his engine, allowed the hull to drift past him, and then carefully pushed it inside the shed and followed from behind. The doors to the shed were quickly closed behind them.

He turned off his engine and sat in the dark. Angel secured the cuddy boat, and carefully made his way to the open pilothouse, and leaned against the bulkhead.

"Think they find us?"

"Quiet," a voice said from the dark.

A few moments later, they could hear the large diesel engines of the cutter idling as it slowly cruised up the river looking for a phantom tug. The vibrations from the cutter's engines thrummed on the metal walls of the shed, creating the sound of a hungry predator nosing the scent of its prey.

They remained quiet for almost fifteen minutes before the cutter made its return to the Sound, unsuccessful in its search. The voice cautioned them to remain silent and, sure enough, the cutter made yet another slow pass. They could see brief flashes of the searchlights through small holes in the shed's riverside wall as the cutter scanned the boathouses and shoreline. Again, the cutter passed back out to the Sound.

Dim lights came on in the shed, and Emmett could see Glaupher on the catwalk.

"Nice driving, Ace."

One of the men with Glaupher must have been a boat builder, perhaps a specialist in converting craft to rumrunners. He jumped into the hull, inspected it from stem to stern and offered his appraisal. "A good one, Virg. Slap a deck and flying bridge on this, reinforce the bulkheads, and she'll carry two hundred cases, easy."

Glaupher nodded and smiled. "Good enough, Jackie. How long before she's ready to run?"

"A week maybe, no more. I'll start on her tonight."

Angel finished tying off the runabout and jumped up onto the catwalk. Emmett joined him, eager to get their money so they could go back home to celebrate Christmas Eve with the old man and Ferrady. When they'd left she was prepping a large bird for the oven. Emmett could imagine how good it would be to be sit down to feast with those who had become his extended family, even if he would have to forego a visit with his actual kin this holiday.

"Got some bad news, boys," said Glaupher. "Don't have the remainder of the cash, but I can get it and be back here in an hour. Or you can ride along and get some hot food."

"We got hot food waiting at home," Angel tersely replied. He didn't like the idea of taking a ride with these men.

"Suit yourself. Jackie's got a percolator in the back if you want some hot coffee."

"We'll tag along," said Emmett, ignoring Angel's hard stare. "Be nice to ride up to the city, maybe get us a sandwich and a beer. Thanks for the invite."

Angel and Emmett followed the other men up the catwalk and steps, where Glaupher's large Buick touring car waited. The weather screens had been lowered, so it was like being under a tarpaulin with cushioned leather seats. Angel was visibly nervous, and Emmett pinched him when no one was looking.

Angel lit a cigarette to calm himself. "You guys got anything to drink?" A pint bottle of rye was passed back and Angel took a hard pull on it.

"Take it easy, that's got to last my shift," said Bradley, taking back the pint.

The drive took twenty minutes, and Emmett was glad to be out from inside the car. Even though he could watch the directions that Glaupher took, he wasn't sure what their actual destination was until he stepped out onto Reynard Delacroix's driveway.

It was actually the driveway for the guesthouse. The main driveway was lined with expensive automobiles. Valets were parking the vehicles, and young men in livery were escorting the guests to the front door.

"Big shindig," said Emmett.

"This way," said Glaupher, directing them toward the backside of a mansion.

The building exterior was well lit, casting up shadows of manicured evergreens and drawing attention to an interesting rock garden. The house was a study in architectural excess, alien to anything Emmett had experienced.

They entered through a side door and went down a hallway to a paneled room. A large desk centered the room. A liquor cart straddled one wall, and a Victrola sat opposite. Glaupher led Emmett and Angel to the front of the desk.

"He'll be here in a few moments," he said. When Angel made note of the liquor Glaupher was terse: "Wait to be offered."

Reynard soon entered the room, his broad smile drawing attention from his pressed white tie and tails. "Gentlemen! Thank you so much for coming. I told the lieutenant you'd come, but he didn't agree. You owe me five dollars, Lieutenant."

"Lieutenant? Is this a set up … ?"

Reynard held out his hands and motioned to the chairs. "Please, sit. Help yourself to some spirits."

Angel got his whisky, and they all sat down.

"From what Lieutenant Glaupher has told me, you're excellent pilots. He hasn't had time to tell me much more than you dodged some bad luck with the Coast Guard tonight. The key thing is that you dodged it. Now, the lieutenant—oh, we're among friends here, Virgil—is purchasing your boat, but he needs to do this thing, and that thing, and it all costs money, something which the lieutenant—Virgil—is lacking. I'll keep the story short. I am now his partner. Our partnership, as regards this enterprise, includes a few assets. Those include Virgil's contacts, the new boat, and my money. We have everything we need to get up to speed except for a crew."

"We just came here for our four thousand bucks," said Emmett. "We got folks waiting on us for Christmas Eve dinner. It's half an hour back to our boat and half an hour across. We appreciate what you're offering, but we'd like our money."

Reynard stood up, looking annoyed, and reached into his pocket. He spread forty one hundred dollar bills on the desk. "There is your money. You may take it anytime. But allow me to make an offer before you refuse it."

Emmett leaned forward and swept the bills into a pile and put the wad into his inside coat pocket. He looked up at his host. "I apologize, Mr. ...?"

"Delacroix. Reynard Delacroix."

Emmett started at the sound of the name, but maintained his composure.

"I accept your apology," Reynard continued, "though none was necessary. And what might your name be?"

"Emmett Dougal."

"I'll be brief, Mr. Dougal. Here is what I propose. I won't bother you with numbers or percentages, but we can afford to pay you fifteen hundred dollars for each successful delivery. You would only make one delivery each week. You figure it out. That's a lot of money. What would you spend that money on ... ?"

"I've never had that much money. I've never had *this* much money," Emmett said, patting his coat pocket.

"Think what you could do for your family. You could build a new house for your wife."

"I'm not married."

"Then think of the women you could court. A whole new class of women! Think of the worlds you could come to know with that kind of money."

"I don't mean to be rude, sir, but can we kick it around for a day or two?"

Emmett remembered Urquhart's ambiguous warning about Delacroix. It was obvious the man had the grit and resource of someone who could command the allegiance of a man like Glaupher—a *cop*. What Emmett really wanted at that moment was to get back across the water and get some of the bird before it got cold and dried out.

"Of course, that's wise. Give it some thought, but don't take too long. Enterprise waits for no man. The lieutenant will be in touch with you. He knows where to find you?"

"Yes, he's got our number."

"Well, then, off to your families. Merry Christmas, gentlemen."

They offered their sentiments in return, and had just started for the door when it burst open to reveal a beautiful young woman, adorned in a marvelous dress that highlighted her physical assets, much to the distress of her brother.

Emmett stood, dumbstruck. It was Noémi. The young woman had become the focal point of his fantasies for the past several weeks, and here she was, in front of him. He stared at her in amazement. If possible, she was even more beautiful than the last time he had seen her.

When she realized that she had almost run right into the mysterious man she had met weeks earlier, Noémi stopped mid-stride and raised her hand to her mouth. The man before her was dirty. It was obvious he had been working this evening. And yet he seemed even more attractive, if that was possible, than he had when they met in the ice cream parlor.

"Hello," was all she could muster, but it was more than Emmett was able to offer in reply.

Reynard noted the look on both faces. "You two know each other?"

Noémi had difficulty looking away from Emmett. "Yes, when I was shopping with Cozette some weeks ago, we met this gentleman in an ice cream parlor on First Street." She immediately looked back to Emmett. "Hello," she repeated.

Reynard arched his eyebrows. "An ice cream parlor?"

"It's true. But what is he doing here?"

"It's just business, and they're leaving, Noémi. We'll be in touch, Emmett."

"Good evening, Miss Noémi, Mr. Delacroix."

Emmett, Noémi thought. Yes, that was his name.

Noémi Delacroix, thought Emmett. He had forgotten about the slip of paper with her address in his wallet. First Hill was as foreign a country as Mexico to Emmett. But the image of her in her party dress would never be erased from his memory. His mind tried to sort out the relationship. Was she the man's wife? His sister? Certainly he wasn't old enough to be her father. Emmett banked on the hope that she was Reynard's sibling, though that gave him no better chance with her than had she been the man's wife.

Glaupher didn't join them on the drive back to their boat. Emmett sat up front with Glaupher's man, a sergeant named Bradley, and Angel stretched out in back and immediately fell asleep.

The crossing was smooth—there was no sign of the cutter—and they were able to tie the cuddy boat up to their dock by eight-thirty. The lights in the cabin were all on, and they could see the Christmas tree as they climbed onto the small porch.

Emmett opened the door and was met with a warm, welcome blast of cooking smells. Atlas was parked in front of the oven, guarding its contents. Seeing Emmett, he quickly got to his feet and lumbered closer to get his ears and neck scratched.

"Come on in, fellas. Kenneth is taking a little nap," Janie said. "We weren't sure how long you boys might be, and the old man talked me into letting him have some of his whisky. Course, now he's gone to Morpheus without wishing you a Merry Christmas."

Emmett shrugged out of his coat and looked at the clock on the wall. "Well, as of eight-thirty, December twenty-fourth, nineteen and twenty-eight, we are … *rich*." He pulled the wad of bills from his coat pocket and spread them on the kitchen table, allowing his fingers to dawdle on the worn paper.

"The boat's repairs are already covered. I'd say we got enough here to clean this place up some, maybe do some painting once it warms up. Repair the roof on my cabin. The old man could use a new chair. That one's a rat's nest. But, most important, we can hire someone to stay out here with the old man when we're fishing."

"I don't mind helping out, Emmett. It gives me something to do with myself besides feeding chickens and collecting eggs. I kinda feel I've become part of this family."

"Well then, get *her* a new chair," interjected Angel. He stood up and theatrically put his nose in the air. "I smell food, but I don't see food."

"Coming up," Janie strode into the kitchen and began to assemble their Christmas Eve turkey dinner while Angel retrieved Urquhart's bottle of Black&White and poured liberal amounts into two glasses.

"Luck turning good," he toasted.

"Luck turning good," Emmett replied and bolted down his whisky. He poured another shot for himself and another for the Indian. "And here's to Mrs. Ferrady. Guardian angel."

Arlyn rounded up the boys, which wasn't difficult because the moment after they had bathed and changed into their little suits they had parked themselves a short distance from the Christmas tree.

The three sat, transfixed. They had been instructed not to touch anything, not to read the gift tags, not to even go within two feet of the closest present. The tone in which these instructions had been given was clearly understood by all three boys. The instructions were inviolable, and would remain so for at least another decade.

Mary Elizabeth had been struggling to become ill for the past three days, announcing each and every twinge, itch, or cough in hopes of being spared another evening at the Delacroix Mausoleum. Arlyn understood her less and less, it seemed. How she could be so critical of another home when that home was the very model for her own?

She didn't like Noémi, which was obvious to everyone despite her attempts at cheerful, if slightly insincere, civility. Having to put on such an act was tiring, and three hours was just torture. Mary Elizabeth couldn't understand why her presence was so important; perhaps it was that they all enjoyed her torment. Wine would flow, tongues would loosen, and they would all have to listen to Miss Noémi recount her college adventures.

But her body refused to provide a credible excuse, and Arlyn simply produced a bottle of aspirin when she started to complain about a headache. Arlyn was beginning to think that this might be their last Christmas together. M.E. was a walking definition of a fallen Catholic. She never went to confession anymore, even when he prompted her. She had begun to swear—nothing major—in front of the boys. And he had caught her smoking. When she started that habit, he had no idea. But if this was going to be their last Christmas together as a family, Arlyn was damned well sure it was going to be a good one for the boys.

He herded them all into the car, and once they had arrived at the Delacroix manor, he marshaled the boys to the game room, where Reynard had installed a pinball machine and a bumper pool table. On top of the pool table were three elaborately wrapped gifts: one for each of the boys. Charles got a baseball glove, and the younger boys got pressed metal cars that sped forward erratically after being wound with a key. One of the cars was a police cruiser that tickled Virgil to no end once he arrived with his brood.

He didn't ask why there weren't presents for his kids. He had come to accept that Reynard had chosen Arlyn to be his right-hand man. Not that Virgil would have wanted that job; he had a bigger vision, and Reynard could never have a subordinate with a vision bigger than his.

He didn't even resent Arlyn's ascension. A year ago, the Dunne family was in a three room cold-water flat. Now they were on Queen Anne, too. He carefully looked over toward Mary Elizabeth, and noted that she was stealing a glance at him. He smiled and after a brief pause, she quickly smiled and looked away. Ah, good, he thought. I'm back in.

Noémi found herself talking to someone that she didn't know, or at least certainly didn't recognize. The young man was intense, and was talking about bonds, or maybe he said bombs; in truth, she hadn't been paying any attention from the moment her brother made introductions.

In her head she was facing the mysterious Emmett. The Emmett that her brother had hired to do … what? What would he have been doing this evening to get that dirty? Didn't he say that he was a fisherman?

Perhaps he was going to supply the restaurant in the new hotel. Why else would he be meeting with Reynard?

The young man had asked a question.

"Pardon me?"

"I asked if you missed New Orleans?"

"Oh. Well, yes, there are *things* that I miss. The food. One cannot find such wonderful food here. Not the same kind of food, anyway. But I don't miss the heat or the humidity. My hair *never* looked good in New Orleans." She said 'Nawlins,' and this pleased the young man.

"I know of a restaurant—"

"I'm sure you do. Would you excuse me, please?" But it wasn't a question, simply a diplomatic dismissal. She left the living room in search of refuge from the three young, unattached men that Reynard had invited in his attempt to strategically match her with someone. She stepped out onto the short terrace that looked over their landscaped yard. By herself, she could focus her imagination on the mysterious 'Emmett.'

"I don't think she likes me," the young man complained to Reynard. This particular young man was on the fast track at Reynard's bank: a junior manager from a good family, who had earned his degree in economics at Penn and was in line to run one of Seattle's largest banks in short time. He was also a nascent political and economic ally of Reynard, and Noémi could help cement that relationship if she could be convinced to give the young man a chance.

"Of course she does, William. She is young and fickle. She needs to get to know you. You mustn't give up simply because she's in one of her moods. Give it a while and get back in there. She'll warm up, you'll see."

But there were no sparks that evening for young William or the other two potential suitors. And there never would be. She would never look at another man in that way again, not after having been reintroduced to Emmett.

As she lay down in her bed that night, the only thing she could see in her mind's eye was that smudged, unshaven face with those brutally piercing eyes. If ever there were a match for her to make, it would be this.

Reynard went to his bedroom in a much less happy mood. His tête-à-tête with Gosford had not gone as well as he would have liked. The pol, whose office Reynard had essentially purchased, was determined to hold Reynard at arm's length now that he no longer felt the latter indispensable.

"While the council recognizes the economic opportunities your project might present, it will not grant the variances you request. The council also happens to recognize what you intend to do with that additional space, and that is illegal."

"Who is to say how that space might be utilized? Is it written anywhere what those intentions are? The plans identify the space as storage."

"But we both know different, don't we, Delacroix?"

Reynard felt his temper rise at the use of his name in such a casual and familiar way. "Why did I bother to support someone who obviously has no interest in supporting me?" Reynard asked.

"Civic responsibility. And that's what I will bring to service each and every day. Your business will only increase the amount of crime in this city. I intend to help you find ways to do business in a manner that brings prosperity and moral authority to Seattle."

"Moral authority? What does that mean?"

"It means more churches, less saloons. It means more sidewalks, more schools, and more families. It means leaving the vicissitudes of crime at the curb."

Reynard laughed. "Vicissitudes? Ah. You mean, the small joys of life. The chance for a working man to salve his daily wounds with a glass of beer or a shot of whisky. Or the chance for a married couple to step out, have a cocktail together, and escape the miseries of daily life—"

"When they should be at home teaching their children about the straight and narrow path of virtue and righteousness," interrupted Gosford. He walked about and waved his hands as he talked, much like a minister fresh from seminary.

Reynard openly smirked and rolled his eyes. "Well, you are correct. I did make a mistake, one that I'll correct as circumstances allow. What you fail to realize, Councilman, is that there must always be a carrot, something that gives the average man a reason to continue his daily slog. Everyone, even the most saintly, needs a bit of candy in hard times, something which allows them to put things into perspective. The Holy Bible does not provide that for a great many people."

"Then they need to spend more time with the Scriptures, for every answer is in there. I looked for, and found the answer in there when I needed to secure your financial assistance. And the solution was there. '*Let the wicked forsake his way, and the unrighteous man his thoughts.*'"

"What is less righteous than deception? You lied to me. You made promises with no intent to keep them. There is another verse, perhaps you're familiar with it. From Proverbs, '*Pride goeth before destruction, and an haughty spirit before a fall.*'"

Gosford smiled. "You know the Bible. I'm surprised."

"There will be more surprises, Councilman. Go home to your family and enjoy the holiday."

Gosford recognized, by its very tone, the hint of a threat contained in that sentence. And that nagging little hint would bedevil him not just through the holidays, but to his last day on earth.

CROSSINGS...

Kenneth Urquhart passed in his sleep on December 28th, 1928. He was 64 years old, though no one knew it—least of all Urquhart, who had long since given up keeping count.

Angel woke on the sofa after his night watch and found the old man cold to the touch. There was a beatific smile on Urquhart's face, framing his reconciliation with death. At his bedside lay the big dog, who would not move, even when the morticians from Port Orchard arrived to take the corpse for burial. Finally, they just stepped over the animal and carefully lifted the old man's body onto a stretcher, which they carried out to their black van.

Atlas went outside with Emmett and Angel to watch the vehicle drive away into the somber, gray morning. Once it was out of sight, Atlas walked into the woods and disappeared.

Emmett watched Atlas go, amazed at the amount of quiet emotion that the dog, in keeping with his humans, shared over Urquhart's passage.

When Janie Ferrady showed up later, she became inconsolable, though all of them had half-expected Urquhart to die. They just hadn't anticipated his passing so soon and without adequate—or what they felt were adequate—good-byes.

"Can I still come over to see you fellows?" she asked, realizing that her job as nursemaid had been commandeered by death.

Emmett gave her a hug. "Kenneth," he said, using the old man's given name for the first time, "would want you to watch over us since he can't. We'll expect to see you over here as often as you like."

Janie nodded and hugged him back. "Fresh coffee, that's what we need." She set to working in the kitchen, cleaning up the dinner fixings from the night before and putting away the dishes in the dry rack. "Where's the dog?" she asked, missing him under her feet.

"Mourning somewhere in the woods," said Emmett. "Where's Angel gone to, now?" He walked outside into the gray morning and looked around the property, but there was no sign of Angel.

In the far distance he could hear a foghorn. Some freighter was navigating the Eastern Passage with zero visibility, marking its progress and issuing a warning with a blast every two minutes. It was a fit morning for Urquhart's departure.

The boatshed door was open, and Emmett walked up the incline to look inside. He pulled one of the doors slightly and he could hear sobbing coming from inside. He stopped and went no further. Angel had lost the closest thing to a father he'd ever had. And that kind of mourning had to be done alone.

Emmett walked back to the old man's cabin. He could see Janie through the window, busy cleaning up the kitchen, giving herself one task after another. He pushed open the door, but the empty, rumpled bed stopped him in his tracks. He closed the door quietly.

There were things that he had to do. He had to go see about the funeral, and check in with the Sheriff to get the word out to anyone interested regarding the service. But he'd do those things later.

This gravelly stretch of beach had become Emmett's home over the past few months, perhaps more of a home than that of his childhood. He stooped by the water's edge to pick up a creamy yellow rock the size of a quarter. Against the gray, black, and brown speckles making up the beach, there were only a few rocks this color. That's what Urquhart had been: one shiny rock among the dull gray and black. He scanned the Passage, but there was no traffic due to the fog, which showed no signs of lifting.

He wondered how many times the old man had combed this beach, picking up the welcome and less-welcome flotsam of small freighters and barges; how many times the old man had given forth drunken soliloquies to the water, sky and trees; or built huge bonfires to scare away whatever devils possessed him. Urquhart's son, Russell, should have been the one shouldering this loss, but instead the kid became more of the emotional flotsam the old man had borne instead.

The old man had been smart, even in the midst of his decline, to take care of his replacement family. They could continue to fish; he had seen to that. And Russell's ill-gotten attempt at rum running had providentially bailed them out. So there was some good to the kid after all, he thought.

The *Aberdeen* would be returned in a little more than two weeks, and though they didn't need to fish, it was something Emmett was desperate to do. Working a seine boat required full attention: attention that can't be given to the horrible losses that life inflicts.

He was beached. He had no boat on which to escape his grief, and crying wouldn't make him feel one whit better.

Where's Atlas, he thought. He wandered back up the beach, past the cabins, and into the woods, following the track that he and Atlas had taken on many walks. He called out the dog's name every minute or so, but the big animal did not appear. Emmett wondered at the depth of understanding Atlas must have, or if perhaps he was transferring his own emotions onto the dog, and the latter was simply making his rounds.

After half an hour spent wading through cane, grass, and bracken, his pants were sodden, so he gave up. Atlas would come back when he was good and ready. If he was mourning then he, like Angel, should be given his space.

Janie had taken off the bed linens to wash. So Emmett took the mattress off its frame and took both, along with pillows and blankets, into Urquhart's bedroom. Then he set the bed back up and put the folded blankets at its foot, ready should its master ever happen back.

"You hungry?" Janie asked, looking in on him.

He shook his head.

"Well, come ahead and eat anyway. You haven't had anything today, and you need something."

"Where's Angel?"

"He came in and got a cup of coffee and a bottle of liquor while you were gone. I think he's in the boat shed."

Emmett sat down at the table and remembered the first meal he had there with the old man and Angel. Janie placed a cheese sandwich in front of him and he ate without tasting it.

She could see he was just going through the motions. "Enough mustard? There, near the end, Kenneth was having me spread mustard on everything but the Johnnycakes."

She poured Emmett some coffee and was liberal with the amount of sugar she spooned into his cup. "Nothing is going to bring him back, Emmett. Lord knows I tried every prayer, every promise, every deal I could think of to save my husband. After he was gone I just wanted the emptiness to go away, but I came to accept that the emptiness was really just the size of the love I had for Lloyd. I still have that emptiness, but now I embrace it. Kenneth will always be with us. Every day you wake up here, you'll be waking up with Kenneth. This place *is* Kenneth."

Emmett took the last bit of sandwich and shoved it in his mouth. As he chewed he smiled at her. "Mrs. Ferrady, you're quite the talker. Thanks, and for the sandwich, too."

He walked up to the shed, pulled the door wide and walked in. Angel was lying across an empty pallet, looking at the shed ceiling.

"C'mon, Angel, we've got things to do. We've got to send the old man on his way."

The funeral was held in the chapel at a cemetery near Olalla, where Urquhart's beloved wife, Lillian, was already interred. The skies were overcast but light, and the few mourners on hand to see the coffin lowered were thankful that it didn't rain.

Janie Ferrady was there, stylish in the same black mourning dress she wore at her husband's funeral. Foster Wilson, the chandler from Gig Harbor, who had known Urquhart for nearly four decades, was there. An elderly gentleman dressed in clean, pressed coveralls paid his respects graveside. Ralph Gerritson, the Kitsap deputy sheriff, came in a fresh uniform with black armband.

Other than those, only two others attended. Both wore ill-fitting suits: one smallish man with a suit too large, and one very large man in a suit one size too small. When the service was over the Mutt and Jeff lingered, waiting for the sheriff to depart.

"You know those two guys?" Emmett asked Gerritson.

The latter sized them up and shook his head. "Somebody's idea of muscle is what I'd guess. You owe anybody any money?"

The mention of money rang a bell. "Ah. That's it. They're collectors for the 'fishing association.'"

"You want me to run them off?"

"Nah, I can handle it. Thanks, Ralph. Urquhart would be happy you turned out."

Gerritson shook his hand. "You've got my number, Emmett. Call me if you need anything."

"The place is always welcome to you, Ralph. You mind taking Mrs. Ferrady home while I clean things up here?"

Angel, who was always nervous around Gerritson, reappeared as the deputy's battered old Ford roared to life and eased away toward the highway.

"What now?"

"We deal with these clowns."

The men, seeing Emmett approach, pulled their hands out of their pockets and stood straight. The larger of the two stood a full head taller than Emmett, but he still strained onto his tiptoes, attempting to impart an image of intimidation.

"Gentlemen, thank you for coming. Did you know Mr. Urquhart?"

The smaller man stepped forward and pulled on the brim of his fedora, something he had seen Cagney do in a recent film. "We're just here for our money. By our accounts, you owe us one hundred bucks. Cash."

"I owe you one hundred dollars?"

"That's what I said. You got it, pay up. You don't, Eldredge here is gonna bruise you a bit."

Emmett smiled up at Eldredge and then looked back at Eldredge's mouthpiece. "For what do I owe you a hundred bucks?"

"Protection—"

Before 'Mutt' could finish the word 'protection,' Emmett kicked Eldredge hard on his right shin, and the big man knelt to the ground. Emmett stepped forward, swung his right fist in a wide arc and brought it up, catching Eldredge in the middle of his face.

Blood splattered onto the ground and Eldredge grabbed his handkerchief and pressed it against his nose, screaming. "You sonuvabitch! You sonuvabitch, you broke my nose. I'll—"

As he attempted to rise, Emmett lifted his right knee into the larger man's shoulder, knocking him to the ground. Eldredge started to reach for a concealed pistol, but Emmett was already on top of him.

Mutt made no attempt to intervene once Angel sidled up next to him, openly fingering a nine-inch boning knife.

Emmett took the gun from Eldredge but continued to sit on the latter's chest. "I want you to go away. Do not ever bother me again. If I see you again, anywhere, I won't be this pleasant. It would be better for *you* to pay my 'dues' than to come asking me. Do you understand?"

Emmett jammed the automatic into Eldredge's chest. "Do you understand, Eldredge?"

The big man nodded and Emmett let him get up. Emmett threw the pistol as far as he could into a bordering canebrake.

Mutt watched both Angel and Emmett. "It don't matter what you want. If they want to come for you they will, with or without us. Frankly, I hope to Sweet Jesus I never see you again. But, they run the show, and they'll just send someone else when you ain't expecting 'em. The money's no big thing by comparison, don't you see?"

"I don't pay anyone for nothing."

"Nothing's gonna get you killed."

"Git. Now."

Angel followed the two men to their Packard and watched them drive away. Emmett joined him.

"He right? They come for us in the night?"

"I gotta make a call. That guy Glaupher, the cop? He can make this go away."

"You thinking mebbe we run some liquor for him?"

"I'm thinking we should do some thinking on that. But first, let's have the man lean on these assholes."

"Who are they?" Virgil asked, his nasal voice fairly rasping through the phone line.

"They call themselves a 'fisherman's association.' Don't know for sure, but I think they're out of Seattle and, according to Urquhart, they shake down the smaller fishermen around the Sound."

"I know who to call. Give me a little time. If you got guns, you should keep them loaded and nearby. Someone warns you, you should listen. But, since you called, you make up your mind? Loyalty goes a long way around here."

"We just had the funeral, Lieutenant. Give me a day. I'll call you first thing in the morning."

"Good enough. Make me happy, Dougal, and I'll make you happy. In the by and by, I'll check out these pricks."

Janie showed up with a baked chicken for dinner. She was looking for any excuse to look in on the boys.

"Mrs. Ferrady, we're grown men and hardly infirm. You don't need to feed us."

She nodded. It was different while Kenneth was still alive. But his passing had removed any need for neighborly assistance. They ate in silence, and Angel finished quickly, departing to his cabin where, Emmett assumed, he had stashed his bottle.

Emmett and Janie made small talk while they cleaned up the dishes. When everything was put away she took stock of the cabin. "Could use some fresh paint. Who's moving into Kenneth's room?"

"No one. We're quite happy where we're at, Mrs. Ferrady. This is still the old man's cabin. That's the way it'll stay."

"Seems like a waste of good living space," she sniffed. "And call me Janie. We know each other well enough for first names."

They walked back to her house on the path that ran parallel to a forest of firs. The rain had come and gone, and mud collected on their shoes as they passed by her chicken coops.

"Guess I'll have time to make up with my hens," she said. At her door she hesitated. "I'm gonna be lonesome again. I just got used to being around folks, and now I'll be back to talking to chickens."

He laughed. "We're not a half-mile away, Janie. That's almost in the same room. What say we make Sundays a dinner day? You cook one week, we cook the next."

"What say I cook every week. I've seen your work in the kitchen. But only one day a week? That's like visiting day at McNeil Penitentiary."

Emmett laughed again and kissed her on her forehead. "Tell you what. You surprise us whenever you like. But I warn you, don't be surprised to see a bunch of half-dressed Turkish dancing girls running around the place."

This time she laughed.

Emmett found Angel stretched out on his bed, the room illuminated by one small candle. On the small side table was the whisky, but the cork remained in the bottle.

"Thinking?"

"Tryin' not to. What we gonna do, Emmett? We got us a bunch of money, do we need fishing?"

"I need something. How about that bottle there, you saving it for some special occasion? Like maybe toasting the memory of the old man?"

Angel sat up and picked up the bottle. He handed it to Emmett. Emmett sat down on the bed and pulled the cork from the scotch. The liquor felt good going down, burning away the grief that still collected in the pit of his stomach. He handed the whisky to Angel who took a long, hard pull.

The bottle was passed back and forth, with little conversation, until it was nearly empty. By then a comfortable numbness had overtaken both of them, and what little talk there was turned toward the old man and then, naturally, to their life on the water.

Angel struggled to stand and hit both jambs of his front door going outside. Emmett followed him, oblivious to the steady rain that fell about them. It was probably no warmer than forty degrees, but both men felt unusually comfortable despite the chill.

Standing on the shoreline, passing the bottle until it was empty, they took in the dim sights and muted sounds that surrounded them. They were somewhere between the glorious heights of drunkenness and the irreversible effects of alcohol poisoning. It was perfect.

In the near distance, it was hard to tell, a soft sound made itself known: a light gurgling, perhaps voices, but unintelligible. The sound made a place for itself within the noise of lapping waves and the wind in the trees, complementing each.

Emmett waded a couple feet into the water in order to hear better but the meaning, if there were words, was beyond his comprehension. Then the sounds began to coalesce, the proverbial mist parted, and he could hear two, maybe three or more feminine voices.

"Come this way," they said, "come this way." Over and over again, punctuated by the seawater slapping on rock, "come this way."

"You hear that?" he asked Angel.

But the Indian just grinned, his white teeth splitting his face in the dim light. "I say we run booze," Angel announced, and grinned some more.

Virgil watched Arlyn pour himself a neat shot of whisky from the bottle on the side table. He hated Dunne. Much of the lust he felt for Mary Elizabeth was steeped in the utter dislike he felt for Arlyn. Fucking Mary Elizabeth was fucking over Dunne. He liked the symmetry.

It made him even angrier to see the office that Reynard had given Dunne. While nowhere as large, or luxurious as Delacroix's, it was the office of someone important. Walnut paneling, mahogany furniture, and three overstuffed leather wingback chairs, one of which he currently occupied. And then there was the fucking liquor cart.

Dunne had come a long way from standing guard on the front porch of some swell's First Hill mansion. The prick wore new suits. He drove a new car. Lived in a big house. As big as his own, he knew, for he had walked the hallways and inspected the rooms while Mary Elizabeth was busy making herself presentable for him.

But now the prick was thinking he held sway over Virgil Glaupher. He was going to have to learn otherwise, but Virgil hadn't yet come up with an appropriate strategy to correct that misconception.

"Have you met with Gosford?"

"I've spoken with him on the phone," Virgil responded.

"After what your department and Mayor Landes did to Olmstead with those wiretaps, I would think you would avoid such phone conversations and stick to private meetings."

"Well, the problem with that, Arlyn, is that the prick refuses to meet with me. I've offered to meet him anywhere, anytime, but he told me that anywhere, anytime would mean that no one else is around, and he thinks I might just have bad intentions for him."

"You do tend to strike that kind of response, don't you Virgil?"

"Look, wise guy, if you think you can do better—"

"We *both* can do better. To be honest, Virgil, your tool bag isn't all that full."

"What the fuck does that mean?"

"You rely on violent confrontation. I admit, it works, most of the time. But this calls for some subtlety. Where is Gosford right now?"

"Home. Eating a plateful of spaghetti for all I know."

"Let's make it our habit to know. Put a man on him. Let's get to know Councilman Gosford. We need leverage, something to compromise him."

"We could pick him up, drug him, and take some pictures with a couple of whores."

"Something more subtle than that, Virgil, but I like your initiative. We play this right, and I'm sure Monsieur Delacroix will make it worth our while, don't you think?"

Virgil wasn't so sure, and he knew Dunne was blowing smoke up his ass; that's what he'd do if the roles were reversed. Still, the prick brought it off fairly well. There were cards yet to be dealt, and he knew he was still in a position to take some off both ends.

Virgil smiled, stood up, and slapped Arlyn on the shoulder. "I knew we'd make a good team. That's why I recommended you to Delacroix. We're both in a good place here, Dunne. Say hello to the wife for me."

Virgil swept out of the room, breathing a sigh of relief while smiling at his inside joke. Meeting with Dunne was like eating Chinese; only with Dunne, after an hour you wondered what it was you had been eating.

Arlyn knocked on the heavy door and was invited in. Reynard was standing in the middle of the room, feet spread, as though he had been speaking to an imaginary audience.

Arlyn was taken aback. "Should I come back?"

"No, no." Reynard waved his hands motioning him to enter. "Glaupher?"

"He's playing us. I don't think he's even spoken to Gosford, though he claims to have had at least one phone conversation with him."

"He's using the phone?"

"Says the Councilman won't meet with him—can't be in public because he can't be seen with Virgil, can't meet in private because he thinks Virgil will kill him."

"That seems to be a common theme when it comes to Lieutenant Glaupher."

"In law enforcement that kind of reputation can be a good thing. Virgil seems to want to take it to the extreme."

"What are we to do, Arlyn?"

"I don't know how much more use he can be to you, Monsieur."

"Has he become a liability?"

"Oh, he's been a liability for some time. The thing is, we're smart enough to make Virgil work for us, even if he's unaware that's what he's doing."

"You're suggesting we give him his leash. He's getting his boat seaworthy, and he indicated that he might be starting runs again as soon as this week. Let's see what we can leverage off the operation before we start thinking about personnel changes."

Reynard did a nifty pirouette and took two steps to the side table, where a decanter and glasses waited. He poured two glasses of aged bourbon and offered one to Arlyn. "I should like to know more about this Emmett Dougal that Glaupher recommended to captain the new boat. Can you do a little snooping for me?"

"Emmett Dougal. You think he's a bad risk? Might take off with the liquor and the boat?"

"No. Noémi has become acquainted with him. She said it was an innocent coincidence, but I'm not so sure. I'd like to know what this character is like, and what he might be up to."

"Consider it done."

"Tell Virgil to set up a meeting with the three of you as soon as possible."

Emmett pulled the cuddy boat up to the public dock and secured the bow and stern lines. Virgil Glaupher was waiting on the dock with Bradley.

"So who's this guy I'm meeting?" Emmett asked when they were heading up First Avenue.

"This guy is someone you don't want to piss off, Dougal." Virgil was sitting in the back like a big shot. He liked being able to watch without being watched himself. "His name is Dunne, late of the Seattle Police Department."

"The department doesn't pay that well, huh?"

Glaupher laughed a bitter laugh. "Ain't that the truth?" He lit a cigarette and felt the nicotine quiet his nerves. This Dougal prick appeared to be as much of a handful as Dunne. Life could be a lot easier if the two of them suddenly no longer existed.

He smiled. Lately his fantasies had been turning more to violence than sex. He could get all the fucking he wanted, but there was a decided lack of physical mayhem available to him. "Anyways, he's watching out for Delacroix's end of things so it would be good for you to keep this guy happy. There's a lot of money to be had here, Dougal. Don't be fucking it up."

He took another drag and wished he had a drink to soothe his throat, but that would have to wait until Dunne was finished with his interrogation of the fisherman.

Arlyn was waiting in his office and stood to greet Emmett when Virgil ushered him in.

"Mr. Dougal," he said, holding out his hand. "I'm Arlyn Dunne. Have a seat. You like a whisky or a cup of coffee?"

Emmett shook his head, taking in the office and Mr. Dunne.

Arlyn turned one of the wingbacks in front of the desk toward the other and they sat down, facing each other. Virgil, who hadn't been invited to sit, took its meaning and excused himself.

"I understand you're a fisherman, Mr. Dougal."

"I am, have been most of my life."

"And this boat you've sold to Lieutenant Glaupher, you came by it legally."

"Yes, I did."

Arlyn nodded. "But you didn't build that boat for fishing, did you?"

"I didn't build the boat." Emmett leaned back in his chair. Typical cop. Why didn't he just come out and ask?

"But you've done this other 'work' before, haven't you?"

Ahh, there it was. "Am I talking to the cops? There sure do seem to be a lot of police involved in this operation. I smell a double-cross here."

Arlyn smiled, shook his head, and leaned back as well. "You have to understand, Mr. Dougal, my job is to protect the interests of my employer. I have no connection, no allegiance, to the Seattle Police Department or any other law enforcement agency. If we are to trust you with our investment, we need to know certain things about you.

"For instance, maybe you don't know this game as well as you think you do. Maybe you'll do something to draw attention to yourself, or take an incorrect course and get nabbed by the Coast Guard. Then, sooner or later, the Prohibition Unit is going to be knocking at our front door. So, it's reasonable to be asking you these questions, isn't it?"

Emmett had to agree with the explanation and nodded.

"So, you're familiar with the transportation of illegal alcohol?"

"Yeah, I've done my share of rum running. Ran the Great Lakes from Thunder Bay to Erie to Toledo, hugged coastlines from the northeast all the way to the Carolinas. I know the do's and don'ts, how to navigate without running lights and, especially, the limits of my boat. I've been shot out of the water twice, but I've never been caught. No one knows my name or my history."

"Well, there's one person."

Emmett realized Dunne had been checking his background. "That's a family matter."

"Obviously. Where does your brother fit into all of this?"

"He doesn't. He knows I fish, but he doesn't know where I live. I'm on good terms with the local law on my side of the water, so outside of his personal beef with me, my brother has nothing to do with my life. I make it a habit to stay out of his backyard."

"You know eventually I'll find something about you that you don't want to be found, right?"

They looked into each other's eyes. They were both at once comfortable and uncomfortable with each other. They understood each other, and how they were very much alike, though their lives had taken much different courses.

"Yes, I suspect you will. But I think that as long as I'm able to deliver on my end, you won't be so enthusiastic about digging that deep, will you?

Arlyn smiled. "Do you spend much time in Seattle, Emmett?"

Now it was *Emmett*. Watch out. "When we come in from the fishing grounds we sell our catch here most of the time, so yes, I do spend some time in the city."

"Saloons, Pioneer Square, whore houses near the waterfront?"

"Didn't realize there would be a morality clause in the contract, Dunne. No, not really. There's a tavern along the waterfront that I stop into, and a cafeteria where they have decent, hot food. But I'm not much one for professional ladies."

"You prefer younger, virginal women then?"

"Look, you can tell your boss that running into his sister was just dumb luck. I wanted some ice cream, they were there, we spoke, and then we met again here in your boss' home. That's all."

"Please take no offense. He's very protective of Noémi, and frankly, he doesn't think that you're a good prospect."

"Not being a good prospect, meaning off-the-rack Filson clothing and the smell of fish. Look, Dunne, I may only be a fisherman, but I'm a hardworking fisherman. I don't beg or steal, and I'm just as good a man as you or your boss."

"You don't find her attractive? You're not interested—?"

"Damn it, of course I'm interested in her—*look at her*! The only men who wouldn't be interested in her would be priests or perverts. Are you saying *you* don't find her attractive?"

Arlyn carefully got up, went to his liquor cart and held the decanter up, eliciting another 'no thank you' from Emmett. He poured himself a good-sized shot. It was refreshing, meeting this man. Virgil had lucked into someone who apparently had the balls to match his brains.

"I think this is going to work out just fine, Emmett. According to Virgil, you know your way around boats and the Sound, and that's good enough for me. You'll get paid by me—by no one else—and only upon delivery. There's one other thing, though. Stay away from the girl."

Emmett stood and they shook hands. They both knew that Emmett was unlikely to follow the last instruction.

Virgil wanted to know everything, and he asked pointed questions as they drove back to the cuddy boat.

"It's just as you said, Lieutenant, down to the letter. You're to get the boat on the water, and I'm to meet an as-yet-unnamed contact above Shoreline, who will take me to the broker in Vancouver. Having seen the determined route, I'll leave the contact in Vancouver and motor over to Monarch Head on Saturna Island. There, a motor launch will meet us after nine pm. We take on our load, head back across, and shadow the leeward side of the Orcas, past Anacortes and into Skagit Bay. All like we discussed. By the way, he thinks very highly of you." Emmett could blow smoke just as well as Virgil.

Of course, none of those particulars had been shared with Dunne, and Virgil could only follow so much of the plan without having it drawn on a chart. To him, it sounded good.

The fact was, based on the little bit of information they had, Emmett was going to have to chart his course at the very last minute, basing his decisions on gut feelings and the amount of ambient light.

"So, when's your man finishing the boat?"

"It's yours to fuel as early as tomorrow. But let me make my calls, line up the goods and the contact. You got a gun?"

"Shotgun. Some fish don't die easy."

Virgil grunted. "Good joke. But I ain't laughing. You're carrying my money, so I insist ..." He passed an army issue .45 automatic into Emmett's hands. "Someone tries to take my money, you shoot the bastard. We clear? This ain't no negotiation, Dougal. This is serious, fucking business. I'll leave a message for you with your neighbor lady. Be sure and check with her. I don't want anything getting lost in translation, we clear?"

Noémi was late. She fiddled with her hair, but she couldn't get it ... right. The clock on her vanity told her she had fifteen minutes to get downtown, and her awful hair was refusing to do what she wanted.

There was a knock at her door. "Come in."

Reynard entered, smiling as he watched her continuing to fuss with a ribbon. "Where's Cozette?"

"She takes this 'day-off' thing too seriously," Noémi said, grimacing for effect.

Reynard stepped behind and took the ribbon from her fingers. He pulled the ribbon tight and tied a careful bow. She turned her head, examining herself. It would do. She stood up.

"Wait a minute, little sister. I want to have a word with you."

"Oh no, Reynard, not another suitor. Can't we just let that rest? And I'm late—"

He patted the bed and she sat down next to him, a bit angry since she would never be on time now. "I'm not in any rush for you to be married, Noémi, but I do want you to be exposed to the kind of gentlemen who will be able to take care of you later on, when you do decide on marriage. You're a prize, Noémi, and not just anyone can claim you."

"I know that, Reynard. Do you think I hold myself in low esteem? That I would be willing to just settle for anyone? That's why I'm not attracted to any of the men that you parade through here. I'm not willing to just 'settle.'"

"Good enough. But you won't mind if I occasionally invite some business associates, who I think you might find interesting, over for dinner?"

"Of course not. But being interested and falling in love aren't the same thing, Reynard."

"Perhaps not. I shall try to control my matchmaking. But on those rare occasions that I do introduce you to someone, I would hope you could feign some outward interest, and show some level of civility."

"You practiced this speech, didn't you?"

"You're the most important thing in the world to me, *ma chéri*. You are my entire family. I only want the best for you."

She stood and kissed him on his forehead. "I know you do. I'm late."

He watched her sweep out of the room, always the centerpiece, always the glue that held his world together.

Noémi was going to have lunch with her friend, Elsie, who was bringing her beau. Elsie was a local girl, a college graduate of the University of Washington, whom Noémi had come to know through mutual work at a charity. Elsie was an attractive, balanced young woman that Noémi liked. Elsie wasn't one of her college chums, which made the relationship special. It represented the new, adult chapter of their lives.

Noémi was excited to meet Elsie's beau, and she imagined he would be attractive—obviously—well bred, and educated. A young man with promise: the kind of man that Reynard wanted her to have. So far, none of those candidates had shown any level of promise, so she wanted to see what kind of man would turn Elsie's head.

They had reserved a table in the restaurant of one of the better hotels. Noémi was shown to the dining room, where she saw Elsie and her young man seated in a corner booth, away from the other diners. Her hat and coat were taken and she was escorted to the table.

The young man stood with a smile on his face and stepped out from the booth to greet her. His hands were warm, but they weren't the soft hands of a banker: they were calloused. He was a pleasant young man, round of face with a ready smile. He had good teeth and was well-mannered.

Noémi seated herself next to Elsie and across from the young man, who introduced himself as "Philip, but you can call me Phil." Elsie fairly beamed each time she looked back at him when he said something.

The lunch was good and the conversation was pleasant, forming around family news and local political gossip. Finally, Noémi got up the nerve to ask Philip his business.

"I'm a machinist," he said. "I have a small shop on the south end. Mostly agricultural, but I've done some marine work as well. Do you know anything about milling or fabricating, Miss Delacroix?"

"Absolutely nothing."

"Don't get him started," Elsie said, playfully tapping at Philip's shoulder. "He lives and dies with his work."

"I wouldn't say that," he protested. "I spend most of my time thinking about you." He leaned slightly forward and puckered his lips, making the ladies laugh.

"Have you met Elsie's family yet?"

That was apparently a sore point, because both of them remained silent for a few moments.

"We're … waiting for the right time. It doesn't really matter, Noémi, we're both of age. We don't need our parents' consent."

"But surely you must announce it to them so that plans for your wedding can begin."

Elsie scooted over and grabbed Philip's arm. "We think we'll elope. Maybe San Francisco … " she kissed him quickly on his lips. "There's something romantic about San Francisco."

"It does sound romantic. Eloping, though? My brother would have an apoplectic fit if I did something like that."

"It's your life, Noémi, not Reynard's. And this is our life, not our parents'."

"So, you're going to tell them? Before you do it?"

"I don't know. Maybe not. I know it'll hurt Mother's feelings, but Daddy won't like Philip at all, I know it. Daddy's just too East Coast. He brought his blue blood with him, in huge barrels it seems. He has always said he would have the last word on my husband, and when I was a child that seemed to be a good thing. Now, I know it's not."

Noémi caught a cab after parting from Elsie and Philip and it deposited her at her home at the same time that Cozette was climbing the last few yards to the house at the top of the hill.

Noémi waited for her as Cozette caught her breath. "Did you have a nice day out?"

"Indeed, I did. Lunch by myself, and a movie. A nice break from the theatrics."

Noémi grasped Cozette by the arm and steered her toward the front porch. "Speaking of theatrics, there's going to be a full three acts at the Burroughs house."

"Why's that?"

"Elsie's going to *elope*!"

Cozette snickered. "Good for her."

"But won't it be a scandal?"

Cozette took out her key, unlocked the door, and waited for Noémi to enter before she followed. "Not in this day and age, unless the chap's reputation is particularly bad, or he's broke. Which is it?"

"I don't believe either, Cozette. But he's a machinist, whatever that is. He works with his hands."

"Lots of men work with their hands, Noémi, and make a good living at it. I don't suppose your friend is going to go without."

"But elopement."

"Saves a lot of bother, if you ask me." Cozette took their coats and hung them in the hall closet. "Let's get some tea. You can tell me all about it. Where are they going, for instance? I hear Arizona is very popular for these sorts of things."

"Where would you hear something like that?"

BUSTING ANGEL'S CHERRY

Angel tied the cuddy boat up to a nearby dock while Emmett began his inspection of the completed boat. The top deck, made of laminated plywood, was painted a dull gray, with several heavy coats of marine varnish. It was solid and well finished. The flying bridge had all new gauges, and dual-throttle controls were mounted in the center console. Jackie had even gone so far as to install ribbed floor decking to provide better footing in choppy seas.

It was a very nice job. There was no name, no port of origin on the stern, nothing that could identify the boat at all. If the Coast Guard got close enough to see a name, they would have already deduced that the vessel's cargo was, no doubt, contraband.

The fuel tanks had been topped off, but there was only room for a couple of jerry cans of additional gas. The rest of the space was already allocated, and designed to hold up to two hundred cases of liquor.

Angel whistled when he stood on the catwalk above the boat to do his inspection. He had been in the bottle for most of the past two days, and Emmett was worried whether Angel would be able to do the job. As the Indian climbed down into the boat, Emmett stepped forward and liberated the pint bottle of rye that Angel had stashed in an inside pocket.

"Hey!"

"Hey is right. No more drinking for a while. I need you, Angel. Getting sloshed is not going to help out. I'll hang onto this for a while. You'll get it back once we get to Vancouver."

Angel wanted to protest, but he knew Emmett was right. He shook his head in an attempt to clear the cobwebs. He rechecked the shotgun and counted the shells before placing it in a rack below the throttles. He straightened a pile of burlap sacks which they would use for additional packing when the cases were loaded. A paper sack held a half dozen beef and cheese sandwiches for the trip.

They were ready. Emmett climbed out of the boat and went outside the boat shed to wait for Glaupher. Angel sat in the boat and smoked, methodically rolling one cigarette after another.

Finally, as the last vestiges of dusk receded, Glaupher's Buick pulled up. Glaupher and his sergeant, Bradley, were alone, the latter bearing a small, brown suitcase. When they walked up to Emmett, Bradley opened it to display a full case of money: ten-dollar bills divided into stacks with rubber bands.

"That's five thousand dollars, Dougal. Do you have your gun?"

Emmett pulled back his coat to show the weapon tucked inside his belt. The gun was going forward into the hold once they were out on the water. He was not going to pull a gun on the Coast Guard. He wasn't that stupid.

"Good. You'll pick up your contact at Tulalip Bay. You know the place, right?"

"I know where it is, I've just never been in there."

"Well, that's where he'll be. He'll park near the spit and flash his car lights when he hears your approach. He's expecting you around nine-thirty, so that gives you four hours to get up there."

"We'll likely have to get past a few Coast Guard vessels to get there, Lieutenant. Is he gonna wait if we get held up for any reason?"

"I'll call him and tell him to be prepared to wait, if that makes you feel better."

"Well, it hardly does either of us any good if we get up there and our road map isn't available."

Glaupher nodded. "Okay, the boat's fueled. Better get your asses on the road."

Bradley laughed. "Road. Ocean."

"Shut the hell up."

It was dark with cloudy skies. The moon was in its first quarter, so even if there weren't clouds there would have been too little light to stand them out on the horizon. The other boats making their way into Seattle and farther south to Commencement Bay were all well-lit, and Emmett stayed well clear of all of them, slowing to compromise any opportunity to make out their silhouette.

By eight-thirty they were through Possession Sound and past Everett. There was little marine traffic in this part of the Sound this late in the evening, and Emmett opened the throttles to give the engines a chance to stretch their legs. The engines were loud, even with the holds closed and secure.

By nine, they were cruising along the Sound side of the spit at Tulalip Bay. As they slowed and turned into the bay, a car's lights turned on and off three times. Emmett shined his floodlights briefly on the car before slowing the boat and heading the bow into the sandy beach.

A man ran down the sand, waded into the water, and took Angel's hand up into the boat. The man instructed Emmett to flash his light once more, and after doing so they watched the car turn and drive back up the spit.

"Name's McElroy." In the dim light on the bridge they could see he was a barrel of a man, though barely five and a half feet tall. "You must be Dougal."

"This is Angel. You're gonna show us the back alley route to Vancouver?"

"Yep, and we'll jump a few fences along the way."

When Angel looked worried McElroy laughed. "Just kidding, Angel. If there was enough light, you could see some beautiful countryside. Our course takes us in and around the islands and makes tracking us that much more difficult. Plus this course doesn't take us into the path of any six-bitters. They tend to be heavily armed."

Emmett and McElroy looked at a chart of the Sound, and McElroy traced the proposed course with his finger. Emmett nodded. He knew the difficulty of navigating without light, particularly on sea-lanes with which he wasn't familiar. It was good they had McElroy.

It took them another hour and a half to carefully navigate the length of Skagit Bay and to cross through Deception Pass. During their transit they saw only the odd fishing boat at rest for the night. After they were back out on the open Sound, they cruised between Cypress and Guemes Islands and circled behind Lummi in their approach to the Canadian border.

McElroy seemed to know the schedule the Coast Guard and RCN were on, so they encountered no vessel that might have an interest in them when they crossed the Strait. By twelve-thirty they had dropped anchor between Galiano and Gossip Island, and Angel rowed McElroy to shore so he could walk down to Sturdles Bay—maybe a half mile—to call his contact in Vancouver.

The three of them spent the night on the beach, fighting a light drizzle with a good-sized fire. They shared Angel's pint and ate the last of the beef and cheese sandwiches before curling up under the shoreline firs to grab some sleep.

They sat on the beach all the next day, waiting for nightfall. They could depart before dusk, but crossing the Strait had to be quick so that they could load and start their return trip.

Angel was becoming more rattled. The pint had long since been exhausted, and there wouldn't be any more alcohol until they were finished loading for the return trip. He scratched his thick shock of black hair and rubbed at his face. “I need a drink, Emmett,” he said.

“I noticed. We don’t have anything to drink but water. You want some of that?”

Angel’s look was his response. Finally, he walked down the inlet and around onto the main part of Galiano.

McElroy, reclining on a wood pallet he had found and covered with fresh fir branches, watched him go. “Is he going to be okay?”

“In the bigger picture, I don’t know. For tonight, yeah, he’ll be okay. He just lost someone important to him. He’s getting used to it, that’s all.”

The afternoon passed and Angel remained gone. When the light began to die, the two men began to get worried. Maybe he had gotten lost, or maybe he was hurt. Either way, they had to find him before they pulled anchor.

They walked back down the inlet. McElroy went north to search the beach, and Emmett headed south toward Sturdles Bay. He hadn’t gone more than a hundred yards when he could see a dark figure running toward him. Before the figure closed the distance, Emmett could hear the hoarse breathing of a man who was just about spent.

“Emmett? Thank god, run!”

There were lights less than a hundred yards away, bobbing as those who carried the flashlights made their way across rough terrain. They were heading toward the spot where Angel and Emmett stood.

Emmett turned and ran, making sure that Angel could keep up. They made it back to the dinghy and jumped in, rowing across the inlet and up the coast, looking for McElroy.

When Emmett finally got his attention the crowd was running up the beach toward McElroy, and he had to wade out into chest-deep water where they could haul him into the boat. Then Angel took the oars of the dinghy and powered them through the water to the gray ghost of a boat.

When Angel shipped the oars, Emmett noticed a dark stain where Angel had been gripping them.

After they started the engines, they idled around the point and headed north into the Strait of Georgia. They had ten miles of open water to cross, and it was still early.

"What the hell was that all about?" demanded McElroy.

"Asshole called me a fuckin' Injun."

"Where were you that you would have a conversation like that?" asked Emmett, knowing.

"Went to get a drink. Had two, maybe three. Started a conversation. Asshole asked what I was doing on Galiano. When I didn't tell him something, things got nasty. I may've hit him with a glass, I don't remember. My hand cut pretty bad."

It was true: blood was still dripping onto the deck.

"Wrap that up, Angel. Jesus, what the hell is the matter with you? We've got a job to do, and you're out stirring up the locals. Well, they saw our boat. Let's hope they don't contact the Coast Guard just to get even."

"We're in Canada. We ain't doin' anything wrong," replied Angel.

"Yeah, well, the moment we cross back into US water, the Coast Guard will have something to say about it. Goddamn it, Angel, get below. I'm tired of looking at you."

Angel retreated like a whipped dog. He lurked in the forward compartment below deck until they idled into West Vancouver, where they were scheduled to make their pickup.

The exchange went smoothly. The bill for the booze was made out to a fictitious import company in Mexico, and Emmett handed over the suitcase to the Canadian broker. The liquor was loaded and secured by the broker's men and they were back out on the open water by nine o'clock. McElroy didn't join them. "Your man blew it, Emmett. I ain't riding on no floating target. The Coast Guard is likely waiting just below the 49th, hoping you stray just a bit too close to the line of demarcation. I'll find a way to the border and cross by foot. Maybe I'll see you on another trip. Good luck."

Angel listened to the conversation and was ashamed. He felt bad and, without Emmett noticing, opened one of the bottles of bonded scotch and took two long pulls. He immediately felt a surge of confidence and took another swig. He took the wheel from Emmett, who spread the map on the chart table. Under the dim cabin light, he read aloud their planned course. "We head back across and follow the shoreline of Galiano to its southern point, continue past Saturna Island, and hole up in the shallows between Tumbo Island and Saturna. We'll make our dash after midnight."

He could smell the liquor on Angel's breath, but he didn't care. He was going to get this shipment to Delacroix come hell or high water.

They dropped anchor in less than twelve feet of water off the southern edge of Tumbo. If Angel drank more, he did it surreptitiously, and he behaved himself, limiting his share of the conversation to "uh-huh" and "okay." They ran a hotplate off the electrical system and made some coffee and oatmeal. Angel drank his coffee black and took watch while Emmett snagged a catnap, stretched out on the remaining burlap bags.

When Angel shook him it was just after midnight.

"See anything?"

"Stars for a while, but clouded back up. Nothing passed in the Strait I could see."

"Let's go. Put everything you might need in easy reach. No lights except on the compass."

They edged back out onto the open water, holding back at first, but then allowing the big aviation engines to open up. The vibrations from the engines could be felt through the entire vessel. The deep V-hull plowed through the short swell with no problem, and Emmett soon figured they were cruising well past twenty-five knots.

Angel went forward and sat down near the bow, leaning against the bow railing, watching for debris or any telltale lights on the horizon. Out on the Strait of Juan de Fuca there would be freighters coming and going, but they were too far north of the shipping lanes to see those ships. Up here, they might encounter fishermen, but the vessels they were on the watch for were also on the watch for them. Angel relished the feel of the moist salt air rushing past his face, and was forced to squint each time their boat plowed through a larger swell.

They passed the headlands at Lummi Island, ducking into Hale Passage, relieved to be off the open ocean and into waters that the Coast Guard rarely patrolled. But once they had progressed farther down the Sound, between Guemes and Cypress Island, they began to get nervous. From that point the Coast Guard patrolled ceaselessly, for there were specific landing points ranging from Anacortes to Olympia that provided the easiest or most convenient ingress of illegal liquor into the barrooms and parlors of the northwest.

The moment they left the shelter of the channel between Guemes and Cypress, they picked up a light on the horizon. Emmett took his binoculars and scanned the light. It wasn't a freighter; the boat wasn't big enough to be a freighter. Who else would be out on the water at two-thirty in the morning besides a freighter or the law?

He altered his course and hugged the coast in Langley Bay, but above Biz Point he began to question his own judgment and that of McElroy. He had planned to cut through Desolation Pass again, but he remembered Glaupher mentioning that he lost the *Marionette* inside the pass after a pursuit. The likelihood that the Coast Guard was camped inside the Pass, or waiting in Skagit Bay, was slight.

Nonetheless, he changed his mind and course, deciding instead to run the windward side of Whidbey and take his chances on the open water. He knew the engines were loud enough to be heard on shore, so the farther he kept from the small communities that dotted the coastline, the better.

Port Townsend was going to be the trick. The Coast Guard kept several smaller cutters stationed there, and the passage between Whidbey and Port Townsend was no more than three miles. Someone at the station was bound to hear his Liberty engines and get the word to a cutter already on station. It could likely be a horse race once he went through that channel.

"Gonna get hairy," he said to Angel. Angel's response was to produce a bottle and take a pull before handing it to Emmett. Emmett swallowed some of the whisky and shook his head.

"Gonna get fun." Angel said and took back the bottle, holding it against his chest. "How fast this thing go, you think?"

"We'll probably find out. It's gonna start getting light in less than two hours. No time to stop and chat with those cutters."

They ran without incident until they passed the Point Wilson lighthouse. The keeper had to have heard the Libertys, because Emmett was throwing caution to the wind. He had opened the throttles so that the boat was plowing through the water in excess of thirty knots.

That question was answered when they could hear a siren on a cutter well in their wake as they passed Indian Island on their way into the inner Sound. The chase was on. No doubt telephones were ringing in Kingston, Bremerton, and Seattle. There would also be more Coast Guard moving to locations that they expected Emmett to pass. He had no options now: only running full out and hoping to not be seen.

In the dim light and cloudy conditions, being heard was the only thing that would get them caught, but slowing to an idle would be foolhardy. They were married to the boat's speed, and only speed was going to save them.

Emmett opened the throttles all the way and the boat surged forward, tracking easily on the smoother water of the Sound. They passed Kingston, wary of a Coast Guard ambush, but could see that their pursuit was coming from the east at Edmonds. Perhaps they had been following, or nabbing, a rumrunner along that side of the Sound.

It didn't matter; the Coast Guard cutters couldn't do more than 22-25 knots full out, and they had nothing on which to fire. The floodlights couldn't find them and, as they left the cutters in their wake, they could see flashing lights stabbing the horizon in a vain search for the loud but otherwise undetectable boat.

They were lucky; or, perhaps, the Coast Guard just wasn't as well organized as they should have been. They were able to speed further down the Sound, even passing a freighter that seemed parked in the water by comparison. That was probably the highlight of the night for that crew, and Emmett would have loved to read the captain's log entry, probably something to the effect: "unknown vessel passed starboard at high speed."

Once inside Elliott Bay, Emmett eased back the throttles and idled the last couple of miles into the Duwamish. Within minutes they had idled the boat inside the shed, shut the doors, and switched off the engines.

They were alone. It would be a couple of hours before they would call Dunne or Glaupher.

"Kid built a hell of a boat, didn't he?" asked Angel. "The old man would be proud."

At six-thirty Emmett rang Arlyn. "Got your goods," was all he said and hung up.

An hour later, Arlyn and Virgil showed up at the shed and went inside, closing the door behind them. They turned on the shed's lights and smiled.

Angel and Emmett had unloaded a fair number of cases, stacking them along the catwalk so that it was difficult to walk past. Virgil walked the line of cases, counting.

"There's still a couple dozen cases forward, Lieutenant. We were kinda tired of stooping and lifting."

Virgil smiled. "I got somebody who can do the lifting. Good job, boys." They watched him counting on his fingers, determining how much money was going into his pocket.

"Any trouble?" Arlyn asked, handing an envelope to Emmett. He was looking at the blood-soaked rag wrapped around Angel's hand.

"Naw, he just cut his hand loading the crates in too much of a hurry. Jitters."

"Too much of a hurry can get a body killed these days," said Arlyn.

He looked at Emmett again. "Nobody saw you?"

"Nobody saw us, but probably several hundred people *heard* us. We need to rig mufflers for these engines before we do that again. You've got a powerful boat there, Dunne. It didn't quibble one bit about the swells or waves that cluttered the course."

"Good enough. Take a few days off, and I'll be in touch." When Emmett was about to turn away, Arlyn laid a hand onto his shoulder. "Listen, Dougal, don't trust that guy," he said, nodding toward Virgil.

"I made him the first time I saw him, Dunne."

Emmett opened the envelope and counted thirty fifty-dollar bills. They were good to their word.

Angel and Emmett stopped at a market near the docks and bought three boxes of groceries and four one-gallon cans of yellow house paint. Angel had refilled his pint bottle from one of the bottles in the shipment, with the express approval of Virgil, who took the remainder of the bottle with him.

Angel and Emmett were immensely relieved that they had survived their first run. When the cuddy boat was nearing their dock they both began laughing, beginning to believe that they had been successful.

"Busted my cherry," Angel noted. "That a new one for me."

The next day the *Aberdeen* was back home and in one piece. Emmett hoped that Urquhart was smiling on them.

DOUBLE CROSSINGS

Councilman Gosford's calendar had been pleasantly overflowing for the past month, ever since he had stepped on the plans for a hotel and restaurant that everyone knew was only a front for a speakeasy. At least, that's how he described his motivations when he spoke to a gathering at a meeting of the Women's Christian Temperance Union.

The hall was filled, mostly by women, and was raucous as the Seattle chairwoman went through the motions of opening the evening. When she introduced Gosford, there was a loud round of applause as he walked to the dais. There, not even needing his prepared notes, he ran through the litany of vices that were hounding the proper growth of the community, and how he intended to address each and every vice.

"Mr. Delacroix is not a bad man. Quite the contrary. He is a good man who employs people and helps fund many improvements in and around the city. My goal is not to punish him, but simply not to reward him for those things that he does wrong. We ought not to be thinking of more opportunities for people to numb themselves, but applying ourselves to establishing the tools that will invigorate our youthful city, such as more schools, libraries, and churches."

He was singing into the maw of an overly emotional choir, and he hit all the right notes. Time and again loud applause interrupted him, and he allowed their fervor to sweep over him like a warm, gentle breeze. He was in his element: he was on familiar turf, and these women were easy political pickings.

After he finished speaking, he took a few questions and answers, and other spiteful inquiries that he diplomatically dodged.

Afterward, enjoying a cup of punch but wishing for something much stronger, a half dozen women approached Gosford, all who sought to touch him or gather some words of praise from him.

One of the women, in her late-forties perhaps, was particularly attractive. In her heels she was only a couple inches shorter than Gosford. Her makeup was tasteful, and highlighted her cheekbones. She was wearing a conservative, but very stylish, black dress, decked out in a fox stole and several pieces of very expensive-looking jewelry. He asked each of them their names, starting at the opposite end of the group, quickly forgetting each name until this dark beauty offered hers.

"Margaret Gardner," she said, "Mrs. Margaret Gardner." She offered her hand for him to kiss. "Actually from Portland. But I—*we've*—heard so much about you. I admire you so much," she said, looking him directly in the eye.

"I am honored," he said, feeling almost faint. He continued to hold her hand for another few seconds before it became awkward.

The group went through the motions of chitchat for a few minutes. Then it began to break up, until there was only Gosford and Mrs. Margaret Gardner.

"Would you care for a drink. Some tea, perhaps?" he asked, expecting to be turned down and forgetting where he was.

"I'd love one," she said.

Later, in her hotel room, he took his time with her, and she seemed to know every move he was about to make, from helping her out of her dress and slip to freeing those magnificent breasts from her bra.

Two men burst into the room, one with a Speed Graphic flash

camera to capture the Councilman *in flagrante delicto*.

While he was hurriedly dressing Gosford angrily swore at her. "That's probably not even your goddamn name is it?"

She was putting her clothes back on, oblivious to the photographer and Sergeant Bradley, who stood behind her.

"Whatever my name is, it isn't mud, Councilman."

"The good Councilman is going to review his previous decision regarding support, and will be glad to sponsor a new request for variance."

Arlyn waited for Reynard's response. But his employer was hardly jumping for joy. Instead, he folded his hands together in his lap, as if he were about to begin praying.

"It would have been better for everyone if he had just lived up to his word. Now, his political career will always remain tenuous at best. He'll be of some use as long as he remains on the council, but I suspect Mr. Gosford is going to find new enthusiasm, outside of politics, for his business."

Arlyn set a bottle of Johnnie Walker on Reynard's desk.

"I see it went well." After the first run went off without any reported hitches, Reynard was satisfied that the operation was sound, and turned his attention strictly toward the money end, allowing Arlyn and Virgil to oversee the enterprise.

Arlyn removed the cork and poured a couple drams into two glasses. "Yes, the second run also went smoothly, although, according to Dougal, the engines are still too loud, even in the middle of the Sound. Virgil's mechanic is testing some oil drums …"

"And Virgil?"

"Got the job done with Gosford, and obviously hired a decent running crew."

"Have you learned anything further about this Dougal?"

"Only that his brother is the sheriff on Vashon Island, and has sworn out a warrant for Dougal's arrest."

"Really? For what?"

"Assault on a police officer. Smacked his brother. Won't stand up in court, though. Obviously, a Cain and Abel."

"Oh, brothers." Reynard sipped the whisky and wrinkled his nose. "Couldn't the supplier in Vancouver get any Black Label?"

"We're kinda a captive market, boss."

Reynard smiled. Arlyn had grown a great deal during the months of his employ. He always deferred to Reynard's decisions, but wasn't afraid to offer his opinions, sometimes in caustic fashion.

"Ask Virgil to inquire of his supplier. We'll require the best in the bar."

"When do you dig the first shovelful?"

"Within two months, if Gosford and the Council follow through."

"You're going to be busy for a while."

Reynard sipped at the scotch and nodded. "And so will you. There are several issues that we'll need to resolve over the next couple of months. First, I want you to recruit a replacement for Virgil."

Arlyn nodded, he knew this was coming. Glaupher had long since grown familiarly contemptible. Whatever value he had could be replaced by the recruitment of any of a half-dozen hungry squad lieutenants around the force. Glaupher had become more of a gangster and less of a cop over the past three months, and the change was beginning to wear on Reynard.

Arlyn was ambivalent. He didn't like Glaupher, but he had no axe to grind. Glaupher was just another greedy bully with a badge. One was pretty much like another. "Any suggestions as to how to resolve that problem?" he asked Reynard, but he knew what the answer would be.

"That's your department."

Virgil looked decidedly uncomfortable as the maître d' took his overcoat and fedora. He was escorted through the restaurant, grimacing and nodding at a couple of acquaintances, to a booth at the back corner. Mary Elizabeth had reserved this very table, at this very time, so that he would have to run the social gauntlet.

"Is this too public for you, baby?" she asked sarcastically as he sat down. She lit a Caporal and took a sip of red wine. She was enjoying his nervousness.

"We could have met at the hotel and had a long chat."

"With no clothes on, right." She watched him fumble for his cigarettes.

"We both know what we want."

"Not anymore, Virgil. That's what this is about. I wanted to meet in public because I know you. I know how you get when things don't go your way, and this is not going your way. We're done. I won't see you anymore."

"Sure you will. You're tired of that prick, and we both know it. You're gonna miss what I can deliver, and you're gonna call me."

She took a drag and stubbed out her cigarette. "Think what you like, Virgil. It was fun while it lasted, but it's over. Good bye."

She stood to leave and he blocked her path. She looked pointedly past him, and he could feel the approach of the maître d'.

"Is there something wrong?"

Before Virgil could say that no, there wasn't anything wrong, Mary Elizabeth said loudly, "I have to leave. The gentleman will take care of the bill."

She pushed past him to exit the restaurant. Virgil quickly collected his overcoat and handed the maître d' a ten dollar bill.

"Hold on, sister!" he said as he followed her onto the sidewalk. He grabbed her by the arm, hurting her with his clenched fingers.

"Stop it!" she cried.

He stepped back, aware of other people walking along the street. His anger was rising, but he was smart enough to realize that a police lieutenant accosting a married woman during the downtown noon rush could result in disastrous consequences.

"You'll call, Mary Elizabeth. No woman quits me!"

Mary Elizabeth thought that closing the door of the taxi was effectively closing the door on Virgil Glaupher.

Though he rarely saw her undressed anymore, Arlyn happened to catch Mary Elizabeth changing into her nightgown that evening, and saw the black and blue bruising on the back of her arm.

"Holy cow, how did you do that?"

Mary Elizabeth was caught off guard. She hadn't even considered the fact that her arm was bruised, much less that Arlyn might see it. She had no story for the bruise, other than the real one. "I got grabbed," she offered.

"I can see *that.* By who?"

Mary Elizabeth realized that she was at the wrong end of a lie. "It was Virgil."

"GLAUPHER? Why would Glaupher have need to grab you like that?"

"I slipped on the steps with some packages, he was just helping me—I might have broken my neck, Arlyn!"

"What was Virgil doing here?"

"He was looking for you."

"You've worked that one already, M.E. It's not gonna slide this time. What the hell is going on with you and Glaupher?"

She hesitated, moving slowly to the other side of the bed, carefully choosing her words.

"He's infatuated with me."

Arlyn shook his head, and then rubbed his forehead with the heels of his hands. "Define 'infatuated,' M.E. What does that mean? A Valentine's Day card?"

M.E. steeled herself. She was reminded of her mother's endorsement of Arlyn as a man who didn't drink and wouldn't hit her. She hoped that last part was right. "We were intimate once—"

Arlyn stormed out.

Emmett and Angel's shakedown cruise of the *Aberdeen* took them across the Sound to Seattle, where they tied her up to show her off. Maakinen's crew had painted her inside and out, buffed out the brass, and re-varnished all the deck hatches.

Angel said he was going to go check out the cafeteria and take in a movie, but Emmett knew where the Indian was really going. "It's eleven. Be back here at seven tonight. You'll be okay? You'll remember? You won't make me come looking for you, will you?"

Angel looked pained. "I may get gassed, but I don't puke, and don't pass out. I'll be on boat by seven. Don't *you* get lost, white man."

Angel fairly sprinted up the steps to the street level and was gone within half a minute.

Emmett made sure everything was secure, and then walked five blocks to a trolley stop that would take him up First Hill. The morning clouds were breaking down, allowing bright shafts of light to angle across the city.

He was about to get on the trolley when Noémi and Cozette exited the car. All three of them stood staring at each other for a moment.

"Miss Delacroix … ma'am." He stepped back, to allow them space to pass. It was awkward, but he had been expecting awkward if he did, in fact, run into Noémi. In a way, he had taken this route with the hope that a chance meeting might occur.

"Mr. Dougal, what a pleasant surprise."

"Surprise, indeed," said Cozette who situated herself between the couple. "What brings you to our neck of the woods, sir?"

"I, we, just berthed our boat, and I thought I'd take a look around this part of town." It was lame, but the women humored him. "Where are you two ladies headed? May I tag along?"

Noémi turned to her chaperone, hoping that Emmett's request would be granted. Cozette's instinct was to tell him to move along, but Noémi had already sidled next to Emmett. Cozette looked at her charge, now a full-grown woman, and how she responded to this man. She looked at her watch brooch and made up her mind.

"Two hours. You two have until one o'clock. You can go get some lunch somewhere. You *do* have enough money to feed her, don't you?"

Emmett nodded and Noémi took his hand, leading him away from Cozette without another word. Cozette watched the retreating young woman and realized that her role as Noémi's surrogate mother was nearing an end. She smiled as she watched the couple walk away from her, their hands entwined, oblivious to the surrounding world.

Cozette knew that Reynard would have a fit. But Noémi's happiness was more important than Reynard's. Big brother was going to have to face living without his pet sooner or later. She turned back in her original direction, but then had to decide where she would go on her own.

Noémi and Emmett ate at a diner on Broad Street. The place was packed and filled with smoke. Workers from the waterfront, small industrial concerns in the Mercer-Republic neighborhood, and retail stores were crammed into the small space, all seemingly happy to be there. The din of conversation made their exchanges difficult, but Noémi was absolutely beaming, being allowed to be "alone" with this mystery man. She ate a grilled cheese sandwich with gusto, something new for her, and laughed at how he nervously consumed his soup.

When they were done they were happy to be back outside, if for no other reason than that they could once again join hands and playfully bump hips as they walked.

"Want to see where I work?" he asked. She nodded. He flagged a taxi, and they were driven down to the waterfront where the *Aberdeen* was berthed. Noémi looked at the line of boats and immediately picked out his. The *Aberdeen* shone bright in new paint, untouched by the inevitable rust marks that would accumulate during service.

Emmett helped her to board and gently held her elbow as he took her on the cook's tour. She admired the gauges and controls on the bridge, asking how things worked, and enjoyed the carefully chosen words he used to describe and explain everything.

"This is *your* boat?"

He nodded. "Well, half mine. I have a partner in crime named Angel. Perhaps you'll meet him."

He showed her the forward bunks, still amazed at the transformation that Maakinen's crew had achieved. The smell of fresh paint wasn't overly pleasing, but it was an improvement to the usual stale stench. With the little light that came in from the overhead hatch cover or the small portholes, the hold was not simply habitable, but attractive. Maakinen had replaced the old bunk mattresses with new ones, and even included some small pillows.

Maakinen was a class act, Emmett thought; the Finn hadn't increased his fee, despite the extra work. Emmett would make it up to him.

Noémi was intrigued that such large people could inhabit such a small space.

"We're not out on pleasure cruises, or to get a good night's sleep. What time we spend in the rack is just to get needed rest in a hurry. But it's fairly comfortable. Try it."

She looked at him quizzically, wondering at his intentions. But the look on his face was one of pride, of wanting to share something that he truly loved, so she tentatively sat on the edge of one of the mattresses while he sat down on the other.

"See? You'd be amazed at how good that thin mattress feels when you've been working a deck for twelve hours."

She leaned back and played with the small wall-mounted electric lamp. He answered her question before it was even posed. "No, not for reading. Just so we don't bump our heads in heavy seas."

"You actually come down here when the boat is getting tossed about?"

He looked around the small space. "You get used to it. Sometimes it becomes your whole world when outside, the ocean is trying to sink you. I once crewed on a freighter when the weather was so bad that we lost cargo overboard, because it was just too dangerous to go out on deck, even with a lifeline, to secure things. Course, that was a big boat, much bigger than this one, and when the weather gets that bad out here on the Sound, everyone just stays in bed, or so it seems.

"The thing is, it's trust. No one could leave the wheel in bad weather and go below to rest if they thought the guy taking the wheel couldn't get the job done. Angel and me have been through hard weather enough times that we know the other won't get us killed. At least, not intentionally." He laughed.

She watched him while he talked: his eyes traveled slowly about his surroundings, resting briefly on her before rescanning the interior. Whatever doubt she had felt about this man—this man with whom she had been alone for little more than an hour—evaporated in that moment. Emmett was inherently good: his language simple but engaging, his eyes honest, almost brutally so; and his touch was magnetic.

She knew this emotion. She had courted it, waited on it, longed for it her entire life, but its intense and sudden arrival surprised her. Emmett was a man of strength, but his was unlike the brute power paraded by many men with whom she had become acquainted while living in the same home as Reynard. She smiled at the comparison, and Emmett took the smile as a response to his anecdote.

"You aren't around women much, are you?" she asked, cocking her head and looking him in the eye.

"You mean, as in courting?" He looked down. "There have been women in my life, of course. But, you mean as showing up with flowers and sitting on porches? No, none of that. I'm sorry if I'm not going about this right."

She touched him lightly on the knee and he jumped, surprising them both. They laughed, and he knew he was doing all right. He leaned forward and took her hands in both of his. "May I ask you something?"

"What?"

He leaned forward and brushed his lips across hers. In that brief moment he could taste her lipstick and smell her hair. In that brief moment he captured her heart.

He leaned back and waited for a reaction, but she just opened her eyes and looked at him.

"You didn't understand the question?" He quickly leaned forward and repeated the kiss, tracing her lips with his, parting her mouth, and tasting her.

They stood simultaneously and embraced in an awkward, mad dance within the tight space. Her hands held his head while he mouthed her neck, allowing herself to be immersed by his passion.

She allowed him to undress her. He was unfamiliar with the number of undergarments she wore, and the way they were secured. She enjoyed his frustration for a few moments, but grew impatient and finished removing her clothing. She stood naked in the cabin, showing herself to him. Her hair had fallen down to her shoulders, and her full breasts were heaving due to her excitement.

His gaze wandered over her beautiful body. His eyes met hers. He undressed and she joined him on one of the bunks, lying side by side. It was cold, so he pulled a wool blanket over them and they spent time enjoying the warmth and each other.

He took his time exploring her: imprinting her fine features, feeling the texture of her skin on her belly. Their mouths had become more than casual acquaintances, and they sought each other out to punctuate the lovemaking. He drew his lips across her taut nipples, making her shiver, and whispered his way along the nape of her neck while cradling her in his muscular arms.

When there was a brief pause, Noémi rested her hands on his forearms, unsure of what to do. He consumed her. It was intoxicating.

In the midst of the passion, Emmett knew that their union was compelled by something much greater than sex. The act of kissing, simply kissing, was as rewarding as the orgasm he experienced a half hour later. It was a metaphysical joining that he had not previously experienced.

They lay there naked under the blanket, propped up by the pillows and sharing a cup of coffee that he'd brewed. She liked the gentle rocking of the boat.

"We're in trouble," she said.

He looked out the porthole toward the dock, but she shook her head. "Reynard will never allow this."

"It's too late," replied Emmett, tracing his fingers around a nipple.

"No, you don't understand. There's more to this than you and me. He's been a balancing act for too long. Everything seems too … interconnected for him, and he's seemingly incapable of separating the many parts of his life from each other. I'm to marry someone that he feels is worthy of me. Someone who is worthy of Reynard. You'll never do."

"I'm as good as any man Reynard has ever met."

"Not in his eyes. Even Reynard isn't good enough for me, in his eyes. His idea of an acceptable suitor has to be someone with pedigree, someone connected. An aristocrat."

"You're right, that's not me. So what? I don't have all the money in the world, but I have a home, I have this boat, and there's a few dollars in the bank. I can take care of you, Noémi. Maybe not in First Hill fashion, but in fashion enough."

"That's not the point. And aren't we jumping the gun here? Are you proposing?"

"Isn't that what's done in these cases?"

"Because we've slept together?"

"Are you saying you wouldn't marry me?"

"We hardly know each other. I look at you and I melt, Emmett, but *is* this right? Maybe I am meant to marry the scion of some blue blood."

"After the last hour you can say that?"

She looked at him and shook her head. "No, you're right, I can't. You've ruined me."

He saw the words form in his head and escape his mouth: "Marry me."

She didn't answer for a while but he waited in silence, fingering a tress of dark brown hair that had fallen across her shoulder.

"Where is this home of yours?"

"Ten miles as the crow flies, but it might as well be ten hundred.

There's a small, four-room cabin, with indoor plumbing and two smaller cabins. Angel and I have used the smaller cabins as our own, but I'm sure we could refurbish the main cabin in a way that you'd like."

"You don't even know what I like."

"Yes, I do," he replied and lowered his head beneath the blanket.

They were late getting back to the trolley stop to meet Cozette. As soon as the two of them walked up, Cozette knew. Despite her charge's efforts, her hair remained slightly unkempt. Cozette shook her head silently, and Noémi could feel the disappointment.

"You go on, now," the older woman said to Emmett, waving her hand as if she were shooing a dog.

He kissed Noémi's hand and Cozette shepherded her onto the trolley. Before it pulled away from the stop he climbed onto the back, out of sight behind a group of riders. He meant to ensure they made it home safely, and to remain close to Noémi for as long as he could.

The trolley made its way up the incline, and the conductor came to collect his nickel, but the women didn't seem aware of his presence. When they got to their stop and exited, he waited until they had turned uphill before he, too, got off.

He followed at a safe distance, or so he thought. There was a man standing in their driveway whom he quickly realized was Arlyn Dunne. He had been seen. Dunne strode swiftly downhill, past the women without any greeting, in order to confront Emmett.

Cozette said, "I knew something bad would come from this. I knew it. I meant for you two to go share lunch, not a bed. I'm ruined."

Arlyn stood in Emmett's face. "What are you up to, Emmett? I told you to stay away from the girl."

"I can't do that. You're too late, Dunne. Noémi and I are in love."

"I don't care if you're in heaven's outer lobby. This is going nowhere. You're an *employee*, Dougal, that doesn't give you privileges."

Emmett looked into Arlyn's face and took a half step closer. "From this moment forward, Dunne, you're warned. Do not attempt to come between me and Noémi."

Dunne took the warning with a nod. "I'm not the one you have to be worried about, Emmett. He's ruthless, and he's not going to take this well."

"Why does he have to know?"

Why *did* Reynard have to know? Arlyn was still smarting from Mary Elizabeth's confession of infidelity; he hadn't even begun to think what he should do about *that.* And now this: the boss' little sister getting involved with a customer like Dougal.

"All right, I won't tell him, for now. But you've got some serious thinking to do, Dougal. He'll find out eventually. This world is difficult enough as it is, without making an enemy of Reynard Delacroix."

Emmett was agitated by his confrontation with Dunne. He knew that Dunne, unlike Glaupher, was a man who was upfront. He was the kind who would stab you in the chest rather than the back. Emmett was bothered as much by the fact that he liked Dunne as by the implicit threat that Dunne presented.

But then his thoughts turned to sweet Noémi, and the lovemaking that had taken place—he checked his watch—forty-four minutes earlier. After more than three decades of turbulent upheaval and aimless wandering, his life had finally crystallized. He knew now what he wanted more than anything else in life: Noémi.

Rather than take the trolley he walked all the way to the docks, revisiting the lovemaking, remembering the look in her eyes when she was sizing him up, hearing her laugh. Her laugh was the best part.

It was early, but he decided he would clean up the *Aberdeen* and make some fresh coffee while he waited for Angel to come reeling onto the boat. He crossed the trolley tracks and walked down the sidewalk to the ramp leading down to the *Aberdeen's* berth.

As he approached, the last person he had expected to see was Virgil, standing on the boat walk and talking with Angel. Emmett stopped and backed up to avoid being seen. He watched as Virgil extended his hand and Angel hesitated before reaching to shake it.

Glaupher climbed the steep stairs behind him to his Buick, and Bradley started its engine. Emmett waited until they drove out of sight before he walked down the ramp. Angel waved at him when he noted Emmett's approach.

"What does that dickhead want?"

"Nothin'. Just curious 'bout the boat. Ready to go?"

"You got back early. Thought you were taking in a movie?"

Angel untied the bowline and shrugged. They said nothing more as they readied to cast off.

The Sound was busy with freighter and barge traffic. The gray skies had opened up, providing a dramatic sunset seascape. The water was calm, which allowed Emmett to open the throttle. She sounded wonderful; better than Emmett remembered. The two of them stood in the face of the wind, letting it cleanse the city smell from their clothes.

"So why would a guy like Glaupher give a good god damn about our boat?"

"Dunno. Got back early, and he was waitin' by the boat. Didn't think nothin' of it."

"I don't trust that son of a bitch."

"Never good to trust a white man."

"Screw you, Indian."

"Mebbe he thinkin' 'bout changin' his profession. Mebbe he wants to crew for us."

That was good for a laugh.

Emmett pulled back the throttle as they entered Colvos Passage. The permanent northward current was strong in the center, so he worked the *Aberdeen* to the eastern and lesser side. This allowed the afternoon sun to shine full into the pilothouse, warming both men.

Angel went below to use the head, and when he reemerged he was shaking his head. "Why'd you bring girl onto the *Aberdeen*, Emmett? You know that bad luck."

Emmett had wondered when that subject was going to be brought up. "It's not what you think."

"What I think it bad luck to bring women on boat."

"It won't happen again, I promise."

Angel scanned the passage for logs and debris. "Bad luck."

Emmett throttled back further as they arrived at their dock, reversing the engine as the boat lightly bumped the dock. They secured the bow and stern and stood on the dock, briefly admiring the refurbished vessel.

"Where's that damn dog?" Emmett said aloud, knowing that question often lured the big canine out of his hiding place. But Atlas didn't appear at the sound of his name when both Emmett and then Angel called out.

The dog had been spending more time away from the house since the old man had died, but Emmett felt it would only be a matter of time before Atlas adjusted to Urquhart's absence. "He's got to be over at Janie's, lying in the middle of her kitchen with a belly full of chicken gizzards and rice. I'll go get him tomorrow morning."

Janie was glad to see Emmett, but she hadn't seen Atlas. As Emmett turned back toward home, Janie went out on her own, walking toward the distant highway, calling for the dog.

Emmett knew that Atlas had been on his own for some unknown amount of time before adopting the Urquhart pack. The dog was smart enough to know that something had happened to the old man, and perhaps some primal grief might have compelled him to move on.

Emmett just wanted to know that Atlas was safe and well. He *had* to know that. When he finally lay down in bed that evening, he had several conflicting thoughts fighting for his attention. It was a difficult night.

In the morning, Janie called Sheriff Gerritson and gave him Atlas' description. He said he'd be on the lookout. "He's basic feral, Janie. Who knows when he'll show up next, or where? I wouldn't give it too much thought."

"I know, Ralph, but Emmett is worried sick about the dog."

"I'll keep watch and ask around."

Emmett sat on a chair in the moist darkness of his cabin, looking out his open front door into the gloom. He was emotionally exhausted after searching the local area for another day. His thoughts of Noémi and how to forge ahead with their plans continued to be shunted aside by his concern for Atlas. Since adopting them, the big dog had rarely wandered off for more than a few hours at a time, and his prolonged absence was beginning to concern Emmett.

He rubbed his forehead and wondered at the timing of life. It gives and it takes, he thought. He recognized his own selfishness, thinking that he should be able to have Noémi, Atlas, and the old man sharing his life. How much good could a person be allowed? He wasn't a bad man, he knew, but he had done bad things. Maybe he had no right to expect happiness.

Now he also had to wonder about Angel. Having seen Angel talking with Glaupher, but offering nothing about the conversation, bothered him. He couldn't believe that Angel could consider doing him harm, but there was *something* going on. He just couldn't begin to identify what that something might be.

Then there was Noémi. He was now committed to her, and the very notion of that commitment called into question his sanity—or, at the very least, his impulsiveness. But their lovemaking was unlike anything he had ever experienced. The union went much deeper than the physical joining; it was born somewhere deeper inside. She was the first person he had encountered that provided the emotional symmetry to which all humans aspire. He was deeply in love and no man, no thing, was ever going to change that.

Mary Elizabeth was hiding in her bath. She had helped to feed and bathe the boys so that she wouldn't have to face Arlyn when he came home. She could hear the front door open and close, and the exchange of pleasantries between Arlyn and the housekeeper. She heard his loud footsteps on the hardwood floors of the hallway as he passed the bathroom on his way to the bedroom. Then there was silence.

She lay in the hot water, submerged to her nose, wondering what miracle could salvage her situation. What had compelled her to confess to Arlyn in the first place? Normally, she wasn't that impulsive. She thought of herself as careful, though not necessarily calculating.

But getting involved with Virgil was not only impulsive, it was careless and—no matter how she might try to rationalize it—the most selfish act she could commit. She knew the first time she saw Glaupher that she would sleep with him, perhaps more to hurt Arlyn than to experience any guilty pleasure.

She ran some more hot water into the tub, allowing the increased warmth to soothe her concerns. Soon she was drifting.

"Mary Elizabeth," Arlyn called through the door.

She jolted upright. "Yes? I'm in the tub."

"I'm going to eat my dinner. Will you join me?"

She was trapped. He'd been home for a while and would, naturally, expect her to get out of the bath to at least say hello.

"Oh, okay." She stood and reached for the towel rack, stepping out onto the bath mat on the tile floor.

The mat slipped from underneath her and she fell backward, hitting her head on the claw foot of the tub.

She wasn't badly hurt, but her scalp was bleeding pretty well. She grabbed another towel and wound it around her head before rising and quickly drying herself. As she was drying her back, she caught sight of herself in the mirror. She looked like a wounded soldier; her 'bandage' now half soaked with blood. "This ought to shut him up," she thought, and smiled.

She exited the bathroom, held the towel to her wound and moaned loudly.

"Jesus Christ, M.E., what have you done now?"

Arlyn rushed to her and helped her to the sofa. He gently pulled the red-stained towel away from the wound, wiped the blood, and examined the laceration.

"Gonna need stitches. Good gosh, M.E., am I going to have to get a nanny for you?" He stood up and went to her closet to pull out a suitable dress.

"Can you dress yourself? That cut has to be sewn up. Do you need help?"

She shook her head and took the dress from Arlyn. The look of concern on his face was as warm as a summer morning. The cut throbbed and she could feel a headache beginning to form behind her ears, but she smiled. She wondered just how far she was going to be able to milk Arlyn's good will.

BROTHERLY LOVE

Reynard had been carrying on an animated conversation for several minutes before he realized he was alone in his office. He turned around slowly, half hoping to see Dunne or Noémi standing there, so as to explain his oratory.

But he was alone. He went to his Victrola and put on a record; it might have been Piaf, but he wasn't really listening. Instead, he began to formulate an idea to better circulate wine stock in the cellars of *La Belle Grande*. He pulled the worn set of plans from a credenza, returned to his desk, and spread them out. He produced a red pencil from his drawer, and was about to insert his idea onto the cellar elevation when he noticed that there was already a note in place, in his handwriting, detailing the same idea.

He thought that strange and sat down. When had he made the note? He couldn't remember. He recounted the previous day's events, then the day before. At some point, he had already given serious thought to his liquor inventory, but no memory of that thought presented itself.

He checked his initial inventory: the Bordeaux, the Burgundy, the Rhone wines, the Ports and apéritifs, the Sauvignon, the Champagne. The stock would fill out two-thirds of the cellar, with the illegal portion of the inventory stored behind a faux brick wall. There would be Scotch, Irish, American, and Canadian whiskies, and a variety of gins, rums, and vodka. So far he had one-third of the hard liquor stock for which he had already paid Glaupher. Where was the remainder?

Currently, his stock was being stored in the boat shed on the Duwamish. But what space was available was half full. He was going to have to find another storage location. And what if Glaupher was pilfering the liquor? What if the bad cop's plans called for something even worse than theft?

He was glad to have Dunne. Dunne was the antidote for a bad case of Glaupher. But, Dunne had been distant lately. Helpful, yes, but not entirely forthcoming, Reynard could sense that. Something was going on with his right-hand man, something about which he knew nothing, and that fact disturbed him.

He looked at his pocket watch. Where was Dunne right now? Another headache began to form at the back of his head, familiar now and no longer surprising, but strong enough to drive his thoughts from Dunne and onto Noémi.

Reynard was losing her. He could see that. He had no idea how much longer he would be able to control her. Her open disapproval of anyone he brought to call on her was evidence of that. And how did this scoundrel, Dougal, play into things? He was certain he had seen the two of them looking at each other in a way that he could not shrug off. He would need to separate the two of them before anything could get started. Where the hell was she?

He started to rise, but the pain was too much, and he sat back down. He looked to the door to ensure he was alone and withdrew a small envelope that held a small amount of white powder. He rose slowly and went to his liquor cabinet, pouring himself a scotch. He wasn't supposed to drink alcohol while using the medication, but he didn't give a damn.

He poured the powder into the whisky and stirred the mixture with his index finger. Then he sat back down and slowly drained the glass.

Within a few minutes, the pain had subsided to a tolerable level, and he felt good enough to seek out his younger sister.

When he called out her name in the hallway, he could hear a muffled reply from her room upstairs. He took the stairs slowly, carefully holding onto the handrail. When he reached her room he caught a glimpse of her quickly putting her diary under a short stack of books on her bed stand.

"I've been looking for you."

"I've been here all morning. What do you need?"

Her beauty pained him. Who could blame scum like Dougal for falling for her? "What have you been up to?"

"What do you mean?" Her quick response suggested to Reynard she had something to hide.

"Nothing. What have you been up to? How's the charity work? What movies have you seen? Whom have you seen them with?" He crossed her room and sat down at her vanity, arranging her brushes and cosmetics.

"Don't they call this 'the second degree'?"

He swiveled around, laughed and motioned to the bed. "I believe they call it the 'third degree.'"

She sat down, hoping this was the old Reynard.

"When a parent says to their child that they only have their best interests at heart it seems natural," he said, leaning forward and placing his hands upon her knees. His touch briefly made her uncomfortable. "When an orphaned brother says it to his orphan sister, it can take on an entirely different meaning."

"I know you worry about me, Reynard. I know you want what you think is best for me. I love you. I'm so thankful that I've had you to guide me through life. You mean so much to me."

She got off the bed and knelt by the bench, putting her arm across his narrow shoulders.

She thought to herself that he must have lost weight. He seemed so slight after having enjoyed Emmett's strong, muscular body. "You work too hard," she continued, "and you worry too much. You should find time to go away for a few days—"

"Can't do that," he replied, suddenly standing. "I cannot allow myself to lower my guard for one minute. I'm having a hard time these days, determining who's a friend and who's not. Our fortune is riding on *La Belle Grande*, Noémi. I need to rely on everyone around me. Can I rely on you, Noémi?"

"Of course you can."

"So you won't see this Dougal fellow any more?"

"Who says I'm seeing him?"

"Don't lie to me, Noémi. Don't let me catch you in a lie." His eyes sought an answer from Noémi, an answer that he could see was not coming.

He left her alone in her room, and she felt vaguely violated. It was the first time in her life she felt anything but love and devotion for her brother. She wondered if Dunne had said anything, or Cozette. She went downstairs and found Cozette in the kitchen, helping to prepare lunch. Noémi motioned to her, and the two went out onto the kitchen porch. "Does Reynard know?"

Cozette frowned and shook her head. "Not from me. Maybe from Arlyn, but not from me. Your brother would fire me if he knew I allowed you to cavort with that fisherman."

"This will all work out, Cozette."

"It will work out, but perhaps not well, young lady. Use your head. You have a lot to lose by making the wrong decision."

"I suppose that goes in either direction."

Cozette considered the response and then agreed.

"Let's get out of here, I need some fresh air."

"I'm not going anywhere if your intent is to meet up with Mr. Dougal."

"No, let's go to a movie. Your pick."

Reynard watched them exit the front door from the top of the stairs. He went into Noémi's room and stood by the window watching them walk down the hill toward the trolley stop.

When he was certain he was alone, he began his search of her room. He found nothing under the stack of books on her side table. It was just a stack of books. He pulled down the covers and searched under her pillows, but there was nothing there. He searched under her bed, inside her bed stand, in her vanity drawers, but found nothing. He opened her bureau and carefully patted down her sweaters, blouses, and intimates.

He finally found it on a shelf in her closet, behind a hatbox: Noémi's diary. Sitting on the bed, he was giddy with anticipation: his sister's secrets. Her diary had always been inviolable. It was an unspoken understanding.

When she was younger, he was amused by her need to record the minutiae of her daily life. But now, committed to the crime, he almost wet himself as he tried to pick the small lock.

He found a hairpin and played around in the lockset, having no idea how to actually pick it. After a few minutes his increased blood pressure began to set off another headache, and he became impatient. He took the diary downstairs to his office, found his letter opener, and broke the lock.

It dawned on him that he couldn't let her find the diary in that condition. But what would he do? Perhaps he could go downtown, find another diary like it, delaminate both bindings, and replace the covers ...

He stopped. What was happening to him? He poured more whisky, emptied another packet into it and quickly drank the mixture. A sober resolve set in. He opened the book and thumbed his way to the most recent entry in order to find the truth.

"Jan.18. R has been behaving erratically over the past few days. Under a great deal of pressure, but there's something else ailing him. He is getting worse. Afraid for his health. He disguises the pain but we see it. What would he do if I left? It might be more than he can bear. His life is his business and, I guess, me. How long until I hear from E?"

He turned back to the previous entry.

"Jan.17. Day with E. Most wonderful day ever. Trying to be responsible but it's hard. Don't want to hurt R but E, oh. Fishing boats are not very

big inside."

There was little doubt who 'E' was. Reynard closed the diary. He didn't need to go any further. He had the evidence. She had been warned. She had been told. Now the only question was the best way to handle the situation.

"You knew nothing about Dougal and Noémi?" The diary sat on Reynard's desk, between them. It might as well have been the Great Wall. Arlyn recognized that things had changed.

"I had my suspicions, but sharing suspicions only dulls the focus, Monsieur Delacroix."

"Stop it with the *monsieur* shit, Arlyn." Reynard picked up the diary and held it up as evidence.

Arlyn noted the broken lock. "She's not going to take kindly to that, boss."

"It doesn't matter. She knows me. She lied to me."

"She didn't actually lie, if I understand—"

"It was a lie of omission. Deception. But there's no way they could have managed to get together without either Cozette or you, or both, being aware. That damned Cozette, she thinks she's Noémi's mother. Well, not anymore."

"Don't be hasty, boss."

"You didn't respond to my accusation."

"I wasn't aware, before the fact."

"*Before the fact*? And what is the fact?"

"I don't know. As I said, I had—I *have*—my suspicions. But neither of them has informed me of what they've done or what they plan to do. It would be better to plan a course of action than to over-examine the who's and what's."

"That's clever, Arlyn. Is that the way they talk in the squad room: *'the who's and what's'*?"

Arlyn sighed. "What do you want me to do, Mr. Delacroix?"

Reynard nearly didn't hear the question. The pain had returned, and was swamping his faculties. The light hurt his eyes, and he was beginning to lose his peripheral vision again. His tongue was tingling, and he knew it was the onset to greater discomfort.

"She goes east. Tomorrow. I'll make arrangements. She's not to know, but I want you to pay close attention to her. You're responsible for her. Fail at this, and I'll set Glaupher on you."

Arlyn felt the hairs on his neck stand. He looked hard at Delacroix, recognizing the look of a dangerous and desperate man. He wanted to ask, why? What had changed? But Reynard was shielding his eyes from the light while simultaneously waving him from the room.

"What about Virgil?" Arlyn asked.

"Don't worry about Glaupher, I'll take care of Glaupher." The hand waved again.

Once the door closed, Reynard poured a full glass of scotch and emptied two of the envelopes into it. He was determined to get some sleep. He crossed to his leather chaise and slowly lay back. He laid his arm across his eyes and focused on his breathing. The pain began to diminish. After a few minutes, he fell into a fitful slumber.

Arlyn was still feeling the sting of Reynard's threat. Setting aside the issues that seemed to be consuming Reynard, there was now a lack of nuance to everything to which his employer laid his hands.

Everyone felt that the surgery in Portland had been a success, but now Arlyn was beginning to think that maybe it hadn't been a *total* success. Removing him from Virgil's watch was not a good thing.

Threatening to exile Noémi was quite another. He wondered how Reynard would, first, break that decision to his sister and, second, how he planned on enforcing the move. Noémi was a grown woman, and the only thing that Reynard could hold over her head was his home and his money. Arlyn believed that the first chance she got, Noémi would make a beeline back to Seattle and Dougal.

Of course, Reynard knew that too, so there was only one thing that Reynard could do: eliminate Emmett. A chill ran down his spine. That the man for whom he had been willing to risk his life was capable of such villainy sickened him.

He was faced with almost the same exact questions that faced Reynard. It had taken a certain level of self-delusion to look past some of the irregular business strategies that Reynard practiced. But he had been able to overlook those irregularities by focusing on the good that could come from Reynard's development. A lot of people would be employed during, and after, construction of the hotel. A lot of money would be poured back into the local economy—an economy that, while growing at a reasonable pace, was beginning to show signs of volatility. Sometimes rules *had* to be broken for the greater good.

And Arlyn didn't kid himself; he knew the prime motivation for his loyalty to Reynard was the more than $800 he received each month without fail. But now, he was beginning to realize that his job was in danger; and perhaps, even his life. If Reynard was the least bit serious about turning Glaupher against him ... he hesitated to think that Reynard would play that kind of game with him.

He thought of M.E. and the boys, how their lives had changed due to his employment, and how difficult it would be for them to have to adjust to what would ultimately be a much smaller income.

Yet, he felt he had to be able to make his next decisions without regard to the money. If protecting his family meant turning his back on Reynard, so be it. And if Glaupher was enlisted by Reynard to exact some form of absurd vengeance, then Arlyn knew he was more than prepared to deal with the ruffian.

While he was sad to see Reynard turning against him and those who had been family to him, he was also glad that he had seen this side of his employer before it was too late.

STEALING HOME

Virgil waited while Bradley supervised the loading of the liquor into the back of a truck. He calculated that he had liberated nearly thirty cases of liquor since Dougal's last delivery. Sooner or later, Reynard was going to pull an inventory, and if those shortages were noted, then all hell was going to break loose.

He had to replace the stolen stock, and he knew exactly how he was going to do it: with the help of the fucking Indian. And, by way of bonus, there would be an opportunity to knock off both the Indian and Dougal. He smiled and lit a cigarette.

Bradley came over to join him and pulled out his pack of Chesterfields.

"You haven't got time, Bradley. Get that booze to Andersen's."

Bradley looked at him and smiled. He understood and accepted the pecking order, and was able to stuff the ongoing indignities beneath the weekly wad of cash that Virgil paid him. He was five years from retirement, and he had been able to stash nearly three grand in extra income since he went to work for Virgil two years earlier.

He despised Virgil, but the lieutenant had established a pipeline of illegal income, which he shared, albeit in small amounts, with Bradley and several patrolmen. He lit his cigarette anyway, and slowly blew out the match. "He's not expecting us before eleven."

"I don't give a shit. Get the booze to his backdoor now. If he's not there, then leave the cases inside his storage shed. We don't have time to be fucking around."

Bradley took another drag, dropped the cigarette on the ground in front of Virgil's well-shined wingtips, and crushed it out. He meant the gesture as one of insolence, but Virgil paid no attention. Bradley hated Virgil's guts, and it was only the money that kept him from facilitating an 'accident.' But, there was still money to be made, so the lieutenant could still count on him. "Six o'clock tomorrow night?"

"Yeah. Bring Davis and Oscar. Tommy guns. I want a lot of noise and a lot of firepower."

"Gotcha."

"And don't forget the fucking hand truck this time."

Bradley climbed into the passenger side of the truck and it moved off. Virgil watched the truck make its way back to the highway leading up to Seattle. Tomorrow night he would not only make up the shortages, he would be able to add to his own liquor stockpile. Delacroix wasn't the only asshole who could make plans and then carry them out.

Noémi wandered through the quiet house. Reynard was not in his office, or the kitchen or parlor. And Cozette was also absent.

That was strange. Was Cozette that angry with her that she felt the need to dodge Noémi? That couldn't be. She was angry, but she had expressed that anger. Cozette wouldn't be spiteful—she had never been spiteful.

She knocked at Cozette's door, but there was no response. Noémi cracked the door open and peeked inside. On the bed were two large valises, both strapped tight. Noémi's stomach sank. Had Cozette confessed to Reynard? Had he found out some other way? How else could he have?

She dashed back to her own room and opened her closet door.

Standing on a chair she kept there, she pushed aside the hatbox, only to find the shelf empty.

Reynard had her diary.

Anger washed over her. How dare he? But, her anger was quickly displaced by panic. Things had changed in a dramatic fashion. Her greatest ally—her *lifelong* ally—now presented a threat. If he sent Cozette away, who would she be able to count on? Who would be her confidant? She wondered if the change in Reynard's disposition was temporary, or whether he would dictate the rest of her life.

Noémi steadied herself and climbed down off the chair before sitting on it. She was sitting in the midst of her childhood and youth. Party dresses of all color and construction surrounded her. Once, they had supplied a great deal of her pleasure, and had signified the rites of passage as she had known them.

There was the pink taffeta gown she had worn for coming out. That had been a marvelous evening. Reynard had escorted her, resplendent in his tailored tuxedo. Both of them were proud peacocks, basking in light that they wouldn't have experienced had they stayed in New Orleans. On the shelf above was the box that contained the red sequined pumps that she wore that night.

There was her confirmation dress, long since outgrown, and the wide variety of tea gowns and dresses, acquired as her taste matured. This was the sum of her life, she thought. And it was all owed to Reynard. Suddenly, she felt constricted by the clothes and the closet, and was compelled to abandon it.

Perhaps, she thought, it was her intention to abandon all of it, to give herself, and only herself, over to Emmett. This had been her world, and she knew little of his, but she was ready to make the change, for better or worse.

She went back into her closet and found her valise at the back. It hadn't been used since their trip to Portland, which now seemed like years past. She lugged the suitcase out and hoisted it onto her bed. She went to her bureau and began to pull out her lingerie and underwear.

Reynard appeared in the door. She hadn't heard him enter the house, or come down the hallway. "Good," he said, "make sure you pack plenty of warm things." There was a large, well-dressed man behind Reynard whom she did not recognize. Reynard noticed her staring at the stranger. "This is Mr. Lyndall. He is your escort. He will accompany you to a new home I've purchased in Baltimore."

"I won't go."

"You will go. One way or the other."

Lyndall produced a small prescription vial and held it out.

"You'd drug me, your own sister?"

"For your own good, to save you from yourself? Yes." Reynard took a step closer and she retreated two. "I understand your anger, Noémi—"

"Do you? You come in here with a thug, threatening to drug me in order to spirit me away to some private little prison? You have no idea!"

Reynard took a step back, turned, and began to pull items from the bureau, placing them on the bed next to the valise.

"Where's Cozette?"

"She's fine. She's waiting at the station. She's already packed her things so that she can accompany you as well."

"I thought you'd sent her away."

"Well, I have. But, with you. Cozette and I have had a talk. She'll be a better guardian in the future."

"I don't need a guardian, Reynard. You're treating me like a child."

"And you're acting like a child. You're infatuated with a rumrunner, a wanted man, Noémi. That's right, a wanted man. You think you'll be setting up housekeeping with him when, in fact, he's either going to end up in jail or some ditch. I'm sparing you from your weakness for strays. Anyway, we're boring Mr. Lyndall. Your train leaves in little more than two hours. Do you need help packing? I'm sure Mr. Lyndall would be glad to assist."

"Get out, both of you. I'll do it myself." Noémi had, in fact, never packed for herself. Whether she was visiting elsewhere or going away to school, Cozette had always packed for her.

She slammed the door behind the men as they exited and immediately went to her window. A few moments later, Lyndall appeared on the steps below, obviously watching the street.

She went to her door and opened it a crack, checking to see if there was anyone in the hallway. It was empty. She tiptoed down the hall to a window overlooking the large backyard. Standing on the grass, smoking a cigarette, was another man, nearly as large as Lyndall.

She was trapped. She felt like crying. She wanted to run, but the men would catch her. Even if she managed to elude them, where would she go? She had no idea how to contact Emmett, or even where he lived. Circumstances had denied them the opportunity to learn the little, but very important details about their lives.

She returned to her room and sat on her bed. She really had no choice other than to go along with Reynard's wishes. She vowed to herself that she would return to Seattle as soon as she could. She only hoped that Emmett could be found, and that he would wait for her. Was he really a wanted criminal? And what had Reynard said, a rumrunner? Or were these accusations simply excuses to keep her from the man with whom she had fallen in love?

"He can make me go," she thought to herself, "but he won't be able to keep me there."

Noémi returned to her packing.

Arlyn needed a drink. As soon as he walked in the door, he ran the boys' gauntlet, giving up the remaining chewing gum in his pockets. Afterward, he went immediately to the small liquor cabinet in the parlor. He poured himself a double shot of bourbon and sat down on the settee. It was an uncomfortable piece of furniture, but Mary Elizabeth had insisted on purchasing it and, worse, had placed it in the middle of the parlor simply because of its rich, red leather.

"Did you pour one for me?" Mary Elizabeth had entered behind him. She leaned against the archway leading from the foyer. She was dressed in a red silk robe, and was made up as though she was going out. Her hair had been pulled forward and crimped to disguise the small, gauze patch that covered her stitches. She was smoking, something that he didn't want her to do in the house.

"I've told you that I don't like that," he said, turning back to his whiskey.

"And I've told you that it relaxes me."

He shrugged. When she noted that he wasn't going to pour her a drink, she went to the cabinet and poured a large whiskey for herself, taking a swallow before smiling at Arlyn.

She was challenging him, he knew, and he wondered at her bravado. Wasn't she aware how thin the ice was under her feet? Did she take him for a fool? His anger boiled up, catching in his throat for a brief moment before erupting into a loud, prolonged grunt.

"Shut up! Shut up, goddammit! You parade around here like some ten-dollar hooker. Is that what Glaupher likes?"

She was stunned, but then happily took on the challenge. "You don't want to know what he likes. You haven't wanted to pay any attention to *me*. You've become Delacraw's pet monkey we can all see that. He snaps his fingers, and you jump. Always at his beck and call, but never any time for me. You leave *me* alone while you run off across the country. You leave me alone every damn day, and you expect me to just sit at home and do nothing?"

That was it? *That* was her defense. It was so silly he almost laughed. "Yes!" He stood and advanced toward her, and she involuntarily cowered from this angry, aggressive man. "You took vows in a church, Mary Elizabeth. And besides those vows, you've broken nearly every commandment short of murder. You lie. You cheat. You've lain with another man. You—" Arlyn realized the boys were standing in the hallway, watching the exchange. "You would be smart to temper things here, M.E.," he said, quietly.

"Where are you going?" she demanded in a low voice.

"Don't worry. I won't leave *you* in the lurch. I'll spend the night elsewhere."

Arlyn was sitting in Reynard's office when the latter entered. "Dunne, what are you doing here?"

"Where else would I be, Mr. Delacroix?"

Reynard stopped, wondering at the question. Should he know where Arlyn should be? He tried to tick off his mental checklist, but he couldn't find it, settling instead for a glass of Johnnie Walker from the pretty crystal decanter.

"Where are the truands?" Arlyn asked.

"*Les truands*? How continental."

"It was you, Mr. Delacroix, who introduced me to the word. Alright, *thugs*."

Reynard swallowed a mouthful of whisky and then slowly shook his head. "They're not thugs, Arlyn, they're bodyguards."

"A rose by any other name."

Reynard finished his scotch, nodded, and smiled. "I think I've been wasting my time with the local authorities' farm system. These are pros from St. Louis, and they're not cheap. But I have it on good authority that they're very good at what they do."

"I'm sure they are. But who are they here to protect?"

"Oh, not me. I have *you*, Arlyn." He poured himself more whisky. "I'm assuming you're still made for the job, aren't you?"

"That's why I'm here. But if not you, then who?"

Reynard crossed the room and sat down hard in his swivel chair, turning it madly. He squealed. But the squeal wasn't delightful as a child's might be. It was disconcerting, and Arlyn felt a sadness suddenly settle upon his shoulders.

The chair slowed and Reynard turned back to face his lieutenant.

"They're here to escort Noémi to safer ground."

"I beg your pardon?"

"Baltimore. That you can know, but no more. You see, Arlyn"—he struggled to lean forward onto his elbows—"I don't entirely take you on your word about Noémi's recent … *complications*. I believe you know more than you're going to tell me. But that's alright, I understand. They would make an impressive couple, *but it's not going to happen*."

He suddenly seemed the sober, calculating Reynard. "Don't you be concerned, Arlyn. Everything is going to be taken care of. Things will be back to normal, or as normal as they can be without Noémi in this house."

"When does she go? I'd like to say good-bye."

"She's already gone but, anyway, I'd rather you not disturb her. You don't mind, do you? She'll be out for holidays, and you'll be able to catch up with her then."

Arlyn nodded, there was no question; it was a declaration. "All right, I have a few things to do. I need to check in with Virgil regarding an inventory of our stock."

"Good thinking, you do that, Arlyn."

At least this time there was no dismissive wave of a hand.

Union Station was busy. It was early evening, and the terminal was packed ass to cheek. Arlyn pressed his way around the baggage area in order to avoid the passenger traffic.

The *Oriental Limited* always departed on track one. Approaching the passenger platform without detection by Noémi's escort would be difficult. He knew that Reynard would have told his new security team that Dougal was a distinct threat, and probably provided an accurate description of him.

With Dougal as their focus, Arlyn was doubtful that they would have been warned that he might rescue Noémi. But while that was all well and good, he had no rescue in mind.

Edging closer to the platform, he saw Noémi and Cozette between the two burly men. He looked at the large clock suspended above the passenger thruway and noted that there was still fifteen minutes before passengers had to board. This was going to be difficult, and he would only get one chance. He needed a diversion.

A porter was pushing a luggage cart nearby, and as he passed by he 'accidentally' knocked over the luggage, causing the thick crowd to part so that the items could be picked up.

During that brief moment, while the escorts' attention was drawn to the disturbance, Arlyn walked by Cozette and quickly pressed a piece of folded paper into her hand before walking back into the crowd without detection.

Cozette clenched her fingers around the paper, recognizing Arlyn just as he disappeared. She knew better than to open the paper to read it in front of the men.

She waited until it was time to board, and with the appearance of helping her young ward, she pressed the paper into Noémi's hand.

The latter was surprised, and was about to ask what it was when she noticed Cozette quickly shake her head. Instead, she placed the paper inside the cuff of her sleeve, and made her way into the hallway of the first class car.

"Which one is ours?" she asked Lyndall. He looked at the tickets in his hand.

"2A and B."

Cozette opened the door to compartment 2A. "Thank you, gentlemen, I'll take it from here."

"No way," replied Lyndall. "I stay with Miss Delacroix all the way to Baltimore."

He opened the wall divider so that both compartments were joined.

"I don't suppose that applies to moments of privacy?" Noémi asked, squeezing by to enter the compartment. It was now one large compartment, sizable enough for four passengers, with fold down bunks on both sides of the bay.

"You'll get your privacy, just not right now, Miss." He took her handbag and put it in an overhead compartment, along with her hat and umbrella. "Sit down, please," he instructed.

"What about refreshments?" Cozette asked. "Did you think to ask the porter to bring us something?"

Lyndall shrugged and stepped into the hallway, flagging a nearby porter. "What do you want?" he asked Cozette.

"Tea would be nice, and sandwiches. We had no time to have a decent lunch."

He nodded and engaged the porter. But before Cozette and Noémi had time to examine the paper that Arlyn had passed, Lyndall reentered the compartment and sat down opposite.

Lyndall was a stoic man, focused entirely on his job. While his eyes were never directly on them, both Cozette and Noémi could feel his full attention. He scanned the people walking by in the corridor and outside on the platform, obviously watching for Emmett.

His partner remained in the hallway until the conductor could be heard yelling 'Board!' When the train jerked into motion, he came into the compartment and sat nearest the door. Anyone streetwise would have noticed the bulge under his coat jacket.

The train moved slowly out of the yard and out to the flats along Elliott Bay before crossing Salmon Bay and heading north along the Sound past Everett. Though it was late in the day, the clouds parted and the setting sun shone brightly off the water. A mile or two out, a fishing boat could be seen making its way toward the Straits.

Even from that distance, Noémi could see it was not the *Aberdeen*. She wondered where Emmett was, and how she might get word to him.

She looked across at Lyndall. "Could I have some privacy?"

"I have my instructions, Miss."

"Do I have to ask permission to use the washroom?"

He smiled. "Of course not."

She opened the door to the water closet and then closed it behind her. There was a small light over the tiny mirror, and she turned it on. She reached inside her sleeve and, for a moment, thought she had lost the piece of paper. But it had just traveled a bit farther up her blouse and she worked it free, exposing it to the minimal light. It was a hastily scribbled bit of writing, which read:

E.D.

Port Orchard exchange 453

Janie Ferrady

She smiled, and wondered how Cozette had come upon this treasure. When she returned to the compartment, she struggled to contain the smile forming at the corners of her mouth.

Cozette could see that Noémi's face had brightened, and wondered what Dunne had written on the small piece of paper. Noémi patted her on the arm. When Lyndall wasn't looking, she and Cozette exchanged a brief and undetected smile of conspiracy.

Reynard didn't like talking on the phone. It made him nervous, made him feel like he was tied down. Often, when taking a long call, he would hold the phone and pace back and forth, as far as the cord would allow. He would step from one floral pattern to the next on the imported wool rug, and the worn path of that pacing was now evident. Reynard regarded the weight of the handheld receiver and the quality of the sound for several seconds before he remembered he was speaking with Glaupher.

" … and Bradley said he got wind of something bad going down, maybe even as early as tonight."

"Where would Bradley 'get wind' of such things?" Reynard compared the color of his patent leather slippers against the woven red rose in the rug. The colors were almost identical. He wondered whether he should get a contrasting throw rug to place over the worn area. Burgundy would make a nice color.

He began to notice the glitter that was obscuring the edges of his vision: a clear indication that another massive headache was on its way.

" … sources that he won't even share with me. What should we do, ignore it? Should we tell Dougal and the Indian? For all we know, those assholes may have set something up. I—*we*—can't afford to lose a load, Mr. Delacroix."

Reynard ignored the pain and focused on Glaupher's comment. "You're correct, of course. We cannot ignore the possibility. I'm beginning to think that, perhaps, we should look at replacing the fisherman. Do you think the Indian can do the job?"

"I know the Indian can do the job, and if I read my cards correct, he's willing."

"Good." The pain was encroaching on his ability to think clearly. The prescribed medication, even in triple dosages, no longer had any palliative effect. He knew he only had a matter of moments to conclude the conversation.

"Virgil, tonight is Dougal's last job. Do you understand?"

"Clearly. Should I call you later?"

But the line had gone dead.

Arlyn Dunne was an unexpected guest at the boat shed. But Virgil said nothing as Dunne watched Angel top off the fuel tanks from five-gallon jerry cans. Emmett emerged from the engine hold and noted the presence of Dunne, Glaupher, and Bradley.

"Aren't you guys supposed to be on the way to Everett?"

"Change of plans," said Virgil. "Got a tip the sheriff there is on to us, so we've moved the drop to Kayak Point."

"That's way out of the way. This boat has too much draft to risk Davis Slough, so we'd be looking at another hour on the water."

"You can handle the slough."

"Not with a hundred and fifty cases of liquor on board. We'll be riding low, and if we get hung up there, we'll be sitting ducks."

"Nonetheless, that's what the boss ordered, so that's what you'll do."

"We be okay, Emmett," Angel said.

Emmett looked at him. "All right, Kayak Point. But make it ten-thirty. That'll give us at least a half hour more." He turned back to his last minute chores while Angel took the sandwiches and thermos of coffee handed to him by Bradley.

"Sweetened that coffee for ya," Bradley noted with a smile. "Watch yer topknot, Injun."

Angel smiled, but inside he wanted to smash the asshole in the middle of his Irish face. When it grew dark enough for them to depart, they idled out of the Duwamish, taking their time. They watched for cutters as well as for freighters, who wouldn't notice a dark, unmarked vessel until it was too late.

They skirted the west side of the Sound, staying clear of Bremerton, and then sped close to the shoreline of Admiralty Bay in order to elude detection by the Coast Guard and lightkeeper at Point Wilson. Things went smoothly, and they were half an hour ahead of schedule when they took on their cargo in West Vancouver.

Just before casting off, Emmett produced a Remington 12 gauge pump shotgun that he had stored without Angel's knowledge. He loaded the tubular magazine and placed the weapon near the wheel.

"Holy shit, Emmett, where you get that?"

"Found it here in the boat shed and thought it might come in handy."

"Well, careful with it. Jesus, you expectin' trouble?"

"Don't know—you tell me."

Angel shrugged and cast off the bow and stern lines. They idled their way back out onto the Strait of Georgia. Their cargo was documented for Mexico, but the documentation was really only good for the Canadians if they were stopped. Once they crossed into American waters, they were only as safe as the boat was fast.

They hugged Galiano and Saturna Islands before crossing into American water. The skies had clouded back over, leaving them nearly invisible without running lights. Emmett opened the throttles and steered by his compass, following the now-familiar course behind the Orcas and between Cypress and Guemes Islands, working their way south.

He eased back the engines a bit so that their roar wouldn't be as loud. The 50-gallon barrel mufflers they had installed were all but useless when the engines ran full out, and Emmett wasn't going to take any chances on tickling the interest of anyone onshore in Anacortes.

They rounded the bottom of Fidalgo Island and cruised through Deception Pass, entering Skagit Bay and making for the Davis Slough. The lights of a good-sized vessel five miles off surprised them, lit up like a Christmas tree. Through binoculars Emmett could see that it was, indeed, a Coast Guard cutter that had stopped and boarded a small boat. Whether that boat was running illegal alcohol they could only guess, but they were thankful that the cutter's attention was elsewhere.

They made the slough and Emmett put Angel on the bow, reading depth with a sounding line.

"Two fathoms, Emmett," he called back.

"Mark Twain," Emmett joked, but Angel didn't get it.

The slough was narrow in spots, making for a slow going, and Emmett could see that whatever time they had made up on the trip into Vancouver had been lost by the time spent in Davis Slough.

They breached the slough, made their way through the shallows heading the Stillaguamish River, and found themselves in the friendlier confines of Port Susan. Emmett held the boat at half speed in order to keep the noise down, and they cruised the last couple of miles in ten minutes. The two of them held their breath, hoping that their landing party hadn't been busted.

As they idled closer to shore, a flashlight was turned on and off twice, giving the prearranged signal. Emmett turned on one of his muted flood lamps to ensure the going was safe to shore. What he saw was disconcerting. Two long banks of rock, each perhaps a hundred feet wide, could be seen every time a swell washed over them. There was no safe way into shore at that spot.

Emmett put the engine in neutral and stepped onto the rear deck, attempting to yell at the small group of men on shore.

"There are rocks here, you idiots! We'll wreck the boat and lose the load if we try to land here! Move twenty yards north!"

But the words were partially lost to the wind and the sound of the engine, so Virgil couldn't hear Emmett's warning.

"Wade into the water until you can hear what he's got to say," Virgil said to Bradley. Bradley repeated the command to another of the men, but before the man took a step Virgil cut in, "You wade into the water, Bradley. I don't want one of the dickheads scaring them off."

Bradley couldn't believe that Virgil was so intent on humiliating him, but Virgil's menacing stance underscored that intent. Bradley took off his overcoat and was starting to untie his shoes when Virgil said, "Leave your fucking shoes on, and get out there now."

The lieutenant was holding a Tommy gun that, while not pointed directly at Bradley, was enough of a threat.

Bradley still took off his coat jacket, folded it, and left it on the sand. He walked into the shallows. It was a sandy shoreline, but there were numerous potholes, driftwood, and ledges that could trip a person foolish enough to be wading without adequate light. Bradley stumbled and heard one of the grunts giggle. He would deal with that prick later.

"What did you say?" he yelled out to the boat.

"Can't … land … here," was the faint reply. "Too … rocky. Going … move"

"What'd he say?" Virgil demanded from the water's edge.

"Can't land, Virg. Says it's too rocky."

"The whole fucking shoreline is sand. The rocks are in his head. Tell him to get that fucking boat into shore."

"Glaupher wants the boat on shore NOW!" yelled Bradley.

"Go … up … beach … find … " but the wind blew away the last part.

Emmett didn't wait for a response. He took the wheel, put the drive into reverse, and began to back his way out. With his floodlight he could see the shoreline a couple dozen yards up the beach.

"What the hell?" Virgil yelled. "Where's he going?"

They ran up the beach, following the boat. There were pieces of driftwood scattered across the heavy sand. One of the men tripped and sprawled face first. He regained his feet and turned on his flashlight. Soon there were five flashlight beams dodging and intersecting the dark. Angel watched with concern from the stern of their boat.

"Yeah, let's bring as much attention as we can to this show," Emmett said. He turned the boat perpendicular to the shore and began to idle toward shallow water.

Virgil noted the movement and hurried his pace along the beach, stopping only to say, "Do not let them get away, no matter what. Let's secure that boat now."

The men continued their mad dash in the sand, some in the shallow water, closing on the boat. One of the men tripped over a rock in the shallows and fell forward, tightening his index finger on the trigger of his machine gun. A burst went off, spraying the dark sky and then trailing down across the bow of the boat, just missing the flying bridge.

Emmett ducked, and Angel dove behind the engine hatch.

"It's a hijack," Emmett yelled. He retrieved the shotgun, leveling a blast toward the flashlights on shore.

This evoked another round of gunfire, this time directed at the boat, before Virgil could regain control.

"STOP FUCKING SHOOTING!" he yelled. But Emmett couldn't hear those words, backing away at full throttle.

"Goddamn it, stop!" Virgil yelled, but he knew Emmett couldn't hear. He aimed his Tommy gun and swept it across the deck and the dark silhouette of the pilothouse, emptying the magazine. The boat continued to back farther from shore.

"Fuck." Virgil stood and shook his head, pulling the empty magazine from his Thompson and replacing it. "Who fired that first shot?"

No one owned up.

"How 'bout I shoot all of you?"

"Fulton fired first."

"The hell I did. You fell down in the water and started firing!"

"I may have tripped, you prick, but you took the first shot."

"Shut the hell up, both of you." Glaupher started walking back to the car. "We need to get a boat. We need to get down to Seattle and get a boat."

"What makes you think he'll head for Seattle, Virg?"

"You got a better idea, Bradley?"

"Yeah." Bradley lifted his service .38 and fired one shot directly into Virgil Glaupher's face.

The remaining four stood over the inert figure, illuminating him with their flashlights.

"Jesus Christ, Jack!"

"Anybody got a problem with this?" Bradley asked.

None of them had a problem with it.

"Take his ID, split his cash between you. Leave nothing that will identify him. We'll leave him for the birds and crabs. Next order of business is saving our asses with Delacraw. This was all Glaupher's idea, right?"

Emmett heard the report of Bradley's service revolver and wondered what that was about. The bridge was riddled with splintered bullet holes, and wood chips and glass littered the deck.

"Angel?"

"I'm okay." Angel lifted himself onto the engine hatch and sat down. "I think mebbe I got in the way of a bullet, though."

Emmett eased back the throttle and lashed the wheel. He went onto the deck with a flashlight to examine Angel's leg wound. He had only been nicked but the wound was bleeding profusely. Emmett took off his belt and lashed it tight above the bleeding.

"Not too bad, but you're going to need some sewing up, Angel." He cut open Angel's pant leg in order to assess the wound. He retrieved a bottle of whisky from the cargo and opened it, pouring the alcohol over the wound.

"Don't waste it," said Angel. He took the bottle and swallowed a mouthful before pouring more onto the torn flesh. "Where I gonna get someone to sew me up?"

"Everett. We'll tie up in Port Gardner, and I'll get you over to the hospital. It's only three or four blocks."

Emmett took the bottle and took a short pull. The whisky took the edge off the adrenaline, and he was able to stop his hands from shaking. "What was that all about?"

Angel was tearing the bottom of his shirt in order to make a bandage, but mostly he was ignoring the question.

"What were you and Glaupher up to?"

Angel looked up. "Wasn't nobody gonna get shot. The cop told me. Said there'd be guns, but no one gets shot. Look at all the bullet holes. How'd you avoid gettin' hit?"

"Luck, I guess. So what was the deal? What could convince you to go into business with that prick?"

Emmett made his way back to the bridge, unlashed the wheel, and eased open the throttle, making for Everett. The last thing they needed was to draw attention to themselves, with a hundred and fifty cases of bonded liquor on board. He would have to find a quiet place to berth, out of sight of the harbormaster.

Angel limped forward and painfully hoisted himself onto the other swivel chair. "He said we make enough from this hijack we never have to run liquor again."

"I do believe he was right. We're done with it. The question is, whether we'll survive it. What are we going to do with the booze? Store it? Where? Glaupher will gladly give us up to save his ass, you can bet. Even Gerritson will be forced to come get us."

"Sorry, Emmett."

"You should be. Why you would ever trust that son of a bitch is beyond me. You were wary of him from the moment you laid eyes on him."

"He put a lot a money in our pockets, Emmett."

"Yeah, so we didn't need some big-time score. We're in for it now. I wonder if we can even continue to live on the Passage, or whether it's time to pack up and move on?"

"I'm getting woozy."

"Loosen that belt a bit."

"Shoulda eaten."

"It won't be long now, maybe fifteen minutes. We have to find a quiet place to tie up."

Angel had climbed off the swivel and sat down on the deck with his back against the bulkhead. "Pretty tired," he said and his head slumped forward onto his chest.

Emmett entered the marina and idled along the waterfront until he found an open slip next to a cannery. He docked and quickly tied off the bow and stern lines. He made sure none of the cargo was visible and then hoisted his unconscious friend onto his shoulders. If he was stopped, his story would be he was just carrying a drunk Indian home.

The hospital was a short two blocks from their berth, and by the time they were near the entrance Angel had regained consciousness.

"Put me down. Put me down," he demanded. He was unsteady, but able to stand.

He put his hand on Emmett's shoulder. "I'm okay. Story is, I'm working a boat, got my leg hurt from loose gaff, boat couldn't wait. Had to get catch to Seattle. Good enough?"

"Yeah. You got money?"

"Five, mebbe ten bucks. Should be enough."

Emmett pulled out his wallet and pressed two tenners into Angel's hand. "That should get you down to Seattle in first-class fashion."

They laughed.

"You got Janie's number?"

"PO453."

"Good. You let me know when you get down there, and I'll bring the boat for you."

Angel held out his hand.

"What the hell, you ain't dying," said Emmett. But the hand remained where it was, and Emmett shook it.

"Don't do nothin' stupid, Emmett. You sink that son of a bitch before you let them get you with the booze."

"Who's 'them'? The Coast Guard, or Glaupher?"

"Either." Angel started to fall but regained his balance. "Gotta go, Emmett. Be careful."

Emmett watched Angel stagger up the street before making his way back to the boat. There was no one around: no lights, no indication that anyone on the planet knew he was there. For a brief moment, he was tempted to remain long enough to rest and regain what composure he had left.

He looked at the sky, wishing he could see the stars. He steeled himself and untied the bow and stern lines, tossing them onto the boat and then pushing off. He started the engines and held them at low speed as he cleared Port Gardner and moved out onto the Sound.

The Sound was empty. He was thankful he was below the Coast Guard station on the Quimper Peninsula. There were cutters out on patrol, of course, but the closer he got to Seattle, the less likely he might run into one. He charted his course so that he ran right down the middle of the shipping lanes between Kingston and Edmonds, cruising at low speed and hoping that some freighter wouldn't overtake him.

His luck held until a cutter emerged from Port Madison Bay, catching him in the open.

At first he thought he had avoided detection, but a floodlight began sweeping back and forth across the water. He couldn't cut his engines or they would surely find him, and idling with the hope of not being heard would accomplish the very same thing.

He didn't like it, but he was going to have to run for it.

He opened the throttles and the engines sprang to life, lifting the bow free of the water, plowing through the short swell as if it didn't exist.

The cutter's floodlights swung madly from side to side, attempting to link a visual to the roar of two aviation engines running at full throttle.

Eventually, one of the lights managed to catch a glimpse of him, and then there were two floodlights. Whistles blew on the cutter as it opened its throttles, hopelessly slower, but armed with a .50 caliber machine gun on its foredeck. The whistles continued. This was a more modern seventy-eight footer, with bigger engines that would allow the boat to cruise at twenty-five knots.

Emmett was pulling away, but the cutter opened up with its machine gun and the half-inch slugs flew just over the flying bridge. Whoever was on that gun was an expert.

Emmett made a hard turn to starboard and dodged out of the light. He was hoping to hide behind Blake Island; if only he could get past Bainbridge without taking fire. The floodlights found him again, and this time the gunfire was not a warning. The projectiles flew past the boat, above his head, and he instinctively ducked just before two rounds caught the fantail, causing the boat to violently shudder.

But the engines seemed okay, and he kept the throttles wide open, rounding the bottom of Bainbridge and angling toward the west side of Blake Island. Then, he could feel the boat slowing perceptibly. He cut the engines, lashed the wheel and looked over the back of the stern.

One of the bullets had penetrated below the water line, and the boat was taking on water. It wasn't a large hole, and he hoped that he had enough time to find safe harbor before the boat took on enough water to swamp the engines. He restarted the engines and hoped for the best.

Once in the lee of Blake, he took a few moments to decide where he wanted to run. By now any other cutter in the south Sound would have been alerted. That he had appeared to angle into Bremerton might slow this cutter, but if he sped into Colvos Passage he might run into pursuit from the other direction. The boat was already losing its ability to plow through the swell, and the engines were laboring to maintain a cruising speed of twenty knots. At that pace the cutter would, sooner or later, come within range again.

He had no knowledge of Coast Guard's tactics. How many boats would they have out on the Sound? How would they coordinate their search? An animal instinct drove him to steer toward a safe harbor: home. But, he knew he couldn't do that, and given the damage to the hull, there was no way he could make it back across the Sound to the safety of the boat shed on the Duwamish.

He had no safe harbor for this boat and its cargo. He decided he needed to scuttle the boat. That meant deep water, which eliminated Colvos Passage. No sense in having incriminating flotsam drifting up on their beach.

He made the south end of Blake Island and slowed, looking through his binoculars for the cutter, but he saw no running lights. He was just starting to idle toward the top of the Passage, where he intended to scuttle his vessel, when he saw that the cutter had not fallen for his bait; it had, in fact, anticipated his move.

His pursuit was closing, and he could feel the hairs on the back of his neck stiffen. They were already as close as they had been when they fired on him a few minutes earlier. The boat sat low in the water, and he could smell the engines laboring. It wouldn't stay afloat much longer. Emmett began to toss cases of liquor overboard, hoping to lighten the boat enough that it could continue moving to a spot far enough from shore to ensure a successful scuttle, but close enough that he could make the swim.

The water was now ankle-deep around the engine hatch cover; it was only going to be mere minutes before it sank.

He was a good half-mile from shore, and the water was ice cold, but he was going to have to swim for it. He waited as the water made its way toward him. The stern had settled, allowing water to pour over the transom slightly, and the trapped air below deck was slowly venting through the cabin door.

Once the water was up around his ankles, he knew it was time to go. This would probably please the old man, he thought. Russell's dream boat sitting at the bottom of the Sound.

He stepped over the edge of the boat and into the cold water. He found an empty liquor case to hold onto. In a few moments he watched the cutter come back to life, turning on its floodlights to survey the wreckage.

As he clung to the wooden case, he was grimly reminded of a similar night at the other end of the country. He watched as the cutter closed on his boat, bright lights focused on the boat's final moments. She steadily began to slip from sight: her bow was the last to disappear into the dark depths of the Sound.

He kicked steadily, pulling the crate along just for buoyancy, for he knew he would have to go under when the floodlights swept over him. He was spent. He assessed his situation. The current was against him, perpetually coming up the Passage from the south, but he could kick against it and cross the current towards shore on the Kitsap Peninsula.

He turned his mind against the numbing cold by thinking about Noémi. Good God, it seemed like weeks since he had seen her, but it was only a matter of days. He thought of her face and her smile, and he felt warmer.

He wasn't ready to die, not before he had really had a chance to share a life with her, but if the cold, black water meant to have him, the memory of Noémi would accompany him to the bottom.

The cutter hove to at the wreckage, and sailors reached out with gaffs to snag floating cases of liquor. They shined their lights about the area, and when the beams traveled past his crate, he ducked his head under and waited until it was dark again. He continued to kick, slowly propelling himself through the current.

Someone on board called out with a megaphone, offering refuge on the cutter. But with no response, the offer wasn't made again. After half an hour, and after most of the floating cases of liquor had been collected, the cutter shut down her floodlights and cruised back north, leaving him in the middle of the cold, black Sound.

Emmett kept kicking with his legs, though he could no longer feel them. Despite the cold, he was heartened by the images of sweet Noémi in his arms. His movements were mechanical, and only the rush of cold water across his face convinced him he was making any progress. He was numb from the chest down, and his breathing was becoming difficult.

He considered, for the first time, that he might not be able to make it to shore. It was too dark to see the distance he had to cover, and perhaps that was a blessing, or he may have given up. He stopped to rest, knowing that the cold would soon consume whatever strength he had left.

In the dimness, he thought he could make out the dark silhouette of a tree line against the gloom. There was no sound of crashing surf to guide him; only his innate sense of direction and the weak promise of that silhouette. He abandoned the crate and went for broke, stretching into a crawl that, at once, provided good headway, giving him hope that he could complete the final distance to dry land.

He forced his arms to pull himself through the water. He was beginning to shake uncontrollably, and his right calf had started to cramp, but he forced his way through the pain and discomfort. He glanced toward what he thought was the shoreline as he stroked. The silhouette was becoming pronounced—yes, he was going to make it!

He was exhausted, and his crawl devolved into a weary breaststroke. He forced himself forward and kept kicking his feet down, hoping to find the bottom.

When his feet managed to touch, he immediately stopped and gasped for air. Both of his legs were cramping, and he was still neck-deep in the freezing, black water. The current along the shore was pulling him sideways, threatening to drag him under.

At the base of the trees, he thought he saw a light colored object move, perhaps an animal of some sort. He wondered if his exhaustion was causing him to hallucinate. The object moved out of sight as he struggled to gain a better foothold, compelling each leg forward, inching his way to dry land and safety. After what seemed to be an interminable length of time, he was freed from the grasp of the cold water, and he collapsed on the rocky beach.

He knew he couldn't stay on the shore long or the cold air would finish what the Sound hadn't. He struggled upright, violently shaking, and turned around a couple of times to determine where he was along the shoreline. He estimated he was a couple of miles north of their fish camp. He swung his arms and lifted each leg several times to get his circulation going.

He was past exhaustion, but he bushwhacked through the brush that clogged the shoreline, and made his way into the forest of firs that bordered the Passage before finding a path.

In the distance, he thought he could hear a dog barking. He didn't give much thought to it, but instinctively set his course to the sound. He fell down several times in the dark, tripping over tree roots or thick clots of bracken and salal. But it didn't matter. He was alive, and unless Glaupher turned him over to the Feds he was safe, at least for a while.

He wondered about Glaupher and what he might have to do to protect himself; then he thought about Noémi and what battles he would have to face liberating her from her brother. But, mostly he thought about a cup of hot coffee, wishing that there were already a pot waiting for him.

Still, he had to go by Janie's to alert her that Angel would be calling. When, in the dim light he could determine where he was, he angled across a clearing behind a dark farmhouse.

Again, he heard a loud bark. Then another. The sound had become a homing beacon, and within fifteen minutes he was in sight of Janie's front door. Once on her porch, he was hesitant to knock and wake her. But a loud eruption of sound came from inside, and as he stood to rap on the door he could see Atlas inside, jumping up onto the door.

Janie came and opened the door, and the big dog leapt forward, nearly knocking him over.

She noted Emmet's sodden state and immediately pulled him inside the house. "He's been going nuts for the last half hour. Musta known you were coming home," she said. She wrapped a heavy blanket around him.

Atlas nudged him toward the kitchen table and leaned against his leg as Emmett collapsed onto a chair; the big dog's warmth was as welcome as a hot bath.

"Welcome home," she said.

ABOUT THE AUTHOR

Blaine Beveridge is a novelist living with his wife and four-legged children on an island in the Puget Sound. For more information about the author, and to read about his other works, please visit www.beveridgebooks.com